immune

immune

A Novel by Sharon Mayes

New Rivers Press 1987

Library of Congress Catalog Card Number: 87-62139
ISBN 0-89823-096-9.

Book design and typesetting:
Peregrine Publications, St. Paul
Cover Art by Caroline Garrett

immune has been published with the aid of grants from the First Bank Systems Foundation, and the National Endowment for the Arts (with funds appropriated by the Congress of the United States).

New Rivers Press books are distributed by:

The Talman Company   and   Bookslinger
150-5th Ave.   213 E. 4th St.
New York, NY 10011   St. Paul, MN 55101

immune has been manufactured in the United States of America for New Rivers Press (C.W. Truesdale, editor/publisher), 1602 Selby Ave., St. Paul, MN 55104 in a first edition of 5,000 copies.

for david

contents

part one

memory

Aﬀﬁ FTER THE POLICE left he stood beside his car a few moments, then walked across the parking lot to where her car had been. His mind replayed the scene of the Marin County tow truck hauling away her car. At the same time his conversation with the detective was forgotten. His brain dimmed in confusion as though a surge of power had blown a fuse. He shook his head. She had to be around here somewhere, and he was determined to find her. This was very inconvenient, he thought, as he grabbed the red backpack and his jacket from the back seat. He checked his pockets for cigarettes and matches and stood there puzzled.

The afternoon sun was setting behind the heavy bank of fog approaching him from the west. To the east the blue sky darkened and thin puffs of clouds raced across the hills to fill the peninsula of Pt. Reyes with fog. This was the end of the road. From this point on he had to walk. He surveyed the familar landscape as he constructed a plan. First, he would search the nearest beach and the small cove on the far side of the giant rock. If she wasn't there he'd search along Pierce Point trail.

The trail covered five miles of wild grassland along the top of the cliffs beneath which steep, rutted, and dangerous canyons cut paths to virgin beaches. There was one beach they had hiked down to in the past, a perfect place to disappear, since getting there involved serious knowledge of the twisted gullies, leaps across deep crevasses and careful clinging to unstable walls of the canyon. The Pacific Ocean below rose and fell in enormous swells. It was foolhardy to hike around here in the fog at twilight, but what choice did he have?

She had to be out here somewhere. Without her sweater — his mind flashed as if it were a camera — her car door was open, he looked inside. Her bag and her sweater lay on the front seat, abandoned. The flash was blinding, and he refused any implications. When he found her she wasn't going to escape the full force of his temper. He summoned up sufficient anger to suppress his worry, his fear that something very wrong had happened. He loved her. They were going to be married in a few short weeks. She must have had a good reason to flee the hospital like that, to leave her laboratory, the slides set up, the blood samples out. In spite of all their shenanigans of late, she was conscientious about her research. They were both serious doctors. They didn't *do* things like this. But the AIDS research and patients, not to mention their tumultuous relationship, kept them under a lot of stress. The pressure could easily have gotten to her.

The tide swept in along the beach forcing him to crawl over the haphazard piles of rock that accumulated along the base of the cliff. The cut to the cove, a narrow passage between the wall of the cliff and the huge granite boulder that sat far into the ocean, was still passable. This black rock shot up into the fog, surreal, like a gnarled hand its fingers curled into a fist gripping the sea. He panted, the damp air mingling with nervous sweat. His glasses were speckled with droplets of salt water. There was little to be seen, but mounds of sand on his left, the green-grey ocean rushing forward in irregular thrusts on his right.

"Suzanne! Suzanne!" His loudest shout was no more than a pin dropping in the sand. The roar of the ocean overpowered everything. The beach was short and narrow in high tide. He searched each of the three small coves along the edge of the cliff until he came to a deep pool of murky water bordered by a sheer face of granite. She wasn't there.

He walked back to the middle of the beach, in front of the cove they called "theirs" and fell into the sand. He had to rest a minute. The last time he sat on this beach he was wildly happy, as happy as he'd ever been or imagined possible. They were together, talking, laughing, running naked on the beach, making love. He felt her lying in his arms on this very spot. "I can't imagine not being wrapped in your strong arms," she said. With her forefinger she traced a line of muscle from his neck across his shoulder down to his hand. Her fingers gingerly played with his until their hands locked together, a Turkish puzzle ring, a Chinese toy, inseparable. She belonged to him. Her face. Her body.

He got up and ran the mile back up to the parking lot. There was not more than an hour of dusk left. The wind pushed him along as he climbed up the hill. His heart beat fast and erratically. He glanced at the weathered barn, remembering that the police had searched there. On Pierce Point trail he ran about ten minutes until he recognized the place where he had to leave the trail and begin to cross the steep slope of the hill to the edge of the canyon. Her voice rang in his ears. "You don't really understand me, do you?" She had said it in the beginning, two months ago; she had said it in the past few days. He had laughed at her both times.

"Of course, I understand you." He always tried to alter these blue moods of hers by making light of her enigmatic pronouncements.

He tripped, falling head first into the tangled vines of ice plant. He rolled down the hill, grasping at the foliage until he stopped himself. On his back he gazed into the sky. Her voice murmured like freeway noise, "Sure you do, just like you understand yourself?"

He didn't like the way his mind slipped and slid from here to there, now to then, like learning to snow ski on ice without poles. He rolled over and rose up on his hands and knees. A few feet away was the edge of the ravine, a very long drop to the bottom. He circumnavigated the winding, barely apparent trail around the fluted edge of the canyon. He was convinced she was down there on that deserted beach. He would put his jacket on her, his arms around her, and they would talk about it.

Small bits of earth fell away as he made his way down the right side of this round, sculpted crease in the earth that looked like a multitude of fat red fingers grasping the edge of the cliff. He jumped over the stream that ran down to the sand. The long beach spread out before him on either side, the ends obscured by the fog. Sandpipers chased the moving shoreline. Seagulls whined a dirge overhead. There wasn't a footprint in the sand. No sign of any human disturbance. Nothing. With his head bent into the wind he started off to the right. He searched until he'd gone as far as he could in both directions. The fog grew denser with the darkness. She wasn't there.

He groped his way back up the canyon. Several hundred feet above the ocean, he found the dirt path. It was too late to search toward the old lighthouse. Shock began to protect him from an encroaching sense of panic. The world around him was a blur. With great difficulty in the wind he lit a cigarette and felt a moment of pride that he'd accomplished it. When he reached his car the possibility of leaving didn't occur to him. He took a flashlight from the glove compartment and methodically hiked back toward their cove. She had to turn up. Her car was gone.

Slowly, using his flashlight and feeling his way along the cold, wet wall of mud and rock, he reached the cove. The first time they lay in this cove together the sand was warm and dry. She slipped her hand underneath his shorts, burying her chin into his abdomen. She melted into him, giving herself over to the comfort of his arms. He held her closer, wrapping his legs around her. His legs, her legs, he forgot whose were whose.

There was an abalone shell next to him. He picked it up, examined it. A leftover of life, a carcass, that's what Suzanne would call it. She collected them — shells — *he* felt strangely like one. He studied it with his flashlight, then noticed that the sand beneath the shell was moving. He never noticed it before, that the sand was in constant motion. " 'To see the world in a grain of sand and heaven in a wildflower.' You know who said that?" She nudged him with a piece of driftwood. "Guess," she demanded. "I'll give you a hint. 'To hold infinity in the palm of your hand and eternity in an hour.' " She grinned at him, "Come on, guess." She pouted, then with a frown said, "Wait a minute, maybe it's 'to hold eternity in the palm of your hand and infinity in an hour.' " Her brow knitted. "Do you think there's a difference between eternity and infinity? I mean, does it matter?"

He smiled, then frowned and turned off the flashlight. Save the batteries, he thought. Is this love? This total absorption, this physical compulsion, this chemical attraction, this instinctual response I have toward her — is this love? Where the hell is she? What the hell is going on here?

He resumed his study of the shell. "I've got you now." Once when they were making love on this beach and he was about to explode into her, she stopped moving with him. She taunted him playfully, "I've got you now; I'll never set you free."

All right, okay, I'll be your prisoner. Whatever you want, you'll have it. With amazement he felt an erection. A prisoner without a prison, it died. He fell on his face in the sand, his arms stretched out over his head, his legs apart. He was exhausted. The sand shifted minutely under him as she had. He drifted toward sleep. His reserve of will, his armour of shock, crumbled. His anger weakened. *Suicide.* The word shot through his brain hot as a bullet. No. She couldn't. She wouldn't. He erased the word, losing consciousness to dreams of her. Them.

*　*　*

It was the end of a cool, hazy August, 1983. The first faculty meeting of the year was in progress. He leaned with his back against the wall, his chair tipped just to the point at which it balanced. His legs were spread to complete this physical feat in which he stupidly risked falling. It wasn't kosher to interrupt the Chairman of the Department of Medicine's report on the insufficiency of grant money generated by the immunology section last year. He tempted fate while this pompous, stringy man gyrated like a marionette, coughed on incipient lung cancer, and chewed them out. Bored and aggravated, he concealed *The Wall Street Journal* between the pages of *Infection and Immunity.* In fits and starts he read the

6

over-the-counter quotations, glancing up to see if anyone took notice of him. As if they cared, he scoffed.

For no reason he became aware of an odd prickly sensation on the back of his neck. Out of the corner of his glasses, he saw the reflection of an unusual looking woman, a new face. Certain that she wasn't real, but a mere hallucination, he continued his half-hearted dabbling in the financial news. Yet, some inner badger nudged him to focus on that corner of the room. She was there, leaning on the arm of the chair with her chin in her hand, a posture of professional conviction. He couldn't believe his eyes. He couldn't believe the combination of arrogance, indifference, and vulnerability in her face, unlike the face of any female scientist he had ever seen. Not that female scientists weren't beautiful to varying degrees, but it struck him that they didn't look like that.

"Must be a new secretary." He poked his nearest colleague.

Too bad he was sitting next to Melvin Forbes, his old laboratory partner and prime competitor for the sparse resources and scarce rewards in academic microbiology. Melvin's interest in women was on a par with his interest in politics: non-existent.

"She's no secretary," Melvin whispered. "She's the new research associate in Mosley's lab. I hear she's got an MD, a Ph.D. in Immunology and a list of publications up to here," he gestured to his neck. "Better be on your toes, Alterberg. She'll have your job when his grant money dries up."

His chair teetered forward and tipped as he lost his balance. He grabbed for stability and found himself with his hand in Melvin's crotch.

"Hey, cut it out!" Melvin, horrified and turning red, pushed his hand away. "What are you? Some kinda pervert?"

Sweat beaded on his forehead as he repositioned his chair, turning it away from Melvin. The chairman frowned at them and let an embarrassing silence go by, but only Melvin was appropriately chagrined. Once the report resumed, he turned again to the woman and positioned his chair so that he saw as much of her face as possible. She looked bored. He tried to imagine whether she was married or not. Would a woman like her be married? Of course. Of course she was married. Look at the way she sat there almost asleep. Look at her obvious boredom with the meeting in which she was one of two women. The other was overweight, gum-chewing, fifty-three and gay-by-choice. There were at least ten or twelve single, thirtyish, attactive men in the room, two of whom were independently wealthy, three who were paragons of academic success, and three who were marathon runners of reputed sexual prowess. Any attractive, single woman would grovel for this array of choices, he speculated. But she, from his brief observation, was in a world of her own.

He coughed and rattled his paper hoping to catch her eye. For several minutes he watched her. She raised her head slowly, tossed her long hair back and fully opened her eyes. When he realized that she was looking straight at him with an expression of bemused indifference he quickly lowered his head and pretended to be reading his journal with a vengeance. God, she could be a ball breaker!

His effort to become indifferent to her presence in the room was a dismal failure. Pride was losing ground to his impulse to stare at her again. In spite of his better judgment, he decided to say something in the meeting. He raised his hand and said that the budget for Xeroxing was so measly he couldn't keep proper copies of his clinical notes. He moved that more money be alloted for Xeroxing. To his embarrassment, while he surveyed his colleagues who seemed stunned by his out-of-the-blue complaint, she smiled at him as though she found his comment vaguely amusing. A lively debate broke out over the Xeroxing budget, and he was constrained to stay since he had brought up the subject. He sat there helpless when she walked out the door without giving him a final glance.

* * *

The ladies' room was particularly sterile, the hospital type with ultra violet light that makes one look pale and wan, that accentuates lines under the eyes. The mirrors in institutional bathrooms always distort the face in a peculiar way. She fumbled in her purse for the red lipstick, noticing the veins standing out on the back of her hand. She hated these reminders of age. In brief flashes and all too often, premonitions crossed her mind, like headlights brightening the walls of a dark bedroom. Decline was imminent, swirling her into a vortex beyond her control. Her hand trembled and the red smeared outside the line of her lower lip. She corrected it with her little finger. An actress practicing expressions, she tried on different faces.

My god, I've gotten old looking. She picked a tiny blackhead, thinking how disgusting she felt at times, or was it how disgusted? Let's not be so morose, my dear, she spoke to her reflection. There was Carol to talk to and wouldn't that be fun.

In truth, she dreaded the time that she was forced to spend with others: colleagues for collaborative work, necessary inquiries for reseach, crucial connections in the administrative sphere. She smiled at herself, recognizing the expression on her face she hated, the one that turned up in most photographs. It doesn't seem to matter how

8

hard I try to put on a happy face, look on the bright side, lighten up. It doesn't matter a damn. I'm irredeemable. I can't "lighten up." I hate that phrase.

A cynical sneer glared back at her, a stranger so real she was frightened into producing another face, a mask of pliability and openness. What if someone walked in? It was one thing to stand in her own bathroom scrutinizing these nuances of expression, searching for some strange ironic truth as if her eyes were windows into the unknown, but quite another to be observed. Appearances still mattered. Indeed, they were her specialty. She was too vulnerable to chance encounters with others in which she found herself offering opinions on everything from the intricacies of monoclonal antibodies to the best kind of face cream for the over-thirty woman. It was awkward to meet the secretaries in the ladies' room. She felt oddly at home with them even though they called her Doctor and treated her with a subservient deference that left her lonely, not quite a woman, obviously not a man. This responsibility for producing appearances, for protecting the illusions she believed others had, made her resentful. Better to encourage distance when she had little to give. But, sometimes, she wished to ask them, those fiftyish matrons, how they managed to look so content, so under control.

In the past, in medical school and when she was an intern, her women friends, few as they were, put such nagging doubts and morbid thoughts in their place. There was late night and early morning gossip over coffee, with lots of sleep-deprived giggling. They touched base on the shared, but fragile world of periods, moods, men, sex. They offered each other advice that kept them down to earth, that left *her* feeling understood. Life was different now. Time had scattered them into their respective specialties. They moved, got married, had children, affairs, divorces. They worked — day in and day out — they were doctors with busy schedules and harried, complicated private lives. Ironically, her personal life, once a tiny island of precious time, devoured by errands and necessities, coveted like a priceless jewel, was a vast expanse of desert. Nothing was funny anymore. Elizabeth Arden was no longer a comical topic with which to pass a lunch hour. Anyway who could talk to a man about face cream or new clothes?

A moment of regret about those lost lunches with her women friends swept over her. What a disillusionment to watch the way they began to compete with each other. She felt sad about the disguised envy among her female colleagues. They all wanted to be "one of the boys," not to mention the constant competition for thinness, for health, for superwoman of the year. She found it all too obvious, too easy, too futile and too boring. Like everyone else she retreated into work, and now work was losing its multi-faceted appeal. AIDS overshadowed all other diseases, all conversations, all cocktail parties, all dates. She hated talking about AIDS, the patients, the research grants, the ever-expanding theories more than anything. But there was no going back. AIDS was her life now, like it or not.

She ran her hands over her small breasts and down across her waist that curved inward and sat atop the bones that stood out around her stomach. She didn't count calories anymore; she hardly remembered when or what she last ate. No, she wasn't fat. She had never really been fat, although she felt fat. Didn't every woman? Now she was skeletal, she had to laugh. Well, who would have predicted it? She had to put all caring behind her. She felt greedy, hungry, thirsty. She dreamt of being someone else, in another exotic life: rich foods, fine wines, a villa overlooking the sea, a fast red sports car, jet setting around.

Was this going forward? *She was frightened.* She wanted to run away; she wanted a drastic change. What if she let go of appearances and faced — faced what? Her actual life, it was so . . . well, so worthwhile. An AIDS doctor. The phrase made her cringe. She wanted to make a sign, a picket on which was written: I am Dr. Normal, the typical, over-achieving, obsessive-compulsive, scientist/career woman. There is nothing wrong with me. Believe me. Please.

Arbeit macht Frei, the words over the entrance to some concentration camp. Work makes you free. Every day she drove to the hospital and worked. Crossing her fingers. But it wasn't the work itself that tumbled downstream, a leaf in the current, a loose thread from her hem threatening to show the ragged edges; she knew this. It was the so-called world of social relations, a world she had once taken for granted. It tilted on its axis and rocked out of balance just when she needed it most. Her conscious decision to detach herself from her zany group of friends was harder than she imagined it would be. She missed them.

She ran a large comb through her hair, watching the strands fan over her cheek in lights of platinum, gold, rust, and some grey. The Timex slid around her wrist and told her she had wasted ten minutes at the mirror staring blankly at herself. Her body stiffened. She gave herself a stop-this-nonsense-look and swiftly tossed open the swinging door.

* * *

He started and began to walk off as if he had been merely passing by. She smiled at him. He knew that she knew he had been lurking outside the ladies' room for ten minutes wondering if he should send in the secretary to see if she was all right. His fists bulged in his pockets. He rocked forward and back, nodding his head at her, flashing a rather silly grin. She walked past him on the way to her office and resisted the impulse to turn and see if he was watching her. She held her head high with a studied poise. Her hair tossed back and forth as she walked, and she was embarrassed by her obvious and irrepressible intention to entice him. The last thing her life needed was another man. But she was going off the deep end anyway.

The desk confronted her with several pink message slips, most from students wanting papers, wanting a waiver for the lab exam, wanting to chat. She slammed her briefcase on the floor and sighed. Why did she ever agree to lecture in virology? It wasn't required by her contract. She volunteered in a weak moment of nostalgia for the classroom, those eager young minds, hands in the air, questions about the microuniverse. Her foot methodically tapped the concrete floor. She fought off the urge to smoke a cigarette. If I had a drug now, I'd take it. The bottle of Valium was in her purse. There was some dope left too, but she couldn't smoke here during the day. The smell was too recognizable. God, for some coke. Little scraps of paper and old gum wrappers flew out of her purse with her hand. She popped two Valium.

There was a stack of mail, unopened, newly put on the corner of her desk. Her curiosity piqued, she forgot her internal dialogue for the moment. She rustled through the mail, advertisements, conference announcements, the usual assortment of journals. There was a letter from *The Journal of Microbiology.* She gently turned it in her fingers, letting herself wonder about its contents, not wanting to read a rejection. Nothing burned like letters that rejected an article for publication. Knifelike words drew emotional blood. This blood might spill over everything and contaminate.... This word was taboo, unthinkable. Her sensitivity was like a raw nerve and required unforgiving mental control. If it weren't for the acceptances and the occasional praises, she might not continue this work; she might quit and disappear. Her enthusiasm heightened; she could tell by the envelope that this was not a rejection letter. Rejection letters were thin, one page.

She was reading the first paragraph: they were going to publish her case report on the AIDS patient who developed disseminated aspergillosis. It wasn't that big a deal, just the results of his treatment with Amphothericin B, but it cheered her up a bit. He had slipped in the door and stood watching her; he noticed her smile. "Good news?" He thrust his hands in his pockets.

"Ah," she gasped, startled by his unannounced presence. She glared at him, her face growing soft, though she tried to maintain the glare. He was awfully cute with those dark brown curls and yellow-brown eyes. "Yes? Can I help you, Doctor?"

"Alterberg, Chris Alterberg." He coughed and cleared his throat, a habit she would soon find familiar, then shifted his weight forward and pushed his glasses high on the bridge of his nose. "I've been meaning to get in touch with you. Didn't you work on the hepatitis B study with Dr. Morgan in Contra Costa county? Some of those patients ended up in our clinic, with AIDS. . . ." he paused. Her lack of response was quite anti-social, but he continued, "Well, I'm running the clinic downstairs, we'd like to get as many patients as possible in-volved in any research trials you've got going. Dr. Forbes said we had some research interests in common," he lied, a little white lie, just stretching the truth. His own insecurity immediately irritated him. Research indeed, he thought, but his desire to know her kept him there, rocking back and forth on his heels, waiting.

She turned her chair away from him and continued to sort her mail, listening with detachment. Her mind wandered to the run in the back of her stocking. She twirled around, better to focus him up-ward. She rose from the chair, smoothing her challis print skirt with a wispy gesture of her hand. "Well, perhaps, but I don't know what your interests are, Dr. Alterberg?" She sat down again and crossed her legs, arranging and rearranging the piles of paper on her desk. "I liked what you said in the faculty meeting. What balls to raise the Xeroxing budget with that old corpse!" She laughed at herself, then noticed the shocked look on his face.

Dammit, she bit her tongue, I did it again. I blurted that out without any warning. Balls indeed! Not very ladylike.

She struggled to think of a way to regain some measure of profes-sionalism with him. "After all, they say that God is in the details, and what more important detail than the Xeroxing. The last thing the ad-ministration here should sabotage is our ability to reproduce." She shrugged her shoulders. "But politics is the same in every medical school, don't you think?" Her eye focused on the poster she had put up, a lithograpic of an Asian woman running in panic with her dying baby draped between her arms.

"Actually, I came here because I noticed you in the faculty meeting for the first time and," he fumbled, "I wanted to welcome you to the department." His confidence grew. He was more in control, not only within his rights, but doing a good deed. He moved closer to her desk, observing how the texture of her face, its infinite shades of mood, produced unrecognizable sensations in him, new, without definition, but with certain excitement. He found himself in the midst of a romantic fantasy. He would touch her shoulders, massage them gently; he would hear her moan with pleasure, then pull her from the chair into his arms and kiss her. Before he jolted back to reality he was standing two feet from her chair. She swiveled it around to face him with a challenge. His hands raced into his pockets and he came to attention like a soldier. "Well, how are you settling in here? Did they give you a reasonable lab?" She appeared not to hear, but was looking straight into his eyes. He shifted from left to right and back again. "What are your major interests, if you don't mind my asking, Doctor?" he persisted with his questions. His annoyance festered. At least she could introduce herself.

She twirled the chair around again, placing her back to him, an infuriating gesture. He considered stomping out without waiting for a reply. "Drugs." She mumbled it, barely audible.

"What? I didn't catch that?"

She gave him a sexy, casual smile, tossed over her shoulder, her eyes flashing past his. "Drugs, I said. I'm interested in drugs."

His eyes grew wider, he thought she must be teasing, then he wondered. He would play along a bit longer. "Oh? Any drugs in particular? I didn't know Mosley had any drug studies going on up here?"

He stared at her, hypnotized like an elk during the rutting season who has his mate spotted. It was intended to offset her, to gain some upper hand, to stimulate her subliminally, although the lack of subtlety was apparent to both. The silence that punctuated their conversation — if it could be called a conversation — was no longer awkward. The more important communication was unspoken. Words were reduced to crude, archaic instruments, means to an end that had little in common with the exchange of information. His entire body felt alive. He was aware of his skin, his eyes, his mouth, the muscles in his shoulders, his small, but growing pot belly. He sucked in his stomach and tried to stand tall, thinking at once how obvious it must have been. And she kept swiveling in her chair like a girl on a swing, dangling her feet, letting them slide with the rhythm of the chair so the shape of her calves and the turn of her ankle became his major focus. Her hair was blonder than he thought, and her eyes were larger, their color difficult to pinpoint. She kept them half closed, averted, but when she opened them and gave him a direct stare, he felt knocked in the head, dizzy. Those eyes were weapons.

"Not exactly what I meant." Yes, she was definitely teasing.

"Not exactly what you meant? Humm." What else could she have meant? He felt another flush of red spread across his face. She isn't going to dangle me, like a fish on a hook. He moved a step closer to her, then sat down on the corner of her desk. His thigh spread toward her, and he kept his legs apart deliberately. "Well, perhaps, I should ask if you mean business or recreation?" He wasn't born yesterday; he knew a thing or two.

"For me, they've become one and the same. It's all part of our business, don't you think?" The softness vanished. Her face became angular, almost hard, bitter.

He stood up, thinking he should leave since he was fifteen minutes late for rounds already. He had never been late for teaching rounds, but he didn't want to leave. This is teenage, he admonished himself, moving toward the door. She turned her back to him, as if he were already gone, as if he were a genie from a bottle that would disappear in a puff of smoke whenever she had finished with him.

"Listen," he called to her from the door, "I'd like to see you later. If you're free, let me buy you some coffee." He wanted to ask her to dinner but felt too uncertain. Better not to risk the rejection nor to risk her thinking that he cared that much.

"I'd prefer a drink."

"A drink? Great. A drink. Let's have a drink then. How about that bar over on Clement and 4th? The one that has free food. About sixish?"

"Fine." She drifted off into the letter from the journal.

He stood a moment, wondering if she really said yes, she would have a drink with him, then he whipped through the door slamming into Dr. Thomas, the chief of their department. She ignored the commotion and the breathless apologies she overheard from the hall. Her watch said four.

*　*　*

She sipped her wine waiting for him to appear. It was 6:20. He was late. She liked that. It showed he wasn't too eager. He had some gall. A shiver sent the hairs on her arm sticking out like a porcupine. She rubbed her arms to replace the natural heat. Cold hands and feet were a plague to her. Ever since she came to California, the land of eternal spring, she'd been cold. Cold sunshine: how she'd come to love it, but at this moment she could do with the cessation of these chills. She felt like crying for no reason. Maybe she misunderstood him. Maybe she was in the wrong bar.

She smiled at her reflection in the dark glass on the table. Calm down, Suzanne. It's okay to wait, to anticipate. It might be better if you could try and look less depressed. The face is still tolerable, a little tired, traced with melancholy, but some men like that. Let's try for some sweetness, some innocence. It will make you look younger. The curve of this smile is a bit crooked, a bit off. How long will you last? How much time will you give him? Let's not think about him now.

She turned to stare out the window where she could focus on the passers-by, blithely strolling along this fashionable, success-laden street. Her mind went automatically to the night before when she had been reading art books in the corner of her living room.

Only that which is etched in stone or made of stone will survive, but not forever. The further back in time she browsed, the more she noticed that only stone survived, stone and color. Human impressions in stone are limited, she thought, so short in the time of this planet. Did we exist before the discovery of the cave paintings in southern Spain? Were these signs of a frail people's first quest for immortality? A plea on stone. A mark that said, don't forget we were here. I was here. Art is too fragile. I am too fragile.

What is this rut I've fallen into? Ever since Dan left again, not that long ago. Every night is longer. Time is expanding with my loneliness. Art is a comfort of sorts. All those books I never had time to read. Is isolation maddening? No. It's necessary. I can't be who I once was. I can't take Dan with me. I can't take anyone. I must be someone new. Perhaps I'll study art history? Everything is new: new job, new friends, new car, new image. I must keep it up; it's working, I suppose.

Restlessness in its current form, peculiar to the middle of the night, had sent her wandering into the kitchen where she poured herself another large glass of wine. Medication. Several new reports, journal articles and letters on the latest in AIDS research sat on the dining table waiting to be read, as they had for several days. Whenever she forced herself to sit down with them for the umpteenth time, anxiety attacked. She gulped the wine. How unbearable would it become?

"Nuclear war will wipe us all out," she said to Carol, her new technician, as they had sat over a late lunch the day before.

"I don't think about nuclear war," Carol chirped. "It's not a political issue to me. It's like AIDS, beyond my control."

Of course, nuclear war is a political issue, she thought. How stupid of Carol to say that, and it's not at all like AIDS, but she couldn't say that to Carol. She felt compelled to twist her flippant statement into something she could agree with. "Yes, well, the total devastation, disappearance, destruction of everything is, perhaps, beyond the political. It's a moral issue, an issue of our nature. Are human beings good or evil? Yes, it is beyond the political in that sense."

Why did she feel the need to agree with Carol? She liked her, but she didn't know why. They were scarcely acquaintances, only co-workers, yet Carol had befriended her, helped her adjust to the new lab and the set up of the department. She gave her tips, bits of advice about the secretaries, the other doctors and techs, traps to avoid, issues to steer clear of. Carol so far seemed the most competent tech she'd ever had. She seemed eager to be her friend.

That was where the problem lay. She was too eager and blind to the distance that allowed them a relationship at all. In their few social meetings, she noticed a tendency in Carol to disagree with everything she said outside of medicine, an unusual, instinctive response. Then she would mute her negativism with a gesture of comradery. It raised curiosity and suspicion. She could be another Dora. Now, *she* was a reason to be ambivalent about close friendships, but with her there was something more, something too complicated to unravel. With Carol there was a simplicity: when she was pessimistic, Carol countered with optimism. When she was cynical, Carol beamed with hope, but in a way that pressured her to comply. A harmless pressure, but she couldn't take it. She didn't want to feel guilty about pushing Carol away. It was a miserable new feeling to be stuck between need and fear.

She wasn't sure she wanted to know Carol beyond the hospital, their work relationship. Her struggle to disentangle the sticky, uncomfortable reliance on Dora was too recent. Maybe she and Carol could be friends in a different way: honest, critical, not too close. No, this would never work. She wasn't prepared to take criticism from anyone right now. She longed for exactly what she couldn't have, because when she asked herself: could I reciprocate? The answer was: hardly. But can I hide? For a time.

She dwelt obsessively on her women friends, past and present. She missed Julia to the point of physical pain. But one had to stand on one's own two feet. Her relationship with Dora had gone bad. Like rotten fruit it had become too ripe, fermented, poisonous. Forget about women. She forced her thoughts to change. That's all too complex. Men are more predictable, easier to play with if they survive the first few dates. On the other hand, recent fun was pretty damned short-lived. It turned to insecurities, needs, demands, and in the end, inevitable combat. Brian, she smirked, he was another dilemma. He, she already knew, would follow the pattern: giving, seducing, sharing, cajoling, pleading, then withholding, becoming vindictive, nasty, perhaps vulgar.

Is there some benefit to lumping men together? It certainly doesn't work with women. Abstract men? Enlightenment? Progress? Civili-ation? What will become of us? None of us are civilized. None of us is etched in stone.

The door opened, and he flew through it, his tie flapping over his shoulder. He was rushing. When he saw her, his stride lengthened. He was pleased that she had arrived first. He was dying to see her and had not been at all sure she would wait for him. He shifted his eyes down, aware of protecting the pleasure he was experiencing.

She immediately looked away from him toward a man who had been staring at her from the bar. He raised his glass to her, and she gave him a broad smile certain that it would be noticed. She had forgotten that she was waiting for him, and she suddenly didn't want him to think what was obviously the truth: she was waiting for him.

* * *

The sun cast a yellowy light on the water. He was covered with dew. Any movement spread the water around, and it seeped into his clothing. The fog hung thick around the shoreline. In the distance the end of it sat, a fat grey mushroom on the horizon. The glow of the water, its glassy texture, alerted him to the sunrise. It came, unobtrusive, the dawn in the west, not like the brilliant ball of fire that rose out of the sea in the east. It came slowly, deliberately, bring-ing the day for better or worse. He slid his parched tongue over his lips. They were swollen, chapped, and sore. His body jerked into consciousness, and as soon as he was aware of his wakeful state a miserable ache tortured him. His legs twitched and his arms felt rub-bery by his sides. No, he closed his eyes and wished, don't let me be awake, don't let me be alive, don't let this be real.

It was a dream, their first drink, their first coffee. "Everything hap-pens at sunset," she blinked at him, then smiled shyly. "Everything happens in transitions, change." She paused, her mood changing too abruptly. "Sunrise . . . sunset . . ."

He remembered the lush green hills, dotted with flashy pink homes, glowing in the reverse light of sunset, the sunsets they didn't see. Their bodies busy, tossing and turning between the sheets. His fingers were stiff, edged in brown, but now he saw those same fingers stroking the peach satin skin of her waist where it blended into her hips and continued in an unbroken line down her thighs. The tips of his fingers pinched her slightly, she moaned, and he pulled her down on him with both hands, the velvet inside of her caressing him, surrounding him with extraordinary pleasure. The blue-black night fell on the hill outside the bedroom, the view became "city stars," her

17

phrase for the random pattern of blinking colored lights, some moving across ribbons of freeway, some steady in buildings, some. . . . Her silhouette graced the glass-enclosed bedroom as she rose to get her bathrobe, to stand staring out into the night smoking a cigarette, miles away from him after coming so close.

He had slept the night in the cove. His stomach rumbled uncomfortably, his clothes were soaked, his beard a disreputable shadow. Despite his frozen body he managed to turn on his back. There was the sheer cliff rising in rings, layers and shafts of sandstone and rock several hundred feet above his head. The waves lapped at his feet, and he heard the baby sandpipers squeal like piglets. He sat up and tried to light a soggy cigarette with shaking hands. Soon he would be forced to go back to town for more cigarettes. Necessity, pared down to the bone, was a constant annoyance like a splinter under a nail. A dull ache that bordered on pain spread through his body, a reminder that it had only been one night without her. Why did she seem more alive to him now than when he last saw her? No, that wasn't true at all. Nothing felt alive anymore, except his memory, that harbor of greed and desire.

Bird dung had fallen on the day pack, her day pack really, a red one with an old anti-war button rusting on the back flap. He brushed it off and opened the aging zipper. When he looked at the black book in it he felt his body fly forward; he was crashing into a windshield, his head shattering on impact with the glass. He stiffened with the command: collect yourself. But the will to obey was lost, impossible. Where was she? Why did she run away? Why yesterday? Why did he break into her house to find her journal? Why? Why didn't she have it with her? She usually did. Why did he need to read it? He wanted to know what she had written about him. For a brief moment that was all that mattered. Was he in there; did he exist for her; did she love him?

His hands trembled as he took the book out and dusted the sand from it. He opened it in the middle where a nonsensical entry confronted him.

Not much journal writing lately. My house is infested with fleas and they're annoying the shit out of me. A friend called today and told me his house is infested with fleas too, but his Buddhist house partners don't want to kill them. If God meant it to be otherwise then fleas wouldn't be here. That's SO Berkeley! I told him they were nuts. Him too, if he listens to that shit. Who cares if fleas are natural? So is the bubonic plague, AIDS, plutonium. As he pointed out, the Buddhists' white blood cells were busily slaughtering many micro-organisms at that very moment or, at least, they better hope like hell they were.

He grinned. This sounded like her, impatient with unscientific ideas, especially those that led to human discomfort. He laughed out loud, remembering several weeks ago when she flea bombed her house, then went to sleep before letting it fully air out. She called him at 2 am to say her knees had buckled from under her when she got up to pee. Did she think that flea poison only affected fleas? She was so hopelessly irrational when she wanted to be. He imagined her sitting on the shag run, tittering hysterically on the phone to him.

Her profile etched double in the window with night surrounding them. She looked at the floor, her eyes half closed, her hair falling forward. He had never seen a lovelier or sadder profile. She smiled wryly, saying without words that she knew more than she would ever say. Maybe it was the angle of her gaze or the slight pucker of her bottom lip in that instant when she averted her eyes from his. Perhaps he might have glimpsed an urge to self-destruct, some sense of violence. But no. Those many nights when they sat in the car under moonlit skies or lay in the bed, lingering over goodbyes, he never fathomed any such thing. And if he had, he never acknowl-edged it.

She was romantic to him, nonsensically idealistic, girlish. Instead of being a scientist, she might have written Victorian romances, Gothic love stories. It was part of her irresistible appeal, her personality filled with contradiction, dissonance, incongruity. Admittedly, he wondered about those times when she became unduly tough, cold, bitter with him. It drove him crazy to see indifference on her face, to watch her mood plunge from gaiety to gloom in a matter of seconds. What was she thinking about when she refused to talk to him? Was there something happening right before his eyes that he refused to see? No, this was unacceptable. He had known her. He had. She had a passion for life. An intoxication with death? She had deserted him now with nothing for solace. No note, no explanation, no goodbye. Only this black book and that unintended.

* * *

She was driving across the Bay bridge in her new silver Prelude, a present from the insurance company after the last one crashed. A radio show announced that Hart was winning in Connecticut. "Yup, yup, yup!" She had no idea what the announcer was talking about, something about Hart's main supporters being "yuppies." She wondered, putting down the joint, if it was possible to smoke too much dope. His drawl clearly faked, he continued, "Yes, the young upwardly mobile urban professionals from New England to Dallas are putting their idealism on the charts, folks." The real acronym was yumup, she figured, but no matter. What a ridiculous world.

Her fingers fumbled with the tape boxes trying to rescue Bob Dylan from his erroneous life in the Joan Baez box. A car pulled without warning in front of her, and she slammed on the brakes, tapes flying from the glove compartment, her joint rolling on to the seat, instant sweat covering her forehead. Goddamn it! These idiots have never learned how to drive. They're probably all yumpies or whatever it is.

Streaks of gold light flashed through the lower levels of the bridge with a hypnotic consistency. She retrieved her joint and took a long draw. "Freedom's just around the corner for you." Maybe she was a yumpy, what a horrible thought. Could this be possible? Am I young, upwardly mobile, professional, urban? Yes to all of them; well, not *that* young. But I'm different. I know I'm different. Probably everyone thinks they're different, and we can't all be different, can we? How did I end up here? There was that strange and sought after feeling again — often drug induced — this peculiar sensation of having no past, no history, of having just dropped in from outer space with strategic amnesia. It was the opposite of deja vu. She studied herself in the rear view mirror: Who are you?

On impulse Suzanne had telephoned Dora earlier in the day. In this moment of panic she had one goal: someone who knew her had to confirm she was still herself. Dora was always by the phone. And they had shared the unfortunate intimacy usually reserved for family. Dora had often played mother to her and vice versa. With two other women this might have worked well, but with them it was like going to bed with an octopus. Suzanne's actual mother was impenetrable. Telephoning her was out of the question. She had never had the least idea who her daughter actually was and she had no tolerance for any kind of mental problem. It would hurt to be ignored or trivialized. Dora was the opposite: available, interested, and all too ready with open arms. When Suzanne reached for the phone she knew it was a mistake, but Dora answered before she could change her mind.

"Hi, it's Suzanne."

Dora's soft voice was cautious, subdued for a moment, then she burst into her loved-and-hated self. "Suzanne, listen, I'm *really* glad you called. I miss you. So much is happening. How are you? Have you heard from Dan?"

"I'm fine." She stammered. "I shouldn't have called." The very mention of his name sent chills up her spine. She felt nauseous with guilt. "But . . . I just wanted to say hello. I'm sorry."

"What is wrong with you? Why are you doing this? I don't understand why you insist on shutting everyone out. You call me then you won't talk. Haven't you even talked to Ivan? Listen, I know you're busy, but come over for dinner. Let's really talk. People still care about you, even if you are acting like a crazy person."

"No." She was getting angry. "I haven't changed my mind." Hearing Dora's familiar voice say these names — Dan, Ivan — it was what she wanted. They still existed. She still existed. "Is everything okay with you?"

Dora's dejection resonated in the silence that followed. She protested, "What do you care? Why in the hell are you so difficult? Why don't you just come over and talk about it? Everyone envies you, you know. You've got everything, Suzanne. I don't understand why you're so hell bent on being by yourself all the time. I know it's hard that Dan left, but there are lots of other men around." She whined like a child's music box winding down.

"I'm sorry, Dora. You don't understand. Never mind. Let's return to the status quo, zero. I hope I haven't upset you. Again."

They both hung up on each other.

What was that all about, she wondered. Forget it. Just forget it.

The dope was working its magic. Stoned. Stoned again. Her favorite state, the only state in which gloom vanished and she metamorphosized from a wicked, evil step-sister into an innocent, sweet Cinderella. I feel giddy, almost happy, she laughed. That's it! That's why I called Dora. My dope connection. What will I do without my dope connection? This is the best dope in the world. I can't live without it. I'll just find someone else. Her eyes scanned the panorama of the East Bay. Thank God for plants in Mendecino and bridges at sunset and tape desks and traffic and me by myself. She sang along with one of her favorite tapes, "Just like a woman and she breaks just like a little girl."

She had a dinner date with Brian, but she wasn't going to keep it. She drove straight home, fell into a lawn chair on her patio and stared at the garden. The blood red roses, the purple and yellow iris, the bristly giant palm tree, they held her transfixed with their intricate detail. The phone rang inside, behind the locked door. She ignored it. He would call back. But the ringing of the phone disturbed her luxuriating in the sensual and moved her on to more left brain mental gymnastics.

Why did life seem easier in the past when it was actually harder? Why does it seem harder now when I've supposedly achieved all the success I worked for then? What the hell did she mean by that: "Everybody envies me?" She had heard this before from Dora, spewed at her like accusations of crime. "*You* have a profession and make good money. *You* have a beautiful house, a nice car, terrific clothes for your perfect figure, AND you're free as a bird, unattached. *You* don't even have to be, you've got men crawling all over you."

Thinking, thinking about not thinking, always not thinking about thinking, by myself, thinking: Why can't I see myself the way everybody else supposedly sees me? Everyone's into this "positive attitude" business: plastic surgery for the masses, triple bypasses for all! Ageing is becoming a curable disease. Dieting, jogging, aerobicizing, transplanting embryos – the newspapers, magazines, T.V. shows are filled with this stuff. Don't worry if you're sterile and fifty, you too can have your first baby! *The Young Octogenarian*, that's what I'd call my new magazine. I'd make a fortune.

What I can't believe is that most people do believe. They have "faith," a concept I thought preserved only in the speeches of wild-eyed evangelists. Religion's not only made a comeback, it's taken over politics, planted itself like a parasite in the national gut. We've come to the time in which many animals get better medical care than the majority of the world's population. But we don't hesitate to torture them by bashing their brains out or depriving them of oxygen. *Save the Whales, Seals, Dolphins*. I'd be happy to pay *Amnesty International* to stop sending me these meticulous accounts of fingernails ripped off, electrodes applied to genitals, children cooked and carved for their parents. Ah, I'm giving myself away with these very sixtyish tendencies. It's not fashionable to care.

Who does cares about the world anymore? Maybe my oft-voiced lie – that nothing bothers me – is true. It's certainly true that another decade has passed me by. When did I start to think in decades? The seventies, definitely a lost decade for me, for people like me who keep skipping merrily back to the sixties wistfully wishing for that mood of liberation to return. In a few months it will be 1984. I remember when 1984 was some distant, futuristic time to be terrified of, but it seemed aeons away. Well, here it is and so what? It was only an Orwellian nightmare. Now it's perfectly obvious that totalitarianism and rampant conformism aren't that scary; they might even make one feel better, more secure. I can take refuge in indifference. If I were me, that would be it; I'd envy my indifference.

And what have I got to complain about, as Dora so persistently reminds me? I have my work. I don't have to moonlight in emergency rooms to pay the bills anymore. I can keep myself in good wine and drugs. I guess I'm upwardly mobile. Can't say I'm on the fringe anymore. Can't claim to be marginal. I've landed smack in the mainstream American Dream. This is my decade: the eighties. The AIDS decade. Maybe the last decade to think in decades. No shortage of brain fodder now. We all have AIDS to think about, as if nuclear war wasn't enough.

The sun had gone down into a cloudy, crimson sky. Sunset often made her want to cry. She didn't want to go into her empty house, but nightfall brought with it a chill. Her mind continued to flip, turning from one channel to another, looking for an image that she could tolerate. He appeared, a frame from a film, Dr. Alterberg, his cute, funny face, his fists balled in his pockets. Best not to think of him. It's too early. But then she did. His image brought a warm tingly sensation to her stomach, a childish delight like chocolate bars and hot fudge sundaes. Risky. Seized with a sudden rush of sobriety, she felt guilty that she hadn't called Brian to cancel their date.

The house was dark and cool. She switched on each light she came to, dumped her briefcase on the chair, put her morning coffee cup in the sink. The usual moments of fantasy, that some horror would befall her alone in her own house, kept her moving from room to room, checking. She turned on the stereo, KJAZ, dinner jazz. Nothing bad could happen during dinner jazz. Being alone felt too easy tonight, too acceptable. Why didn't she keep her date? The phone rang, startling her out of impending regret. Oh God, excuses to Brian. She let it ring, then changed her mind.

"Hi." He hesitated a little, no longer expecting an answer.

"Hi." It wasn't Brian, but him. Her voice spontaneously responded with pleasant surprise. She revised her greeting to a more serious, "Hello." The stereo blared in the background until she shouted, "Wait a minute. Let me turn down the music."

He waited. It seemed a long time before she returned, the silence accentuating the time.

"I'm back. Now. To what do I owe this pleasure, Dr. Alterberg?"

"I was thinking about you, er, about that conversation we had about CMV. Remember? About the role of CMV in AIDS? I was thinking that maybe we should look at some of the gay lymph node patients, you know, for CMV."

"Yesterday in the hall?"

"Yeah, yesterday in the hall." He wondered if this lame excuse for calling her was going to work. It wasn't wholly unjustifiable. They could collaborate on research.

"Listen, Chris," she was still stoned, "let's cut right through the bullshit and get to the point. You want to go to bed with me and that's fine. When do you want to get together?"

He was taken aback and his face went red, but she couldn't see. Maybe she thought life was permanently acting in a Woody Allen movie. Probably a trap he should try to avoid, but caution to the winds. He would call her bluff. "How about Sunday?" Blood rushed to his every extremity. He wished he didn't have a goddamn telephone and the San Francisco Bay between them. Not that he was completely surprised. He knew he would make love to her. It was inevitable and irresistible and terrifying, but he couldn't wait. His fantasies about her were driving him crazy. He couldn't concentrate. He paid no attention to Pat. He ate too much, and he lay awake at night craving her. Every day. Every hour. The wait was too long.

"Well, I don't know. . . ." She hesitated in the grip of a last ditch ambivalence. She knew, too, it was certain to happen.

He took the offensive. "You're not going to change your mind? You said you wanted to be friends. Come on, what are you afraid of? I'm harmless. Ruff, ruff, all bark, no bite." The last thing he intended was to harm her. Anything but.

"Okay. What do you suggest we do?" A movie, a walk in the park, dinner? She wondered which he would choose.

"Why don't you come to my house? We can have a drink, sit around, and, well, talk, listen to music. Nobody else will be there." Why did I say that, he winced, too suggestive.

"Fine. What time?"

"Great!" He felt as if he'd just caught a big fish or escaped a traffic ticket. "Come early, about noon."

"Noon? Don't be silly. You want me to just come over to your house?"

Shit. What was wrong now? She had sounded unreservedly available a moment ago. "Noon's no good? Okay, when can you come?"

"It's just that I'm going to a conference this weekend, and it won't be over until three, I think. I suppose I could leave early, if the speakers aren't very good. Yeah, I guess I could make it by four, say."

"Good. Four is all right. Do you have to go now? I mean, are you real busy?" She sounded anxious to get off the phone. There was a businesslike aspect to the phone call that he was determined to destroy.

"I just walked in the door from the hospital. I'm tired. I'm starved, I haven't eaten all day."

"Why not?"

"Why not? Because I was too busy, that's why not." Her irritation startled him. She could feel him stiffen through the phone wires. "I'm sorry. I didn't mean to shout at you. It's been a hard day."

"Why don't you tell me about it?" Now he felt he might get somewhere with her. He could show her he was a nice guy, that he cared about *her*, not just her body.

"You won't believe it. I get upset over strange things sometimes."

"Try me. Like what?"

"Well, if you really want to know, I heard this stupid thing on the radio about yuppies or yumpies, something like that, and I think I might be one of them. I don't like it. I don't want to be a yuppy. These things are too absurd. I mean, don't you ever wonder what the world is coming to? Stuff like that."

"Stuff like that?" He stifled the urge to laugh. She sounded so naïve, wavering from one extreme to the other: tough, experienced woman of the world to innocent ingenué.

"Yeah, I really have to go now."

"Okay, I'll let you go but, listen, I'm really looking forward to Sunday." The words rolled like syrup from his tongue. This was stickier than he liked, and for an instant he felt artless, sleazy. Maybe he was after her body, but then she seemed like a handful to endure for sexual pleasure alone.

"Bye." She hung up first. Going directly to the stereo she put on her favorite classical guitar tape, then fell onto the sofa like a Victorian lady. Now he would consume her evening; she wouldn't eat much thinking of her waistline. Just a nice glass of dry, white wine, she thought, and where is the servant to bring it? Her briefcase bulged with work, but that was impossible tonight. She tried to rationalize not working with the fact that she'd been working ten hours already. But rationalization was not her strong point these days. Guiltily she rose from the sofa. First she would organize the articles to read, then go over the new data.

Food. She was starving. She opened the refrigerator and stood there looking in until the refrigerator started to buzz. Nothing appealed to her except the Dry Creek Chenin Blanc. Was she becoming an alcoholic or was she already there? Drinking alone was one of the first signs. It was posted on every bulletin board at every hospital. She scoffed at the triviality of alcoholism. In her case it was far down on the list of substance abuse. Of course, she knew lives were ruined by drinking too much, but better that than murder one's children. She had no children to murder and every excuse to drink alone. She was alone.

She wandered back into the high-ceilinged living room and browsed among the hundreds of books. She ran her hands over the Mexican masks, the weavings, the primitive statuary that decorated the walls and assorted tables. She stopped at an antique art deco vase. Dan had given it to her for her birthday two years ago. Tears filled her eyes, and she fell onto a chintz covered chaise lounge. Through the tears she studied the fresh cut flowers, all her favorites — irises, lilies, roses, daisies — each in separate vases. Dan always brought her fresh flowers on Friday afternoon. Since he left she had kept up the tradition, buying them for herself or cutting them from the garden. Somehow with the flowers she tried to convince herself that the house was still the same, the same place the two of them had filled with shells and driftwood and old oak furniture. In three years of weekend browsing in junk shops, at garage sales and auctions, they had managed to fill two houses. Every article her eye fell upon reminded her of a vacation they took: masks from Taxco, rugs from Oaxaca, hunting prints from England, pottery from Quimper.

The dope had worn off and the alcohol was kicking in, bringing with it a state of melancholy, a state she detested and promised herself she would avoid at all costs. The most important task on her many lists of important tasks was: to forget. Quite knowingly and wilfully she was going to reconstruct history. It could be done with patience and perseverance. She had given herself a year to accomplish it, and Dan had only been gone three months. This lapse was due to Chris; yes, a living breathing example that she had made little real progress in attempting to become impervious to affection, to seduction. The possibility of love rears its head and immediately resurrects love as it was. It is the *was* that hurt. *Be Here Now*. God, did that ever work?

Think of life as an experiment, she commanded. Change the ingredients, the components of the environment and, most important, the method of conceptualizing the project and its purpose, then the results are bound to be different. She scanned the room again. It was *her* world. *She* created it. All her stuff, her precious objets d'art, her idiosyncratic souvenirs, her junk furniture salvaged from basements and attics, it was merely an eclectic collection of material possessions: that's all. She stretched out and studied the room once more, without feeling, without memory. She drifted toward sleep.

But what about the bedroom? Could that be transformed again into a place of rest and play? Lately, she stayed away from it. When she slept in there her control vanished. Every night at precisely 3 a.m. she woke up with a jolt, sweat often drenching her

nightgown, her limbs frozen with fear. There was nothing she could
do.

*   *   *

The first Sunday in September, the warmest month in the Bay
area, arrived. She wore an antique white lace blouse and a black skirt
with tiny white roses on it. Not that she was actually going to any
conference. She was engaged in brunch with Brian, her latest lover.
He was not to know of her afternoon, and the newly discovered Dr.
Alterberg was not to know of her morning. They would both think
she was at a conference when it suited her.

Needless to say, her relationships with men were in a shambles at
the moment as they usually were. She never imagined that a time would
come when insecurity ceased to rule. Those who wanted her were
those she responded to. She had never learned to make the first
move, much to her chagrin. Age and experience narrowed the field
of possibility, and she had gotten rather picky. When intellectual,
economic, or political compatibility entered the equation, the
possibilities could hardly be called a field. All the old-fashioned lofty
sentiments had to be thrown out with modern times. Compatibility
itself was archaic, a relic of her pre-marriage, pre-divorce past. Now
she calculated and schemed to put pleasure, sexual pleasure alone, in
the place of compatibility. Another insoluble dilemma. Sexual
pleasure alone. Wasn't this a consequence of pure spontaneity, seren-
dipity? Love, that illusive matter, sent her brain searching like a computer for any reason at all to pursue the opposite sex. In each new
encounter she tried to keep four sentences uppermost in her mind:
She married once for love. She had loved with no strings attached.
She got hurt. Love hurt. Of course, this didn't seem to stop her.

Brian smiled at her, a let's-get-out-of-here-and-go-to-bed smile. She
disliked him intensely. His emotional openness, so very California,
so very new male, struck her as a humiliating defect. His brains are
oatmeal, she thought. Holding an intelligent conversation with him
was like hoping for an oasis in the desert. But his eyes were sky blue,
and his own inferiority complex made him try endlessly to please her
in bed. For this she endured the rest, at least until someone better
came along, and perhaps someone had. Still, there was something
perverse and gratifying about the popular psychology he practiced
on her. She didn't care much about losing him or angering him,
which in any case was impossible to do.

His blatant ogling was driving her to distraction. She groped for a

27

conversation. "Did you read that article on El Salvador in the *Times* this morning?"

"No, didn't see the paper yet." He caressed her shoulder, dismissing the possibility of that sort of conversation. "You look gorgeous this morning," he whispered seductively. Then he leaned over and nibbled her neck, kissing her shoulder, her hand, her fingertips.

A wave of resignation swept over her. Annoyance too. She tried to ignore him and eat faster, but her appetite was spoiled. Here they were: brunch in an outdoor French cafe, fresh orange juice, hot croissants, strawberries with cream, espresso, bright sun, flowers. What could be more enjoyable, more romantic? The vacuum of his company exaggerated the irony. This has to end, she told herself, and hoped for a better afternoon. "I think we have to stop seeing each other, Brian." There was no easy way to say it. She avoided his eyes and scooted her chair far around the table.

"Why? How can you say that?" He held her hand tighter and tried his sexy grin again. "You know we're good for each other. I feel it. There's something between us, something special. We click. You know it too." He refused to take her seriously, searching her eyes, squeezing her hand, touching her cheek.

"I don't think we're right for each other. It's true we 'click' as you say, in certain ways. You know what I mean, but it's not enough. I can't talk to you." Her voice whined too much. She sat back and stopped to think. "I don't know how to say this, but, well, you don't seem to be interested in anything except sex and yourself. I'm tired of discussing your childhood, your ungiving parents, your therapy. I know you are a psychiatrist, but don't you tire of practicing on yourself all the time? It's getting too boring, that's all."

What amazed her was that he wasn't offended. He sat staring at his coffee, sullen, pouting. "I can't help it. I've been depressed my whole life. I'm just coming out of it and realizing the world is out there. I've spent the past five years in intensive therapy to pull myself together. I went to medical school. I *had* to specialize in psychiatry. I wasn't interested in reading books or nature or art or anything. Until I met you. You're the first woman who has made me feel like the world is a great place to explore. We've had fun; that's important to me. I know I've got problems. You do too. Come on, Suzanne, be realistic, our relationship may not be perfect, but it's been pretty damned good. I don't want to give you up." His eyes pleaded with her. "Do I have to?"

In spite of genuine revulsion at his display of emptiness and vulnerability, she felt guilty. She felt pity for him. How could he say that? They had dated sporadically for a month or so, had sex several times, never actually slept together or discussed one serious issue, including their relationship, but his neediness clouded these facts. It was as if she had adopted him, taken on an unforseen responsibility for his happiness that was now coming to light. His confession infuriated her; she had vowed to leave behind all remnants of guilt. It wasn't going to work. "You're manipulating me and you know it." She rose to leave.

He remained seated. "Say that if you want, but you know in your heart that I'm a sincere guy. I'm very sincere. I've never lied to you. I do love you."

The unreality of it made her dizzy. She wanted him to make sense, to act like the thirty-five year old professional he was, to show a bit of dignity. She sat back down. "Listen, Brian, we've only known each other a month."

"That's not true. We met over a year ago." He could argue this point.

"We met, but we didn't know each other. We merely said polite hellos in the cafeteria. That's not the point. The point is we went out. We went to bed. We had a good time. But we don't have anything in common. We're not right for each other."

"Well, you're right for me. What's wrong anyway? Another AIDS patient die?"

"Don't change the subject. Why aren't you hearing me? Isn't listening your profession? I don't think you are right for me. It doesn't matter a damn if you think otherwise. Now I'm going, and I want you to acknowledge that you understand what I'm saying." Her face flushed red with anger and embarrassment.

"Okay. I'll call you later. Is that okay? Can I call you and talk on the phone, just talk?"

As she stood again he pressed her hand. Why couldn't she say no? She couldn't even speak. He didn't let go of her hand. The silence ushered in confusion, bewilderment. She pulled her hand away to take out a five dollar bill. He protested. "All right," she relented, "I'll talk to you on the phone." Would anything ever end at the right time, in the right place?

* * *

At one on this perfect sunny day she drove, aimless, toward the ocean. He wasn't expecting her until four. The morning had soured. An irritating restlessness formed a skin around her depression, a delicate red peel, paper thin, within which she was seedy pulp ready to ooze from any puncture, any crack. Nothing was as it should be;

nothing was as it seemed. Part of her felt a thrill of anticipation for another round of falling in love. It might ameliorate this steady creeping toward the edge. But why did she feel this way about him? She didn't know him at all.

Another part of her anticipated the worst, a silent cancer on a terminal journey. Could it be cancelled? Interrupted maybe? But what was done was done. Forget the past, she reminded herself once more. Yes, one more affair was probable disillusionment, but one last love? It was possible. Facts of life. Her unwelcome knowledge, her wish for doubt, betrayed the simple facts of life. She was older. She had let go of the myth that life started after this or after that. This was life, now, today, in the moment, not in the past, and that was enough. Fact. She had to protect herself from the dangers of repeating history. This depression is normal; it's just a stage to go through. Reactive depression, sadness, it occurs with any traumatic loss. She read it in an article that was supposed to help her understand her dying patients. No reason it couldn't help her too.

Her mind wandered to the soft, rolling hills; those expressionist hills with their weeping eucalyptus trees, the branches fanning out and down in veinlike patterns, random, surely painted onto the landscape by a lonely artist. One tree, by itself, captured the sun-drenched beauty, the sublime peace of this place. She examined herself as usual in the rear view mirror. Her reflection was looking adrift. Don't be aimless, she lectured herself and straightened up in the seat. I know why I'm driving on this country road toward the Pacific. I need the peace of the countryside, this view, the serenity that precedes the rapture of my wild, windy ocean, my cove.

She put in the Phil Ochs tape and searched for her favorite song, "I guess I better do it while I'm here." He committed suicide. It made her feel better when her eyes filled with tears. She stretched a little and sang along. She thought about the lymphocyte study, the retrovirus grant, the next experiments she had to undertake, the eventual papers to write, the clothes at the cleaners she kept forgetting to pick up. Time to smoke a joint. Her right hand searched the glove compartment for the box of Indonesian clove cigarettes, the smell of which intoxicated her. It also hid the smell of marijuana, just in case. Would he approve of her dope smoking habit? This was California after all. If he didn't? So what. Fuck him. She wasn't about to argue over the ethics, the brain cells lost, the consequences to short-term memory, and certainly not the legality of it, the least of her concerns.

Her stomach growled. She hadn't finished her croissant, but she wasn't hungry, not for food. She felt slightly nauseous and wondered if she was losing too much weight. It upset and irritated her. No. No more thinking about deficiencies, limitations or problems.

The Prelude rounded a sharp curve and the cool, watery shade of the redwood grove sent a chill down her spine. When she came to Inverness she would stop at the bakery. There was a house for sale amongst the redwoods. She could barely see it nestled alongside the river. How much would it cost? Maybe they would buy it and spend their weekends in aging blue jeans, stoned, scrubbing mold off the walls. It was no use. She wanted to think about him, to consider the possibilites. The two bowls of pretzels they had consumed with their first drink were a definite sign, a fact. She never ignored the facts. Not the good ones.

Memory. What the hell is it anyway? All those electrical impulses bouncing around from synapse to synapse, information etched into the pathways of the brain, structured biological messages, reinforced repetitions. No, it's not just that. During their first drink she had sensed that he was afraid of her. Already infatuated. All his excuses about being late, parking, his watch running slow, his experiment running overtime.

"Really, forget it. It doesn't matter. I was enjoying myself watching the evening parade of briefcases and baguettes go by." She had ordered a second glass of wine and asked him, "What will you have?"

The waitress stood over him, patient, exchanging the dwindling bowl of pretzels for a full one. These two were good for a big tip. Lots of love affairs began in this bar. She glanced at her other customers, chewed on her lower lip, staightened her spine, and shifted to keep his attention. "Oh, hummm, scotch on the rocks." He never took his eyes off Suzanne's face.

"So, that's accomplished," she smiled knowingly at the waitress. "Shall we get down to business. Who are you?" She played with him, conscious of her enjoyment. He was so like a puppy, squirming at her feet, tongue hanging out, panting, antsy for a stick to be thrown so he could retrieve it with confidence and pride, full of himself.

He felt it, too, the thrill and delight of jumping naked into an icy lake which would take his breath away and leave him gasping. Enervated. Alive. He had thought about it all afternoon. Boy, had he thought about it. He would play with her, whatever game she wanted. "I asked you for this drink. Don't I get the first question?" He automatically began eating the pretzels, one after the other.

"Okay. As long as it has nothing to do with my research."

"Perhaps, I'll begin with your name and phone number? Nothing too formal." They laughed.

"Hasn't Dr. Forbes given you a clue?" She sipped the wine. "I can see you're too impatient." She put out her hand. "Suzanne Keller, doctor of medicine, among other things."

His heart raced. He slipped his hand into hers, pushing aside the pretzels, the wine. He held on a little too long, but she didn't pull away. The warmth of his hand melted in the coolness of hers. She liked this warmth; it was gentle and reassuring. When he finally let go, it was awkward. She caught the wine glass as it tipped toward her splashing into the ashtray and turning her cigarette to mush. How silly preliminaries can be.

"I'm sorry." He hastily wiped the spill with her cocktail napkin. "See what you made me do!" He teased her. "Did anyone ever tell you you're too pretty to be a scientist?" She lowered her eyes and ran her finger around and around the top of the wine glass. There was a blush coming to her cheeks. It was hard to believe. Surely she had heard this a million times before. Surely she knew she was beautiful. Was she going to feign coy? He hoped not. He rather liked her cavalier attitude. He lowered his head until he was practically touching his cheek to the table to catch her eye.

"Everyone. Why can't you men be more creative?" She lowered her head so the two of them looked like children chatting with their heads down at rest time in nursery school. He bolted upright, and she followed suit.

"Ah, come on, take it easy on me. Give a guy a chance." He was serious. The scotch arrived, he gulped it down. "Look before we go any further into this I want to ask you something."

"Sure. Go ahead."

"Did Melvin tell you he thinks I'm a pervert?"

"What?" He must be crazy, another reason to like him. And she did. She liked him already. "No. Are you?"

"Remember the faculty meeting, when I first saw you? I was so knocked out I ended up falling off my chair, and my hand landed in Melvin's crotch, accidently of course." She giggled, remembering the scene. "Melvin's a weird guy, if you haven't already noticed, I wouldn't want him spreading unfounded rumors." Her laughter made him glow. What fun to share their first moment, their first sight of each other. "See, I have other talents besides turning cigarettes to mush. Your pretty face knocked me off my chair."

"Is this the flattery-will-get-you-everywhere approach?"

"Will it?"

She grinned but didn't answer. Of course, it would, but she wasn't going to tell him so soon. "Depends on how perverted you really are."

"Can't I just play the old-fashioned guy and carry on about your gorgeous eyes, your beautiful hair, your twenty-year-old face. How do you do it? Secret potions." His charm was blossoming out of his control. He couldn't remember ever being this nonchalant about his intentions, this open with his compliments. It was all in good fun. Like a drug, she went straight to his head.

"All right, that's enough. Anyway, I'm not *that* pretty and you're embarrassing me." She looked momentarily disturbed, upset, or sad. He wasn't very intuitive, but there was something wrong. He had pushed the seductive banter too far. She repeated herself, not talking to him anymore, "I'm not really pretty. I'm rather plain, and don't tease me about it."

"Ridiculous nonsense." He tried to sound light, casual, but serious, to respect her mood. "Where did you ever get that idea?" Gesturing with his hand, he ordered another scotch.

She seemed to have drifted far away from him, her gaze going out the window and beyond. "My mother. I guess."

* * *

Sand grated against his fingertips until he found the hole in the pocket of his pants. Deftly fretting with the infinite grains of sand he tried to force them out; they tickled the hairs on his thigh and stuck tight in the dampness behind his knees. These physical sensations annoyed him at first. Then he was pleased. He experienced sensation in his own body. The numbness, her erasure of his body that left him stranded, annihilated, that thrust him into the world of pure horror, it had subsided. For a few seconds he thought only of getting the sand out of his pants, but it was a short reprieve. He turned to agony, the agony of memory, associations, connections.

It was mid-morning, the 28th of October, the month of change. Subtle signs of autumn drifted with the wind across the rolling brown hills. The hawks were flying, graceful, invincible birds of prey. A few travel worn leaves sailed over the cliff behind him, scattered themselves among the driftwood, and were swept into the swirling rocks that rattled in and out with the tide. He saw the shadows of the hawks on the face of the cliff magnified as they glided close to the ground in search of field mice. They came in sight of the gull nests lodged precariously on ledges of cliff rock. Baby gulls were as tasty as field mice; the hawks knew only their hunger. He watched them glide on the gusts of wind, passing by the nests again and again, considering their meal with no emotion, no guilt. The life cycle, one bird preying on another, spilling unborn eggs to premature death in the routine search for continued life. This was nature.

She was lecturing him, her voice as alive, as serious and intent on its purpose as the hawk. A superlative bird, she called it, glorious, a perfect combination of intelligence and power, an unambiguous marvel of nature. Hawks terrified her, she said, and she loved them. He put his hands over his ears. His eyes took over, and he saw her, screeching the car to a halt, jumping out with her Nikon, adjusting the telephoto lens to capture the wild hawks not twenty feet over her head. He saw himself, leaning over, tugging on her sweater, fearing she might engage the birds' wrath. Her eyes sparkled when she slid back into the car, her cheeks glowed pink, and her smile made his heart skip. She pinched him on the leg, kissed him on the cheek, reassured him of her safety. He covered his eyes. "Don't worry. What if he did attack me?" That evocative voice, it shifted smoothly as the gears in his Alfa. "Birds can't be held responsible for their actions. They exist to survive. If other life perishes in this cause, so be it. This is the way it is, the way it has to be. Man, and I do mean men, can't understand this; he isn't a part of it. Man has taken nature as his primal other. The other can only be observed. Described, perhaps." She tacked this on to appease the scientist in him.

He had often thought something like this, not in those words, not that clearly articulated. This was one reason he lost himself in the microscopic world of cells, viruses, bacteria, these forms of life as fully alive as they were, but as different from them as the hawk, a rock, a grain of sand. Study, observe, describe, analyze — what he did best for the benefit of his kind. We were of the same kind, the human species, she and I, but so different. She knew how different we were, male and female. She knew. He remembered being envious of her that day. She was a part of the world in a way he'd never been. But he could see it.

Now she really was ONE with the goddamn hawk, or was she? The hawk was alive. He was alive. He was furious, enraged, and he felt more a part of nature than he ever wanted to be. He wished one of the majestic hawks would attack him now. "I'm more food than a gull egg!" He yelled at the hawk with the entire force of his lungs. "Why don't you come down here, you beautiful bastard, pick on someone your own size!" He stood up and started to run down the beach, following the hawk. "Come on, get down here!" He tried throwing rocks, but they fell like dead weights over his shoulders. The hawk appeared to turn his head and notice this strange figure on the beach, his eyes calculating the size of the form, its activity. The bird soared back over the cliff, cautious, in control.

Out of breath, he fell on a rock, cursing, "Dirty, fucking, baby-bird killer!" He lay back on the rock, his chest heaving, his heart pounding. "He knows what's good for him. He knows I would rip him apart with my bare hands. I'd rip off that beak and tear off those wings. He won't come near me. I'd kill him. I'd kill him."

Earlier he had seen a seal swim by, a lone seal with an eery cry, more a whine than a bark. A wet brown head popped between the waves, looked left and right, almost as if it were seeking someone on the beach. A baby seal, he thought, tears gushing from his eyes, blinding him. Crying would be all right, but this wasn't crying. This was disintegrating into salty liquid from the inside out. A river ran beneath his skin. His body — a body he had believed to be flesh and blood, bone and muscle, organs and nerves — was now a vessel of water. He absorbed, he excreted, he rested. He wept inconsolably for that baby seal. It was looking for its mother. It was lost. It was sick. It was cut by a sharp rock. Why was life so cruel, so insensitive? Why did baby seals have to be lost and hurt? Nothing made sense anymore. His head, once a center of control, sat like an old halloween pumpkin, heavy with a crooked carved smile, turning into mush.

He licked the salt from his lips automatically the way a kitten cleans its mouth. This explosion was cleansing. After it he fell into a state of semi-sleep, a state in which dreamy images calmed him, soothed him as she had when his head lay in her lap, when she stroked his hair over and over. He could almost feel her fingertips there. Delicious dreams, experiences of timelessness beyond his imagination pulled him far from any hint of a real world, a material world. But soon enough the sand fleas nipped at his ankles in increasing numbers, and his legs began to jerk in automatic response. It was still there to torment him, his body, his human body.

The seal omen. He sat up. Yes, the seal omen. This he had to consider. He had to clear his mind of everything. Pure concentration. It might lead to an answer, an explanation. They had been to the beach many times, every spare afternoon or evening, every weekend. There was this strange coincidence. The first time he was simply put off, irritated, because it made her sad. The second time he was curious, amused that she made something of it. The third time, the time she named it "the seal omen," he had a twinge of forboding. It was her silliness that misled him, her insistence on making something out of everything, her refusal to believe in coincidence, as if all events were connected to each other in a grand scheme, a scheme she seemed to be hell bent on being a part of.

But why *did* that dead seal wash up in front of them a third time?

Why did it wash up just as they were polishing off a delicious chardonnay, slugging it from the bottle while discussing the end of their brief affair? Why had she been so moody, wanting to break up, saying it would never work, insisting it might as well end before it went too far, before they would both be hurt? Then she noticed it before he did. She stood up and walked to the edge of the water, the empty wine bottle in her hand. He was royally pissed off by this time. There she goes. In the middle of a conversation that threatened to ruin his life, she gets up and walks off. "Come here," she shouted and gestured. "Come here, look at this."

He ignored her. "Fuck you!" he shouted, but knew she couldn't hear, then got up and followed her obediently.

"Look at this," she exclaimed. "It's another dead seal."

"It's a sea lion." She often misidentified species.

"Are you sure? Looks like a large seal to me. Anyway, so what a seal, a sea lion. What do you think it means?"

"I think it means a sea lion died and washed up on the beach." He was caustic. "Who cares what it means. I want to know why you think we should stop seeing each other. It doesn't make sense." He tried to pull her away, back to the cave out of the wind.

"How can you be so insensitive, so concrete? How can you say who cares what this means? A dead seal washes up right in front of us *for the third time* as we're talking about breaking up, and you don't care what it means?" She was incredulous. "A dead seal. Dead. Dead." Jerking her arm from his grip, she stomped back to the cliff, carrying the wine bottle like a club.

He followed her. "Okay. I'm sorry." He put on a solicitous face. "What do you think it means?" There was no choice but to go along with her. She preferred talking in metaphors. But now she wasn't talking. She went far into the cave and lit a cigarette. "Listen," he lay down beside her, "I think this sea lion is trying to tell you to stop being so morbid and morose. Things could be worse." His hand reached up to her shoulder to pull her down beside him to comfort her, to cuddle her, to say whatever disagreements had been were over. "Suzanne, I love you. Why are we having this argument anyway?"

She came back to him. She slid down beside him and let him put his arms around her. She snuggled closer, her arms around his neck, her head buried in his shoulder. "It's an omen." Her words were barely audible but spoken directly into his ear. "It's an omen from the sea, Chris. A seal omen. About death."

The flicker of foreboding came and went when their lips met, when she opened her mouth, hot and wet, sweet with the taste of wine. His tongue explored hers, and they were lost together.

*   *   *

By the time she drove into the beach parking lot it was time to turn around and drive back. That is, if she wanted to show up on time. The last joint was wearing off. The bottle of Perrier was almost empty, and she had to pee. The damp mist of fog near the ocean was pale gold, thin clouds colored by a translucent, white sun. She rolled another joint, filling the pockets of her sweater with necessities: Swiss army knife, Kleenex, matches, roach holder, wallet with cash and credit cards, car keys. Unfortunately, criminals preyed on these deserted parking lots, and once she had lost a special leather bag with her journal of five years in it. The smashed window was nothing compared to the loss of her only photo of Anthony and her. A snapshot of her kissing him on the cheek and him spontaneously, with his mischievious smile, pulling her closer. The camera had caught the magic in that relationship, a relationship she finished with reluctance. Every time she pulled into this parking lot she remembered the photograph, how she had believed keeping it would preserve the memories. And she was right in a way. After it was gone, thanks to the careless thieves, she forced the affair into the recesses of her memory, she felt her sometimes intense longing for him dull. A comfortable gauze curtain fell between then and now. She thought it appropriate that this ritual remembrance of him in this parking lot was enough. It was four years since she'd seen him. Her cataloguing of their time together went with the picture, probably to be strewn across these very hills by those who had no use for words or photos.

The path down to the beach had been made steeper by the ravages of high winds. There were warnings about the water. DO NOT SWIM. RIP TIDES AND DANGEROUS WATER. SHARKS HAVE BEEN SIGHTED HERE. EVERY YEAR LIVES ARE LOST. The ice plants lined the dirt trail with brilliant yellow and pink flowers. Orange poppies were blooming everywhere. The most sensual of flowers, white lilies with their fuzzy tongues poking out, dotted the hills in bountiful clusters. She carefully made her way, wanting to pick the flowers, but knowing they wouldn't last the drive back. Now she was stuck on Anthony. She'd heard he had a new girlfriend, a serious one. She wondered if he thought of her anymore. His letters were sporadic and came only when he wanted a favor. There's no time for this, she scolded herself. Anthony is past. Focus on Dr. Chris Alterberg. He is future.

37

Her hair blew about her face until it stung. Before her was the vast expanse of the Pacific. The first sight of it always took her breath away and made her forget everything. The ocean wind washed out her mind, set it free. She stood for some minutes, drinking in the seascape, feeling her pulse quicken, her lungs synchronizing with the tide. There was only enough time to walk the length of the beach, to check and see if anyone was occupying her spot. Sometimes, rarely, other people were there, couples usually. She considered telling them that this was her special spot, but she never did. It was different when she came alone. There was enough beach to share. She decided she would bring him here. She would, if he still interested her after this evening.

Four o'clock already. Goddammit. Never mind, it isn't fashionable to be on time for a date. He wasn't on time for their first drink. Here was an excuse to drive back fast and recklessly. She threw the car in gear and skidded out of the parking lot. Five or six deer stood perfectly still near the road, stopped dead by her movement, as if they had already been shot and stuffed and set forever regal in the hunter's yard. The car sped by like a bullet, and they turned as one, galloping away from this intrusion of steel. She watched them run as the car twisted and turned around the ribbons of asphalt.

She couldn't shake it. The dope didn't work. The ocean didn't work. The hours of driving weren't going to work either. Remembering. People. Events. Things she couldn't forget, but absolutely had to forget, completely forget. The sadness etched its way too far into her consciousness. Daniel. How was he? She wanted to telephone him, to see him, but he'd only just visited a few weeks ago. It was over. They were over. He was as past as Anthony, but not past enough. Her back ached now, the back of her neck in particular. She rubbed her neck and tried to think of something funny or meaningless. Brian, his pathetic plea to continue their relationship on the phone. How would she dispose of him? How awful. The idea of having to dispose of someone turned her stomach. Every day. Loneliness within plenty, the tortured dominance of the internal and its *au courant* emptiness, it made her choke and want to scream at the same time. Psychic pain. It was no less terrifying than physical pain. Death. Every day.

None of the good radio stations were close enough yet; she had to put in a tape. The least melancholy tape she had was *The Moody Blues*. Too dated, a real relic of hippydom. It reminded her of Anthony. She took out the tape and drove in silence, wishing for the freeway, the grid, where she was one of thousands of other drivers speeding along between the white lines away from the inevitable sunset.

The hills above Sausalito sparkled reds, greens, blues, and yellows, the lights of a permanent carnival. A lot went on in those valleys and hills. The modern, redwood shops with their hand-carved signs offered everything from lodging and food to modern electronic gadgetry and tax preparation. From the Tamalpais movie theater to the freeway entrance there was every luxury known to civilization available at a price, and most inhabitants had the money to pay. How ironic, she thought, to be plagued with the blues in paradise.

The traffic was backed up in San Rafael, not unusual for a Sunday evening. Everyone inched ahead toward the freeway bumper to bumper. Like most Californians she was accustomed to long hours in the car. She even liked it, but now she was in a hurry. At every opportunity she wove in and out of the lanes, jerking herself silly. The police were in their hiding place three blocks from the entrance ramp. She remembered and behaved herself, but couldn't resist giving them a dirty look as she drove by. Losing her license was something she couldn't afford to do. But her mischievous wish to defy authority put her in a precarious position on the road. She crept past them, then once on the ramp it was time to fly.

She stayed in the right lane, knowing that the exit to the Richmond bridge was a minute away. There was a certain exhilaration in turning toward the bridge, in driving past the foreboding concrete box of San Quentin where the unlucky were incarcerated, and she felt a fleeting freedom because of it. Manson was in there, burned or isolated, a hell no different from Sartre's *No Exit*. He *was* alive. Hi Charlie. How ya doin?

The Bay spread out on all sides, punctuated by islands of hills. One could see for miles toward San Francisco, the Bay bridge, and beyond to the San Mateo bridge on the right side and on the left the pastel oil tanks of Richmond, Pinole, the curve of the Bay that went inland by Benica toward the Sacramento delta. She loved to see the San Francisco skyline from this vantage point. It reminded her of the Emerald City, a playground for adults. Dead ahead were the hills of North Berkeley where innumerable women and men stood watching the multi-colored sky from picture windows, drinking in the last moments of daylight, welcoming the dark of night, a respite, a shade pulled down against the eternal beautiful view. It was liberating to enter that bridge at one hundred miles an hour, flying home after a long, tiring drive, after her own sacred Sunday ritual — ocean worship. Home.

* * *

He paced around the living room of the large stucco house. Where was she? Had she had an accident? No one would call him. No one even knew he existed in her life. Would she not come and not call? He ran up the stairs and took out a carefully folded piece of paper. After all that trouble, not to mention the embarrassment he had exposed himself to. He unfolded the paper hesitantly, his mouth watering. Two grams of cocaine. The rocks were like white crystals of quartz; they glittered like diamonds. He smeared some of the loose powder over his gums. It was a surprise for her. She said she liked drugs, he chuckled to himself trying to suppress his exaggerated excitement. If she didn't get here soon he wasn't going to wait. He was jumping out of his skin already.

It took considerable effort, plotting, suggesting, arranging, to convince Pat to visit her sister in L.A. He waited anxiously for the cardiologist's call, suspecting every time the phone rang that the narcotics squad had discovered him before he ever made the request. Could he really trust this cardiologist who didn't know him from Adam? When he put on his best casual approach and asked him, the guy acted like it was nothing. "Two grams of coke? Sure, but the shipment isn't coming until Friday. I get it from my stockbroker. No problem. It's three hundred for two grams and that's a deal. This is pure stuff straight off the boat from Bolivia, uncut." The cardiologist's beeper had gone off, and he raced away toward an incoming coronary, tossing instructions over his shoulder, "Leave the check in my box." So he did. He left the check wrapped in a white sheet of paper in a departmental envelope, and the coke arrived Saturday morning in the same envelope but wrapped in a page from *Playboy* the bottom half of the centerfold — Miss September, not bad.

The distinct sound of a car motor shut off outside. A door opened. He looked out from the upstairs window. She stood beside the car fluffing her hair out in the window, putting on lipstick, straightening her skirt. He turned back to the room. The roses were perfect, right beside the bed. The sheets were new, crispy white, and the pillows were awry as he had arranged them. A twinge of guilt hit him about Pat washing and changing the sheets for the old family friend he said was visiting, an elderly lady, a friend of his mother. He had to put her up for the night. Pat vacuumed the room, did the sheets, cut the roses, put extra hangers in the closet, and cleaned the bathroom. She even put lilac soap in the dish and gardenia bath oil on the edge of the tub. She lent him her matched set of deep purple towels, the soft, thick ones he loved. She'll never know, he dismissed his twinge. The doorbell rang.

He stood behind the door composing himself as if he hadn't expected her until now. "Well, look who's here. Come in." He put out his hand, not waiting for her response and pulled her cheek to his lips. She could have been his sister, his best friend's wife.

She turned her cheek to him with the same benign friendliness, squeezing his hand. "I'm sorry I'm late. I got hung up at the conference. You know how those sessions run on. I was bored to tears, but the time got away from me. Traffic was terrible for a Sunday." She slipped out of her violet angora sweater and draped it over her arm. "What a gorgeous house. Do you live here alone?"

"Er, no, not really. I live with a roommate. A lawyer, a guy. He's not home this weekend, in L.A. on business. So, we've got the place to ourselves." He followed her into the living room where she seemed to be inspecting each object in turn, the wall hangings, the pottery Pat made, the vases of flowers Pat arranged, the large metal and wood sculpture Pat had given him. His nerves were on edge. She stopped at the books, passing them by quickly, but not so quickly that she didn't see the shelf of women's literature. He had to get her out of here. "Would you like to see the rest of the house? As long as we're at it."

"Sure. It's hard to believe two men keep a house this clean. The flowers are beautiful." She didn't follow him, but perused the record collection, Joni Mitchell, Joan Baez, Bonnie Raitt, Phoebe Snow, Chris Williamson, Ricki Lee Jones. There was a woman living here, but never mind. It would all come out sooner or later.

"Let's go upstairs. I have a surprise for you."

"A surprise? Great, I love surprises." Wasn't he going to offer her a drink, something ordinary to begin with? "Do you mind if I have a glass of water first. I'm a bit thirsty."

"Of course. That's a good idea. Let's take some up to my room. It has the best view in the house anyway." He started into the kitchen, then came back and motioned for her to come with him. Her scrutiny of the place was making him very edgy. "I have my own stereo up there, but if there's something down here you'd like to hear, bring it along."

She picked out an old favorite, Joni Mitchell's *Blue*. "I haven't heard this in ages." It was a lie. She had listened to it only two nights ago, but her choice was justifiable. He might object that it was too sad, too female which some men did.

She held her sweater, purse, and the record with one arm, putting her other across the kitchen doorway from which she watched him get out the ice and pour two large glasses of water. He, or someone, had cut fresh limes and put them in a bowl near the bottled water.

The smell reminded her of summer in the tropics where she rubbed limes on her feet and wrists to cool them in the humid heat. He put limes in both glasses and turned to see her standing there, seductively spread across the doorway. Before he could use her stance as an excuse to kiss her, she moved aside and let him pass. "You lead the way."

She followed him up the stairs, watching his tanned hands around the glasses, his soft brown hair curling over his shirt collar. He was wearing faded, tight jeans with a hole in the back pocket and a bright plaid shirt, loosely cut and expensive. He has a nice ass, not too skinny, she thought. She wanted to stand in front of him, reach around his waist, put her hand in his back pocket and pull him close to her. She wanted to say something sexy like, I want to fuck you. Now. But he'd never know, not by her saying it anyway.

She surveyed the bedroom. A huge king size bed on one wall was sandwiched between floor to ceiling French windows and doors. They opened out to a balcony overlooking an enclosed back garden — not uncommon in Berkeley — with several rose bushes, purple iris already on the wane, new yellow chrysanthemums, a lemon tree lush with fruit, an assortment of ferns, jade plants, even a bird of paradise. Its orange and purple flowers jutted forth like a voyeur's nose. A garden of earthly delights. How much we take for granted, she thought. And the room: a small hexagonal antique table — oak, she recognized — sat next to the bed. A white, Finnish glass vase with half a dozen red roses in it filled the room with scent. He certainly has impeccable taste. In one corner was his desk, large, mahogany, littered with papers, medical journals, bills, bank statements. Under the Bay window there was a modern, plush loveseat covered in dark green velvet, the type that swallows one into comfort. She stood at the window a moment looking out from the hill at the grey Bay and the San Francisco skyline beyond. Without waiting for an invitation she sank into the sofa and put her feet up on his coffee table. "Well, I'm impressed, Dr. Alterberg. This is a magnificent room." Her smile was teasing, but her tone meant business. "And how long did you say your wife will be out of town?"

He laughed, then choked and went into a minor coughing fit. "I'm not married. Seriously. The housekeeper was here yesterday. We chip in and have her come once a week. Neither of us have time to, you know, clean. I'm sure you know. You must have a housekeeper too. Haven't noticed much free time in your schedule."

"You've known me less than a week."

He sat down on the other cushion of the sofa and pulled the packet from his shirt pocket, grinning like the Cheshire cat. Meticulously, he unwrapped the paper on the coffee table in front of her. In a glance he saw her eyes grow huge.

"What is that? Is that what I think it is?" Her enthusiasm was unbridled. She threw her arms around him. "Fantastic! Coke or speed?" It had to be coke. She could see that. There was too much of it to be methedrine, a drug she'd sworn off more times than she cared to count. But wishful thinking. Coke was fine. Coke was perfect. It was exactly what she wanted. Goodbye sadness. Goodbye melancholy. Goodbye loneliness. This man was all right. She could be lured. Why not? She tried a moment to mute her total delight, but why bother? He, too, she could see, glowed with anticipation. He hugged her back with his free arm, then got down to business chopping the white rocks into a fine powder, a powder that would erase both their pasts, all their cares, and bring them together as if they had known each other forever. Temporarily.

The lines of coke he made for them were a quarter of a gram each. She watched him. Had he done this before, or was his tolerance that high? Methodically chopping, mashing, and separating with a razor, he seemed to have forgotten she was there. "You've done this before, right?" He assumed that she had. Hadn't everyone?

"Of course." There was no reason for him to know the extent of her past addiction, her unsuccessful attempts to quit, her permanent sinusitis that gave her the most painful headaches imaginable. He might scold her as the ENT specialist had. Dangerous, he had insisted. She was risking her life if she kept it up. In spite of evidence for possible discomfort, she thought only of the incredible sense of well-being, grandiosity and perfection she would feel in the first half hour. Hard as happiness was to come by, it seemed without a doubt worth it. A gentleman, he offered her the first line, pulling a hundred dollar bill from his wallet – she assumed it was leftover from the transaction – rolling it carefully and handing it to her. It was so hard not to look stupid or criminal when snorting a line of cocaine, that she sat holding the hundred for too long. A lot of money. That awful impulse to slip it into her pocket kept her motionless, staring toward the coke, but seeing nothing.

"Want me to try it first?" He sensed some dilemma, not knowing the half of it. He was willing to sacrifice appearances for that first lift skyward away from the cares of reality.

"Yeah." She pulled herself back to the moment. "You go first. That way we'll know if it's poison."

He let out a deep breath, held one nostil, and snorted in the line in one fell swoop. Without waiting he did the next line, then sat up and handed the hundred to her, holding his breath. She bent over and followed suit. The stinging powder traveled to her brain. Straight to the brain without passing go. She imagined the nerve synapses revving up, the re-uptake of epinephrine blocked, the wiry endings stimulated to a frenzy. There was no pain. After seconds there was no burn, only marvelous numbness that expanded, grew, and thrust millions of cells into action. For a minute she felt nothing, said nothing, lingered in the nothingness with supreme enjoyment.

"It takes about three minutes to come on." As if she didn't know. He settled down into the sofa, threw his wallet on the table, and put his feet up on it, indicating they should continue their briefly interrupted getting to know each other. "So, how was the conference? Which group was it anyway? I didn't hear of any meetings in the city this weekend?"

"It wasn't well-publicized. Really, just some molecular biologists up from Stanford presenting some new techniques to detect viral DNA, slicing it up. Stuff like that." She watched his wallet, several hundred dollar bills visible. Why was he carrying around so much money? Her eyes were fixed on it. She tried not to look. God, how she hated money.

"I heard from Melvin you're doing some pretty fancy experiments with retroviruses. I haven't had any time to work in the lab lately. Clinical work is overwhelming, especially now, with this AIDS crisis. It's really amazing. We're seeing more new cases every day. The Gay Plague. It isn't fair. This virus is too smart for us. Did you hear the story of that classics professor who didn't want his family to know he had AIDS? He had never told them he was gay. When he got to the hospital with pneumocystis, he refused treatment. I tried to convince him we could treat it, but he insisted he wanted to die and get it over with. And he did. He died in two weeks. It was ridiculous; we could have saved him." His voice was speeding and he got up to pace around the room.

"For what? He was right about it. He was going to die anyway. I wonder sometimes what I would I do if I found out I had AIDS or even ARC. Go to an island in the South Pacific maybe. Kill myself. Why bother going through the wasting away, the fatigue, the diarrhea, the sweating, coughing, getting desperately sick, getting better, getting sick again, in and out of the hospital, no more sex." She was talking herself into a trap. It started to close around her like prison bars clanking shut. "What are we talking about this for? It's too depressing. I don't see how you can work with the patients. The clinical work was driving me up a wall, really crazy. That's why I took this job. I prefer dealing with it in the laboratory. It's more a game there. The host cells with their unwelcome guests, the trickster virus that evades the first lines of defense, the power of the message it gives to the cell, stops it cold, makes it turn on itself." Her throat was parched. She reached for her drink. He seized her pause.

"What do you think, what are you finding, what is going on with the T-cells? What about this French report on LAV? Have there been any controlled studies on more than one person?" He lit a cigarette with the one that was going out and kept talking so fast there was no opportunity for reply. "What worries me most is the rate the bugger is spreading. At least, in San Francisco. We've got to develop some tests for the blood supply. Another hemophiliac came in last week with spiking fevers – young man, married, two kids. The nurses and orderlies are giving us one headache after another, even some of the interns and residents are afraid to treat them. This isn't going to get better before it gets a lot worse. You're up there in your laboratory playing with it like it's a chess game, and people on the wards are going nuts." Even before he finished the sentence, he realized what he'd said. He hadn't meant to accuse her, to criticize her, but his emotions seemed to run away with him, not uncommon when he discussed this topic. "I mean, we probably need more distance from it, to study it. I just don't get that distance with the patients. We have to have more research, we have to have more money. Money. Money." His agitation was out of control. "I found out last week that the NIH grant we were essentially promised last spring isn't coming through. Not enough money in the new budget, Reagan's budget. God, it makes me mad! How can the fucking Congress and *that actor* make these decisions. It's tantamount to saying who lives and who dies. What right do they have? What do they know about it?"

"They do it all the time. In a thousand ways. It's our system, separation of powers – democracy, remember? Anyway, who cares if a bunch of fags die. That's what people think. Falwell. The Moral Majority, whoever they are. The queers are getting what they deserve. They're perverts. God is punishing them. It's all part of the Apocalypse. You know, the one that's coming around the corner. Wars, floods, earthquakes, plagues. The end of the world is nigh. Time to take to your favorite mountain and pray to God. Supposedly, it's going to be like Noah's Ark all over again. That's what they believe. A few special souls will be saved. Preserved for the future, for God's next grand scheme. Good ole God, playing dice with the universe. I play dice in my laboratory; he plays dice in his." She rather got off on this Einsteinian quip and thought she might play with it all evening if left to her own devices, but he had put *Blue* on the stereo and come to sit closer to her with his arm around the back of the sofa.

"I'm glad the dice rolled my number for a change. How come a woman as smart and gorgeous as you is unattached? Or are you?" He cautiously stroked her hair. His touch was light, barely there.

"I am now." In an abrupt about face she became shy. Vulnerable. Her hands went between her legs which were crossed already. She felt a chill and wanted him to hold her, to warm her up, to give her a therapeutic hug. But it was too early to let her guard down. The coke accelerated everything. Calm had to be maintained. Pace yourself. Could he be trusted? There was no way to know except from her accumulated experience with men and that was a most unfortunate criteria. What if he was the one she wanted — not Mr. Right, an absurd idea she had out-grown — but a good man, kind, intelligent, sexy, understanding? If she had accepted this much earlier would she be here now? Did history always repeat itself? It's the drug, she thought. My mind is going to doubt, to be suspicious, no matter what my body wants. I can simply diminish him, focus on some negative side, then I won't give a damn. I may even loosen up. As she was about to be reeled further into this emotional and ethical dilemma, he bent over and licked her lips with his tongue. His lips were full and soft, his tongue warm and moist. He kissed her until she forgot.

"I've been wanting to do that since the day in your office. Since the moment I saw you." He pulled her hands out and held them in his. "I really can't explain this, but there's something happening to me that hasn't happened before. I haven't ever wanted to kiss anyone as much as I want to kiss you. And that's not all. I want to hold you. All the time. I want to be with you every moment I'm not. I know this sounds unbelievable, but it's the truth. Since that first day I haven't been able to stop thinking about you. I don't even know you. But I do. I don't care if I do or don't. I don't care if you axe murdered you mother. I don't care if you're an alcoholic, a drug addict, a kleptomaniac, a revolutionary, even a Jesus Freak. I want to know everything about you. I want you." His palms were sweaty, and he shook her hands as he talked for emphasis.

The last sentence she believed. But if he only knew. He certainly had let her off the hook in a few areas with his ravings. She softened. He was adorable. He had broken through her doubts, her suspicions, and with the euphoria of the coke melting her judgement, a wondrous sensation of wanting and needing his humanity, his honesty, his body, him, swept her away. Eager to strip off his clothes and her own, climb into his big bed, and luxuriate in him like a hot bath, she let go of his hands and put hers around his face. She kissed him with a message of acceptance and more. They went on kissing until both of them burst out laughing. "Do you think it's the drug?" She joked.

"I didn't pay good money for nothing." Touché.

"Don't you want to know if I have herpes? Or who I've been sleeping with?" She tickled his ribs. "Maybe I've got lovers who are lovers of others." She made a scary face. "Maybe you have? But I don't care; I live dangerously. I like playing with fire." He firmly pulled her hands down and held them so that she could feel his strength. Her words were a taunt, a challenge. The air between them snapped with electricity. She put her feet underneath herself and stood on her knees facing him. He held her hands tight and fell backwards into the sofa until her skirt was draped across his legs and pulling her down onto him required but a slight tug. Her face was crimson around enormous wild eyes. Her pupils were dilated, and her hair fell forward in golden disarray. She was a mirror of what he felt.

"If you have AIDS, I want it." All rationality, all reason forgotten, in another world, another life. They had only passion. Only passion. What he had been waiting for albeit unknowingly. What she had lived for knowing it all too well.

"This is getting ridiculous. I need a cigarette." There was that slight tug, but she resisted. The record stuck on the end, slurping, grinding, ruining the needle. She climbed over him, off the sofa and went to turn it over. Her blouse hung out of the skirt which was turned lopsided around her. She adjusted everything while he watched as disheveled as she, but unconcerned. Without self-consciousness she observed herself in the small mirror on the bureau. There was nothing she would change. At the moment. Then she noticed it, a hair barrette, silver with red and blue cloisonne birds on it. She picked it up and dangled it in front of him, a reminder of his sloppiness. He wasn't clever when it came to deception.

"Okay. Come here. I'll tell you the truth." He sat up, dropped his head forward, and ran his hands through his hair. "Sit by me." He patted the cushion.

She would give him a chance. "All right. Let's hear it, but first tell me if you're married. No lies this time."

"I'm not married. I've been, well, in sort of a relationship for a few years. Her name is Pat. She has a degree in biology. She's a lab tech. She not very ambitious, I guess. She likes pottery and takes tap dance lessons. She's pretty, in a way, very different from you, dark, heavier, zoftig, is that the word? What can I say? She's a very nice person."

"A very nice person." It was time to leave. This was more than she wanted to get involved in, hurting another woman, a very nice person. She probably loved him, probably wanted to marry him, was probably biding her time. She stood up to gather her things, checking the time, finding her shoes.

"Suzanne, since I met you I've realized I have to get out of that relationship. It's hard. I don't want to hurt her. She cares about me. I feel like such a heel. Even worse now. If you leave I'll, I'll, I'll. . .I don't know what I'll do. I've kept this other apartment in the city. Or rather Pat has, because I've insisted on it. She knows I'm not going to marry her. I think she knows. I do care about her. I'd be lying if I didn't tell you that, but, I swear, it's not the same. It's not the same way I feel about you." His head fell again. He talked to the floor, to himself. "Christ, what am I saying?" He looked up at her. "I'm sure I can't let you go. I know it's only been a week, but . . ."

"All right. I won't go yet, but it is getting late, and I have to be at a meeting at seven in the city. I have to go soon." There was compassion in her voice or was it guilt, resignation, disappointment? "Forget it really. It doesn't matter. Any guy your age would be in a relationship with someone, or just ending one, or starting one. I've been seeing someone for a few years. We recently broke up. He got a better job and moved to Boston. Actually, I've been seeing lots of men, sometimes several at once ever since my divorce and that was ten years ago. God. Ten years ago." She took a long drag on the cigarette, time resonated with her voice, experience on her face. She spoke like a therapist. "Listen, relationships are impossible. If I've learned anything I've learned that."

"Oh, no, you don't. You're not getting away with using that as an excuse not to see me. I said before I don't care what stories lurk behind your lovely eyes, and I meant it. Our relationship isn't going to be impossible. And don't compare me to all the others — it makes me feel like a can of Campbell's soup lined up on the shelf. Why didn't you tell me you were married?"

She turned around to look at him. "What? Are you kidding me? Why didn't you tell me you're living with someone? I've been divorced a long time." The nerve, the impudence he had.

"Marriage is important. I would have told you if I were married before or divorced. What happened? I want to know?" His tone was demanding. He clearly had the right, every man's right to know about those who preceded him. The fact that he had been engaged, ending the engagement the day of the wedding, leaving his bride-to-be with all the guests, the presents to return, conveniently slipped his mind. That was a long time ago, it didn't count, they never got married.

"You are unbelievable. A master of changing the subject, that's for sure. Here I am in your fucking bedroom in the nineteen-eighties, and you lie to me about being attached, then you demand an accounting of my past? Am I hearing you correctly? Where is Pat anyway? Is she going to show up? Are we going to have tea together or what?" They were having a fight, their first fight, and it had that peculiar character of indignation on both parts that comes either from a long history or deep involvement, from familiarity that makes no sense.

"She's in L.A. at her sister's. Listen. I'm not staying with Pat. One of us is moving to the apartment. I promise you. As soon as she comes back, I'll tell her. I won't sleep in the same bed with her ever again. I promise. What more can I say?" he shouted angrily.

"Don't do that. Not on my account. How do we know anything will come of this? We're probably not compatible. It's pure lust. Once we've slept together, we may not like each other. These sexual things happen all the time."

"These sexual things! What are you talking about! Sexual things? Did I say I just wanted a 'sexual thing' with you? Goddamm, you are the most impossible woman I've ever met. We haven't even made love and already you're writing the obituary. Don't you know it ruins sex to reduce it to the level of animals in heat? I thought women were the ones to discover that. Isn't that what the women's movement was all about?"

"Don't jump in over your head, Chris." She glared at him, in-credulous. He glared back at her, equally incredulous. Neither had a clue about how they got to this point. They were as tangled in messages as double strands of DNA. "And don't be so foolish as to bring the women's movement into this. You don't know what you're talking about. I'm leaving."

"No. Don't leave. You're not leaving until this conversation is finished."

"It's finished. And don't tell me what to do. I'll leave when I god-damm well want to." That was a problem, she didn't want to leave.

"Okay. All right. Leave then. Go ahead. There's the door."

Her hand was on the doorknob, but she couldn't turn it. She stared at him. He was cold, studying her, erasing any trace of emotion from his eyes. Time had come to a screeching halt. Their passion thrown into reverse left an unnatural indifference in its wake. Within those few seconds the indifference turned to bitterness to hatred. The hatred of a child for a parent, the hatred of wanting too much, of an inescapable bond, of inevitable surrender. She let go first. "I really should go. It's late."

"You know I don't want you to leave." He put his hands in his pockets which sent a rush of affection through her. She let go of the doorknob and put her things down. She kicked off her shoes on her way to his out-stretched arms. Her arms went around his waist and she buried her face in his shoulder. "Can we lie down so I can hold you?" He whispered while kissing her hair, breathing in the smell of her.

She didn't answer but indicated that he should carry on with whatever he pleased. She wanted to be led. She was tired now, too tired to be the initiator. A profound wish to be loved without having to respond, even react, made her almost limp in his arms. They weren't far from the bed. He guided her to it, scooped her up in his arms, and laid her down gently. Her eyes were closed, but she opened them when he took his arms from under her. She watched him slip off his jeans and shirt, then lie beside her, cuddling her with exquisite tenderness.

It surprised him. Never had he felt more comfortable, more at ease with the gentle in him. He wasn't normally like this at all. But it seemed she was meant to sleep in his arms and he in hers, wrapped together. This contentment, this closeness wasn't a simple substitute for sexual desire — that was certainly there — but it fulfilled another, more urgent and unexpected craving, a desire he could not name. She fell asleep, her leg between his, her arm under his pillow and her face still buried in his shoulder. He lay awake, watching her sleep, kissing her cheek occasionally until he was sailing along a river, a strong wind in his face, trees shooting by on a bank which was transformed into sky. He was flying.

She was vaguely aware of being asleep. There were people everywhere. It was a fair or a parade, no, a political rally, a rock concert. There were her friends she hadn't seen since medical school, Alan and Martha, wearing headbands, leather vests, and gypsy clothes. They were singing and dancing. The clothes were flying as they whirled through the air. Too many clothes. Her head was covered with a skirt, a shirt. She couldn't get out. She couldn't breathe. She was suffocating. She woke up unable to breathe through her nose at all. The coke left its characteristic mark, and her head now suffered the reaction. He stirred beside her, groggy and disoriented. Her whole body hurt as if she'd been exercising too much. Her clothes were twisted around her, confining and hopelessly wrinkled. He soothed her groans by fetching water, nose spray, Kleenex and aspirin. "Here, honey, take this."

Honey. As if they already had a history, a life together. She didn't object. His adamant sweetness won her over. She was now along for the ride, hitched to his confidence.

"I guess it's too late now." She mumbled between squirting nose spray in her nose and blowing it out.

"Too late for what?" They both sat up on their pillows, he noticing his erection, wondering if she noticed it.

"Too late to leave. God, I feel like I've been run over by a truck." His legs were tan with beautifully shaped muscles, his toes were pudgy, curling automatically every few seconds. She turned herself around on the bed and played with his toes.

"You fell asleep." He checked the clock. It was three fifteen. "A few hours ago. Me too. Hey, that tickles." He leaned over and bit her exposed thigh.

"Do you mind if I take off my clothes? They're all I've got, and I won't have time to change before work." Her breathing was clear. She was ready to have some fun. She touched the waistband of his jockey shorts, her fingers caressing his tummy.

"I'll help you." They tittered hysterically. She seductively took off her clothes in slow motion, piece by piece. "Hurry up," he cajoled. "We only have three hours." Her unclothed body was as familiar as her mouth and hair had been and as devastatingly delicious. "I adore you," he said it over and over until they were beyond words, a state she entered into sooner than he.

* * *

He found himself crawling on his hands and knees down the beach away from the cove, the one that had the small sheltered cave in its center, the cave they made love in that night, the seal omen night. After some time he discovered he had crawled past the jagged green slate that marked the edge of the granite boulder on the right side. Where was he crawling? To his car? Hell no! He wasn't leaving. He turned around on his hands and knees and began to crawl back along the line of the cliff, that way he couldn't miss it, eventually he had to come to the cave. Some particle of brain tissue insisted that he was dreaming and would wake up soon. The sand was wet. His right hand gushed into the million tiny water holes left by the rising tide. A wall of water was about to grab him with its shattering power. He looked to his left in scant time to scramble away from the full force of the wave breaking on his back. He had almost crawled into the ocean. With her? The sting of the freezing water was muted by the shock of this realization. He forgot himself long enough to risk his life, to give himself away. It was like sex.

The cave was not where it should have been. Mounds and mounds of sand covered the entrance. He tried to dig his way in, but it was futile. The wind had begun to blow wildly, twirling the sand into funnels, shifting the contours of the cove until the sand drifts blocked his view of the ocean. He dug furiously with both hands, his back legs twitching like a dog after a buried bone. The ocean, the sand, the wind, they were against him, his enemies, trying to exhaust him, prevent him from accomplishing his task. The whole world was not supposed to interfere in this, yet it did. All he wanted was peace, time to think this through, come to some resolution. Look at this devastation of his cove! The pack wasn't where he'd left it. He whipped around in horror, ready to see her standing there behind him, dripping, ghoulish, with seaweed as her shroud. There was nothing, only piles of sand, heaps of sand, out of place and silent.

The deep gray-blue ocean with its white fans and crystalline feathers was unchanged, rolling in, rolling out, confronting him with permanence, stability. The wind had died in an instant. The afternoon sun sat in a quiet, clear, royal blue sky. The fog was miles offshore. The red backpack emerged from the the sand beside him. Nicking his finger on the rusty peace button, he almost broke down again, but determination stopped him. His hand frantically plunged into the backpack. He felt the black book covered with sand.

It was possible to open his eyes, he could run his hands over his clothes and shake off the water, a useless, but calming gesture. Nature was allowing him a reprieve, to read if he chose. He held the book in his lap and looked around. It was too quiet. How he had loved that wind storm, the unconscious crawling, the terror of the water, of possible death. With every fragment of energy he wished the wind would come back, continue whipping up the sand, finish off burying him in this cove with his black book, her black book. He could toss it into the ocean. Yes, that is exactly what he should do. She would have done it. She would have tossed in his journal. She would have said, "Well, that's that. If the stupid fool wanted to kill himself, well, he's a fucking idiot, good riddance." Yeah, she would have said that. He could practically hear that particular tone of voice she would use, like a shrill journalist who puts up a front of normalcy while reporting MASS SUICIDE IN GUIANA. We are sorry to say. A ghastly report. Shame.

No, it isn't true. Why was he thinking like this? She wouldn't have been indifferent to such a thing. Or would she? She seemed so determined to live, to love him.

They had taken some incredible drug. MDA, she said it was. He didn't remember the drive to the beach. Somehow she got them there while he sat next to her in the car, giddy, laughing himself to tears, feeling orgasmic rushes through his entire body. He was in love with the red leather upholstery of the car seat and had to shut his eyes to limit these sensations. But he knew, absolutely knew, more certain than words could ever say that she was part of him.

That was the day she threw away time. Rolling naked and sweaty in the sand, drenched in hot sunshine, they had imagined themselves savages in their cave and vowed to stay there forever, to defend their territory against all comers, park police included. The twelve dollar black Timex was her only article of clothing. It slid around her slim wrist, telling her the time, other people's time, four o'clock. "What is this stupid device?" She shook him out of his religious communication with a rock. "I'm still wearing something, something very dangerous. It demarcates events, it slices up life. I've got to get rid of it." Before he could remind her she might want her watch later — it did occur to him, this reasonable possibility — she was running toward the ocean, holding the watch over her head like a sacrifice. Her breasts rose and fell and her slender body stood out against the blue of the sky and sea, a mermaid, a princess of the sea. He watched her in total awe. "I'm throwing away time," she yelled. "I'm throwing off the shackles of civilization and decreeing myself a part of the infinite, the universal, the timeless." Her thin arm flung the small piece of black leather and plastic into the waves. He was as surprised as she that her softball arm managed to commit her watch forever to an early, watery grave.

She jumped up and down like an enraptured little girl, then picked up a long, rubbery piece of seaweed. Three inches across and twelve feet long with a bulbous head on one end, it looked like a gigantic penis from the sea. She wrapped it around her legs, then her waist until the round head sat on her shoulder caressing her neck. She walked back to him and kissed the head of the seaweed that wound around her.

"You are a princess of the sea." He greeted her with a bow. "A timeless creature." He tugged at the seaweed, unwrapping her ceremoniously, slowly. His body ached to be inside her. His penis stood out larger than he'd ever remembered it, the color more purple, the tip more swollen and glistening. Her nipples were a crimson color and beckoned to him, pursed into succulent, sun-dried tomatoes. The hair between her legs was blonde and soft as dandelions gone to seed.

Later, she began to ramble on about nature, the ocean, disconnected ideas, free associations, poetry. She didn't pretend to be talking to him, nor did he pretend to listen. She recited to the elements, as if rehearsing a play, then rose and danced down the beach.

He had sat there hearing her but not listening. His mind was elsewhere, examining the strata of rock and imagining the force of heat that must have sprung from the earth's center to force the rock up or was it forced up by heat? Perhaps an earthquake had split open the ocean bottom and left fallen mountains of rock to be slowly pushed together? He wondered about the new techniques for extracting salt from sea water, an extremely primitive form of separating the elements. A new technique he had developed could probe the very stuff of life. He could now separate viral DNA. He was seized with the urge to leave the beach and rush to his laboratory, thinking he had just figured out why his last experiment didn't work. It was as if he had gone underground, his mind reasoning, calculating, figuring out problems that rested in another realm of assumptions, scientific assumptions.

When he returned to the immediate, she was nowhere to be seen. An instant sweat broke out. He stood up to look for her. Not far away, there she was, naked, draped over a rock, her right arm over her eyes, shading them from the sun, her left leg bent up for stability while the rest of her dangled off the side. She was in a dream of her own, a dream of harmony with the rock, the ocean, the sky. Him. She noticed him watching her and opened her arms, an invitation for him to climb in and become part of her dream, part of her.

He looked toward that same rock now, the same as it was but empty, and yet, the image of her remained vivid in his mind. What difference did it make? He grabbed his head and began to pull his hair out, shaking his head violently. "Just like in the movies." He heard himself screaming, "This is just like in the movies!" He was the one who had to fucking realize it. She was fucking gone. DEAD. What the hell difference did it make? What she would have thought. What she said. Or did. Or wrote. It wasn't going to change anything, but he wasn't convinced. It did matter. He had loved her, trusted her. At least, he could honestly say he never in his wildest dreams thought she would really do it. Commit suicide? He had to admit the thought had crossed his mind. The mere thought. All those ravings about going back to the ocean, the sea, the mother of all things, the creator of life, the universal, mysterious, impenetrable feminine force. It rocked in constant motion, enclosing its endless arms around the earth, the sea creatures, a mother's arms around her babies. It would endure for eternity. This was her ocean.

The book had fallen between his legs. The fog had moved in closer to the shore, but the sun was high behind it. Afternoon was passing. Time went on, noticed or not. He entered into a tranquil state. Emotion had fled his body and now hovered softly around him, a slight reminder of limits. Memory was not reality. Reality was limited. It had beginnings and endings, sun and rain, day and night. Exhausted, he lay his head back on a pillow of rock and sand. He dreamt of his mother tucking him in bed, pulling his favorite red flannel blanket under his chin. Her warm cookie smell, the kisses she placed on each cheek, his forehead, his nose flushed his five-year-old face and left him with visions of fairy tales which he carried into sleep.

He jolted awake. The sun shone on, relentless. His mouth was parched, and the faint taste of blood from his cracked lip was welcome liquid. He opened the book, then closed it. He had to find some water, some cigarettes.

Whenever he stood up, he automatically cried. There was an inescapable sense of life when standing up. His life, reality, the world outside of his head, only highlighted her probable death. Yet, he had reached a moment of physiological need that would not let him continue, whatever his morbid mission, unless he satisfied it. There were some lone beachcombers far from the isolated cove he claimed as his territory. One of them might have water, cigarettes. With water and cigarettes he could continue, survive. But how could he approach them? They were too far away, as distant as the hawk, as poignant as the seal, as dangerous as any representatives of reason. His legs carried him forward, the gusty wind ushering in the evening shroud of fog. A Frankenstein monster who had to learn to walk, he put one foot in front of the other, single-minded, determined to make it the mile to the parking lot. The store was fifteen minutes away, twenty at most. Switch into automatic. Walk. Go.

The parking lot at the general store reminded him of who he once was. BMWs, Volvos, Hondas, and assorted foreign sports cars were parked, haphazard, around the countrified, redwood store, a store unlike any real country store. It was stocked with duck liver mousse, Goumaindaise, peppercorn brie, French baguettes, Amaretto truffles, Famous Amos cookies, boutique wines, Perrier — her staples. Illusions were necessary here, and he tried to brush off his grungy, stained pants, comb his matted, strawlike hair. One glance in the rearview mirror filled his head with excruciating pain. He saw himself. Alive. His eyes were swollen to red slits; his face was burned underneath forty-eight hours of gray speckled beard, but it was his grotesque, twisted mouth that horrified him. His lips, swollen, cracked, bleeding, had curled up baring yellow stained teeth, the way a dead person's face shrinks on the skull, pushing out the jaw, a reminder of destiny. He put on his sunglasses, angry that it mattered. The car door resonated from his slam.

Never in his life would he drink Perrier again. He fell against the cool glass door of the drink case. Shutting his eyes he groped for anything else. Gator Aid, orange juice, milk, soda.

"Hey Buddy, need some help?" A young, well-dressed man stood behind him, thinking he was blind. He reached to hold open the door. "Can I get something for you? Want something in particular?"

"Water." His voice screeched, a soft shrill, the sound of a patient with a poorly done tracheotomy. The kindness of the young man would do him in. He would collapse if he acknowledged it. Beads of sweat emerged on his upper lip. His limbs began to tremble. He kept his eyes shut, knowing his hand shook out of his control, held out like a beggar's.

"Sure. Hang on there, Buddy." The warmth of the man's body, his living breath, assaulted him.

He clutched the bottle offered and ran, stumbling over barrels of cheese and crackers, to the checkout. The pretty, teenage girl looked at him, frightened, disgusted. "Carton of Salem's." Tears rolled from under his glasses and splashed on the wallet as he tried to extract that strange medium of exchange, dollars, money. "No, not Salems, Dunhills." He gave her a twenty, grabbing the carton and his water bottle like a starving child. He existed in the fleeting instant of terror that all was taken from him, that nothing was left. His corporeal body would disintegrate with one more blow, a blow as light as puffing out a candle. He fled with no change, alive in that special way that escape accentuates life.

Dark was coming earlier and earlier. Through the headlights that illuminated the patches of fog, he saw only rolling, dancing, swaying hills, the breasts and hips of the landscape. The road caressed its body, a wide belt pulled snug around the waist. It dipped into curves and brought him back to the line of tall eucalyptus that stood waving him into the parking lot. He was the only one there. This small piece of geography waited for him. He had business there, unfinished business with the sea and her.

It was okay now. He felt calmer. The fog hid him well. He took more batteries for the flashlight from his glove compartment and made his way down the path. Driftwood was abundant. Once in his old neighborhood, he began to collect wood for a fire. His muscles were forced into a perpetual dull ache, lifting the logs, dragging the heavy ones, stacking them in piles. With no knowledge of how much time had passed, he found himself inside a shelter he had constructed around the entrance to the cave. It was rather cozy. He made the fire several yards away near a washed up redwood tree two feet in diameter. He could lean back on it and warm his feet by the fire. He drank half the bottle of water in one gulp, then sat in silence, smoking his Dunhills. Two packs. He smoked with the journal lying in his lap. With a flashlight he could read, but where to begin? Where was the beginning? The first page. He decided to be methodical, to skip nothing to open it at the first page and read every word. No matter what. And there, on the first page, was pasted a crumbling piece of newspaper.

Found in February 1982

Walking the cold winter sand of Florida, I want to believe Joseph Conrad's line: "Life...will close upon a sorrow like the sea upon a dead body, no matter how much love has gone to the bottom.'

And there he had it. But what the hell did it mean? He never knew she liked Conrad. Maybe she didn't like Conrad. Why didn't he ever ask her? Why didn't they discuss it? Questions. Questions. *The Heart of Darkness* was one of his favorite books, and he would never know if she liked it, if she read it.

* * *

She was standing by the centrifuge, her cells spinning down behind her when he walked in. She hugged him and smiled happily. "Hey, I have a fabulous idea." She held both his hands. "Oooh, I can't wait to tell you. It'll be great fun. Promise me we'll do it. Promise me." Her pale green skirt with the pink dahlias on it flounced up and down with her. She wore white ankle socks and olive green flat shoes, an outfit that never failed to enchant. "Promise, right now before you think about it."

"I promise. I promise. What is it?" He put his arms around her waist and nuzzled his chin into her neck. Her perfume reminded him of a dark forest.

"Let's go to Mexico for the weekend, to Puerta Vallarta or Ixtapa. No, I know, Cabo. Cabo San Lucas. Let's lie in the sun and sip Pina Coladas and snorkle and make love under a ceiling fan. Let's just do it. No ifs or buts. Okay? Okay?"

"Suzanne, I don't know." He had promised Pat they would talk this weekend. She knew something was going on when he insisted she stay at the apartment after her trip to L.A. She said nothing then, waiting for him to tell her, accepting his lie about having to work on some articles that required pure concentration. When he left her off at the apartment he wouldn't sit down. He didn't want to make love. He didn't even kiss her on the mouth. A disheartened peck on the cheek was all she got. Last night she had telephoned him. She wanted an explanation. She wanted the truth. A truth she already knew because what else could it be. Another woman. It was obvious, but she loved him, and she wasn't going to get hysterical. These things passed sometimes. Her voice on the phone was quiet, controlled and the effort she invested in being reasonable caused him extreme discomfort. They would go out for a nice lunch at the Zuni Cafe on Saturday. He would tell her then, but not now, not over the phone. She deserved better. He owed it to her.

"How about next weekend? Gives us more time to plan." Her body stiffened in his arms.

"No. Can't you be spontaneous, impulsive? It has to be day after tomorrow. Planning would only spoil it." She wiggled out of his embrace and took the spun tubes out of the centrifuge. "All you need is a bathing suit and a toothbrush. Don't spoil it. It'll be romantic. I can call my travel agent now. There's this wonderful hotel out of the town, wildly luxurious and expensive. You'll love it. Anyway, you promised." Her infectious smile invaded, did its trick. Desire spilled into his muscles. Obligation, responsibility receded into the past.

"Suzanne, will you listen? Be serious a minute. I have to tell Pat about us. She deserves to know. I promised her we would talk on Saturday."

"Saturday! Why Saturday? Why not tomorrow or tonight? What are you waiting for? It isn't going to get easier, you know. Why spoil our whole weekend? You've already broken her heart. It doesn't matter when you tell her. It's not the telling that hurts. Don't make it all messy. I'll be mad. She's going to be mad. You'll feel terrible no matter what." He was learning fast that he couldn't argue with her. She always sounded right, and she usually got her way.

"I don't know. I really hate to do this to her."

"What do you mean? Haven't you already done it to her? Haven't you already promised her love you were never going to deliver? Or do you think she was content just having you around, whether you really loved her or not? Do you know what love is, Chris? I mean, do you love her or don't you? I'd like to know that." She went right on with her experiment. Her hand deftly preparing the slides. She peered at them under the microscope, making minor adjustments that he knew required concentration.

"I guess not. I mean I thought I loved her, sort of. You think it's all that black and white, either/or?" Her work was bothering him. "Are you listening to me?"

"Of course." She moved the tray of tubes closer, quickly looking at a series of slides, making notes in her data book.

"Okay. Let's go to Mexico. Wherever. I can't wait to see you naked in the sand. How could I resist making love on the beach?" He sat on the stool, his eyes on the ground. Resigned, but not unhappy he spoke to the floor.

She threw her arms around his neck, the slides abandoned. "Wonderful! I can't wait either. It will be great fun. If we can't get into Cabo I know another terrific place outside of La Paz." She hugged him tighter. "I'll make the arrangements. Now go on, scat. I've got to finish these slides."

"Tonight?" The perfume made his head swim.

"Absolutely."

"I'll come to your house at six, okay? You better be there." It was his turn to lay down the limits.

"I'll be there. But just in case you get there first the key is in the jade plant next to the door. There's a fresh fish market on College Avenue. Will you pick up something for dinner? Please? These slides will take me the rest of the afternoon."

He kissed her for a long time until he felt her giving in, surrendering, wanting more, until he knew he had made her forget the slides. Then he pulled away, satisfied. "I'll try, but remember I'm the attending this month."

"Chris, one more thing. Do you have any more coke?"

"No, but I can get some if you want it." His hand was on the door.

"Can you get methedrine?"

"Why? That's pretty heavy stuff. Have you done it before?"

"I'm not sure. I think I did, once, in medical school," she lied with a laugh. "You know women, always on some diet. Whatever it was I loved it. Thought we might try something different, if you had the connections. Or both? Why not?" Her eyes were asking intently. "I mean, chemically it probably isn't much worse for you than cocaine, right?"

"Wrong. You know that. Neither one are good for you." He paused. Something told him this could be a touchy subject.

"Well, try to get some. For me? Please?"

"Sure. All right. For you. Anything." How serious could it be, recreational use, that's all. She couldn't have done drugs very much; he'd seen many a drug addict in the ER. They were like AIDS patients, they had a special look about them. Her glee about the coke was patently not that of a regular consumer. The moment of concern passed. "I can't wait until tonight." There was hardly anything he wouldn't do to make her happy.

"Me too." The tubes were already back in the refrigerator. She busily started to draw more blood from the mice. "Till then."

Where was he going to get methedrine? Perhaps his old buddy, Winston, would know. He played the club circuit and lived in the Mission. They hadn't talked in months, but what are high school pals for? He went into his office and called Alan, the cardiologist. His service said he was in the Cath Lab until three. "The message is there's an envelope in his box that's important. Tell him to call me, Dr. Alterberg, tonight at this number, 387-5514. Right." He left Suzanne's number, but not her name. The horrible thought that Alan somehow knew Suzanne flashed in his mind. Ridiculous. He dismissed it while writing out a check for three hundred dollars. He had to call Pat now, and he dreaded it. As he picked up the phone his beeper went off. Saved.

There was a young man in the ER with a fever of 105, chest pain and a cough. The resident met him outside the door. "Dr. Alterberg, this guy looks like AIDS, I mean an AIDS possibility. We tried to draw some blood, but the kid's hysterical — he punched out the new intern. Didn't hurt him though — guy's too weak to be dangerous. Says he's been sick a few weeks. Something about trying to kill himself. Looks around eighteen to me, but he won't give his age or name or anything. A friend brought him in and dumped him. He left. The kid can't even crawl out the door; he tried. Probably doesn't have any insurance. I think we've got a problem here. I told the nurse to start an I.V., but she refuses to go in there." He shuffled around, twisting at the chart as if he wanted to hand it over and leave post haste.

"Give me that, Dr. Collins." He pointed to the chart slowly, deliberately, with the intention of calming him down. He turned toward the nurses' station and shouted, "Get a nurse out here with an I.V., and we'll need X-ray, a blood gas, and get me two red tops, a purple top and a green top tube." He pulled his glasses down over his nose and stared at the resident. "You coming?" Meaning: get your ass in there and do your job.

The boy was lying on a flat gurney with a blanket wrapped around his shoulder. His dark hair was shabby and matted to his neck and forehead. His face was deep pink, and he could barely open his eyes. He shivered like a wounded animal, vulnerable and frightened. A whisper was enough to get his attention.

"I'm Dr. Alterberg. I can see you're not feeling well. I'd like to help you. Can you tell me your name?"

"David." He groaned. "I'm sick."

"You certainly are. That's why we need to talk to you. We'd like to find out what's wrong so we'll know how to help you get better. I need to ask you some important questions." He could tell that the young man wasn't going to resist. He put his hand on his shoulder. His skin was like a furnace, radiating heat. "How long have you had this fever?"

"Three days. This time. It started a while back." Tears came into his eyes, and he wrenched his face in pain. "On Saturday I tried to get up to go to work. I felt shitty. Then in the shower I started to throw up. I threw up over and over and collapsed. I couldn't go to work. My roommate called the boss. I have to work. I have to pay the rent." Silence made the situation all the more pathetic.

"How long ago did the fevers first start, David?" He bit his lip, turned to the resident, and angrily gestured for him to get an I.V. started himself if necessary.

"I don't know. Three, fours month ago. They came and went. I got some penicillin; they got better. Listen, Doc, I gotta get out of here. I got no money. My mother . . ."

"Any other problems besides the fever?" He reached for the blood pressure cuff. "Any diarrhea, chills, weight loss?"

"Yeah. I haven't been very hungry lately. Maybe I've lost weight." A desperation welled up in his voice, and his eyes opened as far as he could manage. He pleaded, "I'm not a homosexual. I'm not a faggot." Tears gushed from his eyes, his fist balled up, and he began to beat his thighs.

"David. Listen, just relax here, this could be any number of illnesses. If I can examine you we might be able to find out what actually is wrong." He was so relieved to hear the kid say he wasn't gay, he almost overlooked the needle marks in his ante culibal fossa. But he didn't. He firmly held his elbow and examined the arm with deliberate care. Yes. He was a drug user. There was no doubt about that. An agitated anger swelled in his throat. Compassion squelched his wish to scold, his wish that it wasn't true. It could still be many other diseases, he composed himself, but who were these young guys: Living in bare apartments with other dispossessed adolescents, working in bars, restaurants, hiding from dreaded or dreadful parents? Were they a new breed of young toughs, fending for themselves in a dog-eat-dog world, seeking any escape from everyday routine? Were they among the growing numbers of youth sustained by a starvation diet, nihilism, going nowhere, doing nothing, being meaningless to a fault? Were they simply ordinary people . . . like him?

"David, listen, I'm not a cop. I'm a doctor, and I have to ask you for your own good, where did you get these needle marks? Are you into junk?"

"Oh, that's nothing. I'm no junkie. I was just shooting coke with a friend. My roommate's friend."

"Shooting coke?" Shit. "Did you know this friend of your roommate?"

"No, he was in from out of town. New York. He was visiting from New York."

"When was this?" He knew the needle marks wouldn't be there from three months ago.

"He's come into town several times in the past year or so. We only do it when he's in town. I can't afford coke."

The resident returned with the drip and started setting it up. "David, I'm going to give you something to make you feel better. I think we better admit you and do some tests. In the meantime you can rest, sleep. I'm going to listen to your chest. Okay?" Too weak to protest, he laid his head back and seemed to fall immediately asleep.

There was a knock on the door, and a too cheerful voice chirped, "Admissions. Can I interview the patient now?"

"Collins, get her the fuck out of here. Now!" His fury had to land somewhere. "Get some X-ray orders. I want a full blood count. Send someone up to Ward 5E, to the nurses' station, and tell them to find a private bed. He's a possible AIDS. After the work up, I'll be up to see him. Make sure that all the blood samples are taken. And let me know as soon as you've finished the routine paperwork. There's going to be extra. My number's 517. I'll be upstairs in Mosley's lab."

He took the chart into the hall to write up his notes. David was out cold on the demerol. The admissions clerk glared at him, looking at her watch, and he glared back and looked at his. It was almost five-thirty. Suzanne. Dinner. Tonight. He was going to be late, but she would understand. Then he realized she was most likely still in the lab. He could consult her. This young man could be enrolled as a subject in her research study.

She sat with her back to the wall, her feet up on a lab stool, her brow knitted into a frown. When he raced in the door, he expected he'd missed her and was happy to see her studying her reports with fierce concentration. He had run up four flights of stairs, but now wanted to appear nonchalant. He would use the excuse that he needed the lab phone to make some emergency arrangements. A moment of awkwardness followed his abrupt invasion of her silence, her work, not to mention the simultaneous realization that each had counted on the other to leave early, fetch the fish, and have a romantic dinner in the works when the tired, dedicated one straggled in the door. He coughed, out of breath, and cleared his throat. "Great, you're still here."

"So are you." She gave him a questioning glance, peering up from her notebook.

"There's a patient on his way to 5E, possible AIDS case, an-eighteen-year-old with what looks like pneumocystis pneumonia. I've ordered the tests plus some extra tubes for you. I've got to get the pulmonary resident in here to do a bronchoscopy among other things. The nurses in the ER are behaving like jerks. That fool Collins doesn't know his ass from a hole in the ground."

"What are you so pissed off about?" She suspected he was trying to deflect her disappointment that he wasn't on his way to make her dinner, but then she didn't know him that well.

"Nothing. There's a lot to do. I thought you might like to be involved. You are working on this, aren't you?" He was completely at home in his position of authority with the regular house staff, but she somehow made him feel subordinate. "Is there a hospital directory around here?"

"Yes and yes." She rubbed her temples, shifting to make her stomach stop rumbling. "So what's the story?"

"High fever, a few outbreaks in the past year, needle marks in his arm, rales in the chest, sweats, weight loss, nausea, vomiting, diarrhea, says he's not gay, was shooting coke with a friend of a friend. That's about all I got out of him. If they get on it in the lab and I can get the pulmonary guy in here we can find out if it's pneumocystis in a few hours. It is, though. I can tell."

"Why don't you start him on Septra or pentamidine, if you're that sure. The tests will take all night, and what makes you think the pulmonary resident will come in to do the bronchoscopy at this hour? He's probably having dinner."

Her questions took him by surprise. It was his responsibility to make the decisions, to take care of the details, to prescribe the medicine. He was the attending physician. "I'm not *that* sure. I'd like to have some diagnostic confirmation before I decide which drugs to start. He could have leukemia, tuberculosis, double pneumonia. It's all possible."

She smiled at him, at his evident sensitivity about his decisions. "Well, you said you could tell."

He dialed the resident's number, trying to ignore her. "Yes, this is Dr. Alterberg. I've got a very sick kid here, possible pneumocystis. I was wondering if I could get a consultation and evaluation on a bronchoscopy. Yeah. I know. Well, I'd really appreciate it if you could look at him. He's on his way to 5E, but may need to be in the

ICU. Yeah. I've ordered the tests already. I suppose. Okay, I'll wait here." He raised his eyebrows at her with concern. "All right, sure, bye."

"He's coming in?"

"Not for an hour or so. I caught him on his way out for a run." Now that his mission was accomplished, disappointment and a moment of purposelessness made him reach for a cigarette. He wanted her approval, her agreement, her involvement. At least, he thought he did. "You want to see him? I'd like your opinion."

"So you're staying here for the night." She was packing her notebook into a briefcase, putting away the slides, tidying up the lab bench. She didn't answer or look at him.

"I'm the attending. I have to. Wouldn't you? What do you expect me to do?" Panic rose with his unnecessary explanations. He wanted her to stay. He wanted to leave with her. He wanted to sleep in the same bed with her tonight. Her promises were suddenly too tenuous.

"If I were you I'd go out and get some dinner since there's nothing more you can do until the test results are back, and the pulmonary resident is exercised, showered, and fed. I'll go see him if you really want my opinion." She slipped on her white coat and stood before him as objective and professional as he imagined himself to be. "I try to see all the possible AIDS patients anyway. There's no substitute for clinical reality, is there?"

She understood. She was reasonable. Now he felt ridiculous, possessed by feelings that tangled his mind in absurd fears, that compromised his judgement. Were there two women here? He wanted to call Pat. There was comfort in knowing the boundaries of a relationship, who was the woman, who was the man. Pat was a lab tech; he was the doctor. It never occurred to him that he would find himself in love with another doctor, an academic researcher, a competitor, a woman who wasn't dazzled by his medical brilliance. Guilt made him fidget. Sexist pig, his conscience whispered, beleaguered and confused. "Yes, of course, I'd like your opinion. Let's go take a look, then get some dinner together, okay?"

"Sure." She held out her hand to him, smiling.

They wound their way through the hospital, discussing the side effects of Septra and pentamidine, the possible differential diagnoses, the latest debates over the causes of T-cell depletion in AIDS. She had just begun to explain her research project to him when they arrived at the ward. The chart revealed little he hadn't already told her. The blood had been drawn. His breathing was described as increasingly distressed, shallow, his color bluish. A respirator had been ordered. His fever was 104.6. Blood pressure was low. She spent a minute considering this and handed the chart to him. He checked the blood gases, he was hypoxic. They went into the room on tip-toes like parents going to listen to a sick child.

"He needs to be tubed." There was authority in her voice, the same authority he recognized in his own.

"Right." He moved to call the anathesiologist, then decided to wait. He wanted to watch her examine the boy.

It was nothing extraordinary. She felt his pulse, listened to his chest, tried to rouse him, then simply observed him carefully, holding his arm, turning it over. Subtly caressing him, he thought, as if some force of empathy might work magic. There was a look in her eyes, complete concentration, a hint of horror, objective contemplation. She seemed to care too much. But could he trust his perception of her? An irrational jealousy of this deathly ill boy made him intervene. "I'll call the anathesiologist now." He motioned that they should leave. "Let's talk outside." It was as clear a request as he could muster.

"I'd start him on Septra right away."

"Why? I thought you agreed we should wait for more confirmation.'

"Why wait?"

"Because he might not have AIDS. He might get serious side effects."

"He does have AIDS. He's going to die. He might respond to the drug. It's indicated."

"I'm not that sure. How can you be so sure?"

"You said you wanted my opinion. I would start him on Septra now or pentamidine, if you like that better."

"I still think we should wait for the bronchoscopy."

"I disagree, but he's your patient." She stood her ground even though they both knew it made very little, if any, difference medically. They were both right.

"Let's go eat." He took her elbow like a boy scout helping a lady across the street.

"Are we going to go to Mexico for the weekend? I called the travel agent." Her question caught him off guard. There was a plea in her eyes. A serious plea. "Let's go far away from this. Far away."

* * *

They decided not to go. They would stay and work on the blood of David. He listened during dinner to her new methods of extracting viral DNA, her theory that AIDS was sure to be a retrovirus.

Several researchers were close to isolating it. The French possibly already had, but no one wanted to seem too eager to believe their report. They both talked at once, excited by the research interests they shared, the endless implications, the possibilities for the future. They were on the edge of a breakthrough, at that crucial stage when dedicated researchers work round the clock, ignoring whatever so-called real life exists outside the hospital. It was the first time since her residency that she stayed up to talk to Paris at two in the morning or Boston at five. In spite of the race to be the first to isolate the virus, hushed tones of solemn cooperation, collective loyalty to this single-minded effort, kept the hospital Watts lines busy. There was no shortage of data, no paucity of subjects. New cases arrived daily. AIDS was the biggest boon for infectious disease since polio. Worst of all, or best, depending on which perspective they took, San Francisco was in the thick of it. The opportunity to make one's career presented itself. There was work to be done, laurels to reap, humanity to help. They could do it together.

His beeper went off in the middle of their second cup of coffee. He went to the pay phone while she continued running the possibilities through her mind. As she was paying the bill, she saw his head shaking back and forth. No. It doesn't usually happen that fast. He was dead.

They stood by the cluttered table, its remnants of wilting lettuce and oily red steak blood congealed under the potatoes. The eaten food somehow exaggerated their life. They tried to speak. Halting stutters, lame rationalizations, an awkward attempt to make light of these deaths that were happening everyday at every hospital, made neither of them feel better. Ashamed, that was all they shared. Her shrugged shoulders, her detachment belied its opposite. His anger was too constricted, his guilt inappropriate. He held her hand anyway, and even though they both wished the other would somehow disappear, be gone for a moment, she didn't let go. It was settled without discussion: Mexico for the weekend.

It was a constant frenzy of arrangements — phone calls, frantic trips to the hospital, the travel agent, Alan's apartment, the drug store. All done in a day. She spent the night calling the airlines and the hotels, making what reservations she could get. She rushed out to the moneymatic for cash as the dawn was breaking, then went home and packed a small suitcase. Her experiments could sit for three days, but the lab tech, Carol, had to inject the mice twice. When a reasonable hour approached, she called her. For good measure she wrote out copious notes with detailed instructions. Carol knew what she was doing, she told herself, and hoped for the best.

He spent the night calling various residents, promising too much to get another doctor to cover for him. After considerable harangue Alan found him two grams of coke, and two drives back and forth across the Bay bridge were necessary to consummate the deal. On his second trip he remembered Pat. He sheepishly left a note in her mailbox. *Next week. Had to leave town for three days. Emergency.*

It was eleven the next morning, two hours before the flight to Tiajuana, by the time he was packing his gym bag. The rain came down in sheets, rare thunder rumbled overhead. She heard on the radio as she drove to pick him up that heavy rains and fog had snarled traffic on the Bay bridge. Neither had slept at all, but they were going one way or the other. There was no turning back; they had to go. Two lines of coke, and they were speeding across the Richmond bridge toward the Golden Gate. She drove like a maniac, but they still had to run through the terminal, barely making the plane. They were screaming curses at each other, sweat dripping from their faces. They stood in the aisle as if they didn't know where they were until the stewardess politely suggested that they take their seats, the last two in the rear of the plane, the ones that don't go back. They were speeding down the runway, the plane shaking violently, when he was gripped with the fear that he had forgotten his passport. He stood up as the plane lurched upward and his head hit the ceiling. She pulled him back into the seat, the stewardess frowning at them. It was there in her bag. She showed it to him. They laughed at each other, not believing they were on this plane. Together.

*   *   *

They lay naked on a twin bed, the ceiling fan humming above them. He lingered in a twilight sleep, satiated, smelling of sex, aware of her skin clinging damp to his side. Her face was turned toward the window gazing at the palms, the bougainvillea, the humming bird hovering over the blossoms. Beyond the tropical garden the ocean rolled onto the sand as calm as waves in a bath. Her left hand played with the hairs on his chest, slid down to his resting genitals and covered them. The afternoon crept by, the languishing time of the tropics. She watched the shadows of the coconut palms grow long and pencil thin. The setting sun bathed the room in rose and gold until even her pale skin glowed a rich melon color. There were no flaws in this light. His breathing grew coarse. When she knew he was asleep, she felt lonely, then relieved. Alone she could think.

Inching away from his sleeping body, she got up and pulled a long knit beach dress over her head. From her make-up kit she extracted an antihistimine, two motrin and a Valium. She'd lost track of dates and times, not having slept much for several days. The sea of Cortez will calm me, she thought. Rummaging quietly among the piles of clothes, bags, plates of half-eaten shrimp enchiladas, empty bottles of beer and tequila, she found her dark glasses and her journal. The colors of the setting sun, the dark blue and crimson of the sky, the rain forest green of the garden pressed her physically into the shadow of the white stucco hotel. Her senses were too raw, too open. But the serenity of the empty picture-postcard beach seduced her onto the sand, a magnet of beauty. She had her choice of several bright yellow beach chairs or the bare sand; she chose the sand. She opened her journal to write.

September 8, 1983

I need to write again. I keep thinking of all the unwritten ideas, the impulses, the desires gone with the realization that I'm coming around again. Can I do it? Can I go through all this? Again? So soon after Dan. I think I'm falling in love and I don't believe in falling in love anymore. I'm in La Paz with Chris. There's a lovely golden and magenta sunset right before my eyes. I can see it. I think of him, sleeping peacefully in the room behind me. I wish I could sleep beside him, but a dream I had haunts me. A young man died in the hospital two days ago, shortly after I examined him. In the dream I was making love to this boy. I thought it was Chris because I had my eyes closed, then I opened them, and it was this boy, dying. But I was close to an orgasm and couldn't stop it. I was sick, horrified, alone. I woke up. After this death Chris and I came here. We cooperate in pretending, and oddly it works. I don't know if I can afford this? Love? I wish I were sleepy, but no such luck. I'll go back in a few minutes and make love to Chris again. I'll make love to him until I sleep. I think the Valium is kicking in. How much should I tell him?

* * *

A coal from the fire burned a hole in his pants. The flashlight battery began to dim. His eyelids fell heavy over his eyes in spite of the dismal damp cold and uncomfortable smoke inhalation. He had skipped from the beginning to near the end, to the time in which he appeared. To read that she was "falling in love" with him brought forth unexpected and conflicting emotions that set in play a deep tranquilization. He couldn't keep his eyes open even to cry. He wanted to read on, to find more comfort in what had been. He wanted to dwell on that wonderfully blissful weekend in Mexico and know more about her falling in love with him. But what engulfed him now was that powerful, unconscious sleep that she wrote about, the sleep that saved him from dreams.

The man stood over him, his hands in his pockets, a cigarette hanging from his lips. He assessed the sight, wondering if he could separate the black book from its cradle in his elbow without waking the protector. No. He chose instead to help himself to a pack of Dunhills, and stood there, rather peculiar, in his shirt and tie, his sweater vest and herringbone sport coat, his Italian alligator shoes. Probably, he reasoned, she wouldn't have written it down. He knew her too well, her type. He had suspected she might do something like this, and he recalled that in this very cove, that he had introduced her to, he told her he believed she might commit suicide one day. Under the circumstances, he supposed, he was legally absolved. It wasn't the police that concerned him now. He wondered who this poor guy was, which one, and a rare wave of pity — a most distasteful emotion — almost made him reconsider. But he had some questions, his curiosity kept him there. He kicked the still smoldering ashes, trying not to dirty his shoes.

Chris jolted to consciousness. "Hey! What the fuck?" His red eyes peered up suspiciously, his body readied itself to fight.

"Take it easy. I'm not going to bother you. I know why you're here. I knew her." He spoke with an accent, European of some sort. Maybe French. German. "Tragic. Life is tragic. The Greeks, they understood this well."

"Who the fuck are you? No. Never mind, I don't give a damn who you are. Get the fuck outta here. Leave me alone." He stood up and brushed his pants, coming across the quarter-sized hole, the red burn on his thigh.

The man didn't move. He offered a Dunhill and lit another one for himself. "I imagine you want to know why she killed herself." His throat cleared. "But this is a hopeless task. I, too, am curious. She was a woman of passion, a beautiful, wild woman. A bit given to romanticism, melodrama, don't you agree?"

"Go away. Go away, or I can't be responsible for your safety," he growled, as frightening an order as possible in his condition.

"You must be Daniel. Of course, you knew there were others, many. I see you have her journal. She never took back her keys. I may still have mine." He pulled out a jailer's key ring and began to study them one by one.

"I'm not going to tell you again." His face grew hot. Blood pumped into his arms, the hair on them bristling, his fingers tightening into fists.

"Hang on there, my friend. I thought, maybe, I could help you. Perhaps not. We, she and I, were, well, associated for quite some time. We were friends in a manner of speaking. An intelligent woman, she was remarkable. She knew how to love," he hesitated, moving slowly away. "She loved easily, but never enough, never completely. You weren't the only one who loved her." He watched the fist uncurl, the arms relax. "The last time I talked with her, she said you two had broken up. You had taken a job back East. Frankly, I'm surprised to find you here. I rather expected that slobbering sentimentalist. What was his name? Bryant, Brian, something like that." Grinning now, he imagined a sense of comradery, the revelations of boys in the locker room who shared the same woman, some knowingly, some not.

Chris sat down and covered his face with both hands. This is not happening. This is an apparition. There is no man standing in front of me speaking of her in the past tense. When I open my eyes he will be gone. He does not exist. He whined, his hands over his face, "Go away. Go away."

"I must go anyway. My clients will be coming soon. I don't suppose you are willing to lend me that book? As I said I, too, am curious about her motives. I'm not the police. I will return it in a day to your home — here, if you wish." He gave a jaded look around, convinced that this man was not stable, perhaps incapable of communication at the moment. "My name is Ivan Wallensky. I'll give you my number, my address. Suzanne was in the midst of doing me a favor, as you say . . ." He reached for the book.

"If you touch that, you're dead. Ivan Wallensky. Now GET THE FUCK OUT OF HERE!" he yelled with all the force of his aching lungs. Wallensky backed off down the beach several yards, concluding there was no hope of reason, yet. He turned and continued walking. "AND MY NAME'S NOT FUCKING DANIEL. I'M NOT FUCKING DANIEL. I'M NOT FUCKING BRIAN!" The herringbone jacket with its leather elbow patches disappeared into the fog around the corner of the cliff.

His fury was unleashed and unfathomable. He stomped over the fire and threw half-burned pieces of wood about wildly. He threw the journal against the rock again and again. He used both feet to kick and bludgeon the book into the sand. He ripped the peace button off the pack and bent it in two, then crushed it into a rock and committed it to the sea. He ripped his pants leg off at the hole with his hands, tearing into the heavy double weave cotton like tissue paper. The durable nylon of the day pack thwarted him. There was nothing left to destroy. Then the water bottle caught his eye. He was about to burst it on the rock when his tantrum stopped. Who was Ivan Wallensky? The name had a familiar sound. He knew about Daniel. He knew about Brian. She had told him during the weekend in Mexico, told him in her playful, story-telling style, accentuating the ridiculous "California mush-brain new male" part of Brian's personality. "Obviously over and done with," she had asserted with finality.

* * *

He stumbled, groggy, with muscles sore from making love, on to the beach. Falling into the sand beside her, he was dimly aware of the darkening sky, more aware of her unwashed smell, the musty, enticing smell of recent sex. He put his arm around her shoulders, hugging her close, her hair tickling his face. "You were right. This place is perfect." He saw that she was engrossed in writing in a hardcover, black book propped on her knees, her pen flying across the page in an unreadable script. "What's that you're writing?"

The book was instantly slammed shut. "Nothing." She turned her head around and kissed him. "It's a silly record of life's trivia. Otherwise known as a diary. A sacred object, you know?" Her look was intended to warn him not to pry.

"Ah, come on. Let me see it," he teased, reaching for the book. "How will I know what you really think of me? If you're writing about me?" The book fell into the sand as he fell on top of her, resting in his favorite position, kissing her neck, her shoulders. He had no intention of starting an argument, nor did he really care about her diary. It was her he wanted, now, in the flesh, not her subjective ruminations which he guessed were only more intimate and explicated versions of their enigmatic conversations.

"Buenos Tardes, Senor y Senora." A handsome, young waiter stood over them, discreetly gazing toward the sea. "Bebidas? Drinks?"

They quickly righted themselves and smiled at him. "Si, si." She

71

smiled at him and he at her, both nodding their heads in agreement. "Dos Pina Coladas, por favor."

With a nod of his head the waiter suggested they take the palapa behind them where the yellow lounge chairs waited next to a rickety table. They complied, settling themselves in under his watchful eye like civilized guests. He dusted the table with his cloth and strolled away.

"The most wonderful thing about Mexico is how long everything takes. In the half-hour that we wait for those drinks we'll have nothing to do but talk and admire the sunset. We'd never relax like this at home." She spoke with her eyes closed, the breeze fanning her hair across the back of the chair.

It was again as though they had known each other for years, her easy way of using "we" and "home." When he thought about it, this familiarity made him just a tad uncomfortable. Marriage. A lifetime with the same woman. It always seemed in his future, and he wanted to keep it there. But he never wanted to be without her. He couldn't imagine living with any other woman. His rationality told him to go slow. The rest of him raced along with her, with no promises, no guarantees. Maybe I will marry her, he thought, as he walked out to the spot on the sand where her book waited to be retrieved. "Here," he placed it in her lap, "don't want history to be deprived, do we?"

She laughed. "Tell me about yourself, Chris. We barely know each other, and here we are. Are you ready for this?"

"Are you?" She seemed to read his mind and speak to him as if she knew the precise depth and intensity of his feelings, his doubts, as if she knew the content and shared them to the extent she chose. At the same time there was always that tone of uncertainty, that note of question even in her statements. There was that quality of . . . of what? He couldn't find the right word. Resignation maybe. Futility. No, it couldn't be that. She exuded happiness. Her face glowed when she smiled at him or laughed with him. And she smiled and laughed since they'd been in La Paz more than he would have ever predicted. She giggled like a child, joked with him, teased him as unmercifully as he teased her. "No answer?"

"Sure, I'm ready for this. I'm ready for anything at this point, but who knows what lurks back in the big city."

"It's too bad we have to go back tomorrow."

"Yeah, that's the trouble with perfectly wonderful anything, it has to end."

"Don't be so gloomy. We'll come here again. Go to other great places." He reached around the table and held her hand. "This has

been a great weekend. I hope it's the beginning of a very long affair."
He squeezed her hand, "Lifelong."

"But this is the best part — the beginning. And you can never go back, never recapture the beginning. It's a special time. It makes me sad that it's already lost."

"Don't be silly. Why do say that? We haven't even begun to discover the limits."

"Have you always been so romantic?"

"Not until I met you."

"Go on. You're unbelievable."

"You better believe me. This is it." His hand had crept down her arm and, before she could resist, he was tickling her again. By the time the waiter arrived with their drinks, giant, frothy white glasses full of fresh pineapple tipping over the edge, they were shamelessly rolling in the sand as before. He kept his presence like a good English butler, then shrugging his shoulders he laughed at them. They fumbled with the pesos, making sure he got a big tip. "Muchas Gracias, Senor y Senora, muchas gracias."

"Did you hear that? Senor y Senora? He thinks we're married, newlyweds probably." She grinned, daring him to suggest it.

"I hate to admit this, but I'm getting hungry again." He was well aware of changing the subject. Not yet. He wasn't that ready, but then he reconsidered. He would call her bluff, accept her dare, whichever. Just as he was about to propose, she relegated the comment to the forgotten, the never-said.

"Me too." She looked at his watch. It was already past seven. "I can't understand it after that gigantic lunch, not to mention breakfast. Well, you know Mexico. We can't eat dinner until nine unless we want to be unfashionably early."

"It must be the snorkeling and tennis," he sighed with regret.

"Are you daft? What snorkeling and tennis?"

"The kind you do with your clothes off."

"Be serious. I want to know about you. Tell me about your past love life."

"It's pretty mundane. Or it was. I had the usual tortured adolescence surrounded by gorgeous beach bunnies and Valley girls in L.A. I wasn't a surfer so I had to cultivate other girl-getting talents. When I went away to college I met my first real girl friend. We dated on and off for years, almost got married, but well, it's embarrassing, but I chickened out. I was a third year medical student, my life was being planned away by her mother and my mother and her. They even had the number and spacing of children figured out, not to mention the mortgage payments on a house and my private practice to support it. I was too busy studying to realize that my life was booked up for the next fifty years. Then there was the ten thousand dollar wedding. Marcy was so absorbed in planning the whole thing we never saw each other. When we did she acted more like a sister than a future wife to me. Sex was never very good. I don't think she liked it. The day before the wedding I got stoned with an old high school buddy. You should meet him. I want you to meet him. Anyway, he said, get out while you still can, so we got in his car and drove to Death Valley. Marcy didn't know I had gone until a few hours before the wedding when my mother called to find me. They both thought I was with the other. So. So they called it off. It was crazy, I know. I should have told her, but I couldn't seem to get through to any of them. They were too wrapped up in the event. I caught hell, as you can imagine. I felt guilty too, but I've never really regretted it. Marcy's happily married now with two kids to a Beverly Hills lawyer. It's just what she planned, what she wanted, money, cars, parties, fancy vacations. I still get Christmas cards from her with pictures of the kids."

"I'd like to go to Death Valley. Will you take me there?"

"Sure." He gulped his drink. "Is that all you're going to say?"

"It all sounds completely normal to me. A typical college romance with a different sort of Dustin Hoffman ending. Terrific. Good movie-of-the-week material, as you well know, but not surprising, not unusual. Don't tell me I've finally found a nice guy with a past only as sordid as a PG movie?"

"So, it's sordid you want? When I was twelve I fucked my au pair in my parents' bed. How 'bout that?"

"You did not. That's obviously something you read in a novel." She was laughing again and choking on her pineapple.

"Hey, take it easy. I thought you could handle sordid." He slapped her on the back and pulled her out of the chair. "Too many cigarettes."

Coughing, she continued, "What about Pat? How'd you get involved with her?"

"No, it's my turn to listen. I told you a mouthful. What about your marriage? What happened to that?"

"You won't believe it if I tell you." Her voice changed; it was sullen, deeper. "I stopped talking about it years ago, because . . ."

"Because?"

"Because it's sad. I got tired of telling the story. It doesn't bother me anymore. I just feel bad watching people when I describe it. They usually get fidgety and wonder what to say, when to change the subject, how to leave gracefully."

"It can't be that bad. Is he alive?"

"Sure, he's alive. He lives in Vermont, I think. I haven't heard from him in several years. It's been ten years since we divorced."

"How long were you married?"

"About five years. Well, we were together five years. We met in 1966 or '67, but we didn't actually become lovers for over a year. It was just after the Chicago convention. Remember *Be Clean For Gene?* McCarthy? That's another story. I was pretty political in my youth. I certainly was young." She was straying form the topic, he could see it in her eyes, the same distanced glaze that came over her when she seemed to get lost in her head. The coughing continued.

"And pretty, I bet." He wanted her to smile again, to laugh, to come back to the moment.

"I didn't think so, but I guess some people did. John did. I suppose I should tell you that John was my second husband. I've been married three times."

"Three times!" He tried not to sound surprised but failed. "How'd you have time to be married three times?"

"Silly, it doesn't take any time to get married. A few minutes at the most. This might sound strange, but it's easier to be married than single. Much easier. Not that I'm interested in another one. I just turned one down as a matter of fact. But marriage is convenient and simple. There's someone around when you come home, someone to take-for-granted, someone to take out the garbage, lift heavy furniture. Besides, you're protected by that little gold band. I guess I needed it, having been brought up never to say no, always to please. I was raised a country girl, you know." She drawled the sentence quite competent with her accent, the one he'd never been able to place. Her comment on marriage lifted his spirits.

"You don't say." Thank goodness she'd relented on the potential explosion of women's rage. He felt allied with her still. "I can see how it would be easier to have one's knight in shining armor around all the time. Slaying dragons and such." He reflected a moment. "I think that's why I got involved with Pat and never changed anything. It was easy. We just fell into these habits that seemed to make everything function. It was convenient. That's true."

The stars were bright in the moonless sky and the air was carrying a refreshing chill. They sat in silence a while, watching the lights from the town in the harbor blink on with a musical rhythm. She went and sat between his legs on the long lounge chair, leaning back against his chest. He put his arms around her. "I'm starving," she mumbled. "What time is it?"

"It's eight-thirty. Let's get dressed for dinner. Shall we eat here, or do you want to go into town? It's our last night. Let's celebrate."

"I'm for that. Let's go to the Lobster Pot down the beach."

"Great."

By the time they stumbled out of the shower, unable to resist the warmth of each other's body, they were almost too late for dinner. Good sex was like food, she remarked as they walked along the beach to the restaurant. "It fills me up, leaves me pleasantly contented for at least half an hour. Aren't you ever satiated?" She pinched him.

"Making love to you makes me ravenous," he said. "If I don't eat soon I'll start eating these cigarettes instead of smoking them." They shared a joint for momentary diversion.

"Slow down," she ordered as he practically inhaled three pieces of bread "You won't have room for the mariscos especialidad," which included shrimp, lobster, huachinango, and chocolate clams the size of oranges. In an amazing display of self control, she nibbled on the crust of a tiny bolleto.

"Why don't you distract me, then," he said. "Tell me what happened to your husband, the one that counts."

"All right, if you really want to know. I've probably overdramatized it anyway. Well, I was nineteen and had already been divorced from my first teenage sweetheart — that didn't last long, but it's another story. When I met John I was young and impressionable. He was handsome, talented. You know, he could do things like play the guitar and recite poetry. He was several years older than me, and I'd never met a man quite so literate and cultured. Besides, he was gentle, kind and funny. But there were big complications. He married a close girl friend of mine. In fact, I introduced them. She was lonely at the time, a starving artist type. He was so handsome he scared me, and she was movie-star pretty. As I expected, they hit it off and married in a very short time. I moved away but kept in touch, mostly with him. To make a long story short, I pined after him for a year until he happened to be passing through New York where I was living at the time. We slept together. He left his wife, and I went to live with him, believing with all my heart that true love would bring forgiveness. We married several months later after his divorce and lived blissfully happy, or so I thought, for a year or two. There were problems, but I only saw them in retrospect after a long, slow deterioration that, God knows, I tried not to admit. I couldn't or wouldn't see anything negative in him, in our relationship. You really want to hear all this?"

"Of course." He had marched through the mariscos like a band of army ants and sat back engrossed, occasionally wondering when he would get to finish off her leftovers. "What happened to his wife? Was there forgiveness?"

"No. I suffered about her for years, guilt, I guess. I often thought he would go back to her someday. Anyway, I got a scholarship to Yale Medical School, and we moved to New Haven in 1970. You know what medical school is like. He had a decent job as a social worker, very idealistic. He wanted to save the poor black children of the ghetto. Our first year, although I was constantly panicked about school, I thought all was well. But I got pregnant in the spring, had an abortion without really consulting him. Later I found out he wanted to have the child, but it would have been the end of medical school. That was one problem. Then he quit his job the next fall with no explanation. He stopped wanting to sleep with me. I was so busy, so tired, I didn't pay much attention to it. We never fought. He never objected to my schedule, never even told me how he felt about the abortion until much later. He stopped talking to me. I suggested a shrink, but he refused. I had to get two jobs to support us, because he slept all day." She shook her head and smiled, "Christ, why am I subjecting you to this?"

"I'm interested. Go on. No kidding, I really want to know what happened." He gave her his most encouraging stare, letting his glasses slide down his nose so she could see he really meant what he said.

"You won't believe this, but he made me move out of the bedroom which I did because it was 'liberated' to have a room of one's own, like Virginia Woolf, you know. And I was getting angry that he did nothing but sleep and scrub the walls. I can't believe how naive I was then." She put down her fork for the last time, the majority of her dinner still on the plate. "I've lost my appetite. Will you order me another drink?"

"Sure." He searched for the waiter. "So, go on. I'm fascinated." She gave him her plate to finish.

"After a while John got a job taking care of dogs at a kennel. I mistakenly believed that disaster had blown over and plunged myself further into my courses and clerkships. Then in October — why does everything happen in October?" she asked rhetorically. "I think it was around the first of the month. He left. He said he needed to be alone for a while. I fell apart for a week, then pulled myself together, went to a shrink and kept going. It was my third year of medical school, awful time. He came back a few times and left again. Finally I stopped it. The next spring I went to a lawyer. The same afternoon I told John I was getting a divorce he tried to kill himself. Next thing I knew he was in a psychiatric ward." She saw his eyebrows rise, a look of disbelief on his face. "That's what happened.

At least, after he was institutionalized I discovered that the problems in our marriage weren't all my fault. His mother who was an evil witch, a paranoid schizophrenic — God, I hated that woman — had screwed him up sexually. She made advances toward him in his teens. All this shit came out in these family therapy sessions. While I was going to school, he was out in the afternoons at porn movies. I found several locked trunks in the attic filled with pornographic magazines. The weird thing was I blamed myself. I still loved him. I thought I had driven him crazy with my constant work, my insistence on the abortion. I kept remembering that he read Buckminster Fuller and Bertrand Russell to me in bed. He sang folk songs to me and patiently taught me to play tennis. His bitch of a mother. I wanted to kill her when I found out what she did. For many years I wanted to murder her, but I knew it wouldn't feel good enough."

"What happened to him? Did he recover?"

"After five years he left the hospital. I guess they considered him recovered. He never was the same to me. By this time, I was half way through my psychoanalysis and a second year resident at Mt. Sinai in New York. I was pretty crazy." She dismissed this with an ironic sort of laugh. "Still am."

"I don't see how you lived through that. You emerged so unscathed." His hand caressed her cheek. "At least sexually." He bent over and kissed her on both cheeks. "The resilience of some people is extraordinary. There isn't a trace of tragedy on your face. How can I believe all this?" There was anger in his voice, an anger that said, I don't want this to have happened to you. I don't like it, and it hurts me to know you were hurt.

"It's true. I've gotten over John. But there's more. My psychoanalysis helped a lot, not to say I didn't almost destroy myself in the process. That's my brief third marriage. I let myself get involved with a real bastard. He was ruthless — insults, beatings, even tried to strangle me once. My analyst thought I was trying to make him kill me to atone for my guilt about John. Once after he beat me up, although I was outraged, I felt this sense of peace, real contentment. I fell asleep almost treasuring my bruises. It was then that I saw what I was doing. Luckily, I came to my senses before I was killed. It took a few months. I think I endured it because he acted out my own secret wishes. I wanted to kill John's mother and that got confused with wanting to kill John, my own mother, my father, my analyst, someone. You know I was a raving pacifist in the anti-war days." Her smile was genuine now. "There was no way I could handle my own desire to murder. Do you know what psychoanalysis is like? It brings out all this primitive shit. It's hell really, because you have to stuff it all back in somehow. I needed it. I wanted to go to hell. But, you know, I never thought about death. Not actually. Not the way I think about it now." Her fingers had folded the napkin over and over into a chain of tiny squares. She twisted it out and tried to put it around her wrist. "I only wanted punishment then. Now I want peace." She showed him her handiwork. "This doesn't fit."

The waiter had fallen asleep across the open air bar, and there were no other customers left. She realized the lights in the town had diminished to a few lone flickers. "My goodness, what time is it?"

"One-thirty. Can you believe it?" He turned around and saw the snoring waiter. "Look at him. For Christ's sake! Why didn't he bring us the check?"

"Mexican hospitality. We were engrossed in my movie-of-the-week story." She got up and went to the waiter and whispered. "La quenta, por favor." He didn't move. "What should we do? There's no point in waking him."

They wedged more than enough money under the sleeping waiter's arm and anchored it with a shell. The walk back under the black silk of the sky with the milky way a dazzling white rainbow and the moon now a pale yellow crescent reduced them to small creatures of the physical world. They were relieved by the night breeze that swept away the weight of their conversation. She wondered if he would still feel that her past was unimportant. He wondered if her telling him this story would create an unnecessary caution in her, a distance, a distrust, a suspicion. She suppressed her guilt that she hadn't told him all of it, that she had left out a few essential details. Enough was enough. She couldn't bear to hear the whole story herself. Would he fault her for it someday? She had an urge to compensate, to make amends immediately.

"You know, Chris, sometimes I get incredibly depressed. Sometimes I don't know how to stop it. There seems to be no real reason anymore. My life is easy. My work goes well. I have a few friends. They're all so far away though. I kind of spiral down. Do you know what I mean?" She was serious, searching, hoping he did know.

He heard the vulnerability in her question, the same vulnerability he could see in her face. "I want to know." His arms went around her, and he pressed her close to him. "I'm not sure I've ever been depressed in my life, not as I've heard it described to me. I never even think about how I'm feeling most of the time. Until recently anyway. If anybody ever had a reason to be depressed, I'd say you have. But it is in the past. Don't worry about it. Next time you feel that way, lean on me." He held her by the shoulders and looked into her eyes. "I love you." He grinned. "It may be the wrong time to say it, but I love you — of this I'm absolutely certain. I'm glad you told me all that, and I'm glad it's over. That *is* over, Suzanne. I'm going to love you a very long time."

She felt her eyes filling with tears, tears of exhaustion, of remembrance, of regrets, of wishful fairy tale endings. "Thank you. That may not be what you want to hear, but thank you, Chris. Maybe I've made it to the point where I can be loved." She put her arms farther around him and hugged him as tight as she could. "I'm so exhausted, I've got to sleep."

*   *   *

The afternoon sun had become razor sharp. A strong wind was blowing, rearranging the sand in another of the infinite possibilities. He had taken the book and hiked up to the top of the largest rock to his right. Powerful waves crashed against the rock, leaving tide pools on the south face, swirling into and through narrow passages on the north. From the peak he could look over the side into a churning cauldron of water, trapped as each new wave rolled over the lower rocks. Rubbery brown seaweed plants were repeatedly smashed by the tons of water in every wave, yet they rose and fell as unaffected as grass in a windy field. Staring down, he could feel the magnetic pull of the watery hole, feel the prickly fear of knowing one slight movement in one instantaneous second could have him churning in that grave. He sat down, not trusting his survival instinct. Perspiration covered his palms and his hands shook nervously on the book.

Some high school kids, playing hooky from school in Berkeley, were stumbling on the lower strata of rock out of his view. They had given him a grocery bag full of accumulated box lunches. In a most sincere effort to befriend him, given their heavily drugged state, they extolled the virtues of sharing, the spiritual benefit they would reap if he allowed them to give away their food. The good that Timothy Leary had wrought, he scoffed, nonetheless pleased that they were there. Despite his less than human appearance, he was quite sure the drug they imbibed, mushrooms, peyote, mescaline or LSD made carrying the sack of lunches only a meaningless weight, a nuisance to them.

They thought he was one of the thousands of wretched, hungry, homeless men roaming the Bay area. The opportunity to do a good

80

deed was upon them. He gratefully accepted the bag of food, pretending to be illiterate, shy and starving. He also managed to mooch their cigarettes and wine. Scurrying away from them, his loot clutched tight, he disappeared into his cave, acting the hermit they envisioned. He buried the bag and marked the spot with some rocks. They – three boys and three girls – had shed their clothes and romped naked in the sand and waves nearby. On top of the giant rock he was spared watching them in their glorious fun.

His reverie took him far enough back into memory that there was no present. The ruthless, blaring sun, the crashing waves, the gale force winds were like the naked children to him, nuisances of the senses, furies from another dimension. He was back there with her, wanting to stay lost in the memories that he prayed would fall into place like pieces in a puzzle. The final picture had to be *The Answer*.

He remembered how quickly the story of her marriage to John was forgotten by both of them. Yes, it was a piece, but it couldn't have been the reason. Yes, he left her in October, but that was mere coincidence. She survived that. Yes, he was certain that if she committed suicide it had nothing to do with John – not that he wasn't part of her vulnerability, her fragility. He studied how the water had cut a ragged edge in the rock. Some wounds don't heal straight. He peeled sunburnt skin from his arm until it bled. There was no tragedy on her face, but how he regretted saying that now. There were scars, invisible scars. There must have been. But she didn't want to kill herself. Not then. She even found someone else to do it for her, this mysterious third husband. And she got out.

Was this all true? Had this really happened to her? She did have a tendency to exaggerate. Death was no exaggeration. He still didn't believe it. Could she really be dead? Did she actually commit suicide? How would he ever know?

On the plane back, she had told him about Daniel. "A kind, wonderful man," she called him. They had been dating on and off ever since she moved to California in 1979. What had she said exactly? That phrase – it had caused him a real pain, a pang of concern, of hurt, of fear that Daniel was a significant rival. "He's a sweetheart." Yes, that was it. "He puts up with so much shit from me, I can't tell you." The present tense. Was it still going on? He detected considerable guilt when she said this, and more worrisome, a tone of tender affection. What she told him about Daniel – his wit, his devotion, his tolerance, his rationality, his creative intelligence, his depth of knowledge – it made him want to drop the subject right there. She insisted they had broken up for good, but she would undoubtedly see him again. He had this way of going away for a while then coming back. When he had in the past, they moved smoothly into a routine together almost as if they were married. She felt married to him, and he had wanted to marry her, she said, just this past summer. She almost married him, but it wasn't right. She didn't want to leave her new job. He was quite a well-known professor of Russian literature.

Suddenly, a gust of wind moved him several feet across the rock to the edge. He grabbed at the crumbling shale rock and dug his feet into a precipice. It passed and he regained stability. Yes, he had known about Daniel. He had known. Compelled to remember as much as he could, he transfixed his gaze over the edge into the swirling pool of white water. It was hypnotic. Daniel had moved back East to Boston where he had a professorship at Harvard. It was the "pinnacle of his career," she had said. He begged her to go with him, to marry him; he even arranged an excellent job for her in which she could have carried on her research on AIDS. For pity sake, why wouldn't she stop talking about this on the plane back when there was no time to renew their own special intimacy? Now they'd have to go back to separate houses. He'd have to think about this alone.

"Why didn't you go with him?" He was angry with her.

"I just couldn't," she replied, unaware of his anger. "I couldn't leave California, the ocean." He could hear her as if she were next to him.

"There's an ocean on the other side of the country quite convenient to Boston, I'm told." He had pushed for a more sensible reason.

"I guess you want me to say I don't really love him." That is exactly what he wanted her to say. Even the memory of her reply registered a pain. "But it isn't really that." He could see her hair hanging forward, her head bent down, the serious, pensive face hidden from him intentionally. "My relationship with Daniel is like yours with Pat, comfortable, convenient. I'd be lying if I said I didn't care about him. But it's not the same way I feel about you. With you there's nothing missing, no doubt." She had taken his hand and put it in her lap. "You can understand this, surely. I have wished − I can't tell you how I have wished − that all my doubts about marrying Daniel, marrying again, would disappear. These doubts feel like the death of me."

Yes. She had said that; he recalled the exact words. "There was something standing in the way. I should've married him." She went on. "He's a good man, a decent man, too decent. I hate that word. He loves me. I just didn't love him enough. I couldn't leave the Pacific ocean, and don't tell me the Atlantic is the same. It's not." This hadn't made sense to him. This wasn't an explanation; it was something incomprehensible. He didn't want to hear anymore.

He had already decided he wanted her for himself and was satisfied that Daniel, wonderful as he may have been, was three thousand miles away. She had put her head on his shoulder, raising her lips to be kissed. "You're the one I love. You're the one I'll stop with. I love you, Chris, believe me."

The waves were smashing against the rock with such a force that he was soaking wet from the spray. He slowly made his way back to the cave. It isn't the same ocean. It wasn't the same love. If only he could ask her now: Was I another John? Another Daniel? Another anyone? You said I was different. You said you loved me completely, absolutely, totally, physically, chemically, instinctually, passionately. You said you would marry me. If only he could have her back for one hour, ten minutes, five minutes. Remember when I asked you? In Death Valley on the trip you wanted to take, our really big one, the first and last big one, the one on which you said yes. We were going to tell my parents and yours, but you wanted to keep it a secret for a week. You wanted to tell Julia, your best friend. Julia, why hadn't you told me about her before? You wanted to talk to some shrink you knew, the one who sounded like a jerk to me. Funny, I remember right where we were, driving past Mono Lake. You kept saying it looked like a moon crater, the surface of the moon. Then you told me about Anthony. For Christ's sake. I was exasperated then. "Who the hell is he?" I yelled at you.

You got angry and wouldn't talk to me. You accused me of being insensitive. Life was complicated, you cried, but you wanted me to know exactly how many times you had been in love. So you had to tell me about Anthony. There was John and, of course, Daniel and there was me, the end of the line. And Anthony. But you never told me about him because we got into a terrific fight. You decided I didn't really love you if I could be jealous of people who were entirely in the past. I really loved Pat. Furthermore, you weren't sure if you didn't really love Daniel and not me. Maybe that is what real love is, you said, tolerance and commitment, devotion and convenience, not this passion stuff, this flash in the pan romance. After an hour of screaming and yelling, accusations and recriminations, we stopped. I'll never forget how agonizingly long that drive was. I kept dozing at the wheel and driving off the road onto the shoulder. You said nothing except that you hoped we were killed instantly when I crashed us up because you didn't want to be an invalid in a wheelchair. You didn't want to be in a hospital.

The box sandwiches were tuna fish, corned beef, and peanut butter and jelly. He ate four of them, methodically, not tasting any difference but having the sensation that he could go on eating in this robot fashion for quite a while. His benefactors had gone, leaving behind a rather dated message in the sand in front of his camp: Make Love Not War. The wind had died down, but the tide was coming in, and the message was already partially washed away. He stood watching it be demolished in the gradual inching in of the tide.

The exactitude with which he remembered these conversations with her fascinated him. It seemed she wasn't, couldn't be dead. Then he wondered why her body had not been found. Why hadn't it washed up here or on some beach? Why hadn't the patrols found her in their search? He had seen them passing over the cove three or four times a day at first, flying low with the big red cross on the side, impossible to ignore. He'd been here a day or two or more? He was disoriented. All he knew was that when they came he scurried into the cave, not to be seen. But he did see them, their objective, antlike faces, surveying the shore, more menacing than rescuing. He didn't want them to find her.

Tears began to stream down his cheeks. The dam broke again. His heart was crushed. He sobbed uncontrollably. As he cried without wanting to stop, more thoughts passed through his mind disconnected from his feelings. Memory was selective. How much had they said to each other that was forgotten, stowed away? How much could he trust of what he remembered, and how much did he create, twist, bend to his own needs? One minute he heard her speaking as if she were there; the words were absolutely as she had said them. The next minute he was plagued with an addition, another word, a missing sentence, a new interpretation, another slant on a phrase. Never would he possess certainty — that was what made him sad, unable to go home, insanely angry. At her. At himself. It might make him insane but not insane enough, he winced. She was insane. He wanted to believe this, but he didn't. The crying spell abated. He blew his nose into the air, wiped his face on his torn off pants leg, and began to read. He started at the beginning again.

*   *   *

March 10, 1982

There is much to be learned in transitions. This is a new journal. I'm going to focus on change. No more outpourings of passion, rage, or self-pity. I'm glad the last one was stolen. It saves me from the embarrassment of reading that old stuff. I don't need intense emotions right now. God! Is this going to work? There is too much disguise in my life. I keep things hidden. I don't want to, but I do. Here I am in London. What on earth did I come for? To keep Daniel company? To see Julia? A change? I did need a change from work. But the illusion was that somehow I could leave the baggage of my life back there. It has to be pulled along, squeezed into this small flat, tugged through the tight spots of doors, elevators, airplanes. Me with my baggage and my positive mask. I came down with the flu the day before we left. D and I had a horrible fight on the plane. He insisted that I bring illness on myself. This made me damned angry. We got into our vicious cycle of accusation, hurt, anger, withdrawal. Guilt, of course. The grand illusion is that both of us think this cycle is about my being sick. It's really about our relationship. I hate to feel dependent. Yet when I'm sick, I am dependent. D finds it impossible to take care of me when I'm sick. He half-heartedly tries. Then he gets angry at me for making him feel inadequate which he absolutely can't stand to feel. I withdraw because I fear he will abandon me. He doesn't abandon me, though, he just makes me feel so bad I wish he would. I want to be left alone. I'd like to be dependent without the feeling of intrusion. I want to feel safe. It's a Catch 22 with D, because I don't feel safe when I need to, when I'm sick.

March 12, 1982

I'm locked in the flat accidently. Speaking of trapped. Now I must reorient my plans. The moment I realized I wasn't getting out of here until someone came back with a key, I was terrified. Time to kill, time to pass in an unstructured, unproductive way. At home I was doing something every waking moment – reading with my morning coffee, off to the hospital, patients, lectures, rounds, lab, dinner (sometimes), dates, sleep. I never had time to sleep late, to dawdle, to think. I rather like it, lying around reading *The London Times*, planning my lunch. I'm getting over the flu, and I started my period which makes me feel better. D is in a frenzy. He runs around the city, shopping, walking the streets, visiting this or that place. I'm content to stay inside the flat or a warm pub. I want to reflect, to let small details amuse me, occupy me. I don't feel bored yet, although I might if I kept it up very long. If D hadn't been in such a rush, locking me in, he wouldn't be waiting for me to appear at Neil's Yard for lunch this very minute. We probably won't make it to the British Museum today.

March 13, 1982

Lunching at a vegetarian restaurant near St. Paul's Cathedral. Spent the morning following D around from bookstore to bookstore. He's off again to visit some university. I didn't want to go. I'm happy on my own. I bought a new jacket, the kind I've wanted for a long time. I asked D to put it on his American Express card. Highly unusual behavior for me to ask for a present. Last night I had dreams about being in risky situations, not being scared and not getting hurt. I was in the water with big sharks. It was OK, and I was even curious to touch them. It was even OK to be hit by a giant wave. I protected myself and landed on my feet. Then the dream changed, and it was OK to get on a scale. I hadn't gained weight; I had lost some. Then I wanted to get on the scale again because I didn't believe it, but they — I don't know who they were — wouldn't let me. I even thought this was OK, that it didn't matter if it was correct, that it didn't matter exactly how much I weighed. I wonder if this dream came from our pig-out last night. D, Julia, her boy-friend, and I got stoned out of our minds. I ended up scarfing down a bag of trail mix, peanut butter, two bananas and a yogurt. I like writing out the food I eat. It doesn't look as sinful in print as it feels when I eat it. D is having a better time. We've made a truce. I still think he's angry with me, but he won't admit it. I'm sure he feels he shouldn't be angry because he's supposed to be perfect all the time, and if he isn't, his conscience bothers him. We both want to have a good time here, but we have trouble agreeing on what to do. Both of us have definite preferences for sightseeing, and they're not the same. I'm sticking to mine, and he to his. Maybe this is a good stage in our relationship, but the going is rough—too rough at times. I wish we wanted to do the same things because I'd like to have someone to share this vacation with.

March 17, 1982

I found William Blake's grave at St. Paul's, 1757-1827. Written on the tombstone is, "To see a world in a grain of sand; And heaven in a wild flower; Hold infinity in the palm of your hand; And eternity in an hour."

March 18, 1982

D went off to the university today; he's obsessed with getting work done. I went to take a sauna. This took all day. I was frustrated with it, feeling like I should spend time in some productive activity. My work compulsion is translating itself into vacation compulsion. I must go to every museum, gallery, theatre, exhibit to enlighten myself. I'm like D! Except he's worse! Neither of us can practice "vacation as relaxation." I want to have a way to justify my being here away from work. One of my goals is to familiarize myself with other cultures, to understand what other people take seriously. Probably goes back to my search for what I take seriously. I want to find myself somewhere. Is the answer in a place?

March 19, 1982

Finding myself . . . I've been thinking about control. I'd like to have it and usually I believe I do, but I'm afraid I don't. Nobody has control really. Like control over illness and disease — as a doctor I act as if knowledge brings control — my patients certainly expect it. But I think knowledge has brought me only more curiosity about and respect for the microbes that defy my best efforts. The first thing a doctor has to learn is humility. Patients may need me to play the all-knowing expert, but I have to remember that I'm not. It's handy to have an entire industry trying to convince everyone that most disease is caused by stress, and it fosters the illusion that individuals can control it. If I believe that I'm in control — like magic — I feel much better. Medicine isn't magic, though, and lately I haven't felt better. I've felt kind of doomed, like modern civilization is going down the drain, and I'm so modern I'm going with it. It's out of control. Yet there's some perverse satisfaction here??? What does this mean? There's a thrill, even pleasure, in letting go of my ironclad control. Liberation awaits?

March 20, 1982

Today we went castle chasing. Leeds was closed. We went to Bodheim and were happily surprised to find a huge Gothic castle with towers on each of its four corners and surrounded by a moat. Just like my childhood fantasies of a castle: dark, dank, moss-covered stone, tiny low-ceilinged rooms which had the feel of a prison. It was the successful conclusion to a cloudy, rain-threatening morning during which we drowned our disappointment at the local pub. The pub food is remarkably good.

I had homemade mushroom soup with big hunks of fresh mushrooms floating in a delicate broth. For "afters" we had brie and sweetmeal biscuits — I love these! Staying in the country is spoiling me, an electric blanket, central heating, and a convenient bath — unlike the flat where everyone camps out in the style of vegetarian anti-vivisectionists. Julia and her friends have been generous with their small flat. They are regular people who work and don't have money or time — for that matter — to spend cleaning up. D feels at home in a mess and dirt is invisible to him. Yesterday we played scrabble, then dictionary. Stoned and drunk, we laughed our heads off, and the cold, rainy outside faded to oblivion. I love Julia. I've missed her wonderful friendship. She's in a spiritual phase and assures me we will meet often in the future. But, at the most, it'll be once or twice a year. I wish we lived closer. She tries to teach me about patience, endurance, and appreciation. It was different a few years ago when she was suicidal and utterly inconsolable. I always knew she would pull out of that. I am completely without doubt about her, and she may very well be the exception to that damnable, eternal aloneness. Still the time we spend togther is too short, miserably short.

March 22, 1982

A wonderful day in the National Gallery, completely transfixed by the Dutch, Flemish painters of the 17th century. The Age of Observation, it's called. Their use of light brings ordinary space, everyday life, out of the natural darkness in their environment and into a visual state of the sublime. The normal becomes the sublime through the use of light. The views of these simple scenes show how an artist can transform life (the unseen obvious) into visual art. I wish I could have been an artist. What an unbeatable contribution to make to humanity. Much better than medicine. I'm indulging in a bit of culinary art: three special cheeses from a local shop I couldn't resist, a camembert with blue in it, a brie with peppercorns, and something pungent like a Bel Paese but stronger. All with a Granny Smith apple and delectable English biscuits. I'm rewarding myself due to a bad dream and that sense of impending disaster.

March 24, 1982

Back to that dream. It was on Sunday night, and I was expecting to see Julia on Monday after the weekend in the country. The dream: I was being taken to the airport by Julia. She kept singing a song, "I'm free . . . I'm free." At first I thought she was just humming along, then I realized she meant to tell me something, i.e. she was free of me. I knew my plane was going to crash, but I still wanted to go. It seemed I would miss the plane. There was snow on the runway, and the actual plane I was to be on was a long way away. There was confusion. Julia left me off in the farthest parking lot as though she wanted me to miss the plane, but in fact I just had a long walk to my demise. She left me promptly in an old beat up car. I was very lonely and scared, deserted and abandoned, then I woke up. When I came back to Julia's flat the next day I found a note. She was at her boy-friend's flat. I telephoned her. She said she was cross and tired, and she didn't want to take the train back to London to spend the day with me. I was very disappointed and hurt and felt the dream was prophetic. She IS free, and I am only her best friend, not the person who will spend the rest of her life with her. At least we have planned a few days in Cornwall together before I go home.

March 26, 1982

Julia and I spent a fantastic day hiking along the Cornwall coast. We took the train from London to Penzance and ended up in Mousehole. The scenery is spectacular, rather like the Northern California coast. Huge rock outcroppings and cliffs overlook a sometimes dark, sometimes bright blue sea — the British Channel, I think. We walked past roaring streams and through fields of daffodils. The ground was wet, muddy in places, and the lush undercoating of spring signalled its arrival. The wood shimmered with sunlight in the early morning dew. We talked and laughed as we walked along. At one point, we walked into a dark forest, a place where primeval fairies should live. The rays of sun picked up the brilliances dancing through the trees and scattered bits of color to the ground. It was magical. Funny thing too, this is where I discovered the camera was broken. Last night we stayed in a lovely bed and breakfast overlooking the sea. We watched the gulls play on the rocks until after sunset then went to the pub next door for crab soup. (I had too much Lager and lime.) We had to share the same bed. I was happy to be close to Julia and even more aware of how much I care about her. Probably these affections were exaggerated by the alcohol. She's the one who takes care of me emotionally. At least I can treat her by paying for things she can't afford. How we walked all those miles without getting outrageously ill, I'll never know. My head hurt a bit, but the English breakfast helped. We carried a picnic and stopped around two to eat realizing we had set our sights too high in terms of distance. It took hours to get to Lamourna, our first stop. On the trail we met an old couple who said they had been hiking four hours from Land's End, and we had already hiked four and a half hours from Mousehole. We were forced to settle for Portneco where we could get a bus back to Penzance. Here we've found a small, but adequate B & B that the bus driver recommended. It's inexpensive. After baths we went in search of dinner, ending up at Admiral Benbow's. It was two hours before we finally got food. It seems we're always starving. Julia's having knee pains, and my lower back is killing me. My clothes are filthy, and a laundrette, a bank and a cafe will do me just fine tomorrow. We're off to St. Ives. Spending this time with Julia is better than I ever hoped for, we chat, squabble, gossip. It's the closest time we've had since we were roomies in college.

March 27, 1982

St. Ives is an ancient village known for its artists, potters, weavers, painters. It has a picturesque harbor and a wide, sandy beach flanked by rocky cliffs and grassy fields. The streets are winding and tiny with centuries old stone houses. The houses are situated on hills surrounded by the harbor, and the main town is a labyrinth of shops, cafes, and daily sundry stores. English beach towns foster the same shops as American beach towns: ice cream, fudge, hats, umbrellas and suntan lotions. Reminds me of New Jersey or Delaware. Today we were so tired from hiking we sat on the beach and didn't move. We began to talk about our deepest feelings, our hopes and plans. Last night at dinner — hysterical from hunger as usual — Julia told me funny stories about her adventures with her boy-friend in Brazil. I have to admit I was jealous. She loves him. There's no doubt about that. We're off to the pub. I must phone D, but don't know what to tell him. He wanted to come and meet us here for more hiking, but we're both too zonked out. Our feet hurt. I can't believe D and I will be flying back next week. It started out rocky, but this has been a treasured vacation. I think I've learned how to relax a bit, how to let go, laugh, and have fun for its own sake. I feel much better about D.

April 10, 1982

I must see a shrink. I had the premonition on our trip that D and I weren't going to make it as a couple. I thought things were getting better. Even though Julia kept me entertained and made the vacation wonderful, now I remember the terrible aloneness I felt. When I woke up this morning, the memory of our lovemaking as close as his body, I felt that same utter aloneness and sadness. There is no real reason for these attacks of loneliness. I find myself close to tears at unpredictable moments. Too often. Now that we're back in the city, D back to work and me overwhelmed by the backlog at the hospital, I'm not sure I can do it. I must keep working without anyone knowing how god-awful I feel. Janet, Dora's friend, mentioned the name of a therapist she likes, Ivan something or other. I think I'll investigate this further. The idea of going back into therapy really appalls me, but what else can I do? Disintegrate? I tried to tell Dora how I felt, and she stood there staring at me with such inquisitive eyes. I immediately felt invaded as if my problems were exciting to her. She fed on them. She wanted me to talk to her, but I clammed up. I made light of it, saying it was nothing but the current "American disease" – alienation, no big deal. Must admit I still have my Easterner's prejudice about psychotherapy in Califonia. I must really be nuts to consider it, but I'm afraid this could affect my work. It's two in the morning and I can't sleep. I don't want to take a Dalmane because I have to be at the hospital by seven. Thank goodness I was able to write myself a script for Valium. Never thought I'd need it, but it's been a lifesaver. Dammit to hell. What is wrong with me? I wish D were here. A warm body. We could make love. This is absurd. Too absurd for words.

April 12, 1982

Dora tells me that Ivan Wallensky is the shrink that Janet goes to and he's not analytically trained, but a graduate of some wacko school in Big Sur. Janet says he's had some training with the Lacanians in France. According to Dora she's in love with the man, says he's a genius. I guess I shouldn't see another analyst anyway. Why repeat the past? I can't go to anyone in psychiatry- too embarrassing, especially since everyone knows I've been in psychoanalysis before. Why aren't I cured? I hate this. I hate how a big city can become a fishbowl; everyone knows everyone else's life history in distorted cocktail party terms. I need anonymity, and this is CA — the world of the open book person. I have his number. Perhaps I'll just try him, make it brief and to the point. I know it's crazy, but if only there were a drug. I'm craving drugs like never before. I want magic.

*　*　*

part two

desire

THE HYPNOTIC, REPETITIVE SHAFTS of light blinking through the bridge were calming her anxiety, but not much. The vacation in England seemed light years away even though she had been back only a month. She was on her way to see Ivan Wallensky for the first time. The traffic was light by 10:30 as it usually was, and she sped along in the far left lane, Joan Armatrading blaring from the tape deck. A sudden swell of anger and panic swept over her; she wanted to light a joint but squashed the impulse. Too early for dope smoking, she reprimanded herself.

This is all Dora's fault, she thought. Nagging, nagging until I made an appointment with this Wallensky character. Janet told Dora the man is a genius, and Dora, as is her habit, wants me to "check him out." Who am I – her goddamn detective! Because she sells real estate she thinks she's an expert in psychology. "If it's broken, fix it. Call the plumber, the electrician, the builder, just do something, Suzanne. Think of your body as a house, if the lights are dimming all the time wouldn't you get them fixed? Can't sell a house without its wiring, now can you?" And I listen to this bizarre stuff! I can't tell her to go to hell and leave me alone. She's too goddamned concerned about my depression. Why did I ever confide in her? Open Pandora's Box – I get what I deserve, I suppose. But Christ, the phone calls! At least once a day she calls to find out if everything is okay, to advise me with some new "house metaphor." And of course, tit for tat she tells me her problems which are variations on demolition: redecorating her house, burning it down for the insurance money, reconstructing it into a duplex! I'm now privy to how much she hates her body, that she fakes liking sex, starves herself, wants more bloody affairs, can't sleep, and worst of all, needs to talk on the phone every half-hour to someone. Sometimes I don't know which one of us is crazier. Janet told me to keep my distance, but I never listen.

Life is complicated enough. My own problems are reaching new depths, and what do I think about – Dora and her house fixation. It's incestuous. That must be what attracts me, keeps me on the damn phone with her. We even argue who's going to come to which house! She wants to come to my house more often – says she does anyway.

Janet says she's jealous of my relationship with Julia; she pouted and fussed all the time I was away, her sales fell off. I can feel the envy and the hate in our relationship like a carnivorous plant that attracts with its flowers then attacks with its tongue. I need a close friend, not a parasite. I feel like she wants to devour me, but I don't know if it's her or me? Have I ever felt this way with another woman? I don't think so. How on earth have we gotten to be friends? I've never had a friend I didn't like before. Whenever I try to put distance between us it lasts about a week. Then comes the inevitable guilt, and my conscience won't leave me alone until I call her. We begin again. Wait a minute. If you live in a glass house, don't throw stones. . . . It takes two to tango. . . . I wish I could blame this on her. On someone.

Dora isn't why I'm upset. It's my cells dying over the weekend. That experiment has to be set up all over again. And that grant from the Rockefeller Foundation — they committed the money to us, and now they say they don't have it. I wish I knew what is happening to me. I wish no one else knew. My fucking psychoanalyst, what the fuck good did he do if I still feel like a basketcase? Dora's spread the word to all our mutual friends: Suzanne's depressed. She can't keep her mouth shut for a minute. Daniel, well, he's about as aware of my feelings as that concrete barrier there. He conveniently managed to leave town this week. It isn't going to work, this relationship. It isn't going to work. That's got to be the core of it. I want something to work.

Poor Dr. Muller, I practically ran over him on my way out of the clinic this morning. I left four new patients sitting in the waiting room. It's incredible the number of sick, young gay guys I'm seeing. When I saw those four this morning I really wanted to rush out. If I only knew what this is, how to find out. If anyone only knew. Those poor, wasting away guys. They're not going to stop fucking each other, ten, twenty, fifty times a night! Nobody's going to stop fucking. Fucking. Now there's something to worry about. Not enough. Too much. What in hell am I going to tell this Wallensky? How can I describe what's bothering me? I should feel some relief that I'm going to get it off my chest, but instead I feel like the anxiety and panic are rising to the surface. I want to do this by myself. It represents failure that I can't. Same old shit. Be stoic. Endure. Whatever you do, don't complain. Doctors don't complain. Big girls don't cry.

The fog had burned off in the East Bay, leaving a golden shimmer on the buildings, the trees, the sleepy streets just coming to life. Instead of being late — she'd rushed out to avoid that — she found herself fifteen minutes early. In light traffic, she forgot, it took less than twenty minutes to get to downtown Berkeley. There was one of the hundreds of espresso and croissant shops on the corner of Telegraph near his office. She didn't want espresso, but needed a bathroom. Ordering was necessary, a pecuniary barrier to the use of the facilities by the hoards of moneyless roaming the Berkeley streets. She fumbled in her purse for the small leather folder. The packet was there. After ordering her coffee, she asked for directions to the ladies' room. Her friendship with Dora was quite understandable, whether she knew it or would admit it. Dora gave her presents, drugs she couldn't prescribe. Dora was the better doctor, Doctor Feelgood. If it works do it. Who could compete with that?

Her hands were shaking. She opened the door of the stall and wiped off the metal box that held the toilet roll. The methedrine was in tiny beads which she carefully poured onto the top of the box. She chopped and mashed it into a fine powder, her mouth watering with the expectancy of that first rush. Speed had a calming effect on her, especially for the first hour or so. It didn't make her think like dope did, it made her feel safe and unselfconscious. There was a woman knocking with persistence on the door. She groped for her coke spoon, another present from Dora, and tried to hurry. The woman's knock was becoming an angry rap. When she emerged from the stall, realizing there were two and that one wasn't supposed to lock the outside door, she released the lock with apologies. The woman, a three-year-old in tow, frowned at her. She knows. But by this time it had taken effect, and she didn't give a damn. A glance at her watch revealed she was now five minutes late. She ran out the door, her espresso on the counter, a redundant drug at this point.

His office was in a shabby pink, stucco bungalow, the favored, old style in local architecture from the forties and fifties. The orange trim stood out, too garish, an electric update from the sixties, she supposed. Her hand was on the door handle of the car. Reconsider. Leave now. No, I might as well "check him out" to use dear Dora's phrase. The speed lifted her resentment and anger; cannibalistic Dora was now the dear friend she wished for. She went in and surveyed the waiting room. What kind of legitimate shrink would furnish a waiting room in post-war salvation army? This is ridiculous, she thought, absurd. But she picked a chair and sat down. The arm fell off, lending a touch of amusement, evoking curiosity about this strange, highly touted healer of the spirit. She knew that he knew that she was there. Shrinks have spy-like devices imbedded in their heads. After an appropriate interval, he would emerge. She began to anticipate this with less dread and a kind of pleasure. The inner door opened.

"Dr. Keller?"

"Dr. Wallensky?"

"Mr. Wallensky. Ivan."

He wasn't at all what she had expected. His European accent was consistent with and exaggerated by his appearance. His well-tailored suit stood out in contrast to the shabby surroundings. One hand held a pipe and the other gestured regally as he rose from a bow, indicating that she should follow him. His invitation to a first name basis disturbed her, a contradiction to his personal formality. He wasn't a doctor. She followed him into a small, but more nicely furnished room. A fraying oriental carpet covered the floor, and two overstuffed chairs faced each other on either side of it. He bowed again, pointing to one of the chairs. She sat down suddenly feeling she had nothing whatever to say.

He smiled at her. "Ah, you are indeed as lovely as Janet has told me."

"Oh?" She gaped at him. He already knew about her. She replayed the conversation with Dora in which she specifically told her not to tell anyone about this appointment. Janet had called that same night, asking her how she was doing, subtly referring to Wallensky as a wonderful man, skirting around the fact that she must have known. She had had lunch with Dora. She didn't want to pry, but Dora was worried about her. She wanted to recommend Dr. Wallensky highly. How unsubtle can one get? "So Janet has mentioned me?"

"We might as well get these things out in the open, don't you agree? You are an intelligent lady and suspicious, I think?" His face lit up with a wry smile. She recognized what it was about him that was so unexpected: he was undeniably sad. This sadness made his face seem older than he was, more distinguished. She could see that he was about her own age, no older. His tinted glasses hid heavily lidded eyes that, she observed, were filled with depression. But not only depression, connivance also; here was a man who got his way. She felt an intimacy with him, an understanding quite like staring at herself in the mirror. She grasped the arms of the chair about to leave. It was frightening her. "Come now." He knew that she was offended, afraid. "You're tougher than that. Tell me why you're here."

"Okay. I'm upset because my cells died over the weekend, a grant I was promised isn't coming through, my boy friend's out of town, my patients are dying of some mystery disease, and I don't trust my friends. Is that enough?"

"That's plenty, but it's not why you're here."

"You seem to know quite a lot about me. Don't you know why I'm here?" Her voice was sarcastic.

"Of course not, but I'm always pleased to see a pretty face." It was hard to believe his words, his compliments expelled from a face turned downward, disinterested, indifferent in a profound way. She mistook it for neutrality. An effort to establish some professional alliance. Her sarcasm passed him by.

"I've been in psychoanalysis before. For five years. The truth is I'm having some minor problems and thought maybe a few sessions would help me. I wanted to see someone analytically oriented. You were recommended by Janet and Dora, the one I don't trust." She added on that sour note, "I don't feel comfortable, knowing that you know Janet, that you've talked about me. It doesn't seem right."

He said nothing. She studied his face. His thin, well-washed brown hair was neatly combed across his forehead. Aside from his eyes there was nothing special about his looks. His square jaw was handsome, she thought, wishing that she wasn't so intrigued with him, with his very odd approach. He was attractive in a Grecian sort of way which, she gathered, was why one would mistake him for older. It annoyed her that he stared at the floor and remained silent. Feeling an attack of stubborness, she folded her hands and joined him.

After some time, in which she had forgotten what she said, he spoke. "Isn't everyone psychoanalytically oriented? You are the doctor. True, I, too, have an interest in Freudian therapy, but I must tell you I'm not a doctor, nor am I licensed to practice in California. Someday perhaps. So you see, I am not bound by any rules. I don't think you know much about me. You see I met your friend, Janet, at a, well, a social function. We are studying together subjects of which I doubt you would approve. But no matter. I do *see* her, as you say in this country. I prefer to say I help her to see herself. Perhaps, you feel misled?"

She let more time pass. "I appreciate your honesty, Mr. Wallensky . . ."

"Ivan."

"Anyway, now that I'm here. Lately, I've had some rather terrible, I should say terrifying anxiety attacks. When it stops, I feel extraordinarily depressed like I'm frozen and I can't move. I think it has to do with the relationship I'm in, with my lover, Daniel. I can't decide whether we should live together or get married or end it. I'm afraid of being alone, without him, but I'm not sure that I love him, that I can be with him all the time either."

"Are you sure you have ever loved a man?"

"Of course." She felt offended again, and she was trying to communicate with him. "I've been married more than once."

"That doesn't necessarily mean love, but perhaps you are telling me you fall in love too easily?"

"No." Her stomach began to feel queasy and a headache was coming on. Her eyes fell to her watch; only thirty minutes had passed to her disbelief. The speed was wearing off, definitely a mistake. Would she be able to finish this hour?

"Maybe I'm wrong, but I have a feeling about you. I think you don't tell me the real reasons you are upset. I don't think it is this man. You have already decided about him, and you are not confused about that, but we, you and I, have something in common, nicht wahr?"

"How do you know I speak German?"

"How does one know these things?" He put down his pipe and took out a pack of cigarettes, Gauloises. He offered her one.

"No, thank you. I don't smoke." As she watched him light the cigarette, she changed her mind. "I think I will have one." He leaned over and gave her one, lighting it with gallantry.

"Do you change your mind a lot?"

"Yes."

"But you are not very confused, I think. I think you are very sad, angry, but not confused. I think we have this in common, you and I."

"You are presumptuous, aren't you?" He was arrogant, she thought, and unfortunately correct.

"Still, am I not right?"

"You do intrigue me, Mr. Wallensky. But I don't think this is going to help me solve my problems. You can send me the bill for this session."

"There is no charge. Please, call me Ivan. I'm sorry if I have offended you. It is better to try and get to the point. I do wish to help you, and I agree this is not the way. I think it is possible in other ways."

He made her feel even more sad when she wanted to feel angry at him, justifiably put out by his unprofessional behavior. Inexplicably to her, she found him appealing, even attractive. All the worse. "I must get back to the hospital." The time was up. He may not be bound by any rules, but she certainly was.

"I don't think we have finished. One doesn't end an important meeting because an artificial increment of time has passed. Yet you are chained by these standards, that I can understand. You are disappointed with me. Perhaps with all men?"

"No."

He laughed, not at her, but empathetically. "You always disagree when you know I am close to the truth."

He was winning her over, and it was true. The more he understood her, the more she rejected him. This was a man she could sincerely dislike. This was a man she might fall in love with. "I really must go, Mr. Wallensky." She started to stand.

"You will have dinner with me on Friday night?"

"No."

"Saturday night then."

"No."

"Yes."

"Yes."

*　　*　　*

The spring and early summer were special times among her friends, always a rash of parties and outings before the fogs of July set in and kept everyone bundled in sweaters most of the day. The flowers bloomed with fresh color. It was as if the earth had stepped out of a long bath. Plants and people came alive; life seemed new again, everything reborn and clean. Many of her friends, herself included, fell prey to "spring depression." The time when everyone wished to feel born again, ready to tackle the world, the time of youth, growth and beauty, was too painful a reminder of the gap between wishes and realities, past and present, nature's perpetual rebirth and one's own perpetual aging. They banded together to ignore their blues and celebrate the inevitable. The parties overflowed with food and drink, drugs and music, new liaisons and gossip.

Most everyone was animated with short-term optimism, mouthing spring resolutions as soon to hit the dustbin as their New Year's Eve counterparts. But there was no revelling in the past, no looking back, worrying about mistakes, or what might have been, no longing for that which was lost to history. This was a solely present and future oriented group in which plans were to be made anew, and the fruits of this new resolve were to be harvested in the grand scheme of life changes. Change could be celebrated when it would lead to bigger and better things. A positive attitude was "in" these days, but it required an enormous effort in the exercise of ignorance, a quality that most of her friends, in spite of their striving for it, didn't really have. From her perspective, this pseudo-idealism, faith in mankind and regeneration of moral imperatives were revoltingly the same from season to season, varying about as much as the content of the reports broadcast on the nightly news. Deadly sameness.

They were an odd assortment of professionals with jobs and without, not that atypical or unusual a group. Many were "changing careers" which meant attempting to survive outside that which they had been educated to do. The majority were over-educated, near middle-age, and ex-radicals of one sort or another. The rest were in their late twenties, still hanging on to their first real job and the hope that

101

it wouldn't be their last. Of course, there were the few professional students who had long since given up on the world of paid employment. They all knew each other's predictable positions on the "issues" and weren't particularly polite when the same jokes and stories were forthcoming from party to party. The new initiates to the crowd were wooed and coddled in hopes that they would infuse some original ideas or perspective into the others. The only threads that kept them together — except for bimonthly orgies — were the fact that not everyone had slept with everyone else yet, and the opportunity to imbibe the diverse consciousness-altering substances of their youths. Since her youth hadn't started until her late twenties, Suzanne seized upon every invitation and looked forward to these events with sincerity. Though terminally skeptical, she always managed to learn something. It was at her last party that she realized she didn't remember who she was before coming to California.

Dora was hostessing her annual "rites of spring" festival on the coming weekend. Suzanne was given the assignment of guacamole for one hundred. Sometimes the party lasted through the night and the next day. Dora spent two weeks in the kitchen making every delicacy known to Californians, more work than she did the rest of the year. This generous feeding ritual was a labor of love, and in spite of the fact that everyone was on a diet and insisted they would eat nothing, there was never a bite of food left over. The guacamole was the first to go. Both Suzanne and Janet complained that the food should be secondary, but both ended up several evenings in the kitchen with Dora chopping carrots and celery until their fingers fell off. Dora's dope connection had supplied her with a new ounce of *Guido's Best* from Mendecino which gave the vegetable chopping the aura of spiritual experience, right up there with love-making.

"Ivan's coming," Dora chirped, spooning the stuffing into the mushrooms. "He actually telephoned to say he would be here. His accent is so adorable." She glanced at both of them, needing to gauge their responses, steeling herself for the criticism she expected to come.

Janet smiled at Suzanne knowingly, with a sense of shared "Tsk, tsk, this is the way Dora is, what can we do." Suzanne tried to show no reaction at all, but she couldn't help colluding with Janet in making Dora the odd one out, the one who carried on with the subterranean desires of the rest. Resisting this comradery within their circle of friends was impossible. Dora was the organizer; she volunteered for the position and had to take the blame with the power. This was no light-weight group of people; they had plenty of ego and enough repressed aggression to power New York City. Only a fool or someone truly innocent would have been in Dora's position. Suzanne wouldn't have traded places with her for anything on earth. Janet was pleased to have her services provided since she had few other opportunities to party. She was delighted that Ivan was coming. "That's wonderful, Dora. Who else have you invited? Lots of cute, unattached men, I hope."

"There's no such thing as attachment here." Suzanne was stoned.

Now Dora and Janet could share a knowing smile. Dora hugged Suzanne. "You're so pessimistic."

"Cynical. Cynical's the word, Dora." She tried to look very cynical. "Did you invite Dan?"

"Of course, but he's going to be out of town. You know that." Poking Janet with a wooden spoon, "Which cute men are you thinking of? You getting a divorce?"

"I might." Janet turned away, reminded of her unhappiness, not eager to share it with anyone. Suzanne felt sorry for her. She didn't take her marriage lightly, in fact, had stayed with it, miserable and not in love anymore for years. Her nightly meetings, study groups, courses, ad nauseam, kept her avoiding the inevitable split. Her three children adored their father who Suzanne also thought was a pretty good guy. Since never-divorced couples were rarer than rubies in the Bay area, she speculated there was more to it than met the eye. It was the one subject she never discussed with Janet. They had agreed, without actually saying so, that only unimportant personal matters were open to discussion in their version of friendship. Dora was oblivious to such agreements. She pushed and pried until she evoked the anger that made her feel justifiably persecuted. Then she pouted like the hurt child she was until Janet or Suzanne forgave her, embraced her. "I don't want to talk about it. Martin isn't coming with me. He's going camping in the Sierras with the kids."

"Oh, that's too bad. I was counting on the kids. Bernie's bringing his kids, and Cheryl too. It's better to have more kids, then they entertain each other." They both knew that Dora wasn't very fond of kids but would never admit it.

"For the parents, the kids are always in the way. They may appear to be entertaining each other to you, but I end up having to watch them. I want to have fun at this party, not be hovering over a bunch of kids."

"We're all going to play." Dora tried to cheer Janet up. The depression that was a permanent part of Janet's company was upsetting her, and, as she did with most friends, she felt it was her duty to make it better. "But which one of you is going to play house with Ivan? Tell me about him." She squeaked.

Suzanne rolled her eyes. "Christ, Dora give us a break!"

"Have you been seeing him?" Janet questioned Suzanne.

"Not formally."

"Not formally?" Dora raised her eyebrows at Janet. "What does that mean?"

"It means I'm not seeing him in therapy."

"But you are seeing him?"

"I've seen him. Yes. Haven't you *seen* him?" She munched on a carrot, enjoying the suspense and absurdity she maintained.

"That's not what I mean." Dora smirked at her.

Janet stopped stirring and turned to Suzanne. "I hope you know there's absolutely nothing going on between Ivan and me. We're in a group together, that's all." She paused. "He is living with someone, I think."

"I know he is, and I know there's nothing sexual between you two. Anyway, I couldn't care less."

"You mean you're not interested in him?" Dora was disappointed.

"I didn't say that. He *is* interesting."

"I'm sorry he didn't work out for you, for therapy." Janet wondered if she was telling the truth.

"Thanks. I'm feeling much better really." She lied.

"Have things worked out with Daniel?"

"Not really. Not yet. My work is picking up though. It keeps me incredibly busy. Did I tell you I'm applying for a fellowship at U.C.S.F. for next year? I'll be able to do research almost full-time. It's a more prestigious position."

"That's wonderful. I thought you liked the job you have?"

"That's great." Dora was factitious. "You'll be even busier. Boo hoo." She made a sad face. "Tell us about this gay mystery disease."

"You don't want to hear about it. It's awful, ungodly awful."

"You're right. Let's not talk about it. Do we know any gay men?"

"Are there any other kind?" Janet joked for a change.

"Let's talk about straight men. It's more fun. Now don't get mad at me, Suzanne. Are you sleeping with him?"

"Ivan?"

"Who else? I know everyone else you're sleeping with?"

"Really? Well, wouldn't you like to know?"

Janet chimed in, "I heard he's a terrific lover."

A lump rose in her throat, but she wasn't going to ask.

"You did? Who told you?" Dora was gleeful, such juicy gossip.
"He did."
They all burst into laughter.

* * *

The party was its usual combination of success and disappointment. After some child broke her favorite fish bowl, Dora burst
into tears and locked herself in the bathroom. Too much coke,
her boy-friend said, and with her wailing in the background, everyone went back to eating, dancing and talking. Ivan had come three
hours late but arrived to his dismay just ahead of Suzanne. He
was hoping to make an entrance, to see her face turn expectantly
toward him.

Suzanne didn't notice Ivan at all. She went immediately to the
bathroom to calm Dora and get something to perk herself up. She
was greeted with a locked door and Dora sobbing that she intentionally meant to insult her by coming so late. Seventy-five other
people weren't enough to keep her company. Suzanne tried to
humor her, whispering through the door. They both knew the
guacamole only had a fighting chance after Dora's primo delicacies
were consumed. Besides, she knew Suzanne didn't want to communicate with anyone who wasn't drugged.

The latter was true. It shortened the obligatory greetings and catching up with the more normal folks: pregnant women, nursing
mothers, and the few couples on their first date. She knew most of
the people by sight but only a handful knew her last name, what she
did for a living, or whether she was married or single. The most ordinary, traditional, getting-to-know-you conversations which included these locating facts were frowned upon, considered gauche.
She was more likely to remember a face from how many orgasms
they had a night or whether they were a victim of child abuse than
from an archaic relic of polite society. Daniel with whom she had
been fighting for the past three hours refused to attend these parties
for this very reason. He was screaming as she left that she could tell
Dora he was permanently out of town for her parties. Rather odd,
she fumed on the way over, since he was the one who liked Dora
and insisted on maintaining the friendship with her after they first
met.

Dora threw the bathroom door open and flung her arms around
Suzanne, hoping to create a scene. But scenes were impossible to

105

create in this context; nobody cared. Suzanne led her back into the bathroom where they had a heart to heart talk. Her diagnostic abilities told her this wasn't cocaine Dora was on; it was another drug, but what? She couldn't get Dora to say in a way that made sense. But whatever it was, Suzanne was quickly convinced, it made Dora happier than she'd ever seen her. Her effusive affections were infectious. Stripping off their clothes, they got into a hot bath together, giggling and squirming to fit into the small tub. Within the garble of love forever, cosmic oneness, the joy of friendship, and such, Dora confessed she had taken some new drug given to her by none other than Ivan who, she insisted in a long and confused diatribe, was Suzanne's long-awaited perfect lover. Ivan had told her so. This was therapy to end all therapy, she exalted. He had given her a lifetime of therapy in one single dose. Suzanne extracted herself from the bath with the promise that she would send in Sidar, Dora's boy-friend, to be with her. A male presence was needed to complete the universal circle, Dora agreed. So this was the *therapy* he practiced. A new drug. Maybe he was the man she had been searching for.

He came over to her as soon as she walked out onto the patio. Taking her hand, he bent over and kissed it, then both her cheeks. "How are you, my sweet?"

"I'm fine. Dora, on the other hand, is raving in the bathtub."

"She needs to rave. Don't you agree?"

"I can't say she seemed unhappy. More like ecstatic."

"Ah, we all need ecstasy." He toasted her with his drink, a shot of whiskey. "Et tu?"

"How many languages do you speak, Ivan?"

"Seven or eight. You don't want to speak of ecstasy?"

"Not here." Out of the corner of her eye she noticed a handsome, young blond man dressed in rugby shorts and a shirt. He was a newcomer and surrounded by an entourage of young women in gypsy skirts, halter tops, or multi-patched jeans. His eyes were a spectacular baby blue, noticeable from several yards away. Not bad, she thought, but young. Too young?

"I know him." Ivan noticed her noticing him.

"That young man?"

"Yes, he came with me. A graduate student in psychology at Berkeley, very bright. He used to be a client of mine. Now's he a friend. Very attractive, Si?"

"Not really." She wasn't interested in threesomes or any sort of bait. "He's not my type at all."

"Not dark and intense enough for a woman like yourself, not angry, or reeking of sorrow," he mocked her, the kind of mockery meant to pass for truth.

"You are a bastard, nicht wahr?" Nothing would hurt him, she knew this.

"That's why you like me."

"Okay, tell me what you gave Dora." He had taken her arm and led her to an empty bench on the far side of the garden.

"Si, if you promise not to judge too quickly."

"Go on." She was pleased that he thought she would disapprove of the use of drugs in this way and very pleased that he didn't know her *that* well. One thing he hadn't surmised.

"It's called MDA. Haven't you heard of it?"

"No. What is it?"

"You are the scientist, Herr Doctor. I don't know exactly its chemical structure, but I've been told it is like a mixture of heroin and amphetamine. Some people use it in therapy, especially with depression. Miraculous results. Of course, I don't believe such results will last." Inconspicuously he slid his arm around her waist. "Nothing does." His eyes were on the ground, his face weighted down with sadness. Then he looked at her with a disquieting intensity. "Come with me to a place of beauty. We can share this ecstasy together."

"I just got here. Dora will be furious if I leave."

His unpredictable and sudden anger surprised her. "Don't give me such a feeble excuse. I have asked you for something special. Don't be so cold, so hard to me." His head shook no with absolute insistence and impatience.

"Listen, Ivan, I'd like to go with you. I'd like to try this drug; it's just that there are people here who will talk if we leave together now. Remember I'm sort of attached to someone. Remember Daniel?"

He was livid. "You don't care about him. Or anyone." As abruptly, he calmed down, softened. "I want you to care about me. You will."

She felt compelled to whisper because several groups of chatterers congregated around them. More people were arriving and the available space was filling up with bodies. "I didn't realize you are so emotional. Another twist of your charming personality? I'm going to mingle for a while. I'll meet you in front of my car, the silver Prelude, in an hour. That's the best I can do."

Two seductive eyes gave her a sulky response, then he scowled and said nothing. She turned to embrace Bernie's eight-year-old daughter, becoming the picture of a mother. Other children came over to hug her, and she was whisked off for a game of tag. He watched her, thinking he would like to have a child with this woman. But he always had this idea with a woman he was unsure of, a woman he hadn't yet conquered. Watching her play was agony. He thought of his own children, lost to him forever. His chest felt constricted and his throat tight; he might cry, finally, after all these years. But no. There were not any tears. More whiskey.

* * *

Suzanne went into a bedroom to think about Ivan's offer. Her better judgment told her she was playing with fire, but her desire to alter her consciousness won out. After calling Daniel to tell him she was spending the night with Dora and wouldn't see him until Sunday, she hastily ate as much as she could and slipped out the side door. Ivan paced up and down in front of her car. "You are late," he admonished. She paid no attention to him, unlocked her door, got in and unlocked the door for him. He stood stubborn, waiting for an apology, an acknowledgement, but after some minutes of staring, he shook his head and got in. "We are taking your car. It's better than mine."

"I like to drive."

"Let's stop at the Mediterranean Cafe for a moment. I must have some coffee."

"Okay." The tires squealed as the car accelerated up the hill. The cassette came on at top volume. She switched it off.

"Do you drive 'like a maniac,' as you say in this country?"

"Yes." She laughed, feeling a surge of freedom and happiness. Sidar had given her the ounce of *John's Best* she ordered and rolled her a few joints. "Do you smoke dope?"

"Kid's stuff," he scoffed.

"I think you should try some of my 'kid's stuff,' then I'll try some of yours."

"If you insist, but it isn't necessary. You won't want it soon. It will seem quite superfluous."

"Where are we going?"

"Have you been to Pt. Reyes?"

"Once. I'm not sure how to get there."

"Up 17 to the Richmond bridge. I'll direct you." They reached the coffee shop and pulled over to the curb.

"I'll wait here."

"Do you take cream and sugar?"

"Cream, no sugar."

While she waited she lit a joint, aware of the policeman on the corner. He looked at her and grinned. She smiled in return, but when he started walking toward her she worried. Christ, what is he doing? This is Berkeley. She quickly stuffed the joint into the ashtray and brushed the ashes away. "Hi."

He leaned on the top of the car and put his head between his arms, his face close to hers. "Hi. Nice car."

"Thank you, officer."

"Do you know you're in a 'no parking' zone?"

"Oh?" Relief flooded her face. "I'm just waiting for my friend, but I'll move."

He didn't say anything or move, his grin growing devilish. She knew he saw her light the joint. She knew he could smell it. "I could give you a ticket."

"I'm really sorry, officer. I'll move." She prayed he would let her go and wondered if she should offer him a joint or what.

"I'll let you go this time, cutey." Her face turned red. "But remember me." He slipped a white card onto her dash board and winked at her.

Ivan stood and watched him walk away, an expression of irritation on his face. He slammed the door getting in. "Are all men attracted to you?"

"Attracted! I nearly got a ticket. I was smoking a joint and that idiot . . ."

"He let you go, didn't he?" He hit his forehead with the palm of his hand while balancing two coffees between his knees — a gesture of exasperation. "You will drive me crazy."

She took the coffee and drove away. "Maybe you'll drive me crazy. Let's forget it." Somehow she wasn't prepared for his bursts of emotion. It was so opposite of Daniel who remained rational and objective at all times, especially when she wanted him to show some emotion. She had forgotten that all men weren't the same.

He took out some inch-long capsules half filled with a beige powder. "We must take these now. It takes some time for the effects to be felt. We will almost be there." He handed one to her.

They were large capsules. She had a moment of reconsideration, then swallowed hers. "These could choke a horse."

"There are a few side effects, nothing serious. You may feel your mouth getting dry. Later you may have a slight headache, muscle ache or a tightness in your jaw. It's easily remedied," he showed her a bottle of Valium, "with two of these. Some people have stomach upset; you won't want to eat."

"It sounds like LSD."

"No. It's much better. You'll see." He fumbled through her tapes and chose Billie Holliday. They drove not speaking, the afternoon sun growing larger on the horizon, the Saturday traffic thick in the opposite direction.

"Janet told me that you're living with someone." She broke the silence.

"Yes. But we won't talk of that."

"What will we talk of?"

"Life. And death."

"My favorite subjects. Rather broad, don't you think?" They were heading up 101 towards Santa Rosa.

"Turn on Lucas Valley Road. Up there." The car veered off into the exit. "Have you been down this road?"

"No. I think we went on Sir Francis Drake before."

"This is better. Turn left at the stop sign."

The landscape began to twist and roll with the car. Her head felt light and thick simultaneously. She was growing too warm and opened the sunroof. A tingling sensation ran up and down her spine with intense pleasure. She looked at him. He looked incredibly handsome, and she knew the drug was taking effect. His slightest movement, smile, gesture was filled with meaning, meaning that she dismissed in favor of the physical sensations. Like Alice in Wonderland she was growing bigger and bigger. Driving began to lose all interest for her. It wasn't difficult. She just didn't want to do it. Her foot eased off the accelerator, but she still had the sensation of speeding up. I can't really think anymore, she thought. Her face grew hot and her body began to melt into liquid. "I'm definitely feeling something, " she said.

"Yes. I know."

"I'm not sure I can drive."

"You can. Watch the instruments and relax."

Did he say relax? Her head was filled with Billie Holliday's voice. The steering wheel seemed to dissolve in her hand. The car was like a toy over which she had mischievous total power. Indeed her essence, or what she felt must be her essence, was completely filling all the available space. Her actual body was no more than a speck, a drain on this powerful substance of her self that within minutes would comprise the whole universe. At minimun she was becoming the universe of meaning. He was no more than a part of her, another dimension of her essence under her control. Of course she loved him. But the word "love" was too trivial, too banal, too ordinary to describe her sensations. "Love" was too metaphysical, too abstract.

Only her body was involved here. Her mind was left way behind; she visualized her mind sitting on her desk in the laboratory, thinking about cells and virus, mice and test tubes. There was a patch of dirt ahead, a turn off near a reservoir. She stopped the car. Her hands wouldn't come off the steering wheel. It seemed to take ages to communicate to him that she could not drive. Words weren't necessary, but he, too, was lost in body. She got out of the car and fell into some grass nearby.

He eventually walked over to her and tried to pull her up. "We must continue." His voice came from outer space, reaching her in a tangle of coded messages. She could not move and tried to tell him with words.

"It's an orgasm with the earth."

"Yes, but we are human, we must go on. You will be happy when we get there." He somehow pulled her to her feet and put her in the car. "I will drive."

She lay back merging into the comfort of the seat, floating with the sound of the music, transfixed by the beauty of the open, treeless hills that in no time turned to forests of redwoods, then a quaint, tiny town swirling by her like time past. That was it; she was in a time capsule, the secret of everlasting life. No sooner then she felt adjusted to being forever in this peculiar life support module, he stopped the car. She didn't want to get out. She never wanted to get out of the car again. "What are you doing?"

"I'm going in this bakery to get a pastry."

"You're what!" He couldn't be serious. She laughed and felt herself literally turning to water. Tears rolled from her eyes, unstoppable. He put his arm around her shoulders and held her tight to him. His lips on hers devoured her face until they were both indistinguishable pools of liquid. "Come with me. It's better to put something in the stomach before too long."

"I can't possibly."

"You can. I'll hold your hand."

She pulled down the visor and looked in the mirror. Her eyes were dark black, nothing but pupil. Huge patches of red covered her cheeks and her lips were the color of red roses. It was quite a shock to see herself this way. "My God!"

"Now you see how beautiful you are."

"I'm a mess; I'm all red." But she did see how beautiful she was. It was unbelievable. "You go. I'll wait here." She wanted to stare at her face, and she did. It was aeons before he returned. She had seen herself in every phase: an infant, a child, an adolescent, a college student, a wife, a middle-aged woman, an old lady . . . a mother. With some force of will she stopped it, and before he returned, she successfully left her body again for the real comfort of car metal, leather upholstery, glass windows. They were moving and Bob Dylan was singing "just like a woman." She closed her eyes and went to sleep, a peaceful sleep, a dreamy euphoria of sleep.

He shook her gently. "We are here." The sun was miraculously still in the sky. There was no wind. They were the only car in the gravel parking lot which was the end of the road. He got out of the car and went around to help her out. His hand on hers was the softest flesh she'd ever felt. The air on her face was like silk or feathers. She leaned against the car to adjust to standing up. He leaned toward her and whispered. "We are going down that trail to your cove," he said, an oracle of the future.

"My cove?"

"Yes. I am giving it to you." With his arm around her shoulders, they staggered down the trail, stopping to pick lilies and wild iris for her hair. About half-way down, the wind began to pick up and signal the coming of the ocean. The roar of it was ominous, then glorious. At the first sight of it, she buried her head in his shoulder and held onto him with all her strength. "Look at it. It's your ocean. It's a mad woman like you."

She stared at the breaking waves and the sun, a red ball of fire throwing a wide triangular shaft of light toward them. Such a rush of impulse to run wildly into it overcame her that she pulled away from him and began to run. Her legs were like jelly, and she fell into the warm sand after a few yards. Everything, especially herself, was suddenly too funny for words. She laughed-cried again, not being able to do one without the other. He fell down beside her, laughing too. "I'm totally absurd," she laughed certain that he understood.

"You are."

They had passed some point with the drug and reached a level plateau. It was very high like the highest point in the Himalayas where the air is thin and movement of the body laborious. But one could still walk and slowly talk, and observation was possible. The sand was warm and her clothes were wet from sweating. They could smell each other. It was intoxicating. "I want to take off my clothes."

"We can, but let's go down the beach behind that big rock." He pointed to his left. "There's a passageway and on the other side is the cove I promised you. You'll see. It's like Italy or the coast of Yugoslavia."

She struggled to her feet and held her hands out to him. "Is there anywhere you haven't been?"

"No." He rose into her arms, and for the first time since they took the drug, he seemed a stranger to her. "But I regret I haven't been with you. All those places are empty in my memory."

"I don't believe you."

"You *won't* believe me. Don't. Don't insist on your loneliness. You must let go of it. What does it matter if one doesn't always hear the truth. It is the fantasies which keep one alive."

"Are you a fantasy?"

"Of course."

Something to contemplate. They walked down the beach, holding hands, chasing the sandpipers, tripping over themselves. It felt better to be in a space she could never fill up, an endless expanse of sky and sea. Her position in the world returned to its place of moderate insignificance. Her mind again inhabited her body. Love again seemed magic and awesome, not to be taken lightly. This immediate experience had to her more the quality of reality than fantasy. There was no doubt of its happening, yet the life behind, at the other end of the road, her "real" life was as remote as her past, as unimportant to her as dead time, history. "I think I'm a materialist," she muttered, "a realist, a physicalist . . . is there such a word?"

"You are a romantic. You will deny it, but it is true. You are a hopeless romantic, as they say."

"They who?"

"English people like you." He spread his arms out before him to present her with the cove they had finally reached at the end of a narrow passage of rock. It was as lovely, as perfect as he promised, and she felt like the princess in *Sleeping Beauty*, trying to wake up and live happily ever after with her prince. It — that feeling — *was* a fantasy. This realization had a powerful mental kickback; her body rejected it, refused to let it be a thought. The sand was not fantasy even if she was. She took off her clothes and lay on top of them on her stomach, her face warm against the soft sand. He took off his shirt and sat beside her.

"Where are you from?"

He caressed her back, tenderly massaging her shoulders with one hand. "Many countries. My mother was from Brazil; my father was German. They lived separately — as wealthy refugees sometimes did — for long periods of time. I lived in Yugoslavia, on Cyprus, in Morocco, France, Brazil, Argentina, many countries. My parents are dead."

"Are you Jewish?"

"No. These things mean something to you? You must know my background to know me?"

"Not necessarily. I'm just curious." She wasn't going to pry. It didn't matter, and besides she had no desire to evoke such questions of herself. Turning on her back, she focused on the sunset, the rays of color brought up in the fog bank hanging off the coast.

"Then I will tell you something. No one here knows this, and I will trust it to you. Ivan Wallensky isn't my real name."

"What?" He was fooling her, she thought.

"No. It's not my real name. Ivan Wallensky is dead. I took his name to get into this country. My passport was no good."

"You're kidding." She covered herself with the sweater, his confession, admission, whatever it was evoking goosebumps on her arms.

"Why would I lie to you? I have nothing to gain." He kissed her on the cheek, and the warmth of his chest covered her. Her naked skin was electrified. She wanted him, his body; the feeling was not romantic, but sexual, raw.

"Don't tell me your name. I'm not to be trusted," she whispered into his ear, biting it afterwards.

His hands covered her breasts, and he slid onto her with force. She sifted sand onto his bare back and raked her nails through it. They rolled over until both were caked in sand, until it stuck like thousands of needles in every body crevice. His kisses were deep, searching for her response, demanding response. He was wild, like no man she'd ever made love to, completely abandoned, touching her in every possible way, exploring her to the limit. She had never liked this kind of sex. It frightened her. He had a lack of shame she preferred to preserve, but she stayed with him and fought back, finding the pleasure on that edge. He rolled her onto her stomach with an unexpected strength, a strength of will as much as of muscle. His face was buried in her neck and she heard him coaxing her to relax, to let go, to let him enter her as he wanted. The sand on his cock burned between her buttocks, but the pain soon gave way to a supreme sensation of fullness. His fingers under her deftly played until she knew she would come like never before. As her body opened up to him, he moaned and cried out with pleasure. Her ass contracted around him. They both moved violently, out of control in an orgasm that carried on until unbearable. She lay exhausted, not very aware of him on top of her, thinking instead of the young man who sat before her in the clinic last week. She had explained there was some medical evidence to suggest his disease was sexually transmitted. He had growled, a kind of laugh-groan, not willing to give up, even to think of giving up sex. What's life without sex? She now understood him better. Not only him.

* * *

114

Dan had spent the night at her house. He got up early and went out for bagels. If she wasn't back by noon he was going out for a run. The landscape sailed by him, his body pushing itself to the limit. He had finished his difficult reanalysis and translation of Dostoyevsky's *Notes from the Underground*. He wrote out a lecture for his students. He refused to sit and wait for her. After building more plastic disk holders than he or she would ever use, doing three loads of wash, cleaning out the garage, changing the oil in the car, reading until his eyes ached, he scribbled a note and left. Around Lake Merit, once, twice. On his third round his bad knee began to hurt. He had hoped she would change her mind and come back during the night. She wouldn't have spent the entire morning with Dora — that was for sure. So where was she? With a man probably. No way would he call Dora to find out. He had his pride. Think it through with reason, he told himself. She's going through another phase. With a hyper-sensitive woman like her, it's to be expected. Some Freudian prob-lem, he rationalized, some career-motherhood conflict; she has to act out against past assholes on a nice guy like me. Life is never boring. She'll come back; she always has. Stay calm. She must never find out how upset she makes me. But I'm furious. Fed-up. She's pushing me too far. I'm going to change her. With patience.

"Hey Dan!" A woman's voice yelled from a distance. "Hey, over here." It was Clara, a colleague in the French department. She stood next to her bike waving at him down the path.

He panted and continued until he approached her. "Hi." His chest heaved. He put his hands on his hips, dropped his head and tried to slow down. "Nice to see you." Coughing, he held out a sweaty hand to shake. "You live around here?"

"No, I live up in the hills. Just riding around. Haven't seen you around the department lately. How's your book coming along?"

"Slow. It's terrible, but don't listen to me. I can't talk about anything when I'm writing it. I hate it. When I finish it, maybe I'll mail it out before I burn it. You still working on, what was it? Feminine narcissism in turn of the century French literature?"

"Yes. Same old theme." They walked along the path, she guiding her bicycle, he stretching his arms and shoulders. "How's Suzanne? You still living together?"

"Don't ask. Actually we've never completely lived together. I have a small house; she has a large one. I stay with her a lot, or I used to anyway." He couldn't help sounding angry.

"Didn't you just get back from a conference in England?"

"A couple months ago."

"How was it?"

"The conference was great." Her long straight red hair strayed in the breeze. He'd thought she was attractive before, but he'd never seen her in shorts and a T-shirt. Her dark tanned legs were long and slender. Her breasts were firm, turned up, and bounced seductively as she walked. She had liked him since they first met, he could tell. The time was coming when Suzanne really would push him too far. Clara was pretty and smart. She even seemed normal. He never heard any gossip about her, never saw her at a party. He could go to bed with her, no problem; he could get involved. "There were especially interesting papers on criticism, new Marxist sort of thing. Reinterpretation of classic texts are big in Europe, some deconstructionist theory that wasn't too bad."

"What about the vacation?" She smiled with a perfect row of white teeth, a strong voluptuous mouth.

"You mean with Suzanne?" He stopped walking and sat down facing the lake. "Sometimes wonderful, most of the time a disaster. That's life with her."

She put her bike against a tree and sat so she could face him. "You must be stuck on this woman. Sounds like it isn't going too well. Tell me to shut up if you don't want to talk about it, but I'm a good listener. It's more interesting than shop talk." She laughed, her teeth sparkling, her green eyes enticing.

"You don't want to hear my problems. It's not that unusual. Man meets intriguing, beautiful, intelligent woman. Man falls in love. Woman is confused, ambivalent, crazy, but she's sometimes wonderful, exciting. What can I say? We've been together off and on for almost three years, two and a half maybe. I've never met anyone more unpredictable." He shook his head. "But, it's that 'but' that gets me every time. I should leave her. I probably will, but . . ."

"You want to get some coffee or a Tab?" She rubbed her legs with oil.

"Sure. We could go back to her house; it's not far. Suzanne's not home and probably won't turn up until late."

"No, I'd feel uncomfortable in her house. Let's go to mine or a cafe?" There was a note of wishful encouragement in her voice.

"Well, I'm kind of waiting to see when she comes home." Hesitating, he thought a moment. "Yeah, I'd like to see your house. You have a view?"

"A great view."

"I'm pretty sweaty. I'll go home first, shower and drive up. Can you give me directions?"

"It would be easier if I come to the house while you shower, then we can drive up, if my bike will fit in your car?"

"Sure."

They walked the two miles back to the house, engrossed in giving each other book reviews, the latest tomes in their respective specialties. His mood had improved drastically, and he heard the animation in his voice, the vigor with which he spoke. She was overjoyed, having admired him for a year, fantasized about him, even dreamt about him once. A sexy dream. At last she would have him to herself, if only for coffee. She wanted to seem composed, even shy, but it wasn't her nature. She dove into the conversation as enthusiastically as he. She wouldn't let this gift of fate escape her.

Engrossed, he was opening the refrigerator before he realized that Suzanne's car was in the garage. Clara's voice echoed through the glass and wood house. His first impulse was to cover her mouth with his hand, but as usual he controlled himself. Suzanne stumbled down the stairs, disheveled expecting to apologize, fall into his arms, get forgiven, and go back to sleep. He stepped in front of Clara as if he wanted to protect them both from an embarrassing embrace.

"You're home," he stammered partly from anger, partly from humiliation. "Dora's party must have been a whopping success." Clara backed away and turned around, embarrassed, superfluous.

Suzanne walked around him and put out her hand to Clara. "Hi, I don't believe we've met. I'm Suzanne." No apologies were necessary now. By accident she was given the upper hand. "Have you forgotten your manners, dear?" Her eyes threw him a I-know-what-you're-up-to glance.

"Clara Barlow." She hastily added, "A colleague of Dan's. We just ran into each other at the lake."

They stood, each averting their eyes, then looking from one to the other, the silence becoming awkward. Suzanne ran her fingers through her hair. Clara, very pretty, she thought, automatically comparing herself. Her eyes had to be red and puffy, her nose too, her hair was matted and stuck out like dry hay. She tried to stand up straight, pulling her hunched shoulders backward and taking a breath. Her head ached and nausea came with the breath. If only Dan were sensitive enough to save me this comparison. Her pride mingled with anger. The guilt and remorse she had felt when she drove in the driveway and saw his car there, the wash done, the garbage out vanished at the sight of Clara. She had been the one in the wrong after all, or she thought she had. He had been waiting for her, behaving like a grown-up, doing the housework, exercising while she rolled in the sand with a man she didn't even know or like. Wasted. Her body. Her unjustifiable expectations. Her decent relationship.

"Well, nice to meet you. I'm feeling a little under the weather so please excuse me." Putting her hand on his shoulder, she kissed his cheek. "I'm going back to bed." Why was he looking so upset? She dashed into the bathroom and vomited.

He followed her. "Clara and I are going out for coffee." She was sick again. "What's going on? Suzanne, what's wrong?" The anger spilled out in his voice. "Have you taken something? We've got to talk. I can't take this anymore, Suzanne. Where were you? I want the truth, goddammit."

"Hand me a wash cloth. Please." He was already wetting the cloth, brushing her hair back, cursing the tears he wanted to cry.

"You bring this on yourself. You're killing yourself the hard way."

"Go to hell. Take your pretty little tart and get the fuck out of my house. I'm sick. I'm sick of everything. Can't you see? You don't really care about me. So shut the fuck up!" Her body was racked with sobs, and tears of fury wet her flannel nightgown. He recognized this rage. It was hopeless now. And his own rage swelled with her irrationality. "I don't care who you fuck," she yelled, choking on the words. "Just leave me alone. Leave me alone."

"Me! What about you, who were you fucking! You bitch. I am leaving. I can't take it anymore. I mean it this time. This is it." The bathroom door slammed, knocking the toothbrushes out of their glass. The back door slammed, shaking the entire house.

Utter misery tore apart her body from inside out. Her heart was like breaking glass, her head throbbed ready to explode, her muscles felt shredded and paper thin. She sobbed, "Don't leave me, don't leave me. Jesus, Dan, please don't leave me." She pulled her knees up to her face and fell into another world, a world of nightmarish sleep, semi-consciousness from which she could not move.

He found her there when he returned an hour later, the odor of vomit and sweat reeking in the strong afternoon sun that filled the tiny airless bathroom.

*   *   *

She woke up in Dan's arms, the birds singing, patches of light dancing on the white down quilt. It was a glorious Sunday, crystal clear, sunny skies. That horrible scene had never happened. Even if he had slept with that woman, she forgave him. He rubbed her back, and she stretched her sore muscles turning over to hug him. His familiar smell evoked a cringe of regret that she had lost her temper, that he had come back and taken care of her. She vowed, as she often did on waking, that it was time to turn over a new leaf. Dora's party was the last one. No more drugs. This thing with Wallensky – never again. They — she and Daniel — would work it all out; they would both try. Today they would drive to the wine country and talk. They would plan for the future. They should live together. It was the only way to make a commitment. No relationship was perfect. She knew that. These doubts, well, they were obviously her problem, relics from the past. But she was tired of letting them prevent her from having the closeness that he, according to her friends, was offering her for a lifetime. He was a good man. He loved her. True, he was a bit emotionless at times, a mite too rational, too sensible, but these couldn't really be counted as major defects. He tried. She knew he tried to understand her. He didn't. But it wasn't his fault.

She snuggled into his neck, his kisses growing hotter on hers. His body stirred and pressed against her into the hollow of her belly. His hand gently, with caution, caressed her breast, not insisting, but wanting. She responded to his warmth. Making love to him felt safe and right, comfortable and secure, dare she think "clean." "I'm sorry I screamed at you yesterday," she whispered, nibbling on his earlobe.

"It's all right. I was worried about you." The words were filled with concern, sweet concern, genuine concern.

"You were right. I bring it on myself. I don't know why. I really don't. I get these crazy ideas. Sometimes I think I'll do anything to change my state of mind. Anything. Maybe it's my work. Two young guys died last week, both gay. It's getting to me. Do you think I'm getting worse? I mean, you've known me for over two years. Do you think I'm crazier?"

"Let's not talk about it now. You're sensitive, you know that, you're erratic, not crazy. Confused maybe, but not crazy. Delicious definitely." He wanted to make love to her. To pour into her physically what she wanted in words. "I'm sorry too. I'm sorry I left." He slid on top of her. "I love you."

He bounced around the kitchen in his underwear, making the coffee, pouring the orange juice, heating the pastries. She sat at the table reading the *Chronicle*. "There are more new reports on this killer disease, GRID, gay cancer. They make it sound like a disco dance." She mumbled, "I should go into the lab today. Do you realize it's only eleven months since the first cases of Kaposi's sarcoma were reported to the CDC and 50% have died."

"I have work I could do if you really want to. I thought you wanted to go to the wine country."

"I do." She knew he was content that they had made love. He was always too eager to work on weekends which raised her resentment even though she had brought it up. "Dan, we need to talk. Really. I'd like to work on our relationship. You've been working or away six out of the past eight weekends since we came back from England."

He bristled. "So have you. You're totally obsessed with this gay disease thing. You've been going to the lab day and night."

"Let's not get into another fight. Okay?" She went back to reading the paper but couldn't concentrate. Here we go again. "Listen, this is stupid. I know I've been out a lot at night. I wanted you to come with me to the party. . . ." she lied. "You're the one who's been to four conferences in two months. How many papers can one squeeze out of *Notes from the Underground* anyway? This disease has killed almost everyone it strikes; it's spreading like brush fires in the canyons, and no one can put it out. We don't even know what's causing it, the most deadly sexually transmitted disease . . ."

He interrupted, "But only gays are getting it. Right?"

"Diseases don't usually discriminate by sexual preference. Gay men may be getting it here and now, but it starts with a rare form of skin cancer that's been seen in Africa and the Mediterranean for a long time. Yet those Kaposi's patients don't die of pneumocystis; that disease progresses slowly. It appears to be the same thing, but it's clearly different. How do we know if people elsewhere aren't dying of it? I seriously doubt there is something special about homosexual blood. Who knows how many unexplained cancers in young heterosexuals are actually caused by the same thing. No one knows all that much about it."

"Tell me about it."

"I'd like to, but we don't seem to find the time to have such discussions. Don't you think we should talk about us first?"

"Okay. But I'm not sure what there is to talk about. Has anything changed? Is it marriage you want to talk about?"

"We could talk about marriage, or we could start with living together, but that's not the point. It's can we be reasonably sure we're compatible. I mean will we be happy? You know I haven't felt that we communicate, I mean, that we understand each other most of the time. There's something missing. . . . I don't know. Maybe there isn't anything missing. Maybe it's just me. Now that I'm talking, I hate talking about this. It sounds trite, like it shouldn't be necessary. You talk. What do you think? Do you think we should live together? I'm not the only one who changes their mind around here. I wish you would say something for a change, goddammit!"

"It would save us both money if I moved in here."

She threw what was left of her pastry at him. "Daniel!"

"Hey! What else is there to consider?"

His complete resistance to serious discussion and his stubborn bright side were impervious to her attempt to extract a believable commitment from him — if that was what she wanted. No matter what he said he never said what she wanted to hear. "Don't you know?" Her voice was resigned.

"I love you. It's simple. I thought we should be living together two years ago. Come on, let's get stoned and drive to the wine country. We can continue this discussion in the car."

She heard the toilet flush, the newspaper rustling. He went to the dope box in the living room and started rolling a joint. The sun fell hot on her shoulders through the window; sweat dripped under her arms. In a gesture of disgust she stripped off her nightgown and sat naked, staring at the blueberry pastry as it oozed down the wallpaper. Her mind went blank. After a few minutes she began humming an old Beatles song. "Baby, you can drive my car. Yes I'm gonna be a star. Baby, you can drive my car, and maybe I'll love you."

* * *

To disappear into the fog at dawn after waking up in bright sunshine seemed a metaphor for her days this week. The bridge was clogged worse than usual, but she wove her way to the far right truck lanes. Trucks were the length of three cars and, although they moved slowly through the toll, once through they were easily passed. For a few moments she watched the speedometer climb. There was an early meeting at the office of disease control in San Francisco. It was time to try to get a handle on this new killer disease. The memo that invited her had a tone of desperation, of severity, of fear that the city was likely to become the scene of not only a deadly epidemic, but a political panic, a plague.

There were a lot of confused and angry people, gay and straight. There were even more terrified people, herself included. Somehow, a stroke of luck or a curse, she had been the attending physician as more and more victims entered the hospital. Her work on CMV — known to some infectious disease specialists in the city — and her extraordinary efforts to treat these patients had given her some local notoriety which at this point was little more than baffled comradery with colleagues previously unknown to her. Without much enthusiasm, she found herself the selected representative from her hospital to any meetings on this new disease. The Chair of Immunology at S.F. Medical School personally called to remind her of this one. Her new fellowship would be demanding; if she got it she'd be expected to get results. Rumor had it that the medical school was going to set up a special clinic for Kaposi's, AIDS, as it was now called.

Thinking about the job, the disease, the deaths, the expectations constricted her chest. Her stomach went sour; sleep threatened to engulf her. The fatigue brought with it another kind of panic, an anxiety that woke her up. Panic that she would fail to perform, to produce, to impress, to stand out among the ranks of the very smart and very competitive young doctors in the city. Her head throbbed, the wheels of her car squealed into the parking garage, grating her nerves like fingernails on a blackboard.

If only I had some speed. If only I hadn't gone to the wine country and gotten plastered. If only Daniel weren't going out of town again today. Nothing was decided. He's not moving in. I'm not agreeing to monogamy. He wants to move back east, no marriage, no kids, no commitment. Just sex and companionship, isn't that enough? When the time comes that I'm certain I really love him, then it will all work out; he's willing to wait. He said that. Don't hold your breath, Daniel.

Her briefcase spilled into the parking lot, charts, computer print-outs, multi-colored tubes rolling in every direction. She slammed her raincoat in the door, hearing the rip as she dove for the tubes. It was going to be one of those days. The ladies' room on the first floor was closed for cleaning. Taking refuge in the coffee shop, she held her face in her hands meditating — praying actually — for composure. Give in. Surrender. She opened the bottle and swallowed two Valium with her coffee. At lunch she could phone Dora. Her speed connection lived in the mission. Doreen? Maureen? Some woman she met once at a party, but God, could she wait until lunch? The ladies' room was open now, the mirror shiny and ready to tell. Okay. She stared at herself: some black eye liner with a little green shadow to downplay the red in her eyes, some peach blush, mauve lip liner and slightly darker lipstick. She pinned her hair back with a barrette and fluffed up the bangs. The pale peach dress was pretty; the rust sweater vest hid the perspiration stains. No runs in her stockings. The I. Magnin shoes matched perfectly. Yes. Presentable. Stylish. Not over done.

I'm okay, she whispered to herself. Am I Okay? There was a thin frown line that ran vertically between her eyebrows. She rubbed it, up and down, up and down. It will never go away. Never.

"Good Morning, Dr. Keller. I'm so glad you could join us today." The middle-aged woman smiled at her with an impression of solidity and warmth. She immediately envied this woman her composure, her rocklike sense of self. "I'm Dr. Fritzenberg. Let me introduce you."

"Good morning. Thank you for inviting me." She shook the hands of eight or ten men, trying to keep faces with names. The Valium was restoring her normality with a pleasant rush of warmth. Then everyone started to talk at once. Suzanne sat there, listening.

"This isn't a gay disease; it's only a *gay related* syndrome."

"I heard one-half are in New York and the other half are in S.F, and they're all gay."

"Those guys who had Kaposi's in N.Y. just happened to be gay; it's pneumocystis that's killing them, opportunistic infections, has nothing to do with sexuality."

"That's bunk! All the victims are gay. In the Bay area over a hundred gay men have been stricken, all between the ages of 26 and 33. Dr. Fritzenberg, can we get on with it?"

"Are you aware that a clinic is being established at U.C.S.F. Medical Center for this thing?"

"I ought to be, I'm one of those setting it up."

"All right, gentlemen, calm down. Let's get on with the facts. One of the major risk factor seems to be sexual activity. Already we've seen a similar pattern to the Hepatitis B studies in New York. The victims have at least two times the sexual activity of other gay men."

"How many victims are we referring to here?"

"Over 65 in S.F. as of May, last month. Nineteen are dead."

"More than that."

"These are the official figures, gentlemen. Let's not quibble."

"It's those drugs they use."

"Are you the representative from the Middle Ages?"

"Gentlemen. Gentlemen."

"I think it's a virus. It's got to be a virus."

"It's probably a new form of Hodgkin's Disease. It's another cancer. We haven't really found out much about how these cancer cells work."

"You haven't done any research in twenty years."

"Listen, I think we need to talk about what kind of research is going on in the Bay area, and how it could be coordinated to find out more about this immuno-suppression. It could be many different things. What about . . ."

"I read a study that said these victims have 1,100 different sex partners versus 500 for healthy gay men and 25 for heterosexual men."

"Now we know whose having all the fun."

"That was uncalled for."

"I've heard that CMV may be the virus that's causing this."

"Well, we invited Dr. Keller here" Dr. Fritzenberg turned to Suzanne who sat in stunned silence in the corner, "to tell us about that. She happens to be doing research on CMV." Ten pairs of eyes fixed on her.

"I, yes, well, I'm not doing anything directly related. As you know CMV is normally harmless in healthy patients. I mean, we've isolated it in people without disease, but in some very sick patients, immuno-suppressed or compromised patients, it can . . ."

"Immuno-compromised, you say? That's what I think; it's all this sex. These homos, I mean gays, get repeated exposure to this agent, this virus or whatever it is, and constant stimulation of their immune systems. It overwhelms the immune responses; it wears them out. They become susceptible to other infections. The city has got to shut down the bathhouses. We can't let them kill themselves."

"Well . . ."

"Jesus Christ! There are other ideas, you know. Anyway what you're saying doesn't account for the upswing in kaposies patients."

"The problem is that they get more than one infection, not repeated infections, multiple infections. You get exposed to a lot of different diseases if you, well, live that way. That's why these gay men are getting it."

"I think it's a new, mutated virus. Probably comes from Africa. There are Haitian patients. Do they come from Africa?"

"So geography's not your speciality either."

"Not only Haitian. There are thirteen heterosexual men and one woman who have been reported to the CDC. Some people do think they have the disease in Africa. The French are on to this."

"Maybe it is a drug. Are there any new street drugs around?"

"This meeting is getting nowhere. We haven't even begun to talk about what to do."

"What can we do?"

"We could start a city-wide educational campaign advising the use of condoms, and letting people know what makes them high risk for exposure: bathhouses, frequent and different sexual partners."

"You've got to be kidding. Tell gays to wear condoms in San Francisco! That's absurd. Would you wear a condom on your tongue? Why should gays be punished anyway? They're always the scapegoats."

"Would you rather they die? Nobody decided to unleash this particular horror on gays."

"What makes you so sure?"

"This man is nuts. Excuse me, Dr. Fritzenberg, I have patients to see. I'll send my reports as usual."

Everyone stood up and left within minutes. Suzanne sat frozen in the corner, a little woozy. Dr. Fritzenberg shook her head and sat beside her. Suzanne said, "I feel as if I were Dorothy and I just dropped out of the tornado."

"Don't mind how they are, dear. They'll all come to their senses in time. I'd like to see your research findings when they're ready. Frankly, I'm at a loss. The city has got to do something. We need more data, more time. These boys are dying."

"*And we* know it's going to get worse, don't we?"

"Yes."

*   *   *

Why did every moneymatic in or near Pacific Heights run out of cash today? She stood in line at the Wells Fargo, her foot tapping rapidly. Maureen waited, sullen and chain smoking in the car. It took her two hours to track down Dora, make up a suitable justification and find Maureen's warehouse hovel in the mission. If she weren't desperate she wouldn't sell to strangers, she whined to Suzanne. The P.G.& E bastards cut off her electricity, the kid was getting thrown out of daycare, and her boy-friend just split with all her cash and her mother's jewelry. But, yeah, she did have some, about a gram. A hundred bucks, she yelled, and not a penny less. And she didn't have no scale, so take it or leave it. Suzanne took it, swearing she would never bypass Dora again. The middle person was worth it. She wasn't prepared to see this. Sickness and death, diseases she could cure, that was what she signed on for, not a birdseye view of everyday, ordinary, terminal misery.

Ahhh . . . the beauty of sailing, of speeding across the Golden Gate toward Sausilito. The speed was good. After eight hours of work, the sun was still high. Ivan had called to invite her to a party in Marin. She said no, but she was on her way. Dan had called to say goodbye right after Ivan. As she said goodbye, tired and annoyed, she changed her mind. They have a hottub, Ivan cajoled, and a view of the Sausilito harbor from the hilltop. They have every kind of amusement, and she knew what he meant when he stressed "every."

Ivan sat alone in the corner, his sad face brooding over a glass of whiskey. Splashing noises came from the deck where several naked bodies bobbed in and out of the hottub and dove into the pool. She stood in the doorway of the cathedral-beamed living room, the far glass wall a frame for a nineteen eighties Bosch orgy. Full breasts, voluptuous bottoms and elongated penises bounced freely, the hot pink, healthy flesh too vivid a contrast to the pallid, grey, skeletal bodies she had examined in the afternoon. The blond preppy she had seen at Dora's party sat in the tub with one arm around an extraor-

125

dinarily handsome young man and the other around a less than pretty young girl. Tears welled up in her eyes without warning, and she clutched the doorknob for support. It was coming again. The panic. Her heart started to race. Ivan was coming toward her. A blur.

The cold penetrated to her bones. Hands were all over her. Welcoming. Dragging. Guiding. Pleading. Hot water rose to her neck. Lips pressed to her face. That healthy flesh was against her own. The blond boy pulled her on to his lap where his erect penis poked at her, bobbing in the water like a bath toy. Laughter echoed in her head, loud happy moans. The girl massaged her shoulders. Someone brought her a drink, and a joint was passed around. Ivan's broad smile expanded from across the deck, the smile of a devil, a set of teeth moving toward her. Closer and closer. A man with a black braid wrapped her in a huge fluffy towel and took her to the table where lines of coke were cut next to rows of tiny black tablets, capsules of MDA, syringes, and rubber bands, your pleasure. Where do you want to go? Up? Down? Out? Where do you want to be? One of each?

Futons covered the floor of an adjoining room. Bodies, healthy, fresh bodies reeking of jasmine, patchouli, coconut and musk rolled around her, over her, under her. Hair, breasts, arms, legs, lips, someone was sucking her toes. Her eyes were closed. Ivan's smell. They were filling her up, spreading her legs, leaving no orifice empty. Penises, tongues, fingers, elbows, knees. The girl was singing. A low resonant tone, a chant, a constant soothing sound. Mantras. Each blended together with the bodies, rotating, taking turns. She didn't exist anymore. Only sensations: pressures, vacuums, entrances, exits, blood pumping. Pumping.

"Fassbinder died today."

"No. You're kidding."

"He killed himself."

"No."

"He was gay."

"I liked his films."

"Suicide."

"Why?"

"Let's get out of here."

* * *

They sat on top of the big rock, the fog thick around them. Her arms wrapped around her body, she shivered from the cold, the drugs. Dawn was beginning to lighten the sky. The murky green of the night waves crashing against the rocks was turning a bruised violet. He struggled to light a cigarette with damp matches.

"I can't see you anymore, Ivan."

"It's all the same to me."

"I can't live this way. I've got to change."

"You loved it. I saw your face. You were in heaven."

"I did like it. At the time. Now I feel ashamed. I'm not like this, Ivan. I haven't done these things before. It's wrong."

"Wrong? You don't believe that. You don't have those scruples, that archaic morality. You may wish you did. You think it would make life easier. Like those Spanish women praying in church."

"I want to change, Ivan. I'm scared."

"You're sick and a good liar. It doesn't matter if you change or not."

"You're the sick one."

"Haven't you ever been to an orgy before?"

"No. Not like that."

"Haven't you ever cruised the singles bars? The gay bars?"

"No."

"Haven't you taken a lot of drugs?"

"Just speed. When I can get it. And dope. Sometimes. This morning — yesterday — I bought a gram of speed. I took Valium with my coffee. That's absurd, isn't it? I really don't want to become a drug addict. Now I feel sick. My head hurts. My cunt hurts. I hate myself for this. Why did I do it?"

"You don't know shit about life, do you?"

"No, I guess I don't. Not what you call life, Ivan."

"You ought to find out about it. Get off that ivory tower doctor trip; get your nose out of those medical books. Life isn't in a book. That knowledge you have about the cells, disease, the way the body works, you think it's going to give you some edge, some protection, some hedge against death. All doctors are into one trip. Immortality. They think they'll be the first not to die. You're so naive."

"Why are you doing this to me?"

"I love you. You could travel. It's possible. But I'm a cynic."

"I don't know what you're talking about. I don't like you, and I don't know why I'm here."

"You lie to yourself." He waved his hand. "You're here for this."

"For what?"

"The ocean, the rocks, the fog. You need me."

"I mean what I said, Ivan. I can't see you anymore. This is it. I'm going to live with Dan. I've got to focus on my work and stop this, this, this . . ."

"This 'living' this 'fun' this 'discovery' perhaps? Don't make the same mistakes again; you've been married; you've been in love. What came of it? What always comes of it. Anyway, you came to me."

Her foot slid unsteadily on the wet rocks as she climbed down with caution. The sand was wet and cold. Hundreds of seagulls sat along the beach with their heads tucked under a wing. They walked along the edge of the cliffs where rivulets of water streamed over the layers of geological time. A herd of deer ran, all sinewy and glistening, over the rolling grassland near the top. She was so tired she crawled part way up the steep path. He walked on ahead, thankfully, letting her make her own way back. At one point she sat on the trail and wept. A familiar determination returned when the tears ran dry. She picked up a dew-covered poppy and stared at it. Yes, she found herself thinking about the articles on CMV in her office. She felt stronger, stubborn, calm. This weakness, this erratic carrying on, this crazy panic, she could conquer it, she could control it. She would. She got up and walked faster, anxious to get to her office, plunge into the journals, begin some new experiments. When she got to the car she studied his face and he hers. He knew she was through with him. For the moment.

* * *

The New England Journal of Medicine, The Journal of Virology, Infection and Immunity, The Annals, stacks and stacks of journals, clipped articles, memos, lab reports, patient charts were spread across her desk, piled on the floor, the file cabinet. There were no bare surfaces in the office. Dirty coffee cups growing mold were scattered on top of it all. Sugarfree Vitamints, Bubble Yum, Lifesavers and cans of Tab spilled from the waste basket along with the unopened junk mail. Her beeper had gone off eight times before eleven in the morning. There was little point in leaving the hospital except to sleep, and a few nights she had found herself sleeping on a cot in the lab.

The S.F. Chronicle confronted her with the headline: "Gay Plague Called Epidemic." The CDC was quoted for the current statistics, "413 cases reported since 1981, 155 are dead. There was one case per day reported in the last half of 1981. Since February 1.5 cases per day. In the past 6 weeks 2.5 cases per day reported. And it is now hitting heterosexuals." Two point five cases. I haven't seen a point five human being yet, she thought. There was a photo of the Pan Am crash in New Orleans, dead bodies and parts of bodies littered with the pieces of metal, priests and firemen walking among them, their faces covered. She went back to tearing articles out of the journals. A month of trying to get organized, constant interruptions, a slow but steady stream of young men with coughs, fevers, diarrhea, malaise. At least half of them were merely frightened, wanting to be checked, wanting to know if they were sick yet. Beep! Beep!

"Dr. Keller, paging Dr. Keller."

She took a last sip of cold coffee and grabbed her stethoscope. The phone was ringing, but she left it. There was no time to answer messages during the day anyway. The emergency room was a tumult of activity. Every examining room was filled and the waiting room had run out of chairs. The nurses scowled and tried to hide harried frowns. There were three or four suspect gay patients waiting. Or to be more precise, the staff had come to think of anyone young, male, thin, and good-looking as gay. A loathsome paranoia had set into the clinics. Hostility born of fear hovered in the staff meetings. The nurses and technicians wanted some assurances of their safety. The doctors hated to show their ignorance, their bewilderment, their fallibility, their vulnerablity.

The middle-aged woman was sitting on the examining table in the skimpy hospital gown clutching her purse to her chest. For a moment Suzanne was relieved. But the examination puzzled her; nothing fit into place. The woman was baffled herself. Never been sick in her life. Fit as a fiddle. It was her husband who was the sick one. He'd had strokes and heart trouble, triple by-pass surgery. Now his lungs were acting up. Couldn't understand it, she began to feel tired all the time about a month ago. He was already back on his feet. Thought maybe all that nursing him had plum worn her out, but now she had this fever sometimes and terrible runs. That had never happened in her whole life. She laughed, a jovial laugh that expressed her sense of disbelief. First time in her life she hadn't suffered from constipation. And the weight she'd lost. Well, God had finally answered her prayers; she'd been trying to diet all her life. "Fat peasant stock, my lot. Now I'm thin as my daughter. She's jealous too." Suzanne laughed with her, liking this woman, admiring her spunk.

"We'll do some blood tests and stool cultures." She smiled at her. "I'll give you some medicine for the diarrhea and some antibiotics. I'm sure you'll be back on your feet in no time." She listened to her chest. Something was there. "Let me ask you a few questions. Now don't be offended; it's just routine."

"Oh dearie, nothing much offends me at my age. You just ask anything at all."

"You say your husband had surgery recently. When was it?"

"Oh, back in November of '81, over there at General. Big hospital, that, but the doctors were so nice."

"That was eight months ago."

"Guess it was."

"Do you know if they gave him blood? Transfusions?"

"Oh sure, lots of blood."

"And has he been recuperating all this time?"

"Oh sure, but he's been up and about for a couple of months now. For a few weeks he was like a new man, walking everywhere, even helped me around the house. A miracle, that surgery. I tell you, dearie, you doctors can work miracles these days. I'd have never believed it, not me, never been in a hospital, had all my kids at home. But I was real thankful, real thankful."

"You're 59 now, Mrs. Canner?"

"That's right."

"Do you and your husband have sex regularly, I mean since he's gotten better."

Her eyes grew wide and she stifled a giggle. "We didn't use to, not much, not for several years — his heart, you know — but well, like I said, he was a new man for a few weeks there."

"I hope I'm not embarrassing you. This is just routine. So you have had sex in the past few months, is that right?"

"I'd be a liar if I said no." She bubbled, her eyes dancing bright with fever. "No harm in that, is there? We've been married forty years."

"Of course not. It's completely normal. I'm going to send you to the lab now. You feel up to walking?"

"Well, I feel a bit weak, you know. A bit queazy." A loud hacking cough erupted, the tissues covered in yellow pus and blood.

"I'll get you a wheelchair. Now lie back here and rest. A nurse will be with you in a moment. I'll see you later. Perhaps we should keep you overnight. Is your husband outside?"

"Oh no, no, dearie. I can't stay overnight. He doesn't cook, you know. He can't manage on his own."

"Well, let me speak to him. We could arrange for him to eat here with you. How about that?"

"I don't know. I don't much like it. I've never been in a hospital before."

"Don't worry. We'll take good care of you. Think of it as a vacation. Just for a night or two." She left before more arguments came. Something troubled her about this woman; something was sticking in her throat. It couldn't possibly be, she told herself. There were loads of other possibilities. She put a rush on the lab tests, but how could she know for sure?

There were phone messages from Dan, Dora, Janet, Dr. Fritzen-berg, Dr. Thomas, numerous patients, and Julia had called long distance. She sorted them in order of importance and the time it would take to respond. Her stomach growled, her hands shook from too much coffee and a familiar headache had begun. Clutching the messages, a new preliminary report on interferon, and two articles, she ran to the cafeteria. Two residents and some interns sat engrossed in heated conversation. Jerry, the smartest of the lot, motioned for her to join them. Soon she too was swept away in the hot debate about — what else? The mystery disease. The gay plague. The hysteria rising like the tide, but with no signs of ebbing. Everyone had a theory, everyone had seen something different in a patient. They fell into two camps: those who thought it was going to get worse, and those who thought it was another legionaires type scare, a swine flu problem. It would peak and level off. "Anyway," one brash young intern grabbed her report on interferon, "this drug looks promising. The real issue is not knowing how much contact is necessary to catch it."

She sat, silently eating her yogurt, peeling an orange, thinking of Mrs. Canner, watching her colleagues grow edgy and shift nervously in their chairs. "Do you mind?" She wrested her report from the in-tern. "I've got to get back to work."

"Wait a minute. You haven't said a word. What about the CMV cultures? Are you getting anything from the pneumocystis patient in isolation? He's in pretty bad shape, seems confused and disoriented. Do you think we should do a spinal tap?"

"Has he had any seizures? Any CNS involvement?"

"I don't think so. I wasn't on his case until yesterday."

"I'll stop by and look at the chart. Let's talk about it at the after-noon rounds. I've got to go."

Her head rested on the stack of articles. She was dozing. Visions of bombed out cities drifted by, empty cities with no people left. A siren wailed in the distance. Her phone rang, and she jumped, awake too fast, so fast it frightened her. "Dr. Keller speaking. Can I help you?"

"Hi, hey, where are you? I've been waiting dinner for two hours. Remember me? Dan? Your friendly cook and bottle washer. Didn't we agree on dinner tonight?"

"I'm sorry. I dozed off at my desk. What time is it?"

"Nine-thirty," he humored her sarcastically, "at night, July 15, 1982."

"I'm really sorry. I'm so tired. Dan, you wouldn't believe what's happening here. I saw three more patients today who, I'm almost sure, have it. One is a middle-aged woman, absolutely heterosexual!" Her voice was shrill. "I had to go over to General after rounds to check on her husband's records. He had four transfusions about eight months ago. Dan, do you realize that the blood supply isn't safe. Do you realize that a hell of a lot of people could already have it! In their blood!"

"Calm down. Suzanne, you're getting obsessed with this thing. You're working too hard. We've barely seen each other in a month. What about dinner? Are you coming over or not?"

"I can't help it. Yes. I'll be there in half an hour. Don't you care about my work? Do I complain when you spend every Sunday buried in *War and Peace* or *Crime and Punishment?*"

"Yes. Jesus, you go from one extreme to the other. Last month you wanted to talk and spend time together. Now you work seven days a week. Listen, I've got something important to talk to you about. Get here as soon as you can." He softened. "I miss you."

"Okay. I'm on my way."

* * *

August was unusually cold and foggy. Dan had moved into her house on a trial basis. His house was being redecorated by the owner who planned to sell it when Dan's lease was up next June. That was a long way off, she said, when he mentioned that he'd have to move elsewhere sooner or later. It was nice crawling into bed next to his warm body every night. They had settled quickly into a comfortable routine, both leaving for work between six and seven. He volunteered to shop during the day, and since his schedule was more flexible, he did the cooking too. She was free to straggle home at seven or eight, smoke a joint, drink some wine, eat and collapse into bed. He didn't even notice that she often fell asleep while they ritually made love almost every night.

Her nightmares and panic spells had abated. But on weekends she became curiously agitated, pacing the house, not able to read or lie on the patio. She couldn't get through the front section of the *New York Times* without being overcome by restlessness. They had taken up jogging a few miles before dinner when time permitted, and she thought that her body had grown dependent on some kind of constant motion, contant movement. Dan seemed happier than she ever remembered. It dawned on her while she ran that he had never told her whatever it was that had been so important several days ago. Nothing unusual — their conversations were often left hanging, or stopped before they started. Raising certain issues left her exhausted, depressed, confused, and always unsatisfied. He wasn't much on talking in the first place, and she had abandoned discussing their relationship. After all why rock the boat? It seemed a moot point whether they would make a commitment to each other. Here they were, living together albeit temporarily. Take comfort when it comes, while it exists. Her work did consume her, and Dan was a welcome link to the world of health. He reminded her that a world outside the hospital, away from AIDS remained — literature, art, food, flowers.

"Can you believe they're really going to execute Coppola? They're going to put him in an electric chair. I can't believe this is still done. God, it infuriates me," she said.

"He's a murderer."

"That's not the point, Dan. Why should the state, of which we are a part, turn around and kill in cold blood just like murderers do? It's not right. It's stupid."

"It's economics. Why should the state spend a fortune keeping cold-blooded murderers alive at our expense? We're the tax-payers you know. What good does that do?"

"You never agree with anything I say."

"That's not true. I agree it's not right, but it has nothing to do with what's right. It's economics that determines who lives and dies. You used to say that to me, remember?"

"But it's not all economics." She fidgeted in frustration. "You're right, I suppose. I just don't like it."

"That's different."

"Dan, let's do something. Let's go somewhere. It's Friday night. I'm bored."

"You want to get stoned?"

"Sure. But let's go out. I've been wanting to go to the Castro, you know, to some of the bars."

"Oh no, come on, Suzanne. The traffic is terrible. Let's go to the movies."

"No. I want to go see what it's like, what's going on. You never want to go to bars with me. Come on, please, just this once." She put on her most seductive plea. "Please, Honey."

"Okay." He rolled a joint, and they sat by the empty fireplace smoking it. "How's the research going, your CMV study?"

"Why are you asking me that now?"

"You haven't mentioned it much lately. There's a guy in the Drama department who's sick. Did I tell you? You met him once at a faculty party. He's in the hospital. I'm beginning to think this disease could get serious. He's a real nice guy, a great actor."

"I can't talk about it now. I think about it every day, I see it every day. Now there's this interferon. A new drug that some people think might block the course of the disease. The protocols for using it are impossible though because it's barely out of the animal model stage. I think they're going to try it on an experimental basis at S.F. General, but I don't know which patients they'll select. Probably those at death's door already. See, here I am talking about it. Let's go. Let's look while there's still somebody to look at."

"Isn't it kind of perverted to go staring at those guys like they were lepers or something?"

"I watch them die; I want to see them live. Maybe I *am* a pervert. Sometimes I think the whole world is perverted. It's all turned upside down."

"That's why I love you. You're a Dostoevsky character, 'swarming opposites' in your 'over-acute consciousness'." He pulled her out of the chair into which she had sunk, her face brooding now. "Let's go cruising, Babe."

* * *

Standing room only greeted her at the hastily called meeting to update the house staff on the interferon drug protocol. The room was abuzz with nervous gossip as the hospital administrator rose to speak. "As you all know tests at Sloan Kettering Cancer Center indicate that interferon has caused partial or complete remissions in about half of the Kaposi's sarcoma patients."

A nurse raised her hand. "For those of us who don't know, could you say what this drug is."

"I'll defer to our chief of medicine on that one."

"Interferon is a naturally occuring substance produced by living cells and apparently acts as an anti-viral agent."

"But," one of the research fellows added, "it has to be extracted in extremely small quantities from animal or human tissue."

"That's true. And now another marvel of recent genetic engineering permits it to be manufactured in large quantities by bacteria. It is, for the first time, possible to get enough to treat some patients."

"How does it work? I mean, how do they know it will work? We've seen remissions here, but they always come back."

The administrator interrupted, "I haven't time to discuss the medical aspects of this treatment, gentlemen and ladies. We want these protocols for treatment read and understood by the entire medical staff. Our legal department has informed us of the necessary caution in using experimental drugs. To save everyone from disappointment, we have decided it will not be used here except in the extreme cases as outlined in your handout and after full review of the case by an independent medical board."

Most of the audience were paging through the packet of forms, frowns on every face. Suzanne didn't bother to look at the handout. She tucked it under her arm and watched the others.

"But this means people who might benefit from the drug could die before it was approved for their use." It was only a matter of time before someone said it.

"We have to be extremely cautious. They've selected ten people for these drug trials at General. We'd rather wait and see what, if any, results they get."

"Then why were we called to this meeting?" The intern hadn't slept in thirty-six hours. He was in that state of diffuse emotion – angry, burned out – yet for less reason he was not alone. Hostility crackled, a current around the room.

Suzanne stood leaning against the door frame, examining the faces as some, one by one, took their leave. The administrator groaned on about procedures, record-keeping, the importance of public relations in the hospital. Professionalism. Bureaucracy. Order. Decorum. Must be preserved.

Her mind wandered back to the Castro where hundreds of perfect heart-shaped bottoms in tight jeans bobbed up and down. They strolled with their arms around each other, sometimes a hand in their lover's back pocket. The traffic was terrible, not a parking place within twenty blocks. The bars were over-flowing, music of all sorts filled the streets. In jeans and white shirts, black leather and bald heads, pin-striped suits, over-alls, cut-off and ripped T-shirts, all looking like Giancarlo Gianini, Robert Redford, movie stars, countless variations on style, class, camp, persona. They were alive. Rough and ready. Alive. Parading happily or with the affected pout of a wounded darling, they exuded sexuality. The night colors of neon and headlights framed different faces, different groups, expressions of the search, the potential, the promise of pleasure, the tease of pain. The sidewalks were so crowded one had to weave a way through, giving way or adopting an attitude of "Move over man I'm coming through." Suzanne and Dan were weavers, trying to keep up with each other, to meet on corners, or duck into a bar to reconnect. The place was a buzz of activity, a center of life, like Piccadilly or Leicester Square where thick throngs of regulars mingle with tourists, gawkers who come for the thrill of watching.

The bars were filled to capacity. Guys were sitting on other guys' laps; bar stools were shared, asses of strangers bumping on purpose. There were very few women except some who weren't really women, and they were a surprising few. It was almost impossible for a novice to know anyway. And novices they were. Worse than novices, they obviously didn't belong here. Dan kept tugging at her arm to leave, trying to be friendly in response to the winks, smiles, and gestures he was attracting. She was entranced, hypnotized by the openness with which these gorgeous young men slid easily from one to the other, fascinated by the colored bandannas that meant something she didn't know.

They walked past the shops — some still open at midnight — selling all kinds of leather and metal contraptions, sexual aids, enhancers, highlighters, magazines, and what looked like instruments of torture: whips, harnesses, pokers and similar non-identifiable objects. Sex: in the shops, in the streets, in the bars, in the music, in the people, in the air. Sex and life. Health. It was everywhere, and therefore invisible, not simply taken for granted, but a non-issue.

It reminded her of being a child at the state fair, the glittery lights of the rides, the gruff and enticing voices of the game callers, the view from the top of the ferris wheel where coming over the front edge took her breath away, but only for a moment. And in the next, laughter, her laughter, spreading on the wind and merging with the countless other bliss-filled eaters of cotton candy and caramel apples. Childhood. The harmless ignorance of childhood when being grown-up meant being free to do whatever one wanted — all those secret, nasty things that had to be even better than the roller coaster. She stood by the tent where the women in harem dresses, the see-through ones, rolled their hips, raised their eyebrows, and slid their tongues over ruby red lips. The men stood, their feet wide apart, cigarettes dangling from their mouths. Then they went in slowly, with a hesitant swagger, acting as though it was nothing, as though the women were pulling them by an invisible string. Her stomach would tingle, but she didn't watch long because it made her uncomfortable, restless, anxious to grow up and go behind that curtain. She remembered not a blissful ignorance, but restraint, the restriction of age. Her father calling her name, time to go home. It was always time to go home and do something boring, like watch T.V. And she hated it each time a ride was over, longing for that freedom of hanging on the edge, dangling in her chair high above the others, wondering what would happen if. . . . Flying over the top of the roller coaster with her hands in the air — it made her want to pee in her pants. But there was no fear, only regret that the end came so soon. Later she curled up under her blankets in the dark and dreamt of growing up. To be free. Freedom. Free at last.

"Hey, Dr. Keller, Suzanne." Jerry shook her by the arm. "The meeting's over." He stood beside her, scratching his head. "Isn't this a bitch. Isn't this insane."

She came to, staring into the empty room, chairs askew, styrofoam coffee cups dotting the brown tables. "Yeah."

"You okay?"

"Yeah." Her back was sore from leaning too long. "Yeah, fine, just day-dreaming."

* * *

"Listen, Suzie," he only called her Suzie when he was worried about her response, "I can move back into my house next week. What do you think? Should I?"

"Finally there's an article in the *New England Journal,* a study that gives us some real leads, real data."

"Suzie, did you hear me? Should I move out or not?"

"Dan, I've got to read this article. Now."

"Okay. I'm leaving then. I'm moving out next week. Don't say I didn't tell you." He went back to grading his exams. The phone rang. It was Dora inviting them to a picnic, a celebration of Cheryl's birthday and all the other September birthdays. He would be out of town, he lied, but he'd tell Suzanne. No, she wasn't at home. She was at the grocery store. Yes. He'd have her call back. He returned to the living room where she was crying.

"What's wrong?"

"Princess Grace died. She was so young."

"Are you crying about that! Give me that article." He snatched the *New England Journal* from her hand. The medicalese was beyond him; he couldn't even understand the abstract. "What does this mean, what the hell are OKT-4 lymphocytes?"

Tears streamed over her cheeks and dripped onto her sweatshirt. "Are you really moving out?"

"I wanted to discuss it with you." He put both his hands around hers rubbing them gently to warm them up. "They've invited me for an interview at Harvard, Suzie. Harvard. That's the top. The pay's lousy, but just think, living in Cambridge. Boston. We could get away from this place where reading *The Sunday Times* qualifies one to be an expert in world affairs. Think of it. Serious intellectual discussions, real scholars, autumn in the Bershires." Now he was grasping at straws. "You could work there. New York has more AIDS than San Francisco. Boston can't be far behind."

She stared at him in disbelief. "You think I should go with you

137

because there's more AIDS there? More death. More *serious* death? Are you crazy?"

"I'm going for the interview, Suzie. If they offer me the job, I'm going to take it. I want you to go with me. I think we should get married and plan a normal life together. You know, like most people our age do? Marriage, buy a house, maybe have a kid."

Now she was bawling, her shoulders rising and falling with the sobs. She covered her face and ran from the room to get a box of Kleenex. The tears kept coming, unremittant. At first she kept repeating everything he said. "Normal life. Marriage. House. Kid. I'm too old for all that." Then she wailed louder and louder.

"For Christ's sake, calm down. Are you about to start your period?"

"AAHHH." The heavy ceramic lamp sailed toward the plate glass door, hit the door sill, and smashed on the floor. She ran outside onto the patio and threw the wrought iron chairs into the garden. When he got to her she was stomping on the basil and oregano plants, her fists clenched, her arms moving like a boxer's.

"What the hell. . . ." He ducked as she swung at him, wrestling her to the ground and pinning her arms down with his knees. She was stronger than he imagined, and they rolled in the dirt, crushing an assortment of vegetables before he subdued her. She refused to open her eyes, and he wasn't going to let her up until he could see that she was calm enough to trust.

"Let go of me."

"Not until you promise to calm down. You're destroying the garden."

"It's my garden."

"I planted it."

"It's in my yard."

"I bought the plants."

"Don't be ridiculous, Dan. It is my garden."

"All right. It's your garden, but you broke my lamp."

"I'll pay for it."

"Will you please open your eyes and look at me?"

"Don't ever ask me if I'm going to start my period again."

"Don't worry. I won't."

She opened her eyes and saw him covered with dirt and pieces of plants. It was funny, and much as she hated to do it, she smiled at him. He kissed her, tasting the dirt and the salt from her tears. "What makes you think they'll actually offer you that job?"

"I know people there. I know the competition. My book just won a prize, remember?"

"Must be pretty stiff competition for a job at Harvard." She sat up, brushing herself off in a haphazard fashion.

"What if I do get it? That's the point. We need to talk about it."

"I can tell you now the answer's no. I'm not leaving the Bay area and that's that."

"But you grew up on the East Coast. You said you loved it there. The first year I knew you all you talked about was how great it was there, how flaky it is here. You hated it here, remember? You said everyone you met had the brain of a beetle, remember? A bunch of geeks. You said this was a plastic world, a fake, pseudo-culture trying to become more unreal than it already was. Remember saying that?"

"Not really. Maybe. It doesn't matter. I've changed my opinion. I'm entitled to change my opinions, aren't I?"

"Suzie, are you saying I should turn down the best job of my life to live around a bunch of beetle-brains and geeks?"

"I didn't say that. You do what you want. You will anyway. But I'm not going." Her face was set in a blank, emotionless expression, a look he'd never seen before. It was as if she had gone away, taken flight, retreated deep inside herself, leaving a rigid, fragile shell for the onlooker. He felt reduced to someone she barely recognized, refused to acknowledge, a mere stranger whose actions — much less words — were of no consequence to her. Aside from an angry hurt that made him want to hit her — a feeling he'd never had in his entire life toward anyone. There was another new feeling: she frightened him. He had to look away.

* * *

The cafeteria had plenty of empty tables. Her table — the one in the corner behind the post — was the hardest to find, and she assumed solitude there. The blood test results from her study of the AIDS patients and the healthy volunteers were sitting in front of her. They confirmed the pattern published in the *New England Journal*: the AIDS patients had far fewer OKT-4 lymphocytes than the healthy homosexuals who had fewer "helper cells" than the heterosexual volunteers. She had found the same abnormal ratio of helper to suppressor cells, OKT-8's, in her CMV studies and knew this appeared in hepatitis, and probably in innumerable viral infections. But the AIDS patients — those with the severe opportunistic infections — all died. In other types of infection these balances of helper to suppressor cells could and would correct themselves. The immune system was beautiful, subtle and complex in its ability to self-correct, to produce antibodies when attacked, to surround and isolate foreign agents, to retreat when necessary. She felt like an Army general in a losing battle. The enemy was too crafty, too unpredictable, already behind the lines of defense. The enemy was within . . . wasn't that some anti-communist treatise from the past?

Her concentration was especially poor. Taking the newspaper from her briefcase for a breather, it confronted her again: "AIDS, the new CDC name for acquired immuno-deficiency syndrome, has struck 585 people in the U.S. in the last 16 months; 241 have died. Reported cases have jumped from 1 to 2 to 3 a day recently. It attacks the immune system lowering the ratio of helper to suppressor cells which inhibit antibody output. Sufferers have less than one helper cell to each suppressor, while healthy people have two times as many helpers to suppressors. Too little is known."

She rested her head on the table thinking. The news reporters know almost as much as we do about this mess. It was disheartening. Why carry on? Yet the whole medical-scientific community had launched into the fastest, most serious studies of this syndrome imaginable. She was only one of hundreds of doctors collecting data, searching for clues, designing studies, looking for answers. The resignation. She had to shake it. Only yesterday she'd gotten word they were reviewing her fellowship application at U.C.S.F. Strictly off the record, it looked very favorable. Closer to the pulse. Better facilities. More clinical data. More patients. Grants. Her career was blossoming.

"Is anyone sitting here?"

She looked up, then around the room at the many tables, still empty. "Yes, I am." She gestured to her papers spread across the table.

"I know. I've seen you in here before and have often wanted to speak to you, but you always look so busy. My name's Brian. I'm in psychiatry." He precariously balanced a plate of veal parmagiana over a cup of coffee. "Do you mind if I join you?"

"Well, I'm working. Sort of."

"You look like you could use a break." His bashful smile gave away the effort it took him to approach her. His eyes were full of such empathy she couldn't refuse.

"Yeah. Okay, sit down."

"So. Shall I call you Dr. Keller?" He read her name tag.

"Why not?"

"What's your speciality?" Her sarcasm was ignored.

"Disease and death."

"Mine's psychic torment. Guess we have something in common."

"I doubt it." She wasn't in the mood. He continued to smile, but with less enthusiasm.

"I hate to sound like a psychiatrist, but is something bothering you?"

"Yes. You." He looked her in the eye, then lowered his head, playing with the fork in the veal. She gathered her papers into a stack. "I'm sorry for being so rude. One of my patients died this morning. I'm not much on conversation just now. I need to be alone." She rose to leave.

"It's forgiven. I'm sorry you have to leave, but I understand. I really do. Next time, maybe?"

"See you around."

She went back to the lab and sat at the microscope. Hours passed like minutes, and it was pitch dark when she dashed into the bathroom. There wasn't any point in going home. Daniel was gone, not only back to his own house, but out of town again. I should have gotten his last name, she thought, sitting on the toilet. He was cute. C'est la vie. There were lots of men out there. With nary a twinge of guilt she went back to her office, locked the door, and rolled a joint. Her tiny stash of speed had to be replenished. She called Dora.

"Why don't you come over? I've got an enormous pot of spaghetti on and nothing more exciting to do than my nails. I closed that $250,000 deal today. Isn't that fantastic!"

"Yeah. Listen, I'm at the hospital. I was wondering if you had any speed or anything. Why don't we go out on the town tonight? We could check out some bars in the city, listen to some music, get high."

"I thought you'd given it up. The consummate, devoted St. Joan healing the sick, raising the dead. Or is that St. Theresa?"

"Very funny, Dora. You game or not?"

"I can't, Suzanne. The bank opens early, you know. Come to my house. I do have some coke and some great dope. There are bars in the East Bay, you know."

"I need to buy some more dope. Coke, humm. Okay. About an hour?"

"Fine. Oh, I'm so glad you're coming over. We haven't talked girl to girl in so long. Can't wait." Dora's high-pitched tone rated up there with harmonicas, an instrument that hurt her ears and her nerves unbearably. She hung up, already inhaling the sweet Sinseminna. The night felt endless and the options all less than satisfying. A gnawing discontent, like trying to sleep with sand in the bed, made her squirm in the chair, restless. She shrugged her shoulders and dialed Ivan's number. No answer. She dialed Julia in New York, forgetting it was one in the morning there.

"Hullo," her sleepy voice answered.

"Julia. Did I wake you?" Of course, she knew she had.

"Suzanne. No. Yes. I mean it's okay. What's wrong?"

"Nothing. Nothing really. I just wanted to talk to you."

"Sure. Anything special?"

"No."

"Where are you?"

"In my office."

"Are you all right?"

"Sure. How are you? I was wondering how you are. Do you like New York?"

"I'm fine. The job's going fantastically. I miss London, Colin, but basically all's well. Suzanne, I know you better than this. You don't call me in the middle of the night for no reason. Tell me what's going on."

"I don't know. I'm a little down. Daniel's gone to interview for that job at Harvard. The AIDS thing, I guess. I don't know."

"You sound terrible. Or this is a bad connection? You sound like you're under water."

"I'm stoned. Sorry for mumbling. I just wanted to hear your voice. Go back to bed now. Bye." She hung up before the reply.

The phone was ringing as she left. It had to be Julia, worried, but she'd call her tomorrow. The time wasn't right.

* * *

A few bites of spaghetti, a few lines of coke, back over the bridge, the headlights coming at her in hypnotic bursts. What if? What if? What if she just barely turned the wheel, just enough to lose control of the car. It wouldn't be hard at eighty or ninety miles an hour. Into the bridge, of course. Would the weight of the car crash through the barrier and send her flying into the icy waters of the Bay below? Or would the concrete bounce the car back into traffic, possibly endangering other drivers? How would it feel to go flying off the bridge in the Prelude? It was too light a car; it would bounce back. Only the slightest move. In less than a second she wouldn't be able to turn back. In an instant, she'd be out of control. The palms of her hands were sweaty on the wheel. The wail of Bob Marley was at top volume in the tape player. Her head swam, dizzy from the power she had, the power of life or death, a horrifying power. Julia would really be pissed at her. Dan would be furious. Her parents would be in shock, never in a zillion years expecting such a thing, never understanding. No one would understand. They'd label her a nut case, definitely out of her mind. No. They'd all think it was an accident. Of course. An accident. Traces of coke in her blood, the stash of dope in her office, regrettably under the influence. As soon as she considered the reactions, it was over. "Wake up and live! Yeah! Wake up and live! . . ." Good ole Bob Marley. The Fell Street exit was coming up.

The streets were deserted, but the bar was crowded with women and men all of whom were dressed with meticulous and studied attention to the casual, tossed together look. Since she was casually tossed together, she fit right in. There were more women than men, some dancing with each other, others draped over bar stools, surveying the competition. Her cheeks and nose were glowing from the coke and the chilly night air. Going straight to the ladies' room, she stood in line for the mirror, carefully correcting her make-up, brushing her hair back to show off her high cheek bones. Her fellow mirror users laughed and joked about the shortage of straight men in the city, the never-fail bathroom conversation of San Francisco women. Shoulders shrugged, and sympathetic smiles were exchanged. They didn't resent each other. It was a city full of good sporting women most of whom went home alone night after night, wondering when, if ever, they'd find a warm body of the opposite sex. Some decided to switch. Any warm body was better than none, and besides there were many lovely women. Suzanne found herself contemplating the possibilities while waiting in line. What would it be like? Making love to a woman. Easy. Safe. Too safe.

The bartender recognized her and recited the nightly specials on white wines without asking. "The Pine Ridge Chenin Blanc is the best," he shouted over the roar.

"Great." She was fishing about in her purse for a five when a bill went over her head.

"It's on me," a deep voice insisted.

"Thank you." The bartender winked at her. She turned to see a tall, handsome man with a balding head and grey speckled beard. His rust brown eyes were deep set, and he had the most elegant nose she had ever seen. He wore a tailored suit, more personal than a designer one off the rack. Rich. Jewish. A bachelor. She knew this already because she often attracted them, and they, predictably, ended up falling in love with her too fast, hating her soon thereafter. Not her favorite role: shiksa goddess, but they were sometimes good in bed.

"Will you join me?" He gestured to a coveted table guarded by a friend who stared at her with a shit-eating grin on his face.

"Who's he?" She had no time for an obvious nerd.

"He's leaving."

"My name's Suzanne." His arm went to her elbow; he escorted her like the gentleman he was to his table.

"Jerome Kahn." He put his card in her hand with a slight squeeze.

She read it, the polite thing to do. "A stockbroker? How interesting. I'm terrible with money. You can teach me about it."

His smile was infectious, shy and self-conscious. "Certainly. What do you do?"

"I work in a hospital. Secretarial work, that sort of thing."

"Do you come here often?"

"Oh no, this is my first time. I never go to bars, but . . ."

"Don't apologize. I never go to bars either. My business associate was meeting his girl-friend here, but she never showed up. Lucky for me." He raised his glass to toast their meeting.

She looked around furtively as if she were expecting someone. "I was supposed to meet my girl-friend here, but I guess I'm too late."

"Again my good fortune. I'm a very lucky man, you know."

"I'll bet you are. You must need a lot of luck to be a stockbroker."

He laughed. "Luck, and good friends, connections. Do you mind if I ask your last name?"

"Williams. Suzanne Williams." She smiled back at him as coyly as she could feign.

"A lovely name. I suppose you know you're quite beautiful, Suzanne. You must be all of twenty-five?"

"I wish." Now she was forced to stop her pretenses. He was going to play the "older, experienced man" with her, his maturity a complement to her youth. It was going too far. The coke was wearing off. She knew the bartender would sell her some, but she didn't have enough cash. She studied him. Should she continue this charade or come off it? Would he buy her some coke? No question he could afford it.

"Younger?" His eyebrows rose to suggest he didn't go younger than that, as if he was in danger of committing some crime with her.

"No, silly, I'm thirty-four. I've been teasing you." She hoped he'd find it amusing. "I'm a physician, an immunologist, you know, science?" Hah, hah. "Don't be upset, I find these little games entertaining. I'm sorry." He suddenly looked captivated, not angry, but more interested than ever. "I've been coming here quite a lot lately. The music's good, don't you agree?" Why doesn't he say something. "You must be annoyed that I lied to you. I better go now. All in good fun. Right?"

"Don't you dare leave." He leaned over and took her hand. "You're the most interesting woman I've met lately," he glanced around, "and the best looking one here."

"Interesting" was not her more important quality, just the current catch-all for personality. Twenty-five years ago he might have said "I like your personality," as much a little white lie then as now. "You flatter me. Compliments will get you everywhere."

"Everywhere?"

"Why not? As the song says, 'What did we come here for?'"

"I can't believe you're serious."

"I'm not."

"Do you live around here?"

"No. In the East Bay."

"I live on Russian Hill."

"Nice. It's closer."

"Would you like to dance?" A slow song had come on, and the bar was about to make last calls.

"Sure."

His arm went around her waist, warm and tight. He danced expertly, leading her with confidence, his well-kept body lending her complete security. Tall as she was, she could just rest her head on his shoulder. It was like cuddling up to a big bear and being swirled into a dreamland of soft music, muted light, like dancing with Daddy as a little girl. She loved it. Maybe he was the one?

His breath warmed her face, and he bent over to kiss her neck. She turned her face toward him, responding in kind. "Will you come home with me?" he whispered.

"Yes, but . . ."

"But what?"

"There was something I wanted to get from the bartender. Some . . ." she hesitated. It could ruin the whole evening.

"Some coke," he laughed. "Where do you think he gets it?"

Pushing herself back, she looked at him, asking . . . ?

"I've got enough coke to supply half the city. Come home with me, you crazy lady."

"You talked me into it."

* * *

The panel had been assembled to talk to a small group of representatives from several gay organizations and the press. She was asked to participate along with two other doctors, a sociologist, a psychologist, and a representative from the mayor's office. The gays in the audience were furious. It didn't surprise her, but their questions led only to increased fury. They wanted answers. They wanted a treatment. They wanted to know: Why them? They had fought damn hard out there on the front lines of the sexual revolution. Hadn't they suffered enough? Was there any possibility that this was *given* to them by some Anita Bryant type crackpot, some mentally deranged Dan White, some homophobic CIA men? Clearly the psychologist and the sociologist were more in demand here than she. It was amazing to her how people in general consistently overlooked the impartiality of the elements. Diseases didn't have motives or axes to grind. There were too few facts to report: In sixteen months 634 cases had been reported to the CDC, and there had been 260 deaths. The causes and cures were still elusive. She mentioned pneumocystis carinii, toxoplasmosis, CMV, Epstein-Barr virus, Burkett's lymphoma, herpes simplex type II, hepatitis B. Drug use had been shown to increase statistical chances of getting sick, but this was based on very limited evidence and studies. She cited the very few relevant medical publications and suggested that frequent and many sexual contacts increased one's risk. Simultaneous hostile groans rose from the audience. Will they lynch me? She was flushed with vulnerability and felt inordinately stupid, wishing she had never opened her mouth.

The sociologist jumped in to change the subject, gathering support from the psychologist's nodding head. He said the socio-psychological impact was far greater than the medical reality at this point. This meeting needed to focus on education and prevention. The gay organizations had to publicize where to get information, where to get help. The press had to cooperate, striving to reduce public panic. The mayor's rep insisted the city wanted to do everything possible to prevent more discrimination against gays, but the public was concerned. Parents' groups, restaurant associations, tourist agents, hospital workers, sanitation workers — the city represented all of these constituencies. It was a big problem. A major problem. People were afraid. The gay community had to recognize that; they had to organize their own programs, spread the word. We all had to pitch in; we all had to cooperate; we all had to be as positive as possible about this. Constructive. Be constructive.

"You fucking assholes!" some guy shouted from the back. "My lover's dying right this minute. You motherfucking-asshole-shit-faced-imbeciles, motherfuckers. . .!" His friends dragged him from the room with the help of two security men. "We're all going to die! We're all dyyyinng, dyyyyinng." His screams echoed in the hall, resonated in her head.

Her office was its familiar shambles. She picked up the phone to call Dan who had left three messages for her. "Hi, it's me. What's up?"

"I want to see you tonight. Let's go out to dinner."

"Can't."

"Why not?"

"Have to work late. I wasted my morning at this useless meeting. My cells won't be ready until late, I have to stay here and feed them. I can't ask my tech to stay late again this week."

"How 'bout if I meet you later at your house. We could have a drink?"

"All right. But I'm not talking about moving back East, Dan. Promise me you won't bring it up."

"When can we talk about it? We've got to talk about it, Suzie. I mean eventually we've got to discuss this like rational adults." Exasperation rang over the lines.

"Since when are we rational adults anyway?"

"Suzie!"

"Dan, I have patients waiting in the clinic. I have work waiting in the lab. I have to go be a rational adult, as you say. I've got to go, and if you plan on talking about this tonight, don't bother to come."

"Is our relationship over, Suzanne? I mean, over just like that?"

"Have they offered you the job?"

"Yes. Can't you be happy for me? It's the job I've worked for all my life. Can't you celebrate with me?"

"I am happy for you. Congratulations. We will celebrate. But I'm not going with you, and I've got to go now. Bye."

She unlocked her special drawer and popped two Lorazepam. The tears were going to come anyway. Big deal. He's leaving. Good riddance. I don't give a shit. I don't give a damn. I hate him. The tears were driven away, the unwanted drops of a fool. She swore she'd never cry about it. Plenty of fish in the sea, Mother used to say. Plenty of fish in the sea.

There on her desk were messages from Brian in psychiatry, from Jerome, an old one from Ivan's blond friend. They went ripped together into the waste basket. Her beeper went off, and she was lost again in a series of consults, patients, rounds, lab work, her hectic routine, her saving grace.

As she drove home, earlier than she'd anticipated and stoned as usual, welcome thoughts of mundane, domestic chores floated through her mind. The plants needed watering, the cat was due for her feline leukemia shot, there were a few buttons to sew on, and the damn frostfree refrigerator had to be defrosted. Weeks had passed since she had written any letters, and her journal sat on the night table beside her bed, untouched since the spring. Glorious October weather with crystal clear blue skies, warm temperatures and fogless sunsets. How had she neglected her favorite time of year, her favorite month? In the rear view mirror she saw the sun, an orange ball of fire low on the horizon. Pt. Reyes, her beach. She was due for a day off, a day of lazing about on the rocks, writing in her journal, reading a good novel. What in the hell had happened to Ivan? He was the only person she knew who had MDA. Call Janet. She put that on her mental list. A day at the beach, some MDA. It made her feel there was something to look forward to.

The phone was ringing as she fumbled with the lock. A long box tied with red ribbon and a bottle of Dom Perignon sat on her doorstep. Racing, she answered with an out of breath choke, "Yeah."

Silence. About to hang up she heard his low voice, brimming with excitement. "Did you see the paper? Did you see the paper today?"

At first she didn't recognize the voice. "What?"

"Did you just get home?" Sensing her disorientation. "This is Jerome."

"Uh, Hi. Yes, let me catch my breath. Just walked in the door." Her phone cord stretched back to the door where she picked up the bottle of champagne and the box of two dozen long stem red roses. "Did you . . . ?"

"You obviously haven't read the headlines. The stock market hit the second highest volume in history today, over the 1000 mark. I hit it big, Suzanne. Really big. And it's all legit."

"That's wonderful. Fantastic. So you're very rich today, not just a little rich like the last time I saw you," she teased.

"Can I come over and drink it with you? Are the flowers nice?"

"Gorgeous. Beautiful. You shouldn't have, Jerome."

"Our night last week, I hope you realize what it meant to me. You must know I want to see you again." A naked plea, he was laying his cards on the table, his favorite expression.

"Jerome," she hated to say no, he seemed so innocent for a middle-aged man, "we will get together. Soon. But I can't tonight. I'm committed to dinner, with a friend." She added, "I'll save the champagne." This was going to be a sticky mess. She made faces at the cat. I'll give it back, she reasoned to herself. He was so nice, so rich, so available. But not at all good in bed. She couldn't tell him that. She wasn't that cruel, and he was very unaware. Some men, she supposed, were not acquainted with the female orgasm. How could they be expected to recognize its absence?

"Can't you break it? This is special. My treat. Anywhere. The Elite Cafe, The 4th Street Grill, Chez Panisse, that new Japanese place in the city, you name it."

"I can't, really. My friend's only in town one night. I promised her." Lying was much easier than telling the truth, not to mention kinder.

"Are you going to break my heart?"

"Now, don't start using lines from old movies on me. I watch the late shows too, you know."

"You mean you're not susceptible to Jewish guilt?"

"No. Only Baptist hellfire and damnation."

"I'm not that kind of man."

"I know. Look. I, well, you're a sweetheart. Thanks for the flowers. We'll be in touch, okay."

"I've got something else for you."

By this time she had wrapped herself in the telephone cord from head to foot. He had promised her an ounce of coke, uncut, free. The shipment must have arrived. There was no resisting this, bad sex or not. "How about tomorrow night? A rain check till tomorrow?"

"I may have to go out of town tomorrow. The firm wants me in Houston. I'll be gone two weeks."

Two weeks, Christ! She really wanted that coke. His true colors were showing; he was stubborn, determined. His business success was no longer any mystery. He got what he wanted when he wanted it. Money talks. Everyone had their price. Their weakness. Hers certainly wasn't hard to figure out. Now he felt less an emotional underling and more an equal to reckon with. Ah, the old-fashioned battle of the sexes; her indifference would come in handy later. "All right. I'll try to reach my friend. But let's not get together over here. I'll meet you at your place. In an hour?"

"I can't wait to see you."

Daniel got a note on the door: *Emergency. Had to go back to work. Call you tomorrow.*

*   *   *

Armed with five grams of coke, ten joints, a bottle of Valium and a case of Perrier, they set out to drive up the coast road to Mendecino. Dan made reservations at the Albion River Inn. She had agreed to discuss the situation with him, including the move back East, marriage, the whole bit. It was the least she could do before he left. Being together — now tranformed by his impending departure into an intolerable, dutiful chore — was in any case a state she had lost contact with; being alone was the constant. The dawn broke into a soft tangerine light, a stripe of grey fog across the city. The tops of buildings stuck out over the clouds, a city built in the sky. There was almost no traffic heading up highway 17 toward

149

Pinole. They both sipped their large espressos and tried to wake up. He was driving for a change, and she enjoyed the freedom to drift into the scenery, to forget everything remotely concerned with medicine or AIDS. Why couldn't they be together like this, on their way to Mendecino for the rest of their lives?

What an impossible question. And she wasn't going to ask it. "Is it too early to smoke a joint?"

"Yes, but let's do a little of the coke. Get things moving."

"How can we do it in the car?"

"Just get out the mirror and cut it up. I got some straws from the coffee shop. I can snort while I drive. I breathe while I drive, don't I?"

"You are really funny, Daniel. I wish to God I understood you. How can someone so straight, a future Harvard professor no less, snort coke while driving at six in the morning? I'm sure there's a contradiction there."

"Don't underestimate me, my dear. I mean, the Russians discovered contradictions."

"That is absurd. Which Russians?"

"Lots. Mayakovsky, for instance."

"How could he 'discover' a concept that historically preceded him? You literature types really think metaphysically, ahistorically, I ought to say."

"You scientific types are linear in the extreme. History doesn't even begin for you until the unfortunate discovery of the scientific method. I said, 'for instance.' Since I have to spell it out for you, I was using the term 'discovery' in the sense of finding out, knowing, and knowing that you know, like Dostoevsky in *Notes from the Underground*."

"If that's what you mean, there are plenty of French, English, Japanese, African, Indian, et cetera, et cetera, discoverers of contradiction." She had chopped the coke into a fine powder and separated it into four lines. She cut the straw with the scissors in her Swiss army knife and swooped up her lines. After a sniffling silence, she asked, "What in the hell are we talking about?"

She held the mirror for him while he did his lines.

"Contradiction." He let out a breath.

"Didn't Mayakovsky kill himself?"

"Yeah. Shot himself after being jilted in love."

"How old was he?"

"Thirty-six, I think. Esenin's even more romantic."

"Who's he?"

"Another Russian poet. Hung himself. Thirty years old. He wanted to be famous.

'I greet everything, I accept everything,
I am glad and happy to abandon my soul.
I have come on this earth
To leave it soon.'
Not bad, eh?"

"Why'd they do it?"

"Why do you think? Why does anyone kill himself? Fed up, I guess. They knew each other. Mayakovsky wrote after Esenin's death: 'To die — in life is not so hard. To make life — harder by far.' "

"That's beautiful. I should read these guys. Can you imagine killing yourself, Dan?"

"No. I can't. Hey, let's talk about something else."

"I can. I can imagine it."

"I don't think you can or could. What would be the point? Don't be silly. You're just provoking me."

"What would you do if I did?"

"I'd kill you," he joked.

"In a few months you won't be around to stop me."

"You won't be around either because you're coming with me."

"Let's not get into a fight about it. You said we'd discuss it like rational adults. I never said I'd go. In fact, I always said I would never go. Why don't we just face it. Our relationship is going to end when you leave. I don't believe in long distance relationships. I've tried it, and it doesn't work."

"A year ago you wanted a commitment, remember? You wanted to settle down with one person and struggle through everyday bullshit like normal people do, remember?"

"If you say 'normal people' one more time I think I'll throw up."

"All right, all right then, I want you to tell me, do you love me or not? Because I love you, and I've been under this delusion that you loved me. You say you do anyway."

"I'm a notorious liar." Her tone wasn't serious. "Actually, I think I do love you. I think I do. But I'm not moving to Boston. If you loved me, then you'd stay here. Why's your career more important than mine?"

"You can work anywhere! You're a doctor. I'm an academic. I don't have that luxury. I have to take what I can get."

"I wouldn't call Harvard 'taking what you can get.' They wouldn't like that."

"Well, what are we going to do? I love you; you say you love me. I've got a job at Harvard; you've got a job here. Someone's got to give," and it wasn't going to be him, but he didn't dare say it.

"You give then." It wasn't going to be her either.

"You're not being rational. You're not being fair. You're not listening to me!" She was raising his blood pressure.

"I could say the same to you." The madder he got, the calmer she acted.

"Okay. All right. Suppose I stay here. What then? Will we get married? What will I do when this fellowship ends at Berkeley? There are thousands of Ph.D.'s in Russian literature here. Will you support me?"

"Thousands. That's an exaggeration, Daniel." Her hands were trembling, and the anxiety made her freeze all over. He had hit the nail on the head. Was she prepared to marry him? Wasn't his eventual departure part of their negotiations from the start? Had any of that romantic talk been more than talk on her part? The idea of a permanent commitment scared her more than death despite the many nights she longed for it, dreamt of it. In the mornings it was gone and thank goodness. Her life was finally under her control, at least in the mornings. She locked the door to her own house behind her and went into the world a free woman with her own money, her own career, her own problems. As Ivan said, she'd been married, she'd tried love. How would she cope if another one ended in divorce, in bitterness, in years of getting over it? "I'll be honest, Dan. I don't think I can marry you anyway. I don't think I can make that commitment. I've done it before. You know that. It took me six years to get over one divorce. Six years. Never, never could I survive that again."

"But it won't be that way with us, Suzie. He was certifiable. You were young. Your life is different now. I thought you worked all that out in your analysis? Anyway, we're already committed to each other. We keep going on, don't we? It was wonderful living together this summer."

"But I'm not sure, I'm not absolutely certain, Dan. As long as there's a doubt I can't give up my job, sell my house, and ride off into the sunset with you. We can still visit, I suppose. Be friends."

"Be friends! That's insane. Idiotic. I don't want to be your friend. I want to be your husband, your lover, your *only* lover. Isn't AIDS the best argument for monogamy yet?"

"It depends. Anyway, nothing's changing. There have been 110 cases in the city, thirty-five deaths. All the researchers I know think the cause will turn out to be a sexually transmitted virus carried in the blood. I mean it's obvious already. But the gay bars in the Castro and the Tenderloin are packed wall-to-wall with men looking for someone new. Did you read what Hardman, the publisher of *The Voice,* said? 'Look at the Eighth and Howard Clubs; they're booming.' He doesn't think anybody is changing to any extent. You've been there; you've seen it. So, if they don't think it's a good argument for monogamy, why should I?"

"Because you know more about it. The worse it gets the more they'll change. Most of them will, I bet. The others, well, some people are hopelessly self-destructive. And you're not one of them. You wouldn't be where you are today if you were, so don't give me any psychobabble rigmarole about the joy of suffering." He put his hand on her thigh. "I've never known any woman who was as hell bent on living, enjoying life, feeling good. Much as you try to hide it, you're one of the lucky ones; you love fun, pleasure."

"I do. But. . . ." He didn't really understand her, but the truth was too futile to talk about. It was beside the point now. She put in a tape and gazed out at Tomales Bay, a haven of peace, the home of herons and ramshackle houses that sat lost in time. The cliffs were coming up soon, the end of the Bay where the ocean crashed into the land, transforming the tranquillity into excitement, action. "It's a perfect day, a beautiful day. Let's change the subject for a while, okay?" She lit a joint to mellow out from the jangled come down of the coke. They smiled at each other, singing along with the *Talking Heads*, "psycho killer, qu'est que c'est, fa, fa, fa, fa-fa, fa-fa, fa, fa, fa."

The dope worked fast. "Dan, why is it that we only talk when we get in the car and drive?"

"I don't know. There aren't as many distractions maybe. This is California. I spent my whole adolescence in a car, driving somewhere. I guess I learned how to communicate in a car. When I'm not behind the wheel, my mind just zaps into the work zone. All my early relationships were carried on in a car."

"Now that you mention it, a lot of mine were too. But does that mean we have some kind of car relationship? I mean, if we lived in a car we could get married? Nice and cozy. Never out of each other's sight."

"You think those people who live in mobile homes know something we don't?"

"Oh God, I could never live in a mobile home. God, the very thought of it petrifies me. It reminds me of being poor white trash. I had relatives who lived in mobile homes. It was humiliating. No, I'd rather live in a Mercedes 450SL."

"No, I've got it! A checker station wagon. Those were great cars."

"Did you know I once had a VW van?"

"Didn't everyone? In the sixties, right? And real long straight hair? You wore cut off jeans and buttons all over your workshirt. I bet you were incredibly cute."

"I did have a workshirt. With a big yellow sun painted on the back. God, I loved that shirt. I wore it until it literally fell into pieces. Then I carried it around for years."

"Did you have a leather jacket with fringes on it?"

"No, couldn't afford one."

"I had a long velvet cape, midnight blue, lined in red silk. My mother got hysterical thinking that I was a homosexual. That's why I wore it, especially around the house. It drove her crazy."

"The good ole days."

The car was warm with laughter, the past buying the present.

*　*　*

Daily the AIDS crisis grew. The organizers of the conference at U.C.S.F. were surprised at the turnout. The Kaposi's clinic at General was in full swing. Money was essential, and she was asked to be a co-investigator on a grant proposal to the National Cancer Institute. Cases were now being reported from Europe and Australia. The public demanded to know more. A hastily organized free forum was held at Roland Hall. Standing room only. *Urgent Meeting on Disease That Hits Gays.* Average survival time was now being calculated – dismal figures – months not years. Heterosexuals and women were falling victim too, in small, but alarming percentages. The mayor had proposed spending $293,000 for research and treatment. The handwriting was on the wall: San Francisco was in for IT, an epidemic, but nobody had the nerve to use the term. Yet.

The more the public knew, the more they reacted. As expected. Fear. The sanitation workers were photographed dressed in space suits collecting litter from a gay rally, covered from head to foot, decked out for germ warfare. Laboratory technicians given to jokes about blood born contagions joked a lot less. They got serious, had meetings, threatened to stike, demanded precautions. No group was more in favor of precautions than the doctors themselves, but what kind of precautions? How many precautions? Would these dying young men be shut off from human contact in the last weeks of their lives? How humane was it to isolate them completely? Was it *medically* necessary? The days when medical science might masquerade as objective and neutral were, to say the least, numbered. The calendars loomed on office walls, enemies and prophets of future misery, death. Days were numbered. Emotion overwhelmed an entire city. Dinner party conversation was interminably the same. War was declared. A war waged against an invisible adversary; war with nothing but death statistics; war in which the most a doctor could do was attend symposia, conferences, bedsides, and then admit defeat. The deaths would continue. The battles would go on.

Nightmares, early morning waking, trouble getting to sleep afflicted more than the victims of this wasting disease. Suzanne didn't have to watch it on T.V. — the weeping doctors, nurses, even administrators. It was sickening to see these torturous deaths of people she liked. To see them over and over as they went from better to worse on that roller coaster that runs off the track, to watch their hopes raised by remissions, to suffer their despair when they returned to the hospital; it wasn't an easy or pretty job. Parents, friends, lovers waited, steeling themselves against the ugly stigma; they asked her questions that had no answers, said goodbye too many times. People stopped saying, "It could never happen to me," when shocked and surprised, they learned that someone they never dreamed could perish, friend or foe, had IT.

In spite of sixteen hour days, she volunteered on one of the new AIDS information hotlines. An ounce of coke goes a long way, and she chose to spend her nights writing pamphlets on where to get help for AIDS or ARC, sitting with confused and stunned relatives, and reading backlogs of ariticles on rare fungal infections, parasites, histories of blood banks, public health policies. She even played French tapes while she dozed, hoping to learn the language by osmosis, certain it would come in handy and anxious to read any new studies. There was no time to lose, no time to fool around. And as she suspected, by mid-December it was realized that the incubation period for this disease could be long, years maybe. Who remembered or knew every lover, every lover's lover, every lover's lover's lover for years back? For how many years: two? five? ten? The lies that had been told, the deceptions designed to avoid hurt feelings. Surely she wasn't the only one?

Everyone was a detective, an amateur Sherlock Holmes. The startling illness of a baby, the tracing of the blood donor — healthy at the time, but sick seven months later and dead within a year — raised new questions about blood transfusions, about risk factors, about latency and incubation periods. Some diehards were admitting that this baby probably wasn't a homosexual. The CDC, with its 800 cases reported and its 40% mortality rate, knew already there was an indeterminate number of walking time bombs, human death carriers out there, feeling fine, unsuspecting. But what of the rest of the country, the Midwest, the South, the seat of government? Silence. As caught up in it as those in a hurricane, they could not believe that the vast majority of the population saw the "gay disease" as no threat to them. The unmentionable remained unmentioned. It was too loaded for politicians. If it can't hurt US why worry? A tidy, irresistible illusion: US and THEM. How neat, how efficient a division of the human race; it protected US from all manner of THEIR evil sins. Grist for the mill of the homophobics who, time would tell, outnumbered the gays in their closets.

On the weekends and sometimes several nights a week she drove to the Castro. Selecting different locations she parked. She surveyed the men going in and out of the bars, the bathhouses, the restaurants, the Haagen-Dazs ice cream store. There were no less of them. They didn't look particularly unhappy, sick, or worried. She observed the scene time after time, no longer trying to understand it, no longer wondering, no longer asking herself questions. She simply wanted to watch. The fact that life went on, continued as it had one day to the next, did not seem strange to her anymore; it seemed ordinary, nothing more. Truth. Forces of destiny. Death bargained hard, but that was nothing new. The more she went and watched, the more the actual world — the activity before her scientific eyes — became a mere abstraction, ultimately lost in abstractions. The meaning of life or death? There is no meaning. Desire, pleasure, sex, love — all inextricably linked to death. The choice of solitude, celibacy, monastic retreat — well, that was reserved for those rare few saints, martyrs and Zen masters whom she wasn't so sure of in the first place. Metaphysics, what a wonderful escape into ideas, the speculative, the mind, the unknown, the eternal questions with no answers, all that which she renounced in favor of science. It returned to clothe her in psychic combat gear.

She sat in her car on Castro Street near Market drinking a large steaming cup of coffee. These evenings in her car had become her favorite times of solitude. Time to watch and think without beepers going off, phones ringing, or her name blaring over the intercom. She thought about the young men walking by her, and she thought about herself. Why had she gone into medicine? A question she hadn't raised in several years; somehow it seemed important to understand it now. Was that decision a mistake?

It was long ago when I was twenty-one, making that choice. Everyone was surprised that I even applied.

The words of her favorite philosophy professor rattled skeletons from those many years past. She had bounced into his office to tell him she had gotten into medical school, a real feat with a major in philosophy. Justification seemed necessary, and she carried on about how she needed a career she could count on, meaning: one in which she could count the money. Life had taught her one truth that philosophy neglected: money was indispensible. Ironic, paradoxical, contradictory — she didn't care. She'd been impoverished, and it didn't agree with her. This was the logical extension of her politics anyway: nobody should have to be poor, herself included. His good-natured frown disturbed her. Yes, she admitted she had loved the study of philosophy, art, literature, history. She wanted to dance, to act, to paint. The humanities were her true loves, and she had excelled in them. But. But. But. She couldn't ignore certain facts and trusted them more than any faith in ideas, more than what she would have wished to do in some other world, some better world. She was female, she had no fallbacks like connections or a monied family, her political views were hopelessly unpopular, and she doubted her ability to get along in an academic profession. The economic insecurity of every art form was intolerable. Besides, she questioned her talent. Anyway, these were perfect hobbies. Medicine was success; it was a daily dose of regular contact with people in a social relationship that suited her, one in which she was the authority. More important, it would give her the security of science, cause and effect, manageable truths and an income.

"What fabulous rationalizations! You are wasting your talents, your preferences, four years of study, honors and awards, a full fellowship for your Ph.D. for a tolerable exercise of the brain. It is the other way round, dear Suzanne. Anyone can do science, medicine, but not everyone can create. The time will come when you'll regret this decision. Although your insecurity may not abate, it's not money that will comfort you. You'll have it, and you'll see the old cliché is true, money does not buy happiness, not for someone like you, a thinking person, a creative person. Money is a representation of something else, something you can't speak of yet. You cannot buy authority. Power yes, but it won't eliminate your fears. Self-hatred runs deep as the underground seas." He laughed his Santa Claus, Ho, Ho, Ho laugh that always made her feel two years old. "I have more faith in you than you, yourself. You will come full circle; you will embrace in the future what you reject today."

How dare he say this to me, she winced. How could he? It didn't make sense at all. Her best professor, whom she idolized, sounded like her mother, full of riddles. "But I don't want to THINK all the time about philosophies. I'm not talented enough to be a professional dancer or actress. I have to DO something worthwhile. Anybody can teach or do social work. I want a challenge, problems to solve. I want to see people get better because I gave them the right medicine or made the right diagnosis. I want to work in a field in which it's at least possible to be right sometimes. It doesn't mean I'll stop reading or dancing or dabbling with my paints. It means I'll be able to answer questions, act on proven knowledge, do research that gets results, make a contribution. I'll get rewarded for doing it well. Doctors make money because they get results that people are willing to pay for. Look at you! You've been teaching thirty years, and you make less than a doctor's starting salary! You barely have any furniture in your house!" She was at a loss for any more argumentative fuel and aware of how absurd her speech was becoming.

His bright blue eyes twinkled within his gray bearded and wrinkled face. He loved her spunk. "Yes, furniture is an existential necessity, and you shall have it. Ah, to be young and idealistic again, to be self-righteously impervious to reason. I'm so glad I don't have your choices, my dear. It's not easy to be a young woman with a mind like yours. The sixties, with all its glories and defeats, disillusioned your generation to an extent we have not yet begun to discover. You won't be alone in medical school."

He had said it in 1970. She believed it now. They had lost contact in the years that followed. Medical school: read, study, class, eat, read, study, class, little sleep, and more of the same. The loans, unbelievable sums she had borrowed and was still paying back. Mortgaging her future until failure was impossible. Her economic gains did not yield anything like the dollar signs that registered in her eyes when she read her acceptance letter. True, she had enough money to feel secure, but at what sacrifices? The cost of living kept going up. Her personal life fell apart around her, and she had no time to worry about it. *Your husband left you? He's institutionalized? Wow! That's too bad. Gotta rush.* Personal life isn't meant to exist for medical students or interns. Bodies in beds were no more than their diseases. There were too many of them. Her mice were as human as the patients, and everyone knew that patients weren't people. Steel yourself. You can't even begin to get through anatomy class without it: cutting up a corpse. The first time she felt a kind of amnesia, an out of body experience. It wasn't actually HER cutting open this gut, removing these eyeballs, stripping the skin from these fingers. It was a future DOCTOR. A woman who could take it. A woman who would make it.

So that's when the detachment first began. Hummm. Maybe I should have joined a monastery.

The car was freezing and the fog so thick there was no one to be seen. She shivered inside her down jacket and put on her mittens. Past midnight anyway, time to go home.

The bridge was deserted. Christmas was a week away. Tomorrow she had to do some shopping. This year she volunteered to work Christmas Eve and Christmas Day. It saved spending the holiday by herself, the most depressing experience she could conceive of at the moment. Daniel was going to the Carribbean with Clara, she suspected. Julia left for her holiday in London where her boy-friend's family put on an old-fashioned fest and sat in front of the telly for a week. A young resident and his wife who just had their second baby invited her to Christmas dinner. They felt sorry for her, alone at this time of the year — she could tell by the way he stammered out the invitation, adding the disclaimer that, of course, she probably had plans already. She declined with thanks, so far removed from the appropriate spirit that she didn't want to cast a pall on their day. Most of her other friends were Jewish and off to exotic parts of the world where they waited out this week of crowded shops and traffic jams.

Her parents no longer mentioned the holidays after too many unfortunate scenes over her atheism. Wouldn't she just go to Christmas Eve services to please her grandmother? No. Her mother still sent her a nice Hallmark card and flowery feminine gift. Usually something she never bought for herself — fancy silk lingerie in purple or red, pearls, silver or gold jewelry. Imagine that, she thought, Mom reminding me of the joys of being a woman.

She preferred working at the hospital, eating over-cooked turkey and dry stuffing in the house staff lounge while watching T.V. It made the whole miserable affair pass faster. Besides, there was the uplifting experience of seeing the families of her patients go to great lengths to make their loved ones' Christmas festive and memorable. It could be their last.

*　*　*

part three

reality

THE RAIN SHOWED NO SIGN of abating. It had gone on all night, drenching everything thoroughly. The cave, four or five feet deep at most, gave him little protection. In soaking wet clothes with no possibility of a fire he sat hunched into a ball, snarling at the elements. The waves threatened to reach over the entire cove. White spikey feathers of foam rushed right up to his small patch of sand, wetting his feet until he felt the water squishing between his toes and smelled the wet shoe leather. Waking in the early hours before dawn, the visibility nil, he considered hiking back to the car for shelter but found the ocean blocking his exit. The water had risen high on the rocks to his right, the waves crashing into the cliffs with a killer slam. So be it. There was no escape, no leaving this tiny cave. Fine. Maybe he would drown. Fine.

The journal, his cigarettes and matches were wrapped in the nylon pack and kept in the farthest reaches of the cave. It was wet there, the sand absorbing the water like a giant sponge, but he checked, and they were still dry. If he had cared a damn about being alive, if he weren't completely numb, he might have been freezing, perhaps afraid. The tide rising a foot more meant swimming out which was impossible in the tumultuous storm, the fog, and the invisible rocks. The Pacific, notoriously cold, would gobble him up as it had her. But he felt nothing now, not cold, not fear. What he had achieved with no actual effort of his own was a state of psychic limbo. Out of this state came agonizing explosions, moments of anguish beyond his comprehension, a raging anger he'd never known. During the periods of numbness, his mind functioned like a computer propelled on by an inconsolable need to know the details of her demise. Information was fed in, analyzed, computed, results printed out on a continuous scroll of white paper that moved in his mind from left to right The data base was not very reliable — literally all wet — but he was determined to keep reading. In the end . . . the end of what? Never mind. He had to have an answer. Her journal, this opaque now weathered document, put away when the storm began, was not just a book. It was a place as real as their cove and in it she lived. He wanted to preserve this place, her life, until *he* decided to let go and leave her. He wrested this control from her as though he struggled with the devil himself. There, he told himself, I must finish it off. This storm will finish me, or I will finish it.

What had he discovered? While waiting for the rain to subside he mulled it over. She wrote that she loved him. She loved him. Why did this make it worse, more horrific, less understandable? If she had been falling in love with him as she wrote on September 8, why did she kill herself? Does someone falling in love kill herself? Her holiday in England, how much better he felt to read that her relationship with Daniel wasn't working out over a year ago. When she had talked of Dan, with such ambivalence, such tenderness, even regret, it had caused him grief, but not very much. He was going to give her everything Daniel hadn't. There would have been nothing missing, no depressions, no sleepless nights, no anxieties or fear. His love would have healed. He would have brought her chicken soup and fussed over her when she was sick. He would have taken her with him to conferences or not have gone. He would have . . . What is the point of this? He still would. She wasn't dead. She was not dead. There was no evidence, nothing to indicate suicide.

There was the unexplainable loneliness, disappointment, unrealistic fear that she wrote about, that she wondered about. But not with Julia. She adored Julia, her best friend. They had happy, light-hearted times together. Does someone with a friend like that kill herself? What about her dreams? Sharks in the water, it was okay to touch them? Julia taking her to a plane that was going to crash, rejecting her in a song? And the anger about her flu? It was only a common cold, but she was very upset that Dan didn't pamper her. She wanted to be dependent, and she wanted to be left alone? She was always ambivalent; she had a tendency to exaggerate. The journal was written coherently like any diary, a record of what she did this or that day, what she felt, not many surprises or shameful secrets hidden there. But he hadn't gotten very far, he reminded himself. He had reached a couple of blank pages just before the storm, and his desire not to finish it, to save it, savor it — this last bit of her — gave him an excuse to stop.

Bits of red clay and pebbles were falling from the cliff, and a stream of water, steady and growing, came down a foot from his face. His shoes were covered with debris and the pieces of rock hitting his legs made him consider that the cave in which he sat could collapse at any moment. He stepped out into the rain, the waves swarming around his ankles. Through the fog which was a bit thinner, he saw the outline of the big rock. It was faint, only two hundred yards away. The tiny outlet was merged into the rock on one side and the cliff on the other. Water gushed through the channel, several feet over his head. There was still no getting out. With calculated and strenuous swimming he might take refuge on the big rock. That is, if the violent waves didn't crush him on his way. They were breaking in random patterns on the shore and as far out as he could see. He would never make it trying to preserve the journal in the pack. A thunderous roar sounded right over his head. Instinct made him throw his arms up for protection, but nothing fell. A moment later he thought he saw a huge metal object hanging from the sky. A helicopter. They know I'm here. He jumped back into the cave and tried to hide. He didn't want to be saved. After some time the sound went away. Somehow he managed to light a cigarette. It was an hallucination. Thunder perhaps. Wallensky? He was here, was it yesterday? The day before? He knows I'm here. She wrote about him, at the end when his eyelids were being pulled over his eyes by fatigue. What had she written? He couldn't remember, and anger came burning back, searing into his head. He drifted into semi-consciousness through tears and curses. How selective is memory?

They were driving along the Russian River, tipsy from visits to four wineries. The road was horrible, potted and narrow with branches fallen here and there. She was rolling a joint and singing along with Joan Baez at the top of her lungs. Her voice was funny, soft and terribly off-key. Singing was definitely not one of her many talents, he teased her. Then he sang too so they could both laugh at their equal ineptness. It was a hot Saturday only four days after their return from Mexico. Neither of them wanted to go back to work, to the gloom of AIDS, the new admissions, the endless piles of charts, questions, relatives, despair. They agreed not to talk about it after work or on weekends, but they thought about it. Separately. Silently. In four short days Mexico had dissipated, a sweet dream forgotten. She had an awful cold, staggered around the lab in exhaustion, coughing too much. Somehow she'd managed to lose four pounds over that weekend. Never too thin or too rich, she chuckled, delighted by the scale. She took a hit off the joint and began to cough violently.

"Hey," he patted her on the back. "You shouldn't be smoking with that cold. We've both got to stop smoking cigarettes."

She handed him the joint, choking, coughing, nodding in agreement.

He took a hit. His head swirled immediately. The desire to smoke a cigarette now lodged in his head. He wouldn't be able to think of anything else until he had one. What a goddamn annoyance. "How long till we reach the coast road?"

Still catching her breath, she took another drag off the joint. The second one always goes down more easily. "About twenty miles, I think." In spite of ill health and too much work she had insisted they drive up the coast for the weekend. There was another special beach – the sculpture beach she called it – he had to see it. No one was ever there. They could lie naked amongst the driftwood. They could make love in the sand. There was this fantastic place she knew to stay, cabins with a Japanese outdoor bath. A friend had given her some psilicybin mushrooms. They would chew them and travel together to new worlds, other universes.

His subtly-made, reasonable suggestion that they put this off a few weeks was greeted with incomprehensible rejection. She was adamant that they do everything now. Any free hour, any free day had to be filled with an adventure. Let's just have fun, fun and more fun, she confronted his every sensible hesitation. He told her she was a whirlwind, a tornado that swept him off the ground, tossed him around and down, and then came back to get him again. Even though his reason told him otherwise, he went merrily along. Reluctant at first to put aside his obligations or make use of the many favors he was owed, he found himself, within hours of their escape from the hospital and the city, delighted she had insisted on having her way. How many times in a lifetime does one fall in love like this? He was totalled, convinced, captivated. She said it was the beach, the ocean, the drugs; he knew it was her.

He even wondered – why her? True, she was pretty, smart and full of lust for adventure, but she was also stubborn, unreasonable, moody, and made him miserable in a way that Pat never did. None of this mattered though; he had no choice. Love doesn't give one choices. He was learning it the hard way. But it was bringing back parts of him long lost to the demands of his work.

His boyhood obsession with cataloging trees, flowers, rocks came back to entertain them both. He had forgotten how much he knew about plants, birds, geology. His old binoculars, dug out of the trunk in his basement, were fought over. The truce negotiated was that he would look first to tell her what it was, then she would gaze at the bird as intent as if it were the last bird she'd ever see. How amazing, how cute, how unusual, he'd thought. She really does love to look at birds, rocks, animals. But she was different. Unlike any woman he'd known in this respect, she was not content to simply look. She pried deeply into the world as though every particle of it contained the mystery of life and time. Her questions were endless and needled him at times. He had to remind her sometimes that he wasn't the great reservoir of general knowledge that she imagined. On the other hand, he wanted to give her an answer to every question; he wanted her to think he was the smartest man on earth.

What wonderful, long evenings they had spent reminiscing about their past interests, the ravages of years in medical school and the dulling of aesthetic sensibilities. She told him that she majored in philosophy as an undergradute, that she danced professionally for three years, that she secretly wanted to be an actress, that she drew and painted in her spare time. If she had any spare time now, she'd study sculpture or art history. He told her about his ambitious study of geology, his teenage decision to become a furniture maker, his avid passion for science fiction, and his years of playing saxaphone in a jazz band. He hadn't talked about these interests, his past or life before medicine in years. Every minute erupted with fresh commonalities, nourishment for the future. At least, as far as he was concerned. He thought, we're perfect for each other. Life works out just the way it's supposed to — I waited for the right woman to marry and here she is. He never thought, this is too good to be true.

Did she know even then? That very beautiful Saturday on which they would travel the cosmos together, that perfect evening in which he had read to her without pause T.S. Eliot's *Wasteland*. Had she planned to leave him already? Was she plotting her death as he, ignorant and blissful, read the poetry of her choice to her. Her urgency to do it all now. Then. Impossible.

"You're getting too skinny," he said while they sat in the outdoor Japanese bath with drizzling rain and the gray foggy night around them.

"It's the mushrooms; they've distorted your vision." The water cupped in her hand flew into his face. "Don't you find me sexy anymore?"

He wrestled her under the water. "I'll show you how sexy I find you." The soft flesh of her body, softened further by the drug became voluptuous through suggestion. "What's this bruise on your arm?" He noticed it in the tussle, but he hadn't the guts to say needlemarks, and there were definitely needlemarks.

"Oh, the needlemarks. I've been using my own blood as a control for the T-4/ T-8 study. I bruise easily. I could use some of yours actually. I need more controls. But no shop talk here, you promised."

Of course, he thought, all researchers do that. He was ashamed at how relieved he was and wondered how paranoid his work with AIDS patients had made him. "Sure." She covered his mouth with hers and then they were gone.

After they made love more than once, and after he finished reading to her, they had fallen asleep. He awoke in the early morning to find her fully dressed, staring out the window into a thick fog with that impenetrable expression. There *was* something wrong. He went back to sleep, and when he woke up again, she had made the most enormous breakfast of sausages and eggs, hash brown potatoes, sliced tomatoes, whole wheat toast, and a pot of steaming black coffee. They feasted until he thought his stomach would burst, and to his pleased disbelief, she ate as much as he.

Was it then she told him she was going back East on the following Tuesday? She was going to see Julia for some garbled, mysterious reason. He knew she was going to see Daniel, instinctively he knew. Why? He had tried to be fair, to be calm. No lies. He just wanted to know why she was going to see Daniel. "Don't be so suspicious and ridiculous," she insisted. "I'm going to see Julia." Stony silence dominated their morning. She smoked two joints, then admitted she might see Daniel but only for dinner or lunch. It was primarily Julia she had to visit. She'd be gone only two days, and he could have his obligatory talk with Pat. Get that out of the way. "Trust me." And he did. Or he sort of did. He wasn't worried in the long run. Dan was 3,000 miles away; he was here. But jealousy, a most unpleasant, unfamiliar emotion ruined the rest of their day. He needled her for more reasons, the timing, where she would stay, where she would sleep until she refused to talk to him at all. They drove four hours back to the city, without a word spoken.

When he looked up again, the rain had stopped. The gray sky still surrounded him, a steaming smoke, but the tide had begun to recede, and some beach was visible to his right. The rust, red and ochre sandstone rings in the cliffs were highlighted by weak rays from the sun. The channel to the larger beach and the trail beyond was impassable, but a new assortment of driftwood was strewn about the beach in the waning waves. The sickening, grotesque idea that her body might have washed up in the storm made him instantly vomit. With dread and loathing, he glanced around. Nothing. Could he fully believe she was dead until he saw her?

Before long he could assemble wood for a fire, dry out his clothes, and contemplate another trip into Inverness for supplies. His stomach rumbled, loud and angry. A cold sweat broke out over his body and with no warning, he fainted and fell on his face. He had never fainted in his life, and although he didn't completely lose consciousness, he recognized the imperative of the physical; he had to get food and drink. It felt strange to have any will to take care of himself, to bow to necessity, or to give up on his obsession here. As the rage welled up, he pushed it down. No more memories now, he pleaded with his ragged self, as if his body and mind were on the brink of forever splitting in two.

February 10, 1983

It's been so long since I wrote to myself. A year almost. What's happening? Dan finally admitted he met Clara in the Carribbean. They slept together. I shouldn't care, but it made me furious. I wanted to kill him. Then I found he was more sexually appealing to me than he'd ever been. We fucked all night. Passion has its sadistic elements. Found out yesterday I got the research fellowship at UCSF. Mixed emotions. Dan was quite upset when I told him. He's leaving the end of May and I'm staying. My job begins July 1. I've been thinking of seeing another shrink, a woman this time. Find myself too removed from everything, not depressed or anxious, just removed. This fellowship is a great opportunity to continue the lymphocyte study, better techs, more money, better equipment. I should be thrilled, but I'm not. I think the clinical work is affecting me. I can feel little bits of my emotions sinking into oblivion everytime I examine another AIDS patient.

February 14, 1983

Valentine's Day. I had a car accident. Nothing major except the entire front of my car is in ruin. I escaped the full impact of the car that hit me. I could have been killed or maimed, by inches, but I wasn't scared. Afterwards, I stood there, staring at the mangled steel, trying to make sense of it. I turned left in front of a car that went through the yellow light fast. I heard the screeching attempt to stop, felt the crunch of the impact. It didn't make sense that my car was totalled, while I stood there perfectly well. I did hit my head on the windshield and thought for a minute that I might be in shock, but I knew I wasn't. Dora picked me up after they towed it away. We had some drinks, did some coke and went cruising. Who should we run into but my old friend, Ivan, and his blond boy friend. Too high, we went to some dump in the Mission and fucked all around, but what bothers me now is free-basing more coke. My first time. God, it was fantastic. What a rush! Ivan says I might as well go all the way and try some smack. I think I better find a shrink soon.

March 1, 1983

This AIDS situation is getting heavy. Sometimes I want to strangle the patients. I'm so enraged that this is happening. It's giving sex a very bad name. Two more died last week. I flipped out, went out with Ivan and shot some smack. It was awful. I vomited and vomited, and the euphoria wasn't nearly as good as coke or speed. Suppose I should be thankful that's one drug I can do without. His boy-friend is really addicted. He doesn't look well at all, but that's Ivan's problem, not mine. Every time I have one of these evenings of debauchery, I decide I must give it up, especially the drugs. Sex with Ivan is like being in a porn film, and it feels like that too, curiously perverse, but distanced, removed. I feel as if it isn't me that's doing it. Once I hallucinated myself in the corner watching us from above. Actual pleasure is impossible if I'm "out of my body." Found out he's been sleeping with Janet and even Dora, God knows who else. One of these days I'm going to say to hell with everyone I know. Create a whole new life. Dan doesn't come over much anymore. It's too sad for both of us. I can't wait until he leaves, and I start the new job. Maybe I'll move to the city. New job. New house. New car. New men. New shrink. New life. Clean break.

March 10, 1983

Went to see a woman shrink in the city, very businesslike lady. I told her about Dan leaving, my fellowship, my work on AIDS, but couldn't bring myself to tell her about the drugs. She said almost nothing which was fine, it's what I'm used to, but during the session I felt distanced, removed, like before — I was hovering somewhere else in the room, watching myself talk. She did say I had a lot on my mind. Not exactly the most scintillating or original remark of the century. I doubt this will work if I'm not honest with her.

March 21, 1983

I've been trying to write two articles on the detection of retrovirus and on my lymphocyte study, but I can't do it. The work with patients is interfering with my concentration. Sometimes I don't believe or don't want to believe what I see. One of the lab techs hasn't been feeling well — all the classic symptoms. He's gay. I have to run some tests and talk to him about it. God, I wish I didn't have to! This is too awful to believe. I've noticed that some of the patients in the later stages become like their diseases. They won't let go of life. They live in excruciating pain and utter confusion, and they still want to live. It's partly their youth I think. They've never before confronted death — this thing that happens later, when one gets old, and it's all right then. I wish I could help them. Medicine seems so impotent now.

April 1, 1983

There's a job at Mt. Sinai in Boston, a clinical infectious disease position. They want someone working on AIDS. They called me about it yesterday. Of course, Dan gave them my name, but Dr. Zola remembered me from ICCAC last year. He wanted to know if I'd be interested in applying. I can't stand this terminal ambivalence. One day I've given Dan up, the next day I'm reconsidering. The job sounded good actually, but it's much more clinical work than the fellowship. Do I really want to do research or not? Damn him! Damn him! Why won't he let me be, let me go! The shrink says I've already made my decision, and I'm only torturing myself by reconsidering. She wonders why I punish myself with ambivalence. *She* wonders why!

April 8, 1983

I don't know what to write anymore, but I'm so restless I have to write. I slept with Jerome last night and actually thought I could fall in love with him, then when I opened my eyes, I didn't recognize him. The sex was awful, as usual, but I convinced myself I could only love someone with whom sex was awful. Now this is crazy! I was imagining that he is everything I ever wanted in a man, making him into another person. Me and Dr. Jekyll.

April 11, 1983

Dan came over tonight and suggested that we elope to Tiajuana. I considered it. For a while I really wanted to do it. He's so sweet, but I'm a fucking basketcase. This shrink isn't helping much. If I could get myself together maybe I could marry Dan. Maybe it would work. No matter what I tell her she just says, "Humm." She says, I'm "not responding to the stress and pressure in my life well." I'm "not coping" as well as I could. Jesus Fucking Christ! Coping. Everything sounds like trivia to me. Even worse, I find myself at work blurting out what's going on in my head without censorship. Nobody dares tell me to keep it to myself. They know I'm leaving soon. It's disgusting to me, though, like exhibiting myself on a street corner. My intern and I got into a discussion about mice shit in which I said, lying as usual for no reason, that I loved it when they shit on my hand or bit me, it took away all the guilt when I murdered them. It was the word murder that did it. In the name of science I've killed hundreds of mice and guinea pigs, but I never called it murder before. I suddenly felt very Out of Control and was grateful when he changed the subject.

April 12, 1983

My birthday's coming up. I hate birthdays. Today, during rounds, I became obsessed with an irrelevant idea — that I get too much money to focus for a few moments on another person's pain. This idea wouldn't leave my head. Then I started thinking that friends are dangerous. I can't believe that anyone would be my friend unless I paid them. Somehow these things are connected?

April 13, 1983

Dan says all he wants is monogamy. It sounds reasonable and easy enough — monogamy — but why? I used to think life boiled down to money, then and sometimes still, I think it all boils down to sex. Now, at this moment, I think it's neither. It all boils down to death. Death is THE question. How can so many writers, philosophers, artists, and even ordinary people be wrong? They're not. But the word itself has little meaning to me, no energy, no reference point. It could be garbage or dinner or dress, but it's death. Death is what we're all so supposedly upset by, our own limited existence on earth, and its pitiful lack of significance. I'd like to know death better, to feel it, see it, smell it, hear it. I see it all the time, everyday, but I don't. This is morbid, but I feel totally alienated from death, lost in life. Life is everso present, heartlessly reminiscent of itself, with a vengeance.

April 14, 1983

I said I would come for an interview for the job in Boston since I was going to be there anyway at the end of the month. A lie. Now I guess I have to go because they wanted me to come, and I thought they would say they hadn't had time to review my application yet. Why do I get myself in these situations? I started to feel sad about leaving the hospital this summer. I felt tender toward the janitors and the security guards, people I've never stopped to notice. I was my twenty year old do-goody self again. I wanted to do something out of "the goodness of my heart," but nothing seemed good enough. I could never DO enough. The world needs an indestructible good heart, and I'm not indestructible. I'm fragile, indeed, and feel on the brink of self-destruction more than I'm comfortable with. The shrink says I'm still trying to prove to my parents that I'm worthwhile. Every shrink says this sooner or later to every patient, I think. Could this be it? How could it be so simple? Anyway, I didn't want to embarrass her by saying that I found that out in my analysis, and it hasn't crossed my mind in years. How can anyone be expected to take this therapy stuff seriously?

April 16, 1983

Jerome got me some more coke, but this time I had to pay for half of it, the rest being a birthday present. I guess sex is declining in value with the stock market. Can't complain since I've managed to acquire several hundred dollars worth from him. This is sick — trading in flesh — but no sicker than letting Ivan wrest money from my wallet, pretending I don't know. He gave me ten caps of MDA for my birthday. I'm saving them. Dan is in the garage making boxes to pack his books in. He insists he has to do it in my garage. He asked me to marry him again today, quite serious still, and told me to write it down which I'm dutifully doing. Recorded history. We're going to Boston together at the end of the month. Julia's flying up from New York, for a quicky weekend. I can't wait to see her. Hearing Dan in the garage makes me think I will marry him, but not until I'm more stable. He hasn't been feeling well lately, very unusual. He's never been sick a day since I've known him. I'm sure it's the leaving. I told my shrink I wasn't coming anymore. She implied this meant I was getting better. How she overestimates me. Ran into this guy Brian again; he keeps pestering me about having lunch or dinner. Maybe I'll give him a try, but not until Daniel leaves. No time. I'm so sleepy and it's only 10:00.

April 18, 1983

Woke up crying hysterically. It's my thirty-fifth birthday. I'm a 35 year old sex maniac drug addict without a sense of identity anymore.

April 24, 1983

Last Friday we flew to Boston and spent four hectic, crazy, emotional days. By accident I was able to combine the interview with a virology conference. Got the latest on AIDS — very little news, and no news is not good news, it's bad, bad news. The real eye-opener was visiting several of my old friends who happen to be in Boston. There was so much I had forgotten. In the midst of it I got sick, started throwing up and had terrible diarrhea. Chinese food poisoning, I'm sure. I never liked Chinese food. Dan didn't feel well either, but he wouldn't stay in bed. I actually wondered if I could have IT. Could I have been careless in the lab? With the patients? My lovers? Nonsense. Julia said that everyone is paranoid about this disease, and it was only natural that someone working with it would be more paranoid than most. I wish I believed that it won't get me. . . . I'm not a gay man. But I know better than that. Julia pointed out that I'm not in a high risk group. True enough, as far as we know. BUT we know next to nothing. I was so relieved just to articulate this fear to her that it seemed a heavy weight was lifted off my head and shoulders. I realized this could be the core of my problems lately, especially not being able to write the articles. The other docs at the conference got to talking about it, and lots of them have had weird and unusual emotional problems lately. These psychological consequences of AIDS haven't begun to be addressed.

April 26, 1983

I'm feeling stronger emotionally after the trip back East. I know I don't want that job, and I do want the fellowship. It's not the right job for me, and as much as I loved visiting my friends, life has changed. Martha and Alan are divorced. Robert is engaged. Julia travels constantly. Anthony has a girl-friend. Everyone's absorbed in their work, their lives. Another decade. Thomas Wolfe was right: "You can't go home again." It will never be the same as it was. I can't be a serious East coast intellectual anymore. California has captured me. My work here is back in its rightful place — number one priority. It is the mainstay of my life. Dan and I will either work it out in the future or we won't. It's as simple as that. It was talking to Julia which made me feel better about myself. She's such a source of strength for me, of calm and consideration. She said we choose our battles, and I choose the toughest ones, the ones easiest to lose.

* * *

The air cleaned thin by the storm entered his lungs with the effect of pure oxygen, heady and disorienting. The sun blazed down on him, scorching his skin. His clothes, now nothing more than tattered rags, steamed on his body. He discarded them all save his jockey shorts. The sand, the rocks, the ice plants imbedded in the cliffs shimmered and shouted at him with their washed brilliance. This small piece of coastline glowed in a spotlight, the sun, the universal torch. It was too grotesquely bright. What was he supposed to do? Get up and make a speech, a fool on nature's stage. He shut his eyes and waited for the fog.

Why me? Why am I sitting here now, imprisoned without even a dark, damp concrete cell? Searching in the world's most beautiful place for the ugliest of realities. For someone irretrievable, lost, someone I love.

Because her car *was* in the parking lot with her African bag, her Mexican sweater, her empty Perrier bottles, her ashtray full of roaches. This is no joke. I remember them searching the car meticulously, inspecting every object, every scrap of paper, opening every lipstick tube and eye pencil, every tape box, even an unopened pack of gum. The policeman raised his eyebrows when he discovered her dope box, smiled when he found the coke spoon, mirror and razor blade, and frowned when he opened the empty Valium bottle. They dutifully scraped her ashtray into a plastic baggy and recorded their inventory like drones. The driver of the tow truck paced around the car impatient to get on his way. I pretended to be a mildly curious by-stander. They could take it all, her bag, her car, but they'd find few clues there. They didn't know her; I did. She was perfectly capable of outwitting the law, but not me. I was certain then that she had staged this fiasco. But why?

He forced himself further back to those initial crazy, disjointed hours after he found her lab unlocked and empty, the tubes of blood beside her microscope which was focused on a slide. Carol said she had gone across the street for coffee, but she hadn't come back. He rushed over to the coffee shop; she hadn't been there. Her car was gone from the doctors' parking lot. He phoned her house. No answer. He sped over there to find the door locked as usual, the cat meowing, rubbing his legs, ready to be fed. The key wasn't in the jade plant. Something was out of order. Instant dread. Panic. Out of order. He broke the glass on the door and went in. Nothing was askew, everything sat undisturbed, ordinary, but in a holy silence, a ghostly silence. The journal lay on the floor by her side of the bed. He grabbed it along with the red pack on a hook behind the door, and automatically knew where to go. In the car he raced without thinking toward the beach. Her car was there as he suspected. He gave it a cursory inspection. Her checkbook, her wallet with eight twenties in it, her woven make-up bag that she'd bought in La Paz, cigarettes, lighter, wads of used Kleenex, her dope box, her tapes — everything was there in its place. He held her sweater to his face, the smell of her, the odd mixtures of perfumes and bath oils, the way her hair always smelled. She had to be around somewhere. At the moment he started down the trail, the park police followed by a tow truck and a Marin County police car with its siren on came careening around the corner. He stopped and watched.

"What's going on, officer?" He feigned mere curiosity.

"Who are you?" The officer stared at him as if he were a criminal.

"Chris Alterberg, a physician, out for a hike on the beach. What's going on?"

"I'm afraid I'll have to ask you for some identification, sir." His tone implied suspicion.

"Sure, officer." He pulled out his driver's license and his faculty ID from the hospital. "What's the matter? Something wrong?" His innocent act was working.

"Some lady's missing. This vehicle fits the description of her car. You seen anyone around here?" After examining his ID and looking closely at the picture and his face, he turned around satisfied, and pointed to her sweater, her purse, the ashtray. "Get going. Let's have a look here," he barked at the uniformed officer who held a box of baggies in a gloved hand.

Chris backed further away, aware that the reality of watching these unfriendly strangers touch her possessions was about to unleash a volcanic explosion in him. The idea that she was . . . well, gone, missing, he just couldn't believe it. It wouldn't sink in. He clutched the journal under his arm and went down the path. He walked to the other end of the beach while they conducted a thorough search. He pretended to be collecting shells, examining rocks. Most of the men retreated finally, up the trail, no trace of her there, no body, live or dead. Nothing. The detective in plain clothes walked toward him again, his face tucked down away from the wind, a face that had seen too many horror shows. Foul play could be involved in this woman's disappearance, he sugested. This beach might not be safe. Why didn't he leave?

"Foul play?" The conversation come back to him with merciless exactitude.

"There've been three women murdered in this general vicinity, sir. Ever heard of the trail-side murders?"

"Murder? No? I'm leaving soon, officer, soon as the sun starts to go down."

"I'll have to ask you for that ID again, sir. We might want to question you later. Seems you're the only person here." He wrote down his license number and name. "Park closes at sundown, Mr. Alterberg."

"Officer, I . . . I hope you sort this thing out. You don't think . . . I mean, this woman, murdered?" He stuttered; the word was impossible to think much less spit out.

The detective gave him a resigned look and shook his head. "No, no, I've been at this a long time and I can usually tell. This one'll either turn up, or she's a suicide. My bet's suicide." The man kept shaking his head in bewilderment. "Can't understand why they do it. Suicide. See a lot of it these days." He turned to walk away. "Sun's going down."

The word wouldn't penetrate. Suicide. Suicide? Suicide. It barely pricked his consciousness like a hypodermic needle slipped into a vein, painless, effortless. Then he saw red, the blood coming up into the syringe, a light-headed rush close behind. Numbness, the euphoria of numbness, made him capable of following some distance behind the detective until they reached the top of the trail. There was the tow truck, pulling away with her new Prelude. Suicide. His head filled with exotic vision and sound. A man in a saffron robe with a shaved head banged a giant gong: SUICIDE. A deafening, unending echo, reverberated across the green dales in front of him, over the awesome cliffs behind him, through the weeping eucalyptus trees, and back with the wind. The sound was like a wild animal crouched to rip into his chest and tear out his heart. In this instant, he knew with finite certainty that she was dead. Dead. Here. In this ocean. He knew the very spot where she lived her last moments. Then, as if he had walked into a pitch dark room from bright sunlight, he forgot.

This seemed like an eternity ago. The park police had appeared in person only once after that vague scan of the beach. This time he made sure they did not see him. Helicopters had flown over twice and one light plane, but it wasn't much of a search, he thought. Not much at all. Why? Why had they stopped the search for her? Why hadn't it mattered to him before? Did they believe she was dead? That it was hopeless? Did he? How many days had he been here? He opened his eyes to look at his watch. It was October 31. Four days. Only four days. Halloween. They were supposed to go to a masquerade party tonight, a benefit for the San Francisco AIDS Project.

He caressed the journal, turning it over and over in his hands. Tears welled up and spilled over his cheeks. She had felt alone. She was hanging on by a thread, that was clear. But she was trying to get help, going to some shrink, looking forward to her new job, talking to her friend, Julia. She wanted to sort herself out. She was trying hard to let go of Dan. Any idiot could see that. She was quite a pretender. An actress with talent. How together she had seemed when they met, how confident and cool. The "if onlys" started in his head. If only I knew the name of that shrink. If only I could hold her and tell her it's going to be okay. If only she had confided in me more.

He stood up, his body aching with sorrow, and began to collect wood – robotic, automatic movement; he had to do it. Dizzy and disoriented he kept it up. Collect one piece at a time, pick it up, take it back, put it down, go get another one, each separate. Out of the corner of his eye, he saw a woman walking toward him. She leaned on the side of the rock as she passed through the small channel. There was a familiarity about her. Lights flashed in front of his eyes. He went crazy. It's her! It's her! She's alive! He fell over a large mess of seaweed and was terrified to look up. Another hallucination. "I can't stand it!" he screamed into the seaweed, salt burning his mouth. "I can't stand it!"

She saw him and began to run toward him. Her arms went round his shoulders. She tried to pull him up. "Oh God, you poor thing, you poor thing. Chris, Chris, it's me. Pat. It's me. I'm so glad I found you. Look at you. Poor, poor baby." She sat down and tried to cradle his head in her lap, to smooth back his hair, to stroke his face. Tears streamed from her eyes and fell on his neck.

Pat. Pat? Pat. It was Pat. How? How had she found him? Maybe if he stayed mute, acted deaf and dumb she would leave. But how wonderful her real voice was in his ears, how gentle her hands, how warm, how alive she was. He was paralyzed with emotion. She didn't say anything. She didn't leave. She sat there, his face in her lap, for a long time, crying over him, with him, for him.

There was no choice now. The betrayal had already been completed long ago. She must have come for a reason, her own reasons. He no longer had anything to hide, to feel ashamed of or guilty for. She had known it all, and she was here. A friend. He had forgotten that he was a person with friends. Friends could help in times like this. Yet he didn't feel helped; her presence only heightened the grief, made it rise to the surface like a fever breaking in clammy sweat. But he was curious too. "How did you find me?" The words came out, long, broken spaces between them.

"I've been searching every beach at Pt. Reyes for three days." She stroked his back and arms. "Let's move over there, I've got some sandwiches and soda, a handkerchief. Come on, Chris, let's wipe you off and get some food into you. I want to help you. Honest. I'm really terribly sorry about this. I know what it's like to lose someone you love. Remember?" He let her pull him up and lead him to a small ledge where they could sit off of the wet sand. He let her wipe his face with the handkerchief. His ability to resist was about on par with his childhood ability to turn away his mother's comfort. Silent and reluctant hostility simmered in him, but he showed absolute deference to her skills.

"How did you find me?"

She wanted to wait until he had eaten, had gotten used to her presence. But finding him in this state, she knew he was going to be single-minded and stubborn. She pulled a small clipping from *The Chronicle* dated October 29, 1983. "This came out in the paper."

AIDS DOCTOR MISSING: SUICIDE FEARED

Co-workers became alarmed when Dr. Suzanne Keller (35), a specialist in immunology at U.C.S.F Medical School, failed to return from a coffee break early yesterday morning. The police found her car abandoned in a beach parking lot at Pt. Reyes. Her personal effects were undisturbed. There was no evidence of foul play. Co-workers said she had been "preoccupied and distressed" in the past few weeks. Dr. Keller, described as a "serious, hard-working researcher" on the deadly AIDS disease, "was under a great deal of pressure, as we all are," said Dr. Thornton Thomas, the Chief of Immunology. Dr. Keller had recently joined the U.C.S.F. staff. "We are confused, shocked and saddened," said another colleague. Anyone with information on this case is requested to call Detective Sanchez in the Marin County police department.

He read it over several times, wondering which co-workers described her this way. Why hadn't anyone mentioned that he had been looking for her? Why didn't the police notice that her house had been broken into? Was this some kind of bait? Trap? Didn't anyone care about him? How did Pat know this was the same woman he had told her about? He handed the article back to her and covered his face with his hands. "How did you know it was the same woman?"

"You told me her name, Chris." He obviously wasn't thinking straight. "I've been trying to get in touch with you for days. I called the hospital the day I read this, and they said no one had been able to reach you for twenty-four hours. Your secretary told me that everyone was worried because of what had happened. They knew so little about her. Except. . . . Evidently, everyone knew about the two of you. Gloria told me the article in *The Chronicle* was as much as they knew. The whole bloody hospital staff is pretty upset. The police keep snooping around, asking questions, but only Carol could tell them anything as you can see." She crumbled the article, its use outlived, and sighed deeply, "I didn't want to get you involved so I wasn't about to talk to the police. Neither was anybody else for that matter. Carol told me you rushed in and out again, that you seemed quite upset and angry. She was afraid when neither of you came back. People wonder, Chris." She added, "I know Carol quite well, you know; we went to graduate school together. She told me, well, that you and Suzanne had a pretty stormy relationship. She couldn't help overhearing you fighting on the phone several times in the past week. I don't know, maybe she thought, well, that something happened, an accident or something." Her eyes had grown wide while telling the story; a questioning look pleaded with him. "Chris, please tell me, I'm your friend, are you involved in this? I mean did something happen."

A bolt of lightening might as well have struck him from the cloudless sky. Here was a woman he had lived with for several years, who knew him very well, asking him if he were capable of murder. He grinned, then chuckled, then laughed so hard his stomach ached. "Are you, do they, I mean, are you asking me if I killed her?" His laugh bellowed into the wind. It exploded from beneath his grief, swirled from his gut in a huge tight ball to his mouth and spewed out in big gusts.

She moved away from him slowly in an effort to prevent him from detecting her doubt, her fear. What if he had killed Suzanne? Had that unbelievable, unexplainable thing happened to him? Had he snapped completely? No. She didn't think so. She couldn't believe it. She studied him and waited until he eased back to silence with a heavy sigh. "I'm glad you can still laugh."

"I loved her, Pat, I loved her more than I've ever loved anyone. If I could kill her now I would because I loved her that much. Or I thought I did. I experienced. . . . God, what am I saying? No, I didn't kill her." His laughter changed into little racking sobs. Hot, angry tears rolled over his cheeks. "I've been trying to find her. I don't know. Wait for her maybe. Hope that she'll come back here." With his fist he kept beating a repetitive rhythm in the sand. His elbow and forearm became a metronome.

"So she did kill herself? Is that what you think? Are you saying that maybe she ran away, maybe she's not dead?"

He stared into the sand, then glanced toward the ocean, an angry look on his face. "I don't want to believe it, but I do. She didn't run away. She's out there." He pointed to the ocean.

What could she possibly say? Her head bent down and her body shook with cold in the hot sun. The woman who took the man she loved away was most probably dead, dead by her own hand. A tremendous shame that she wasn't sorry this woman was forever gone haunted her. She wanted her to be dead. She feared that she wasn't, that she might come back. On the surface she felt sad, angry, disgusted to be a party, an injured party, in this disaster of the past two months, but deep down inside there was hope. Hope that Chris would recover, come to his senses. She could help him, comfort him, make him forget. It was only two months. In time the whole affair would be a story to tell bored dinner guests, a twisted memory like fighting in Vietnam or being cured of cancer. The feelings he had for Suzanne would fade and be replaced by continuing his work, the love of his friends, and the security she would give him, an ordinary marriage, children, bills to pay, real problems to solve together. Their future was still possible. These hopes steeled her for the present battle with him, and she knew it was going to be a battle to get him back.

"There's no point in staying here, Chris. Everyone is worried about you. I told Gloria to find someone to cover for you. I probably shouldn't have, but I made up a story that you were at my house, recovering for a few days. It's over. Nothing is going to change the fact that she's dead. You might as well come home with me, get some rest, and go back to work. It might sound cruel, but she did leave you. You haven't got much choice. Chris, let her go."

"I want you to leave, Pat. Please. I don't want to hurt you, but you don't understand this. Go. Now."

"I'm not leaving you here like this."

"I'm telling you I don't want to hurt you. I have to stay. I want you to go."

"Why? Why do you have to stay?" Her face grew red and puffy as she fought off tears of defeat. After three days of sloshing through rain and mud, after two nights in a crummy motel, after worrying, crying herself to sleep, after thinking he was dead too, she wasn't going to be treated this way, sluffed off like flaky skin. "This doesn't make sense, you know. Eventually, I'd have to send someone down here to get you forcibly. Should one more tragic thing come of this. They'd put you in the psych ward. You're certainly not behaving like a mentally competent person. Remember the seventy-two hour hold if you're a danger to yourself or others? Can you still think, Chris? Have you any reason left! Look at you! Your clothes are rags; you're practically naked, thin, burned over most of your body, talking about hurting me. Laughing about murder. Crying. Let's face it, you're a wreck, and it wouldn't take any convincing to have you hauled out of here in a straight jacket."

After quite serious reflection: "Pat, I know you have my best interests at heart, but I'm not ready to leave yet. You know you've never had the bark of a seal, much less a watch-dog. Tone down. I'm in complete possession of my faculties, I assure you. There are reasons why I have to stay."

His calm voice disarmed her more than his emotional outbursts. Maybe he really was a basketcase already. But he wasn't unfriendly. Her hope overrode her suspicion. She reminded herself that she knew him well, that she'd known him for years, that he was the same person no matter what had happened. Whatever that was escaped her. "Okay, I'll stay with you. I won't bother you. I'll stay as long as you do."

"Why? You don't want to stay here. It's not very comfortable." He grinned at her, nudged her to be reasonable as he used to do the very few times when she was stubborn about something. He was almost acting like his old self. "Listen, I really appreciate the story you told the hospital for me. I want you to go back and tell them I'm getting better, but I need more time off. I don't know how much time. Just tell them that. Will you do it for me?"

"Chris, as you can see, I'd do almost anything for you. But I can't leave you here. I'm worried about you. At least, let me get some camping equipment, some supplies, some clothes for you. Let me come back and stay with you. I'll call the hospital from Pt. Reyes station. Okay?"

"No, Pat. I need to be alone."

"Please, Chris. Please."

He got up and walked down the beach to pee. The sun had almost dried everything, and the cove was wide with rearranged sand dunes, pale white driftwood and huge piles of greenish brown seaweed. They're going to find me sooner or later, he thought. Someone from the hospital or the police. They will come and take me away. She's right. Pat might be able to put it off. Gratitude. The emotion he'd felt most toward her. Her indefatigable loyalty to him, her indelible mark on his life, a godmother of sorts, protecting him, covering for him, insisting on making his well-being her concern, her job. A pang of recognition. Her feeling for him, her irrational need to care for him, to love beyond the realm of sense or duty, he understood it now. He didn't deserve this from her, but then nobody gets love because they deserve it. It can't be earned or learned. With her here he did feel a bit better. Some human ability — the necessity to think about an interaction, to negotiate to get what one wants — was undergoing quiet restoration. The journal. It had to be finished. It had to be considered, analyzed, understood. Then he would leave. Pat could not be involved, but she might buy him time. She could go for supplies, bring him cigarettes, make some phone calls, and find out what they thought out there. She did offer. He would accept.

"Pat, I don't know why you give a damn about me, but I trust you. I always have. I have Suzanne's journal. It's the only clue I have of discovering why she did this. We were going to get married." He saw her eyes look away and was sorry he had to tell her bluntly, with no preliminaries. "I have to know why she did it. Can you understand that?"

"Yes, I think so." It couldn't be true. He was going to marry someone else. After two months? All those years she'd loved him, waited for him to ask her, believed in it, accepted his feeble excuses that put it off. But she was too tired to be upset. It had all gone wrong anyway. There wasn't much left to believe in. The damned bitch was gone. Dead. She was alive, sane, well, and she had found him. He was alive. "I'm curious too," a meek little whisper, "about a lot of things."

"Listen, I broke the glass in her side door to get the journal. That wasn't mentioned in the paper, but the police must know it. They may suspect me. They even have my name and address. Can you find out about this? Call this Sanchez person? Call him from a phone booth. Tell him you may have some information, then find out what he knows." He sat beside her and patted her shoulder. "You may have to go to the East Bay. There's someone else I want you to find; his name is Ivan Wallensky. I want to talk to him. He knew Suzanne, and he knows I'm here. Find him and tell him I want to talk to him."

"Chris, I'm not a detective. I want to stay with you. Here. What's in that journal anyway? Did she leave some note, anything?"

"I can't talk about it, Pat. Please don't ask me." He kissed her on the cheek to her surprise, and uncontrollable tears floated in her eyes. "I'll explain it all to you when the time comes. I promise I will if you help me."

She held his hand, kissed it, and pressed it to her face. "Oh, Chris, I'm such a stupid fool, but I still love you. I wish I didn't, but I do. You've hurt me too much. Is there any hope this will ever heal. Is there any hope?"

His arms went round her shoulders, and he hugged her tight. No, at the moment there was no hope, but he wouldn't say this to her. A sense of fair play, of kindness kept his mouth shut. "You've always been too good to me, Pat."

She dried her eyes and let go of him, refueled by his physical embrace. "What should I get? What do you want?"

"Cigarettes, matches, water, food, dry clothes, tennis shoes, a jacket, whatever you can think of to camp out a few days."

"A few days!"

"I don't know how long, Pat. Maybe less, maybe more."

"Then are you coming home?"

"I don't know that either. Please, make those calls. Don't tell anybody where I am. That's all. Now go."

"Chris, this is crazy. It all feels, well, insane. Do you promise you'll be here when I get back." She paused and searched his eyes which she could no longer read. "Will you be safe?"

He sat down at the entrance to the cave. "I promise you I will wait right here in the cave. I promise."

She left him the food and supplies she'd brought and walked away hesitantly, turning around several times, reconsidering with every step.

When she was a few minutes past the channel, out of sight, he took out the journal, carefully separating the damp pages, trying not to blur the ink. It had to dry for a while. He stretched out and tried to piece together the journal entries he'd read before Pat had distracted him.

The drug use is surprising, he thought to himself. Somehow I'd never suspected that she was a user to that extent and for that long. How had she gotten so much work done? How had she managed such a competent, collected image? The perfect workaholic admired by everyone on the staff for her broad scope of knowledge, her perceptive comments, her usually correct angle on a difficult diagnosis. Dr. Thomas told me once in the men's room that she was the most talented female researcher he'd ever worked with, adding that he might even scratch female. She was brilliant, he said, she had a unique talent for bringing research to bear on clinical problems. Dr. Thomas was not given to such compliments, and at the time, I wondered if Thomas was interested in her in more than a medical capacity. Not possible, I decided, taking it personally. This was Thomas's way of telling me to get on the ball. Always comparing myself, I always compared myself to her. Why. . . ?

There was no question of her dedication, and it's obvious where she got the boundless energy to stay late at her lab every night, to go to every conference on AIDS, to see all the new patients and do her own research too. If anything, she was considered rather socially backward by the other fellows, interns and residents. She wasted no time on lunch or coffee breaks. She disappeared if personal conversations began. She never went to hospital parties or picnics, and at absolutely necessary occasions, she only drank mineral water. I especially liked that about her, her social reserve. I didn't want any competition. There was a mysterious aura about her, about us. When we started seeing each other, I thought I gained a new measure of respect from the other docs. Hah! Maybe they just kept their distance like sane people do from earthquake faults and war zones! I just stumbled right in. How could I have been so blind? What about this veritable chasm between the woman I loved and the person who wrote this journal? It wasn't all my misperception. I refuse to believe it. When she sailed into a room, looking like she just stepped out of some fashion magazine, every head turned. Then she acted like an unapproachable Brahmin. Until I made my fatal approach this is how I saw her. It seems so ludicrous now.

But she'd only been there four months. Less than four months. She couldn't be blamed for the impression I had of her or the impressions I thought they had. What about her impressions? God, I never even asked her! Considering how absorbed she was in her own problems, she probably wasn't aware, probably didn't care. I never had any idea anyone could be this complicated. If I had been told about her sexual escapades, her drug habits, her detachment from reality would I have believed it? All hidden well, these secrets, but I have to admit she never tried to hide any of this from me. No, she didn't, but I tried not to hear her when certain topics came up, like other men, past loves. All right, I wasn't the only one who didn't hear her.

She did go to this shrink. Not much on that, the woman saw her as the rest of the world did. "Over-estimates," that was the word Suzanne used. It is no wonder she was sick all the time! Now that makes sense to me. No one can lead a life that way and not get sick. Those drugs did have physical effects, but the psychological ones were more profound. Her constant, low-grade illnesses — were they a hypochondriacal reaction to AIDS? She took drugs to cope, to keep working, to function. No doubt her work had become an emotional liability. But I didn't see it. She seemed to take the unpleasantries in stride, the way I do, the way most doctors do; patients die, but life goes on. For her it was more — that was clear from the way she wrote about it. Too much more. More than I realized. If I could have talked to her about it. And all that fun we had. If I had asked her why we had to have fun every minute, every day, every night, what would she have said? I think I understand that. She wanted an escape.

There is more to it. She was confused. Removed. Detached. Paranoid? Losing touch with reality? Or too in touch with reality? Death was sucking her in, and she wasn't putting up much of a fight. Her life was overrun with irresolvable and paradoxical conflicts. Conflicts she dwelt on. The obsession with death isn't such a surprise. Her work, what she called her "number one priority," "her mainstay of life," AIDS, that shitty, miserable disease was making her a failure, something she couldn't stand to be. It was pure coincidence that she got mixed up in it. She should have continued her CMV studies, chicken pox, VD, anything else. Maybe she should have gone with Daniel. All that phoney stoicism. Pretenses. She embraced her work, a deadly disease, and rejected her own life, a man who loved her. She did it again! To me! Why did she think she could handle it? How does anyone know they can handle it? A preoccupation with death: "THE question," she wrote — is that the most important point here? Well ... is it?

There was a different person writing in the spring of 1983, different from the woman writing a year earlier, different from the woman I knew. What had happened in that year, that long gap? Those blank pages. Detachment replaced anxiety. She was disturbed over a year ago, but her vacation in England was ordinary compared to the sex and drug orgies, shooting coke, heroin. Recreational drug use. Back to that again. I do it. We all do it. But we don't all kill ourselves. That couldn't be the reason. This country runs on pills. There's no one who doesn't find a pill to their benefit sooner or later. It is one of those things that never go too far, one of those "never happen to me" things. Addiction. A thin line. And I bought it for her, did it with her. Fun. Fun and games. It was.

The pages were curled and crispy. The ink was dry. He pulled himelf up to a seated position in which he could lean against the rock. His chin jutted out in determination as he opened the journal once more.

*　*　*

May 13, 1983

Dan is leaving soon. I'm crying. Too many memories of leavings. I keep thinking of John and the time we sat on the roof of McDonald's, eating Big Macs, drinking beer, laughing. I've never had the guts to hang on to someone I love. I told Dora today that once I've really loved someone I always love them, and it's true. But it's strange that I can't hang on to love. Leaving causes pain, but it's a relief too. I do love D, but it's love on top of love. "Too much love gone to the bottom." I wonder if I've ever let go of John or even Anthony.

May 31, 1983

The night before Dan leaves. I'm totally freaked out and unprepared. Memories, shemories, blah. I don't give a hoot about them anymore. I hate this. I hate myself this way. Who ever said getting it all out in the open makes it easier. I am hysterical in the classical conversion sense. I'm paralyzed all over. Dan is trying to be nice, to be normal which is throwing us both into a surrealist nightmare. He doesn't know. I'm stoned, smashed, drugged.

June 2, 1983

It's over. He's gone. I'm calmer. Julia and I talked on the

187

phone for two hours, and I'm taking her suggestions to heart: work. I'll be leaving the hospital soon for the greener pastures of research. I'll have as much time as I want in the lab, and my work with patients will be only consults. Unfortunately, there are plenty of AIDS consults. At least, I won't be their primary doc. I can maintain a safer distance. Dr. Thomas wants me to teach an advanced virology seminar. I like that, working with students, people who aren't dying. It's quite exciting to be in the thick of it, research geared toward isolating the damned thing. I have some ideas. The French are sure it's a retrovirus in the family of human T-cell leukemia viruses – HTLV. The pattern of lymphocyte studies is born out, but you can't really argue much on the basis of one patient. It is only a matter of time before we find one or more subgroups of this virus. Viruses invading the T-cells, perhaps not the cause of the disease itself, but responsible for the paralysis of the immune system that results in AIDS or ARC. Similar to lentivirus, or one of them? There are so many important questions to ask. I can't wait to start the reverse transcriptase assays. . . .

Well, who am I trying to fool? I should be writing this in my medical notes, not in my diary. Work isn't on my mind, Dan is. He looked so sad when he left. This perpetual cold he's got is affecting his looks. I couldn't help crying, really bawling when I hugged him for the last time. He promised me he'd see a doctor in Boston if he didn't get better soon. We're both agreed that it's the stress of parting. I haven't had an appetite either, but then I never had. Shit! Maybe we will get back together, but I can't afford to think that. He'd be happier with someone easier, Clara perhaps. I've cried myself to sleep for three nights in a row. I'm going to be lonely. Lonely and free. Am I doing the right thing?

June 14, 1983

The anniversary of our first engagement three years ago. D and I always went on a picnic to celebrate, but no use crying over spilt milk. Right, Mom? I hesitate to write. A wish to punish myself is returning. I'm afraid of this. When I isolate myself, it gets better, but then it begins to grow. I have no choice. I have to write, because I can't tell this to anyone. Julia hasn't answered my letter, and I'm mad at her. The struggle to protect myself is mine alone. I've been watching the paths that other people take: religion, therapy, exercise, hobbies, family . . . all varieties of faith in something. I'm cutting off contact with my old friends. Just as well, Dora said, she's had it with me anyway. Jerome is moving to Houston. He met and married some starlet in Las Vegas. Gave me a going away present of five grams. I'm tired of coke. Downers make me feel better, but they're rotten for sex. Sex. Now there's a path that's interesting enough. The coke comes in handy for my pursuit of living dangerously. Casual fucking. There's no shortage of material. I like the men who seem a bit effeminate. Playing with fire. One guy I picked up wanted to use a condom and I objected, no need for birth control since I can't have children anyway. It's Russian Roulette. The excitement is indescribable, playing with a weapon of love and death. Afterwards, I like to go out into the foggy night, the time when no one is awake except streetwalkers, criminals and the police, then drive as fast as I can across the bridge to my own house. My beautiful, empty house, dark and cold and frightening as I grope for the light switch. Death feels closer then, as if it waits up for me. I'm getting to know it. When I switch on the light, I imagine a crowd of people, old friends, jumping out from behind the furniture, Surprise! Surprise! It's only us, your friends, here to comfort you, to take you home. But I am home. And I have no friends. I'm exhausted, but never sleepy. I take Dalmane and Valium and have a drink and listen to jazz until that heavy, drugged, dreamless sleep grabs me and pulls me into it, way deep into it. Indifference. A state I reach now with little effort. I like it. No guilt, no shame, no regrets. I'm left with pure curiosity. I'm not going to be disappointed anymore. I'm not going to be hurt.

June 20, 1983

Everything is transient. Doom, nuclear war, AIDS – it's all too close for comfort. Perilous. It's closing in on all of us. At least me. I feel uncomfortable in the world, very uncomfortable. I walk past a glass storefront and see a woman frowning, an angry, restless woman, a bored woman, a woman who wants to start making speeches on the street corner but won't. I've no tolerance for boredom. I create conflict to

alleviate it, to punctuate the loneliness. I wonder if I can
see anymore, if my brain is damaged? The core problem is
that I don't believe in anything. I've lost my beliefs as if they
were my house keys. It makes me feel insecure in that
way. I don't know. I keep doing things and pursuing life for
no reasons. When I talk to others, especially men, I often decide what to say on the basis of what I think will make the
conversation easier. I don't say what I really think, except about
patients. When I stop to think about it, there seems little left
to say. I can see the dilemma of this position, but I'm not
taking it as much as it's taking me. The path of least resistance.
Everywhere. I'm starting to do this with AIDS patients; I sur-
mise (and it's too easy) what they want from me and tell them
that. What they want from me is all I can give anyway, false
hope. There's no meaning in anything else, no truth. What am
I saying? I don't know. Am I a slave, a servant? With the usual
feeling for an unknown master? Murderous? This doesn't make
sense, but who cares anymore?

June 25, 1983

To add to my list of complaints, it appears I'm possessed by
yet another problem. I can't go to sleep at night. I lay in bed
afraid. I imagine burglars, rapists, psychopathic maniacs, breaking in, standing over my bed ready to slit my throat, but I
know it's just my morbid, wild imagination. Would
understanding put an end to it? I fear the answers won't set me
free. I know answers mean death. But I *want* the death of this.
Only ubiquitous conflict can rescue me, so perhaps, I don't
want to understand or find answers? The moment conflict sub-
sides (and the experience of peace is at hand), I am utterly terrified. I manufacture a new one, a new threat, a new dilemma,
an insoluble problem to solve. Life can't go on without it. The
reversal of progress is the truth, and the illusion of progress is
the defense against the truth of perpetual regress as one "grows"
up, old. . . . I must isolate myself from others. It's not their
fault.

June 27, 1983

I have come to the conclusion that I believe only in the

primitive, the irrational, the "dirty tricks," the fantasmagorical. I don't want any morals, and I don't have them. I don't respect tradition. I don't have standards. It's awful. I wonder how society survives with people like me in it, and it seems there are a lot of us. But not most people! Certainly not! I should hope not! Let's confine this to yourself, dear self. Most people aren't anti-everything. Are they? Freud, old boy, you were unfortunately too right: when the primitive is uncovered in oneself, life in "civilized" society is a hellish experience. One, always, on a daily, hourly, momentary basis has to choose. The mental awareness of choosing the social, proper, moral course of action or trying to get away with the immoral, illegal, anti-social course of action is staring me in the face. A horrible burden. It is much easier to have no choice, to follow automatically some habitualized course, some ideology or doctrine. I couldn't stand watching the pain anymore in one of my AIDS patients. He told me months ago he didn't want so-called heroic measures, but his parents — they wanted him to live no matter what. His brain was more or less gone, complete confusion; he'd lost most of his sight, his body so feeble he could barely lift an arm, but I might have cured the pneumocystis. I asked them if they wanted me to stop treatment, even told them he was never going to recover, but they wanted to push on, to put off the inevitable death. I ignored them and, instead of the IV Septra, I put him on a morphine drip, gradually increasing the dose. I did it myself. I killed him. It's not uncommon, I justified to myself. It happens all the time with terminal old folks. I've done it before, but never without the family's consent. Never outside the boundaries. How's twenty-four as an age to die? I don't believe in reality anymore, I don't believe in society. Where did this come from? This tiny, baby retrovirus of mine. Society didn't construct it. Science can't even find it. It's a little piece of purity with no harm intended, untouched by any human notions, just looking for a comfy place to be fruitful and multiply. So dumb it kills its host, but boy, it's got a civilization full of cells to march through.

June 30, 1983

My last day at the hospital. Said goodbye to everyone, the patients, the staff, the secretaries. One of my patients cried and said he'd miss me. I almost cried too.

                              *   *   *

The tide had receded far into the sea. The sun rested in the afternoon sky invisibly radiating waves of heat onto his face. Sweat ran
in rivulets over his forehead into his eyes, forcing his glasses to slide
down his nose. The burn contracted his skin and suddenly convinced
him that he had a fever. He put his palm to his forehead, wiped the
sweat from his eyes and nose and stared at the words blurring on the
paper. "I almost cried."

They were speeding along the freeway past Daly City toward the
coast road to go south to Santa Cruz. The *Psychedelic Supper* was on
KFOG, and the sun was a burning orange globe in the western sky.
When they passed the rows and rows of wood frame houses in
Pacifica that ran over the hills like stationary box cars in a crowded
railroad yard one of them mentioned Seeger's "ticky-tack" song from
the fifties. It denigrated such conformist, milk-toast housing
developments in which families settled to pursue "the American
dream." "That's where I grew up." She spoke with her head turned to
the window in a matter of fact tone. "Not here, but they're the same
everywhere, aren't they?"

He remembered glancing around then and seeing these rows of
houses facing the sunset with their picture windows reflecting the
glare like giant happy eyes, with garage doors half-open in smiles.
There were worse places to grow up or even to live in, he thought.
"The 'burbs, yeah. Same everywhere, but they don't all have that
view."

They were on their way to have a seafood dinner in the tiny harbor of Princeton. It was a Friday night. They both had had a hard
week. Three patients died, and she was still sick with her "cold." But
tomorrow they were going to spend the day combing the beaches,
watching the seals, wading in tide pools. A friend of his had loaned
them his house in the Bonnie Doon hills where they could hike in
the redwoods, sit in the hottub and be quietly together. A song that
she liked by the Pretenders came on, "It's a thin line between love
and hate. . . . It's a thin line between love and hate. . . ." She turned
up the sound, and he turned it down again. "Hey, Suzanne, where
do you think we should live after we make ourselves legal?" He put
his hand on her knee and squeezed it; he was in a very good mood.
"This may be fifties ticky-tack, but some of these houses have great
views, and they're big. This isn't a bad commute, and it's as close as
we can get to the ocean since you don't want to live in the Sunset.
I don't think we can afford Marin yet, even if we combine our
resources. But in a couple of years. . . ."

She looked at him as if he'd said, let's throw caution to the winds and move to Fiji or something revolutionary like that. "We can't talk about that yet!"

"Why not? These things have to be planned ahead of time. If we move into our own house we can start out on neutral territory. I think that's better than me moving in with you or vice versa. Besides commuting from the East Bay takes too long. Traffic on the bridge is getting worse and worse."

With what appeared to him as effort, she smiled and held his hand. "We haven't even decided to get married yet. You haven't formally proposed, and I haven't formally accepted."

"Well, let's just suppose that we have the formalities over with, and we've decided to get married. Hypothetically speaking where would we want to live?"

"Hypothetically speaking, my darling Chris, I just want to live."

The sun beat down on his back. He had turned away from it toward the cliff. The fissures that ran through these rocks split centuries of time like lightning bolts through a stormy night sky. Fragile tufts of feathery grass grew on this edge of nothing for a mean, short season. But the grass kept coming back. Not the same blades, but new ones. The rocks stayed the same from his human perspective. The rocks never died. They preserved the dead past; they were the housing, the shelter, the casing, but not for the content of life, only for the shell, the form. Some baby gulls screeched from their nest in a shallow hole, and a mother gull raced on the wind to pacify them. Her wings flapped with grace as she hovered over the nest, and her spindly legs touched down with care. She had food in her beak which instantly quieted their screams. He watched without thought. He thought without comment.

The Alfa pulled with centrifugal force out of the hairpin curves of the two lane road that cuts across the edge of the cliff above the Pacific, the beginning of the scenic drive. There is nothing built here, although there are the remains of some building on one precarious out-cropping of unstable earth. Some drunk teenagers once went over this cliff and miraculously survived. Their pick-up truck hung by its axle on a three foot ledge and was thus saved from plunging into the ocean. They crawled out and up to the road. Everyone said it was a miracle. He liked to believe in such miracles and told her the story because it proved how some people got reprieves, some people were meant to live. Like her and him.

"Some people do and some people don't," she tried not to sound fatalistic, "get reprieves."

"Imagine what a shocking experience! Then to crawl to the top and look down at the truck just hanging there! It actually did fall when they were trying to hoist it out."

"Well, if they were drunk that probably made it easier. They must have acted on instinct. I bet they laughed."

"Might as well laugh. What could be a better occasion to roar with laughter — an escape from certain death, a mangled, twisted death too."

"But people in those situations, like plane crashes, never know what hit them. Even if they have an inkling it's over so fast, it doesn't matter. Not like AIDS."

"No, it's not like AIDS." No matter how hard they tried, it always took Friday night and often half of Saturday to reclaim their private life from the constant focus on AIDS during the week. It hung in the space between them, a spectre of the unknown, of impotence, failure, and death.

She rolled a joint and took a long draw of smoke. They were cruising along the flat lands now, the ocean pounding safely on the white sand to their left. It was not only more secure, but restful and serene to be level with the sea. It reminded her of long, lazy, summer evenings when she sat in a swing, fighting off mosquitos, and watched the sun set over Chesapeake Bay. She told him about it. How she spiked her iced tea with her mother's vodka, got happily smashed, and went skinny dipping with her brother. The flat lands of Delaware where she spent several summer vacations were much like the artichoke and brussels sprout farms that lined the road to Santa Cruz. "If I had my real 'druthers,' I'd live out here in the country."

"It's not practical." He had trouble distinguishing between her dreams and her actual, realizable wants. This got them into numerous petty quarrels, because as soon as she grasped his dilemma she insisted her dream was attainable. The mere mention of the word "practical" raised her hackles.

"Why not? It is too. So we'd have to commute two hours to work. Big deal. Or we could have an apartment in the city and a house out here. We could live here every weekend. Oh, let's not talk about it." She finished off the joint and lit a cigarette. Her face turned to the window, she slumped in the seat and gazed at the darkening red sky.

When they got to the restaurant he pulled into the parking lot and reached to get his sweater from the back seat. Tears were streaming down her cheeks from under her sunglasses which were merely dramatic accoutrements since night had fallen. He pulled her over to cry on his shoulder. "Okay, come on, tell me what's wrong."

"I can't," she stuttered. A stopped up nose made her gulp for breath.

"Sure you can. Come on. It doesn't matter, I'll understand."

"Will you, Chris? Will you really understand?"

"Yes. If you explain it to me I'll understand. I promise."

"It's about Dan." She stopped, fumbled in her purse and took a long time blowing her nose.

"Okay. Go ahead. Tell me. What about Dan?"

"He's sick, Chris. He's really sick." With this she burst into tears again, burying her face in his shoulder and shaking her head back and forth.

"There, there, Suzanne, baby, honey, it's okay. It's okay. Calm down. What's wrong with him?" So this was it. This was why she jetted off to the east coast to see Dan. He knew she had gone to see Dan and not Julia. Now she must feel guilty about their relationship. He felt relieved. It was workable. He just happened to be a doctor. Sickness was something he could fix.

"I'm not sure. The doctor in Boston says it's Epstein-Barr mono, but . . ."

"That's awful, but he'll get over it. You know this problem. It takes a long time, but he'll be fine eventually. Epstein-Barr mono? Jesus, that's unusual. Look, Suzanne, I'm really sorry to hear that he's sick. I know you care about him, but you shouldn't feel guilty about us. You decided not to go with Dan before we ever met. You're not jilting him for me."

"Chris, no, you don't understand. That's not it." Her huge, watery eyes blinked at him with an urgent, but obscure message.

"Well, what is it then?"

"I don't know. . . ." She pulled away from him and put down the visor that had a lighted mirror behind it. She smiled weakly at herself, for his benefit, he thought. Then she busied herself with lipstick, eye-liner, hair barrettes and the like until she seemed satisfied. "I can't go in there like this. I'm a mess. Anyone can see I've been crying."

"You look terrific, fine, beautiful as usual. They keep the lights down low in the bar, remember? That's why you said we'd eat in the bar — lights down low, romantic — remember?"

"Never mind this stuff about Dan." She kissed his cheek softly. "I kind of lost my cool. It's been a rough week." She hugged him. "I'm sure he'll get better. I wish I didn't feel so responsible." She sighed and let go of him.

"Let's go eat. I'm famished." He took a mock bite of her finger and saw the sparkle return to her eyes.

That sparkle in her eye had misled him. He had not even considered then that there was something seriously wrong with her, or that she feared Dan might die. An idea, as real but as unformed and unknowable as a baby at conception, germinated in his mind and took root. But he felt frustrated as though he was being asked to choose the right door in a corridor of doors and being given a handful of keys, the frustration multiplying with every fruitless turn of the wrong one. She told him she wanted to live. She cried about Dan being sick. But she was playing with fire before they met. If this journal was to be believed and that was becoming a bigger IF every moment. If she wanted to make someone think that she was dead and that she was crazy enough to do herself in, this is just the sort of stuff to write. She isolated herself from her friends; she placed little hints about transience, death, impulses, doom. She painted a neat little picture of herself digging her own grave, but she ruined it with one admission: she had trouble saying goodbye.

*　*　*

July 16, 1983

Life is HARD. I don't feel entitled to say that because it isn't really hard for me. My new job goes well. I'm alone in the lab most of the time. Summer is slow. I read a lot. My tech, Carol, is very competent, and she does most of the actual work. We don't talk much. I've taken to compulsively reading two or three newspapers a day, *The Chronicle*, *The New York Times*, *The L.A. Times*. They all say the same thing: the world's teeming millions are out there in trouble. War, fighting, killing. I feel lazy and down. I don't want to play anymore. Drugs are boring. Sex is worse. Actually, on my way home, I do think of going out to play sometimes, but I'm worried someone from the hospital might see me in some bar on some drug. Now I must confine my altered states of consciousness to home or the beach. I have a reputation to maintain. Hah! I decided to start smoking cigarettes regularly for the hell of it. Maybe I'll get to the point of sniffing glue, drinking sterno, whatever. I don't seem to stomach alcohol well these days or I'd drink a lot more. Now I don't just see myself, hovering from a corner in a room, I can hear myself as if someone else were talking. My body is the other person and it says, "Stop poisoning me!" But I, my mind, we don't listen. I say, "To hell with you. The sooner, the better!" I like talking to myself; it prevents any unpredictable comment from anyone else. It's all a game and I know it. I'd like to convince myself that I'm crazy, then I could check into a rest home and have a vacation. Trouble is I know it's a chicken-shit act. I'm on to myself. I've been having terrible headaches lately, chronic sinusitis from too much coke. I hate the pain. I want the impossible, pleasure with no pain. Fun with no price. A free lunch. Relief even costs. I'm about 0-5 years old, somewhere in there. I want the breast I never had. I want to suck it dry, bite it off and swallow it. I want to fight for something. AIDS? Myself? Losing battles. No one knows what's happening to me. What would they think?

July still

It's amazing. As I keep on pretending, my pretenses are more effective. Everyone here thinks I'm quite normal, even more normal than they are. My colleagues are very nice, polite, and unobtrusive, but inquisitive about my work. I decided to begin seeing someone, an acquaintance or colleague, for lunch, coffee or afterwork drink, at least once or twice a week. It's the normal thing to do. This keeps up appearances. Appearances, so it seems, are a great substitute for reality, more acceptable than reality. I'm looking good now. I'm invisible.

Everyday July

My work goes incredibly well. I'm getting organized in the lab. My experiments are working out. Nothing to complain about. I drove out to the beach by myself on Sunday. Sat there and did nothing, stared at the waves. I've limited myself to one joint a day and Lorazepam at night. Coke is gone, and I've lost all my contacts. Life isn't as much fun, but it's more peaceful. I'm keeping my fingers crossed that calm doesn't turn to boredom. Daytime: Work, work, work. Nighttime: Watch T.V.

For God's Sake – July

Is there anything I can't forgive myself for? I was strolling absent-mindedly down Clement St. when a young black man came up to me and pulled out a gun. I thought, he's going to kill me, but he wanted to sell it to me. It was a big gun, a 38 caliber. I shook my head, no, too stunned to speak, but then I couldn't get the gun out of my head. I wished I had bought it. I even went back to the corner to see if he was there. It was so sudden. Later, I wondered if I imagined it – no chance. But it was a strange message from fate. Last week I had lunch with Carol. We talked, like women do, about the rapists, muggers, the reports in the press, what we would do if, etc. She said she'd been mugged one night by a man with a knife. Not thinking, she screamed and he ran away, but he could have slit her throat. She bought a gun, registered it with the police and took lessons on how to use it. I've always hated guns. The idea of having one is more than appalling, but I wanted to see her gun. We went to her apartment and she showed it to me. Then this guy, a coincidence? There's more. The next night I went to an obligatory cocktail party at the gorgeous home of our chief of surgery. After having a heady conversation with some bigwig from Johns Hopkins, I excused myself to pee. There was this loaded gun in the top drawer of this famous surgeon's night-table. I don't know why I was rummaging in his nighttable, but when I saw it, snap. A loaded gun right next to his pillow. I'm not the only one, I thought. It looked very similar to the one the guy offered to sell me. I stole it. I put the damn loaded gun in my Gucci handbag which isn't all that big. It barely fit and the barrel kind of stuck out the end. Worst of all, in playing with the thing in the bathroom I managed to cock the trigger and I didn't know how to uncock it without firing the gun. I went back out and asked the friend who I came with if he would mind taking me back to my car. Bad headache, I said. He, of course, agreed. There I was riding in this car with a load-ed, cocked gun in my handbag. Nobody noticed the bulge or the barrel sticking out. They had no idea. I couldn't believe it myself. We drove with death, and an obvious psychotic, me, in the car for fifteen minutes. Now I've got this stolen gun, a 38 caliber police special. When I got home I had to fire the damned gun out the window to get it uncocked. I just pointed it toward the sky and fired. What a kickback! Then I realized the bullet had to come down somewhere — gravity and all that. This is beyond the pale. Now what the fuck am I going to do with this gun?

Nearing the end — July

Don't be surprised — that's the crucial thing to remember if sanity is to be preserved, and if I am to survive. Expect nothing — second thing to remember. My shrink made one perceptive comment that stays with me. "No one will ever be with you always; no one will ever stay with you forever." I said, "You're so pessimistic." "No," she insisted, "I'm realistic. This is the way life is, life goes on. You're only going on with your life." Realistic? I need to become more realistic. I live in a dream world. I must stop expecting anything, wanting anything, trusting anyone. Dan's coming to visit me soon. I've got this gun. Can I show it to him? I suspect he's really coming to visit Clara, pretty, young Clara. He sounded hostile on the phone. I don't know what to think. Why is he coming back again now?

Aug. – beginning

Dan arrived yesterday. We had a date to spend the afternoon together, but an hour before he was supposed to come over, he called and said he had to change his plans. I knew this would happen. He spent the afternoon with Clara. He doesn't give a damn about me really. Now he's going to be sadistic, hateful, to try and get back at me for not going with him. Well, it won't work. When he came over this morning and tried to hug me I pushed him away. I told him I had a gun and he laughed. He didn't believe me until I showed it to him. He said I better be careful and asked me if I planned to use it on someone. He was lucky, I told him, I still have pacifist leanings. We got stoned and it became quite funny. I don't care if he sleeps with Clara. What difference could it possibly make anyway. We're going to try and be friends. Does that ever work?

Aug. 4, 1983

D is staying a week. By coincidence I ran into the psychiatrist, Brian, and figured now's the time. I need someone to bargain with. After all, Dan's got Clara. I took Brian up on his millionth offer for dinner. It wasn't that bad. D is as predictable as a period. He smells other men and asked me who I was dating now. It wasn't hard to make Brian sound better than he is, tit for tat. We argued, but neither of us had our hearts in it. Decided to call it off and go to the beach. We're lounging about on a deserted beach right now. We hiked down from Pierce Point Trail. I objected to this — as I have many times — because we never hike the trail to the end. But it's fantastic here and the climb back up the ravines won't happen for a while. The ocean is angry today, rough, roaring, pounding the shore, bashing the rocks, back and forth, in and out, polishing the jasper and churt varied hues of blood and mustard. I found a perfectly preserved abalone shell wedged between two immovable boulders. I dug it out, a treasure from the sea. I tried to give it to D, a gift, but he said no, I should keep it. My first thought was that I deserve nothing, certainly not a present from the ocean. A gift of nature. Free. Doesn't seem fair. D is way down the beach, collecting shells. He looks like a tiny doll on the horizon. I wish we could talk, really talk, but we never did. I'd like to tell him what's going on, but I don't know what I'd say. He says he's feeling better and gaining some weight. He loves his new job. But his hair looks thinner. He looks older and kind of pale. I was relieved to hear he went to a doctor in Boston who agreed the stress of leaving here and me was probably the source of his physical problems. Dan said he tossed the vitamins he gave him but kept the sleeping pills and Valium. He says his problem is not smoking enough good California dope. Probably.

Aug. 6

Why am I taking up with this guy, Brian? He's like the rest. No, worse. He's a rather uneducated, sycophant from a wealthy family, totally self-absorbed, and a deluded drug user like me. He's pretty good-looking and has a nice body. His most redeeming quality is that he's been so involved in himself he hasn't given a thought to the possibility of external reality. Now that's interesting. It's one thing to give it up voluntarily after a struggle, but it's something else indeed to have never even known it was (is) out there. Could this be the reason he's in psychiatry??? I wonder how he ever got through medical school. Anyway, he's done me a good deed. He's made me look at the external world more than I have lately. I couldn't believe that after five years of living in S.F. this man had never been to the ocean. He's like leading around a baby: See, this is a rock, that's a flower, that's the ocean, those are eucalyptus trees. Those are lilies. You know the flowers one sends to funerals?

Aug. 8

Brian's got some great coke. When it's put there in front of me, free, I can't resist it. After being off it for a while the high is terrific, up there, but. . . . Why do I ramble on like this? Can't be afraid of life I tell myself, but. . . . I get up every morning and say, today, I'll be different. And I never am. I keep on acting the very same way over and over again. More self-destruction, more depression, more immobility in everything, but work. I have this inability to care about ordinary things. Life or death, life or death, beepers go off in my dreams. Emergency. Code Red. Emergency. I'm so screwed up — the only phrase that fits — I don't know what to do. I've tried everything. My energy is at an all time low. In the early evening I can only head for my bed and lie there in a state of maddening consciousness, not sleep, but not awake either with loud ringing in my ears, buzzing in my head, pains in my chest, nausea. I get up and take a drug for the worst symptom which then aggravates the other symptoms for which I take other drugs, ad nauseam. Finally, I fall into a stuporous sleep, wake up the next morning and say, I won't do whatever made me feel that way again today. But it goes on.

Aug. 9, 1983

D will be leaving in two days. The same old shit again. But it's lessened, thankfully. He's had a bout of flu, similar to the one I had a few days ago. We seem fused on the level of viral transmission. Reminds me of that Paul Simon song, "All that winter we shared a cold." Sad song. Well, hell, I'll miss him again. Out of the frying pan, into the fire. Right, Mom?

Middle of August

I won't write anymore. It's useless. I thought it over, but something tells me it's just beginning. I always feared getting into IT to the point that I couldn't write about IT. The time is coming. . . .

August 19

The AIDS patients are pouring into the wards like wounded soldiers evacuated from the front lines of battle in the war to end all wars. I could work twenty-four hours a day and never be close to finished. The lab is swimming in blood.

"Any day now . . . any day now . . . I shall be released."

* * *

The wheel of Dan's bike caught on the loose board in the weathered old wood of the porch. He jerked it up the steps with more force than necessary ripping the board farther out of its place. This old crumbling Victorian house was a compromise, but its advantages far out-weighed its disadvantages, especially now that he was so tired all the time. He rented the downstairs flat which had two huge bedrooms, sixteen-foot ceilings, a fireplace and a big bay window over the porch. The upstairs was easier and cheaper to heat, but he couldn't climb stairs without gasping for breath everytime. Anyway, it was big enough and had elegant hardwood floors, built-in bookcases and a buffet in the dining room with the original beveled glass doors — Suzanne would love it, if she came. Plus, it was within walking distance to the campus and the bustling town of Cambridge. It was, by Boston standards, the find of the century — affordable, close, no landlord on the premises and not tackily redecorated for students. He fumbled with his key, balancing the bike on his thigh. Everything he did required patience and perseverance.

It had been years since he experienced an eastern autumn. The first chilly nip hit the air weeks ago like the cold breeze that blew off the Pacific in the winter. A kind of excitement seemed to lighten the steps of people in the streets, an enthusiasm that beckoned the coming of football games, apple pies, cosy nights around a fire, Halloween pumpkins and parties. An old maple tree that towered over the house in the tiny front yard had turned a bright banana yellow. Now faded to rust, the leaves drifted to the sidewalk where neighborhood children raked them into huge piles and threw them at each other. The street was populated by couples his age, most with one or two kids from babies to teenagers. He spent many a restful afternoon sitting on his porch watching the mothers wheel by their progeny in strollers or old-fashioned prams. They welcomed him to the neighborhood, even brought him casseroles and brownies and bowls of fruit. Almost everyone had some connection to Harvard as graduate students or as faculty or staff. They seemed without exception just as he had imagined they would be: intelligent, serious, well-read, hard-working, thoughtful and well . . . normal. This was the life he had envisioned living with Suzanne. If only he could get her here for any length of time, he was certain it would work.

When he let things get him down, when he felt sick, he experienced a new indifference about Suzanne that he found difficult to believe. Sometimes he thought about Clara — how she would fit in here, how they would produce beautiful red-haired children, and she would blossom as a happy young wife and mother. It made him angry that the mysterious passion that swept him away with Suzanne just wasn't aroused by Clara. Not that he didn't enjoy sex with Clara — he did — but it didn't have that quality of satisfying a tremendous hunger, of making him feel electric and alive in every cell of his body. Clara was just as pretty, just as smart as Suzanne, even closer to him by profession, yet he had grown used to Suzanne's spontaneous — he should call it unpredictable — behavior. He wondered, when he spent days and nights with Clara, if this was what was missing. In fact, he'd never realized that something could be missing from a relationship until he experienced it with Clara. She was so available to him, so easy-going, so sensible and understanding. But after a few hours with her he began to long for Suzanne, for their crazed, drugged drives in the country, their knock-down-drag-out fights, their tender hours of love-making, their tension-filled discussions. He thought about this a lot while watching the maple out the bay window go through its marvelous fall changes. He wanted to think that passion wasn't important. What was important was consistency, predictability, loyalty, trust, companionship. More than this, he needed a wife. Someone to take care of him. Unfortunately, he still loved Suzanne.

He stumbled over the boxes in the hall and collapsed onto the sofa, tossing his dirty clothes from yesterday and a wet towel to the floor. Dishes sat scattered on the tops of tables and unopened boxes of books. The haphazardly placed furniture was covered with newspapers, folders, lecture notes and so many other things that he had lost track of where anything was. This mess bothered him only in so far as it hampered his getting work done. His health was his major concern, next to preparing his courses, and that meant rest, rest and more rest. Sleep, eat well, and do as little as possible the doctor had said, and don't waste any energy worrying about anything else. He followed these orders exactly, but even if he hadn't been a good patient, he couldn't have done much more. Riding his bike five blocks to his office almost did him in, and he bought a sofa from the Salvation Army so he could lie down there. The doctor had told him not to expect to feel well for a year. A year! It was a damned good thing that his contract ran for six years and that his tenure looked pretty definite.

The newspaper lay on top of a morass of papers in front of him. He lay back, stretched out and tried to read it. There was a front page headline on AIDS which he read with reluctant curiosity. This article — one of many like it — detailed the symptoms of ARC and AIDS and gave the current statistics of incidence and death. Whenever he read these almost daily reports he couldn't help wondering if it was possible that he had it. The doctor was vehement that he did not — no history of homosexuality, no blood transfusions, no shooting of drugs, and a relatively monogamous sex life the past four years. But. . . . He crumpled the paper and closed his eyes.

But why didn't the diarrhea stop? Why was he still losing weight? Why did he forget what he was saying in the middle of a lecture that he knew by heart? "Don't think about it," the doctor said. "Your mental state is weakened by the EBV virus. It's very serious, and you musn't deplete your resources by dwelling on this AIDS problem. If you can't stop worrying about this, you should seek psychological counseling. Lots of young men with real risk factors come to me with the same fears. Please, Mr. Lowen, count your blessings." He heard some variant of this lecture every time he went because no matter how hard he tried he couldn't stop asking.

He floated in a twilight sleep; only chills were keeping him partially awake. Night came early and he heard the distant calls of mothers to their children. "Dinner's ready!" He had to get up and turn up the heat and fix his own dinner. He had to write his lecture for tomorrow and attend to some correspondence. Sleep seemed to reach up from within the sofa, put arms around him and pull him uncomfortably into the springs. It soon felt like a heavy weight had fallen onto his chest and was crushing him so that he couldn't breathe. He struggled to wake up. The ringing of the phone jolted him like a cattle prod. He fought to move a leg off the couch without opening his eyes. Groping frantically, he picked up the receiver just as the line went dead. He fell into a straight backed chair and shook his head. There it was again — that sensation that he didn't know where he was — confusion. Order, a state he'd never especially needed in his home or his head, had to be constantly nourished. He had a mental system for doing this: he pretended he was studying Russian and counted backwards from one hundred. The phone rang again and startled him out of his mental exercise.

"Hello. Lowen here." Static crackled in the wires.

"Dan. Dan. Is that you?" The connection made the caller sound as though she was in the midst of a wind storm.

"Yeah. Who's this?"

"Dan. This is Julia. I'm calling from London. It's about Suzanne. Have you seen her? Have you heard from her in the past few days?"

"No. I don't think so. Wait a minute. Yeah. I spoke to her on the phone about . . . let's see. When was it?" He looked at the calendar on the wall beside his phone. "Last week sometime."

There was a dead silence. The wind had stopped and he thought they had been disconnected. "Dan, I don't know how to tell you this, but . . ."

"What? What's wrong? Julia? Julia, can you hear me?" His stomach turned over, and he suddenly felt very weak.

"Dan, something has happened to Suzanne. She's disappeared or something. Her brother called me here because the police asked her family to contact her friends and see if anyone had seen her."

"What! Where is she? What happened? What are you talking about?"

"I don't know. All I know is what he told me. She was reported missing by someone at the hospital. The police found her car at Pt. Reyes. It was unlocked with her purse and sweater in it. They called her parents who called her brother who called me. I thought, maybe, she was with you in Boston. I hoped. . . . How are you feeling?"

"How am I feeling!" His emotions were like an elevator gone beserk racing from floor to floor without stopping. "I feel sick, but I always feel sick. Never mind. What do you think is going on? When did you talk to her last?"

"I spoke to her about a week ago on the phone. She sounded pretty good, but. . . ." She had no idea what Dan knew about recent events in Suzanne's life. She knew little of substance about his illness. Suzanne had mentioned it the last time they spoke — that she feared Dan had ARC. Up until now she had rejected this out of hand. It was Suzanne's occupational hazard that she believed such things. She couldn't imagine Dan having a homosexual affair; she couldn't imagine him having any kind of affair, although Suzanne had told her about Clara. Perhaps it was a mistake to call Dan, but she had to find out what happened to Suzanne. She blurted it out. "Dan, the police think she committed suicide. I'm going out there."

"Don't be absurd! She'd never commit suicide! I don't believe it. I don't believe it." He was shaking all over with rage and fear, hanging on that edge of disbelief over a bottomless pit of truth.

"I don't believe it either, but I'm going to find out. I'm flying out of here in the morning. I've got a five hour lay over in New York. I guess I'll call you when I get there and find out what's going on. I'll keep you posted, Okay?"

"No. I'm going too. I'm going with you. I want to see her. I knew there was something wrong when I saw her three weeks ago. Don't worry we'll find her. She's got to stop being so god-damned stubborn. I want her here with me."

"Well. I don't know what to say, Dan. I'll give you my flight number out of New York. Do you want to meet me at JFK or in San Francisco?" He obviously didn't know about Chris. Now she had another problem on her hands, but she wanted company. She was scared, but at the same time she didn't know if she could handle Dan's reaction when she told him. How could Suzanne do this to her? If she weren't so frightened she would be furious.

"I'll meet you at JFK. We can fly out together. When did this happen?"

"I'll tell you everything I know on the plane. It's really late here. I've got to get to sleep." She wanted time to think, to plan what she would say to him. He was going to find out about Chris sooner or later. And where was Chris anyway? She'd called his house a dozen times. She called the hospital at least that often. He seemed to be missing too, but no one thought he'd committed suicide. Maybe they ran off together. But why? Now she'd dragged Dan into this. She regretted it, but it was too late. "I'm on TWA, flight number 54, leaving JFK at 9 pm. Okay? Got that?"

"Yeah. I'll be there." His grip was loosening on the phone, and he stuttered, "but, but, Julia, don't you know anything more? I mean, do you believe that this is really possible? Is this possible?"

"Dan, anything is possible. Right?"

He hung up. Anything's possible. Anything's possible. Oh God, Suzanne, what have you done? In a calm, calculated manner he telephoned every one he knew in Berkeley and San Francisco. No one had even seen her in two months. The secretary at the hospital had left to go home. The police bureau of missing persons was closed. Some woman in her lab told him about the article in *The Chronicle*. She read it to him over the phone, then asked him if he was a relative. Not a relative, he replied, just a friend, an old friend. He phoned the airlines and got a seat on the plane out of New York. He arranged to get on a commuter flight from Boston. He called his teaching assistant to take over his classes and asked him to stop by and pick up the lecture notes. He packed his suitcase, ate a box of pasta with cheese, fell on the bed in his clothes, and cried himself to sleep.

*   *   *

End of August

The fog has lifted. Summer is about to begin. Christ Almighty, it's happening again! I met another man, a doc at work. When he first came to my office — followed me from the faculty meeting no less — I wanted to toy with him, same as the others. But he's actually quite adorable, funny, and cute. I caught myself liking him before I could stop it. We met for a drink. Nothing happened, except that we talked and for the first time in a long time everything seemed real to me. Real and new. Fresh. A wonderful few moments of blissful unselfconsciousness. I forgot about myself, but no floating away or anything like that. I was there, simply there, being appropriate and sociable on a first date. Is this possible? Can I be real again?

August 31

His name is Chris. I try not to think about him, but he called and I was thrilled. This is silly, ridiculous, absurd. Never again. Never again. How many times have I said this? How many more? I agreed to see him again. A real date. You know what that means. I'm supposed to see Brian the same day, but this is a good excuse to get rid of him. Yet, do I want to do that? Isn't it better to keep myself from getting involved? My idiotic, uncontrollable feelings! Now when I see him around the hospital, I get this little rush.

Sept. A New Month

We had our "date" and Oh Boy! Am I in trouble! I really like this guy. He doesn't let me get away with my excuses, my rationales, my efforts to trivialize relationships. He's smart like Dan, but not nearly as easy to manipulate. I can't believe that I slept with him, that he felt so familiar this way and comfortable. But what am I doing to him? He's been involved with someone who sounds like a nice person for a long time. I'm pretty shaky right now — to say the least godammit. I don't want to hurt him, but I'm weak. I don't think I can resist the temptation of feeling good again, feeling love.

Sept. 3, 1983

There are a lot of problems with seeing Chris. One of us should have the sense to know that mixing business and pleasure isn't a good idea. But I'm desperate. There's not enough time in a lifetime to be in love. Being alone has made me all the more sensitive to longing. I want him now, immediately. The future is what I want to think about, the future is all we might have together. Memories. I want to have memories of Chris, a history with him.

Sept. 5, 1983

Death is in the present. In the future too. Death is the end of memory. What if Chris died? I was thinking today about Koestler's suicide. His statement in *Dialogue with Death* about time: something to the effect that time collapsed when he left prison after four months on death row. Every second in prison felt like an eternity, but an eternity in which nothing happened. After he had been out a while, he said it felt like it never happened, because nothing happened. I felt like I knew what he meant. I've been on death row. I know what that's like. I've heard many people on their death bed say this — nothing ever happened. There was no time at all. Life is short. The only way I know it exists is by feeling. At least, my brief subjective moment hasn't been emotionless. I've had all that's possible. Almost. This makes me think of having a child. It hurts. It makes me want to fall on my knees and pray or beg.

Sept. 15, 1983

The journey continues. Chris and me. Traveling. Boy, am I scared. It isn't a good time to be in love. Work is a harassment. Chris is as absorbed in the AIDS horror as I am, but he deals with it with courage. I envy his bravery, his persevering. I wish we weren't working on the same disease with the same patients in the same department, same hospital. It's hard to play down our involvement when my tech finds me kissing him in the lab or we end up shouting at each other in the cafeteria. I wish I knew what he said to his old girl-friend while I was in Boston. I'm jealous. I know he'd find it hard to say anything that would hurt her. Our weekends are such fun. I've probably told him too much about myself, yet in another way not enough. Sometimes I think: this is it, this is the man Julia told me about, the one to stop with, to settle down with, but it's way too soon for that. I'm rushing to get the preliminaries over with, but why? I don't really want to rush into this. I have bad premonitions, can't shake them. In my dreams I'm always running to catch a train or a plane or trying to find someone, but it's too late. I'm always too late. Just once, just once if I could stop time. Please, let it be now.

Sept. 19

Ivan called. I told him I could never see him again. Never. Ever. But this time he has a legitimate problem: his boy-friend, Peter, is at General, and the doctors won't tell him anything because he's not next of kin. I agreed to find out his diagnosis. The resident said pneumococcoyl pneumonia, but I'm worried.

They didn't do a broncoscophy. He's got no insurance, no money, and seems to be responding to treatment. They want to get him out A.S.A.P. Ivan thinks it's AIDS. The kid was shooting a lot of smack, and he was bisexual. I'm going over to see him tomorrow. I can't believe this is happening. Too close. I told Ivan AIDS is a pretty hard disease to catch as far as we know. Sharing needles, multiple sexual partners, blood to blood contact, that sort of thing. Right. Well. My old out of body thing came back, I heard myself talking to him as if I were across the room in another space. His classic philosophical response: life's many twists and turns, death is only another conversion of matter into energy, blah, blah, blah. He said he hasn't shot any smack or coke with him since that night in the Mission with Dora and me last February. A night I wish I could erase. I did insist that we boil the needles, I remember that, and we each had our own. I didn't go to medical school for nothing. Ivan wasn't impressed. He says he feels fine, just existential Angst as usual. What if this kid does have AIDS? My God. I've got to get some of his blood. I've got to stay calm.

End of September

How could I live with him? Marry him? What would we have? I have a computer, a color T.V., a cassette recorder, good stereo equipment, a Cuisinart, a house, a shitload of books, art, furniture, clothes. He's got all this too, plus mutual funds. I even have some CD's. He'd have me to do his laundry on Saturdays, and I'd have him to balance the checkbook once a month. We could fuck a lot. God, I wish I could stop thinking about him for one stupid moment. I don't want to be a doctor's wife. I'm a doctor. It's so typical, so sterile, so pointless. There's nothing to be gained for either of us by marriage. It's irrational. Chris is a normal person, I think. Like Dan, not very screwed up, few actual emotional problems or psychological hang-ups. I'd rather be outright California pointless with Brian. No fooling myself. I'd rather drink myself into oblivion but it won't come. Anxiety absorbs alcohol like a sponge. Come here baby, come here baby, come here to me, come here . . . fuck me baby, come here, come now, come. . . .

* * *

The general store had almost everything Pat needed. Now for the hard part, a call to the hospital. The quarter fell into the phone slot, the dial tone came on, and she dialed the number, her last handful of change ready. "Please deposit one dollar and twenty-five cents, please deposit one dollar and twenty-five cents, please deposit one dollar and twenty-five cents." Her shaking hands fumbled with the quarters. Finally, she heard the familiar voice of the department secretary. "Department of Immunology, Gloria speaking, can I help you?"

"Gloria, this is Pat."

"Pat. Where are you? Where's Chris? The detective was just here again. They come everyday. Several other people have been here looking for him. I don't know how much longer I can hold them off." A distinct note of irritation rose with every word.

"Well, listen, please keep trying. Chris isn't in real good shape. I've gotten a little out of him, I mean, he's talking about it now, but he can't come back to work yet. He's not implicated, you know. He didn't have anything to do with it." Her desperation matched Gloria's in tone. "He wants to know what people are saying? What do the police say? Anything?"

"Hang on a minute. Someone's on the other line."

Her feet shuffled around the phone booth. The afternoon fog bringing its usual damp chill.

"Okay, hello, are you there?"

"Yeah."

"That was this woman, Julia Carmichael again. She says she was Suzanne's best friend for fifteen years. She insists she has to talk to Chris. It's very, very important, something about information he needs to know. She's really upset, Pat. She calls several times a day. She flew here all the way from London and is staying at Suzanne's house. The two of them — she's with another friend of Suzanne's, Daniel. They have been over here twice. Really concerned. Can't you convince Chris to talk to them?"

"Your three minutes is up, please deposit one dollar and twenty-five cents, please deposit one dollar and twenty-five cents."

"Shit! I'm out of change, can you call me back? 707-865-9120." The line went dead. She didn't know if Gloria got the number. Jumping up and down to stay warm, she surveyed the main street of Pt. Reyes Station or what was still visible of it. There was a seedy Mexican bar across the street — a warmer place, perhaps with a pay phone. The phone rang finally.

"Pat?"

"Yeah, I'm so glad you got the number."

"Where are you anyway?"

"Uhh, I'm at my aunt's in Petaluma."

"Well, what shall I tell this woman? I know she'll call again."

"Give me Suzanne's home number, I'll call her."

"Are you sure you want to get mixed up in this?" Gloria's mother hen voice crackled. "After what he did to you? I don't understand you, Pat, such a nice girl. Why are you protecting him?"

"Don't think I haven't asked myself those same questions. But we were together a long time, you know. I care about him. You should see him. He's in pretty bad shape. What he did to me is nothing compared to what she did to him."

"Doesn't surprise me. The way those two carried on around here. Well, poor girl, I don't understand you young people these days. I just don't understand this. Why would such a smart, pretty girl do such a thing?"

"Gloria, I haven't got time to discuss it now. Is there anything more you can tell me about the police? What quesions are they asking?"

"Same questions everyday: Did we notice anything strange about her behavior? Can we give a recounting of the last time we saw her? What was she wearing? Did she say or do anything unusual? Who were her friends? Who last saw her? Was she depressed? Things like that. Poor Carol, they've had her down at the station twice. She was the last one to see her alive as far as we know. But no one around here knew her at all personally. She just started working in July, kept to herself, seemed very reserved, dedicated, serious type, you know. We haven't had much to tell them. The most excitement we've had around here in a long time, I'll tell you. Dr. Thomas refuses to discuss it. He's upset. Looks bad for the department. The paper's playing it up as an AIDS suicide, you know – depressed, overworked, young doctor can't take the pressure of the AIDS crisis. Besides, he's all worried if it will affect the grant. That's about it."

"What about Chris?"

"Well, frankly, Pat, I hate to say this to you, but everyone knew he fell head over heels for her. You couldn't avoid seeing it. I guess they think he's grief-stricken. Dr. Thomas told me to put in sick leave papers for him until we heard. How is he anyway?"

"He's okay. Getting better, I think." A gush of emotion sent tears spilling from her eyes. She choked. Gloria shouldn't know, but why not? Her feelings were hurt too.

Gloria, after thirty years of listening with a mother's third ear, could tell she had hit a raw nerve. "How are you holding up?"

She bit her tongue. "Oh, I'm hanging in there." Now the crying worsened. That minutia of sympathy, of which she wanted more, stirred her anguish. This was no time to break, and more tongue biting kept her together. "So the police aren't interested in Chris?"

"Well, they might be if they knew about him. But so far nobody here has mentioned him. That's why you have to talk to this woman, Julia. She's going to tell the police about Chris if she doesn't hear from him soon. There's trouble if she does, Pat, although the police seem convinced that this is a suicide. Dr. Thomas told all of us not to say a word about Chris and Suzanne, that they were entitled to their private lives, and he still was. I don't think the police want to waste more time on the case, as they call it. You know, cut and dry, suicide closes the case. On the other hand, this one detective acts like it may be some act, that she ran away or was abducted, but he told me they didn't have much evidence to go on for that possibility. Hang on — the other line again."

Gloria could go on forever about this, Pat realized. It *was* the most excitement she'd had in thirty years of running the department. There was bound to be curiosity. How much did she really know, and how much was her own unique speculation? Well, if anybody knew anything it would be Gloria. She kept tabs. The conversation was taking on that intimate tone of juicy gossip in the mill. It unsettled her. The whole thing was a Fellini circus.

"I'm back. Hello?"

"I'm still here. Gloria, thanks so much for your help, especially keeping Chris out of this. I'm sure he'll be able to call you himself in a few days. Can you give me Suzanne's home number?"

"Sure." She searched her directory and recited the number. "There's one thing I forgot to tell you. I don't know if it's important, but some Dr. Wallensky has called several times, too. He says he was a friend of Suzanne's and wants to know about some of her research results. Something about a friend of his at General. He wondered who would be taking over her AIDS studies. Of course, I told him that information couldn't be given out to anyone. He sounded like a real character, threatened to come over here and have a word with the chief of medicine."

She had forgotten about Wallensky but remembered Chris's request when she heard the name. "I'm glad you mentioned that, Chris asked me to get in touch with this guy. I don't know why, but did he leave a number or anything?"

"Yes, it's right here. I don't know if I'd call him; he sounds very strange, foreign." Gloria could never resist meddling, but in her pivotal position, she seemed to have every right.

"I'd better go now. Gloria, thanks again. And tell Carol thanks too. I'll call her when I can, soon."

"Pat? Can I ask you something? I hope you won't mind."

Oh, God, here it comes, she stiffened. "Sure."

"Well, do you think she killed herself?"

She breathed a sigh of relief. "Yes."

"Do you think it has anything to do with AIDS? I mean, my husband thinks I should quit my job. I get a little worried, you know. It's frightening. . . ." Another roll was about to begin, the tension rose in her voice.

"No, no, Gloria. Don't worry about that. I'm sure she was a very careful researcher. I don't think it has anything to do with AIDS. We didn't know her. She must have been very unhappy. I don't know. I've got to go now. Thanks."

"Okay, tell Chris to get better soon. Our thoughts are with him."

"Bye."

"Bye."

She stood, freezing, in the phone booth and tried to think. The afternoon was passing away too fast. Her head ached, and she realized she hadn't eaten since yesterday. The dingy bar began to look good to her. Across the street she dashed and entered the dark, *La Cucaracha*. A woman sat with her head on the bar next to a glass of whiskey. Two older men in ratty clothes stared into clouds of cigarette smoke over their beers. The bartender, a fat, ageless, Hispanic woman wiped newly washed glasses with her apron. Except for the drunken woman at the bar who was dead to the world, they gave her a mere fleeting blank glance. Chili with beans or chili without beans and tortillas, that was it for the menu, scrawled over the bar on a blackboard. Without beans, she decided. Yes, there was a pay phone in the back. The woman pointed down a dark hall. First, Julia, then Wallensky, she had to stop this woman from going to the police, and she had no idea how much or what she knew about Chris. What information could she possibly have for him?

The phone rang ten times, and she was about to hang up when a weak male voice answered. "Is Julia Carmichael there?"

"Who's this?" His voice was suspicious, hostile.

"My name is Pat Silvino. I'm a friend of Chris Alterberg from the hospital. The secretary told me Julia was looking for him. It's about Suzanne."

"I know what it's about. I'm Daniel Lowen," a loud cough interrupted him, but after a few moments he continued, "also a friend of Suzanne's. More than a friend. Anyway, we know she was involved with him until," he paused again, "until she disappeared. We'd like to talk to Alterberg, that's all."

"Well, he's pretty upset."

"He's upset! How do you think I feel. Listen, I don't know this guy, but you tell him he's going to be a lot more upset if he doesn't come up with some explanations." There was a female voice in the background, then a scuffle.

"Hello. This is Julia Carmichael, who am I speaking to?"

"Pat. I'm a friend of Chris Alterberg. Gloria, the secretary at the hospital told me you wanted to get in touch with him."

"Yes. I've known Suzanne since college. We were very close." Her voice started to break. "I want to know what happened. I loved her. I can't believe this. I don't want to believe this. Her family is in shock. Anything you could tell us we'd really appreciate." Her efforts to maintain composure were failing.

"I don't know very much really." Julia's sorrow touched her in spite of her own feelings about Suzanne. She saw no reason to hide anything from her. "I just talked to Chris myself this morning. He's pretty broken up too." The Mexican woman was gesturing to her chili. She waved back to pacify her.

"We're going to run out of time any second. I'm in a bar at Pt. Reyes Station, a pay phone. Here's the number. Call me back."

She raced to the table and took the bowl of chili with her to the pay phone. The woman, shaking her head, brought her a chair.

"Hello."

"Yes, this is Julia. Is he there with you?"

"No. I left him at the beach. He's been there going on five days now. He won't leave."

"Where they found her car?"

"Yes, it's rather far out. About an hour and a half from the East Bay, at least. Chris is out there, and he refuses to leave." She heard Julia ask Daniel if he knew the beach where her car was found. A muffled answer she couldn't hear.

"Daniel thinks he knows this beach. We'll come out there."

"No, not yet. I mean, it's getting late. You might not find us in the dark. Anyway, Chris is determined to stay the night. You might as well come tomorrow. I'm going to camp out with him."

"Why's he staying out there? I don't understand."

"Me neither. It's her journal. He says he has her journal and wants to finish it there. Believe me I've tried to talk him out of it, but he won't budge. Maybe if you talked to him?"

Another muffled conversation began. She heard Daniel raise his voice, more coughing, Julia's hand was over the receiver. The chili was swimming with fat, now congealed like scum over a stagnant pool. She put it on the floor and ate the tortilla. "How do we know you'll be there tomorrow?"

"Well, he's not leaving, and I'm staying with him. I don't know. I guess you've got no reason to trust me. I can't predict what he'll do, but he says he's staying there. I'll give you my apartment number in the city if you want. Gloria knows me. You can check it with her if you don't believe me. I just spoke to her."

"Okay. Have you known this guy, Chris, a long time?"

"Several years. We were living together before . . ."

"I'm sorry."

"Yeah, well, we're all sorry now. I guess."

"I don't know if you ever knew Suzanne, but . . ."

"No, I never met her. I saw her once."

"She and Dan had been living together, dating steadily for three years. I guess you two have something in common." Pat heard choking sounds, then Julia blowing her nose. Dan's talking went on in the background, a Greek chorus.

Suddenly, she couldn't bear anymore. Her emotions were dry as a bone in the desert. "I have to go now. I'm sorry. I know you've come a long way. You should talk to Chris. I don't know what else to say."

"Tell Chris we'll be there tomorrow. Thanks for calling." Her sniffles continued as the phone went dead.

Wallensky's number glared at her from the piece of note paper. Not another one. She couldn't face it. It was four-thirty. The sun would be setting, and soon there would be no light at all. A shudder shot through her. She had to get back down the trail before dark. The woman at the bar still lay in her drunken stupor. The men sat in their cloud of smoke. The Mexican proprietress wiped her hands on the dirty apron and sold her two bottles of liquor — tequila and brandy. As soon as she sat in the safety of her VW Rabbit, she took a big slug of brandy. Unlike herself, but hell, nothing was like it was before, why should she be an exception. The warm brandy felt good in her throat. One more swallow and hit the road, she said to herself.

* * *

The fog was rolling in again. Chris looked up from the journal into the grey mist. Nothing beyond the shoreline was visible, but he imagined he saw people walking in the mist, back and forth, like ghosts on patrol. He dismissed this vision and pulled out his last cigarette. His mind was reeling from what he'd read. She had loved him. He was in there. It was what he thought it was. He recognized the caution she had about their working together. He recognized the doubts she had about rushing into a serious relationship. He recognized the arguments, pro and con, about marriage. For the first time in what seemed like an eternity, her words comforted him, made him feel almost happy.

At this moment he decided there was no doubt: she was not dead. She could not have commited suicide. She ran away because she was afraid of commitment. She was over-burdened at work. But she was not dead. Now it was only a question of finding her. Perhaps she had somehow switched cars here to throw everyone off. She must have known what she was doing. She might have been upset, but it wouldn't have affected her ability to engineer this sort of disappearance if she really wanted it. He felt the most wonderful certainty now that she could be found. She left her journal for him, because it contained the clue. That was it; she planned the whole thing, knowing he would find it. His task was de-coding the message. He was smart. She said so.

What were these things that she didn't tell him? Do they have anything to do with where she might be? Journeys? Traveling? Together. What would have made her flee so hysterically though? Like a stinging nettle or a recalcitrant thorn, AIDS insistently crossed his mind. If he could get his hands on Wallensky now. . . . This guy had scared her to death. No. That's only a manner of speaking, a turn of phrase. Anger rose into his throat. Okay, he was going to continue. He felt stronger. He put a new battery in the flashlight and began to read again.

* * *

October – My Month

I want to walk into an analyst's office and say: listen, I've got a problem. I am falling in love. And it's impossible. Because love is behind me, in my past, and love isn't the problem. You see, I've lied and cheated. I've abused drugs and alcohol and myself. I'm obsessed with death. I think I'm a child of the ocean, and I want to go home to Mommy. Nothing is ever enough. And furthermore, I keep many secrets. I imagine that I am dying and people I care about are dying? People *are really dying!* Am I crazy?

Oct. 5

Good morning, Mr. Freud. My lover makes me feel too good. We discussed this last hour if you'll recall? I'm a woman and I like sex. But I'm getting it all confused with death. Have you

216

ever heard of such problems? Well, my last analyst hadn't. You better be careful or I'll fuck you and kill you right here in your office! I'm trying to put one over on myself. I don't have my wits about me anymore. I'd like to set a good example for the kids. I'm suffering for my injustices, yours too, and for my lack of control. I want to stop taking and start doing something about this. I want to fight my way out of this. Can you help me?

Oct. 6

Too much happening. Can't keep up. Had to fly back East to see Julia. I cancelled my grand rounds talk. Chris is covering for me. Everything is going berserk. Julia's boy-friend had some sort of breakdown and won't talk. To anyone. She's leaving for London to try and sort it out. I can't help her. She's too far away. Dan flew down to New York to have lunch with me, but I chickened out on telling him much about Chris. I did tell Julia, but she isn't very interested under the circumstances. Dan's doctor in Boston thinks he has Epstein-Barr mono. They're running a series of tests. Says he feels better now that someone has given it a name. I didn't want to tell him how long it takes to get over this type of mono, if he has it. Chris is angry with me for leaving again, even for two days. On the plane I thought I was going to crack up for sure, heart palpitations, broke into a sweat, couldn't breath, classic panic attack. I was completely certain the plane was going to crash every minute we were in the air. I took 20mg of Valium and it barely fazed me. When we landed the stewardess helped me off the plane. Found Koestler's *Scum of the Earth* in a used bookstore. Love the title.

October 9, 1983

We are getting closer and closer. Both feeling the same, both setting sail on a life-raft into the ocean, the two of us, in a storm. Our need for each other is rising with the waves. I love him, and I'm going to marry him. What a surprise. Life does start over and over.

Oct. 11

I have to stop being crazy and get myself through this. For both of us.

Oct 12

Chris is too nice to me. I don't deserve all the things he gives me. The cosmic balance sheet doesn't balance when I feel I'm getting more than I'm giving. Yet he seems to feel blissfully happy. I wonder sometimes if I've made him enter my fantasy world, and thus, neither of us is real. But most of the time I know he's not a delusion or a fantasy. He keeps reminding me that we both have to deal with reality. The only discrepancy between us is that he thinks this is going to be fun and easy.

October, October

We're in the mountains. Mountains like I've never seen before. Jagged peaks with streams of snow falling like lava from the heights that surround vast areas of high desert, scrub brush, a few pines, giant grey boulders....

Later

Chris and I spent the day driving through Death Valley. He met a geologist, Winston, another rock person. We followed him around all afternoon, collecting wonderful rocks and minerals. I found a large, beautiful pyrite crystal, half red from iron deposits. I now know more about rocks than I'd ever imagined I would. But it's still the feeling of a rock in my hand that fascinates me, its shape, texture, form, not what it's composed of. I snuck away from the motel quite early to be by myself for a while. I find that when I'm with Chris all the time, I begin to feel like I'm not with him. I'm just tagging along. I don't do what I want when I'm with him. I do what I think he wants then I resent it later. Old ghosts. He seems to know so much about everything in the world, but so little about people, especially women. Last night we shared our celebration dinner with the geologist. Fitting, in one sense, Chris gave me the most gorgeous diamond ring in an art deco setting, an old cut that catches the light and color in millions of facets. I didn't want to invite Winston. After all we were celebrating our decision to get married, a pretty intimate, romantic occasion for us, but I did what I thought Chris wanted. Funny too, because I got on better with Winston than Chris did. Chris didn't talk much, and I felt the burden of conversation thrown on me. Then I wondered if he didn't talk because he knew they would talk about rocks, and I would be bored. It surprised me since I thought that's why Chris invited him, to pump him for rock data. All the same . . . peculiar. I was aware that I had been feeling neglected by Chris, ignored in these most crucial of days. I liked having Winston to talk to, but it was all backwards and disjointed. Chris said Winston wanted to impress us. But why? He was the expert. Is this what living with Chris all the time will be like? Peculiar?

Oct. 16

Death Valley is spectacular. There isn't enough time to explore it. Some day. The tourists are bizarre, middle America, from all classes, places, ages, centuries, walks of life. Young couples with children, babies, old folks in Bermuda shorts. They all look odd, unattractive. Some of the men are really Neanderthal. I've been in San Francisco so long I've forgotten about the rest of the country, the solid citizens of the U.S.A.

Yesterday I saw a huge mountain of "waste" from a rock dump, a mine. Winston said it was a pile of cyanide, the potential for death grossly exaggerated, yet pitifully minute compared to other substances, plutonium, for instance.

Death Valley, the valley of death, where very little survives and almost nothing lives. I think only humans have the potential to live; everything else exists. Survival is a human concept. Plants and animals don't survive; they exist, growing and dying in tune with themselves. They are nature, not a part of it, but nature itself. We are not part of it anymore. Somehow we've been cut loose, adrift in a physical, cosmic space, disconnected from the earth, alienated – a purely human concept – from our "environment," i.e. nature. There's a tremendous temptation to view this as horrible, bad, irreversible movement toward something that nature does not "know" since nature "knows" nothing; that is death. We can come to Death Valley, never dreaming of death. The canyons, the dunes, the mountains of rock don't laugh or cry at our concocted relationship to them.

Oct. 17, 1983

I sit here in the motel restaurant, drinking coffee and thinking about the dream I had last night. I wonder if it's related to the out-of-body experiences I've had. Or maybe all this nature stuff I've been thinking about? I was hiking in the Sierras with my father and brother and some other man. They all got ahead of me and I began to feel cold, but not unhappy. I came to a stand of pines. The trees were so thick I had to use my arms to part the branches. I didn't mind because the pine needles were long and soft and very green. Then I looked down and realized I was walking in the tops of the trees grown out of the side of a mountain. I was walking in the air on precarious branches over a magnificent plain. Very suddenly I realized I couldn't walk on air. I was going to fall. I frantically looked down through the trees for the ground. As soon as I saw I couldn't get back to it I woke up. The dream was so sensual. I felt elated, but then terrified. The last moment of the dream I remembered the men had been with me.

Oct. 18, 1983

I think not eating gets one closer to nature in a strange way — bones, frames without flesh on them are closer to death, removed from the pull of need or desire. Thrown into the struggle for control, one's senses are more acute. Lack of food leaves a grating, gnawing sensation that accentuates the other senses, throws the body on hyper-alert. One looks at a plant or animal differently as a potential source of gratification, a potential object of one's own ability to destroy, consume, devour. Refusal of food is a triumph over one's humanity, need, desire and a surrender to nature at the same time. I'm not near this level of deprivation, depravity, but I have been. I'm concentrating now on eating as I should and as I please, comforting myself with the freedom to satisfy, to give myself that often unnecessary pleasure of "filling up," being the bringer, the controller of new ripples of flesh. I have to put some substance between myself and others. The armor between my bones and death is equally satisfying, although unlike starvation it doesn't heighten the senses. It dulls them, satiates them. The body becomes "more" natural; it demands rest, relief from the work food imposes. Food takes me to the internal in a comfortable, physical way, an animal way almost. I want to curl up and sleep it off.

Oct. 20, 1983

I was standing in the kitchen eating a Carr's biscuit with

peanut butter, and I suddenly became aware of a terrible sadness. About Daniel. I may be marrying another man, and Daniel doesn't even know it. It's especially sad that he's nobody's husband, nobody's father. He doesn't have me anymore. He's alone now. I have left him. I'm sure I loved him — those rivers of tears such a short time ago. It makes no sense. It's nonsensical that life should take away from him and give back to me without any logic. Why me? He should be the one, the deserving, kind person he is. I wish he would tell me he is marrying someone else and let me off the hook. I don't want to be THE ONE, the Medusa, the Salome. (Earlier this evening I talked with Chris about death, or I tried. It seems to upset him, but he won't admit it. He's so stoic in areas where I'm all coming apart. He doesn't seem to feel too bad about Pat.) I couldn't get death off my mind. I was obsessed with it the entire evening. Probably it has to do with Daniel, maybe even Pat. Then I found myself locked in the bathroom trying to remember the words to the Lord's Prayer and that verse about walking in the valley of the shadow of death. Death is around the corner, close to me, and I don't know why now? Where was death when I wanted to know it? Am I the one it's after? That would solve the problem of never having to deal with someone I love dying. If I die first I save myself that inevitable confrontation, that meeting with the real thing in the most unlikely and wrong place.

DEATH IN THE SUPERMARKET

The basket stops as if under its own
Power
By the meat, red and brown, turning
It's dead
And my mouth gobbles a handful of peanuts
To ease the pain of meeting death
In the supermarket
Minding my own business
In line at the post office
He tapped my left shoulder
Chuckle, a raspy throat, a snort
The Dead Letter File
He showed me the way to
The Dead Letter File
It's there all right, it's everywhere

Dead whale on the beach, seal, sea lion
Washed up with no shame

I want to kill the killer in myself.

Oct. 21

Lillian Gish: "I was never young, therefore how can I ever feel old."

I've been slowly reading *Under the Volcano*. Finally got to the end tonight. The man was a genius, no doubt about it. I could feel myself in that ditch with the Consul, feel it as if it had happened to me. Chris had fallen asleep. I wanted to wake him up and talk about it, but it seemed a bit extreme, over-reacting again. That's me. I settled for hugging up to him, tight as I could. The sky was lightening before I managed to get to sleep.

Oct. 22

Only one and a half hours before we go out. I started my period. I decided to spend the day in bed. I'm pretty fucked up, stoned and drunk. I watched T.V. awhile, then read.

Oct. 23

I'm not sure I'm capable of worthwhile existence.

Oct. 25

All day long and all night long a line from a Dylan Thomas poem — I think it's Dylan Thomas — played over and over in my head, "Do not go gentle into that dark night." I spent two hours looking the damn thing up when I got home. It's not "dark" night; it's "Do not go gentle into that good night." I can't get it out of my head. Dark is a scarier word than good.

Oct. 26

The blood samples that were supposed to arrive from General today got hung up somehow. Now I won't get them until tomorrow. I've been dragging my feet on this anyway. I'm totally swamped at work, but I'm anxious to see the final comparisons on the lymphocyte trials. We've got a huge sample of

AIDS cases and controls. If I stay late tonight I might be able to get the preliminary data printed out. I'll finally be able to tell Ivan something more about Peter and get him off my back. I'm goddamn exhausted from not sleeping well the past few nights, and I promised to cook dinner for Chris, my turn. Always the same battle. I wish I could get that line to stop playing in my head.

Oct. 27

I had a dream: I'm taking a short trip, driving East to get away for a while. Miles and miles of wheat fields, grassland, prairie. Lots of people appear: God-fearing, nice, normal Americans. Families with literally 2.5 children, and they all had campers. Housewives in curlers, with fat bottoms straining their Bermuda shorts, swept off fake grass patchs outside their mobile homes. Monuments every few miles: To the Great American Hubby. Billboards advertising COKE (a cola). There were cowboys and Indians out there, and I stopped for a hamburger. My waitress was a Sioux Indian. She lectured me on how her people were butchered, cheated, thrown off the land. I was ashamed, humiliated, but the other people paid no attention. Then they huddled around me and began to gawk at me, pointing fingers. I was desperate and ran as fast as I could to my car. I drove all night to a motel in Colorado in the mountains somewhere, but they wouldn't let me stay there. I had to get back to the ocean, the edge of the earth, California. It was a matter of life or death. I woke up exhausted. Chris is still asleep. He was on last night until late. I don't want to wake him. I do, but I won't. I'll make a pot of coffee for him and wait till lunch. He looks so sweet in my bed, snoring away. All bad dreams must go.

*   *   *

He turned the page. Blank. Nothing. He kept turning the pages. All blank. He wanted more. That couldn't be it, all of it. He examined every blank page for any mark, any scribble, a drop of ink. Blank. Nothing. The hard black cover of the book closed against the blank pages. There were so many words, so many entries, but all he could think of were the blank pages. Not enough. Never enough.

Her words, would they always be there to remind him? His life, the future, relegated to one of her blank pages.

The earlier mist had blown over the cliffs and afternoon lingered slowly giving way to evening. The sun retreated far into the western horizon, a pale yellow saucer about to dip behind the next encroaching bank of fog. His legs and arms were covered with goosebumps. The damp chilly fog fell on his sunburned skin. His bones froze inside him, radiating cold outward in concentric circles to his extremities; each movement felt capable of cracking an arm or a leg. His head vibrated, even though he held it deathly still. His red eyes watched the day subtly become night, a spectrum of grays in hues from light to dark, arranged, as on an astral artist's pallet. Decisions. The fire, long since dying, glowed from one red ember about to surrender to ash.

His brief moments of certainty that she was alive had changed back again to doubt. Those last few days had been hectic. He was on call on the 27th and, as usual, ten patients walked in right before he was supposed to get off at eleven. By the time he tip-toed into her bedroom at 2:00 a.m. she was fast asleep. Quietly, he crawled into bed next to her, kissing the back of her head, her right cheek, rubbing his hand down her back, patting her bottom as he drifted into a dreamless sleep. When he woke up, too late, she was already gone. A note sat next to the espresso maker. "I'll be in the lab this morning, hope to see you for lunch. Got to rush. Love, S"

He had rushed off to the hospital himself, thinking, this sort of schedule would never do: one of them asleep before the other came home, one of them gone before the other woke up. If not for the weekend excursions she demanded, when would they ever see each other? Around 10:00 he had a break in the clinic and phoned the lab to confirm lunch. She answered, her voice – in retrospect – subdued, disturbed, but when she recognized him she shouted a brusque, "What do you want?"

He had wanted to tell her he missed her and was looking forward to taking her out for lunch, but her curt tone got under his skin. "What's eating you?" he yelled back. Her voice took on an even stranger tone. She whispered that she was in the middle of something important and couldn't he just bug off. Bug off! She hung up on him before he could retaliate. As he instantly reached to call her back, Melvin interrupted to ask him some questions about a medical student's exam. He was caught in the fray. By the time he ran into the lab, ready to chastise her for being so rude on the phone, she was gone. Carol said she seemed upset, went to get some coffee, but that was over an hour ago, and she hadn't come back. Without thinking he raised his voice to Carol, something inappropriate like, "Why didn't you stop her?" Then he ran out without waiting for a reply. The world spun out of control — what he did, why he did it — a wild blur of activity, running, driving, running. Then here.

The last time he saw her she was asleep, peacefully and soundly asleep. The journal sat propped in his lap. He looked at it. Everything was there. But nothing. His mind quit. Night was falling, the only absolute to confront. There was a mere hint of red in the ashes. The waves were crashing in closer with every new surge of the tide. Soon there would be little fire material left on the beach. More wood. Move. Get wood. Nothing. Now I'm like her, he muttered, talking to myself from another place, giving commands that my body rejects. Frozen. His legs refused to move. His arms refused to lift him up. He shut his eyes and the line that had played in her head now played in his: "Do not go gentle into that good night." Not now. Please not now. The time to swallow, digest and pick the bones of what he'd read had to come later. That knowledge, her thoughts, hopes, fears, ambivalences, confusions, dreams, were too pregnant, too close, too real, too powerful to touch in the dusk of a new night. Numbness: the state to strive for. Blank. Be blank like the blank pages of the end. Blank was not enough. Never enough. Collect wood. Move. Prepare for the end of the light, the dense black of a foggy night. The journal fell into the sand between his legs.

Pat struggled with the down sleeping bag, the pack filled with groceries, water, matches, cigarettes, new clothes and tennis shoes for him, a water-proof ground cloth and two bottles of liquor. It was more than she could carry, but she did it anyway, shifting the load from shoulder to shoulder, arm to arm. Every five minutes she had to rest and re-shift. She asked herself more than once — What the hell am I doing? A stiff slug of liquor and on she hobbled. The trail was downhill with a few difficult navigations, shaky boards across the ravine, narrow, steep paths on one side of the canyon. As she neared the bottom of the trail and heard the roar of the ocean, she knew the rest was a mere mile hike to the cove and hoped the channel was still passable. Like a ram on a hill, she bent forward into the wind and descended into the fog bank. She rummaged through the pack to find the new flashlight and batteries. How in the hell will I ever pay this Master Card bill? She thanked her lucky stars that they didn't phone in for validation at the general store because she knew she was already over the credit limit. With the flashlight she stayed close to the cliff and crawled over the new boulders strewn over the beach from the storm. She imagined Chris huddled in that tiny mud overhang he liked to call a cave and tried to walk faster. Finally coming to the channel between the rocks she could barely fit herself and the baggage through. She did see a faint glow that had to be his fire. She shouted out as loud as she could, "Chris! Chris! Come help me with this!" She saw nothing, no movement, no one. She heard nothing but the crash of the waves.

The idea that she was fool enough to come all this way back and that he would have gone was too humiliating to consider. The fog was spooky. Biting her lip, she pushed on toward the faint glow of red. Suddenly, the pack was lifted from her back, and she fell forward on her face screaming automatically.

"Hey, it's only me." He stood behind her quiet as a ghost.

Face down in the sand, exhausted and terrified, she didn't want to look up at him. The telephone conversations, the trip from the car, her Master Card bill, the uncertainty, and the insanity of it overcame her. But not for long. She scrambled onto her side, tangled in the bags. "Chris, you scared me to death, goddammit!"

He put down his load of firewood and tried to help her up. "I wasn't sure you were coming back." The truth was he'd forgotten she'd gone off on these errands for him.

"I told you I'd be back. It took longer than I thought to get this stuff." A little appreciation would have gone a long way with her at that moment.

"Let me help you. God, look at this. What did you do, buy out the store?" The waves were fanning in closer and he scurried with as much as he could carry farther down toward the cove.

She followed, dragging the pack and two bags. "Chris, listen, there's a lot more beach on the other side of the channel. There are big boulders we could camp behind for shelter. The tide doesn't come in as far. Look at this, we could get drenched or trapped, and there's no way out." She pointed the light up the sheer, unstable, sandstone cliff behind them. "Let's move before the waves get into the channel. There's not much time."

"No, I've got to stay here. But look, Pat, why don't you leave. You don't have to stay here with me. There's still time for you to get back to the other side and up the trail. I don't want you to endure this because of me. I'll be here tomorrow."

He doesn't want me to *endure this* because of him. She was insulted, tears filled her eyes, but she was determined not to let him see, not now. "I'm not leaving until you do, Chris. I'm not some slave with a back and a Master Card permanently at your disposal, you know!" The tears spilled over the bottom of her eyelids. She hadn't wanted to say that.

"I know. I know. I'm trying to think of you, of your safety." He gripped her shoulders. "It isn't very comfortable or safe here. I didn't ask you to find me. You came here of your own accord. There's not much time for gathering wood. If you insist on staying, that's what we have to do." He had to shout over the unending thunder of the waves. Her dark brown hair was covered with dew drops from the fog. The top of her head would soon be soaked, and he watched the drops float down her back into the dense watery air surrounding them. Her deep-set, wide brown eyes gazed at him with a stubborn disbelief and brought him a moment of tenderness. He really wished she would leave.

Her eyes never moved from his, "I'm not leaving and that's *that*." She turned away and began to collect any sticks, twigs or logs that would burn. He walked back to the place where he'd left his arm load of wood. They worked in silence, neither knowing if or when conversation would be possible.

She noticed that he wrapped the journal up — after carefully brushing off the sand — and put it away in the red nylon pack. Did she dare ask him what he'd read? The conversation with Julia and Dan — should she tell him they know where he is, that they could show up at any time? Later she would tell him about Gloria, the hospital, the concern everyone had for him. The police believe it's a suicide. He's not been implicated. That should reassure him, she thought. Would he be upset that she hadn't called Wallensky? Judging from his state of preoccupation, she hoped he'd forgotten. There was always tomorrow to sort it out. What about the detective Sanchez? After talking to Gloria, she didn't want to call him. What purpose would it serve? Surely Chris would agree with that. He didn't want the police breathing down his neck.

The fire began to crackle and smoke. He tended it with care, blowing on the near caught logs, arranging and rearranging the kindling. She sat as close as she could, her sweater pulled over her knees where she could rest her head and warm her hands. The air was so damp that the best they could hope for was warmth, nothing would be dry. He stood, his back to her, putting on the new khaki pants, the flannel shirt, the sweater, dry socks and tennis shoes. When he walked around the fire he looked almost human again. His smile was not genuine though; she could tell he plastered it on to please her. She tried to smile back that it was okay, that no forced thanks were necessary. It occurred to her that they had only one sleeping bag. She wondered if it occurred to him. By mutual consent silence continued.

* * *

They were high upon a hillside, on a balcony of some marvelous villa, a medieval chateau. Her blond hair blew away from her face in the breeze and she laughed with him at some private joke. From their vantage point they watched a wide, fast running river some hundreds yards from their perch. An impossible combination of oaks, acacias, maples, palm, and flame trees were scattered between them and the river where the banks were lined with an arboretum of equally unlikely foilage. "Let's go for a walk along the river." Her voice echoed from far away. "Yes, let's." They held hands and seemed to fly down the hill to the path in this ethereal garden. She wore a sleeveless white dress with red roses scattered across the loose, full skirt. It was tropical, hot, and sweat dripped from his forehead. They strolled along the river, gaping at the magical environs until they came to a small clearing where grass, soft as cotton, covered the ground. "Look, isn't this perfect?" She pulled him down into the tall grass. "I want you." In moments her dress lay underneath her, and his naked body pressed close to hers. They were both sweating and the beginning of her was indistinguishable from the end of him. They made love for what seemed like hours, the heat wrapping around them, a blanket of security, love, a reminder of infancy in mother's arms. "I'll never leave you." Who said it – him, her? Without warning she began to fade. A heavy curtain on the stage was closing. He groped in agony to stay with her.

He held on too tight, and Pat, much to her regret, had to pull away gently. His moaning went from the familiar – what she remembered – to something new like a growl, a howl. "Chris," she hugged him, holding his arms around her waist, hoping to ease him into consciousness, fearful that he would regret what had happened, that he would blame her. But it wasn't she who had crawled into the sleeping bag with him. He had insisted on sleeping curled up by the fire, and she had no idea when he had taken off his clothes and slipped in with her. When she felt the warmth of his naked body pressed close to hers, she thought she was dreaming, a dream much to her surprise and joy, but she knew she was awake. Making love to him was a first step back, a step toward what she was certain would be a new beginning. He had to leave his grief behind. He had to return to life, to love because he was alive and she was with him. No rationalizations – in spite of the fact that she considered many – were necessary. She loved him. That was enough.

"Oh, my God." He realized where he was, that he was naked, that his cock was dripping semen, that Pat's dark hair lay across his face, that her full breasts were crushed against his chest. A sinking, anguished feeling overwhelmed him. What had he done? How could he have done this? He felt sick and gradually extracted himself from underneath her. The cool air dried the sweat on his naked body. This shrewd body that deceived him and made him a liar, a louse, an irresponsible dreamer. This body that still had to relieve itself, that still wanted to smoke a cigarette and drink a cup of coffee. How he hated it.

Pat lay snuggled in the wonderfully warm sleeping bag that smelled of him and her, that reminded her of the happier past, that gave her confidence in the future. His will to live was unquestionable. It was only a matter of time. She watched him tentatively as he walked down the beach and very slowly wove his way back. Weary. They were both weary. She grabbed her sweater and pulled it over her head. She would stoke up the fire and try to boil some water. When he came close enough she smiled at him, "It's okay, Chris. Please. It's going to be all right. In time." He didn't answer but pulled on his clothes with his back to her. She opened the brandy and took the last swallow. This was no time to cry. Just stay calm and go about trying to make coffee. But she hadn't bought any coffee. Well. Her clothes lay in a tangled mess, and she busied herself getting them on while he walked away again. There were still remnants of a fire, but the fog was already out and the sun had risen to shine over the cliffs. The day would be warm. No point in making a fire. She was shocked to find her watch said 10:15. They had slept a long time.

He climbed high onto the big rock that sat, as ever, out in the sea, that was never fully enveloped by the waves. He could see Pat sitting on the sand and imagined her confusion; she had every right to be confused. But more than anything he wanted his dream back. He climbed farther around until he couldn't see the cove anymore. He could see the long beautiful beach on the other side, the aquamarine waves smashing against the rocks, seals lolling on the lower ones, seagulls swooping with the air currents down to the water, up into the wind. There was a hole, a deep pool, carved out of the granite by centuries of oceanic will. He stood on the edge peering straight down. It was no more than a hundred feet down. If he jumped, it probably wouldn't kill him quickly. Yes, eventually. He'd be smashed on the rocks, some broken bones maybe, then the whirlpool would suck him under. Eventually. He leaned into it, wanting with every fiber of his being to go, to jump, to have that instant of loss of control, just one second, enough to dislodge him, to enter that point of no return. He couldn't. I don't have the guts. He cried, sitting down with his knees pulled up to his chin.

Peculiar. Why did Suzanne wonder if life with me would be

peculiar? There was something peculiar about this entire disgusting travesty. A coward. All right. I'm a coward. I can't kill myself, and I don't want to live. What now? She was obsessed with death. No doubt. It was too late by the time we met. But she had loved me. No doubt. She must have known I would hate her for this, hate her until any memory of her was bitter as that mountain of cyanide, dry as Death Valley, hard as the diamond I put on her finger. Can I hate her yet? If only. How could she have feared my knowing everything about her? Didn't I tell her that nothing mattered, nothing could have changed how I felt about her? Nothing. Didn't I tell her that?

There was a lone figure way down the beach, turning off the place where the trail came out toward him. A moving speck drawing closer, but slowly, in no hurry. It looked like a man. He didn't walk toward the sea the way most people do. He didn't seem to look at the ocean or in any other direction but down. He bent over and walked as if he knew where he was going. The closer he came the easier it was to observe the neglectful attitude he had toward the surroundings, a sign that he wasn't here to relax and enjoy. Chris scrambled to his feet and took his glasses from his pocket. A sports jacket, the man wore a sports jacket and leather shoes, a shirt and tie. The police? No, he dismissed that, they wore uniforms to arrest people, didn't they? The man seemed familiar, his gait, his stature — this was someone he knew. What about Pat? What he suspected and what she might discover made him tremble, a fierce shake that upset his balance. Holding on to the rocks as he scrambled down fast, he bolted back toward the cove. He wanted to protect Pat, but from what? He wasn't sure.

Pat was pacing up and down along the shoreline. When she saw him, relief flooded her senses. Thank God he was coming back. This helplessness and agitation were almost more than she could stand. She wanted some coffee, some breakfast; she wanted to go home. While he was gone, she considered reading the journal, but decided against it. He was too fragile, too volatile. She had to consider each step, take it easy, go slow, stay calm, and by all means, do nothing to anger him, to evoke his suspicion. Why was he running toward her? Her instinct told her to go to the sleeping bag and sit down. He couldn't knock her down if she was already there.

"There's someone coming," he panted, his lungs heaving for oxygen.

"Who, I mean, where?"

"Down the beach towards the channel. I know it's someone who knows I'm here. It's got to be."

"How do you know? It could be anyone, Chris. Here," she patted

the sand next to her, "sit down. It's a beautiful day, it's probably someone coming to the beach. That's all." She had to tell him about
Julia and Dan. They were going to turn up for sure. Maybe this was
them. "Listen, I didn't tell you last night, but I talked to Julia Carmichael and her friend, Dan Lowen, I think his name was . . ."

"What! Why didn't you tell me?" He refused to sit down and his
shaking was frightening her.

"You didn't seem to be in the mood for conversation. Anyway,
calm down, will you? They want to talk to you. Gloria said they'd
called and been around the hospital several times. I told them you
were here. They're probably going to come. I couldn't help it, Chris.
They were her friends too. They want to know what happened." Her
excuses sounded feeble and exaggerated at the same time.

"It's not them. It's only one man. What else didn't you tell me? Did
you call Sanchez?"

"No. And I didn't call the other guy either, Wallski or whatever
his name was."

He grabbed a cigarette, trembling like a madman. "That's it. It's
Wallensky. He knows I'm here. He was here before. Of course.
That's the man. I recognize him now." His head nodded, but not at
her. He wasn't in contact with her anymore.

"I didn't call him, Chris. What are you talking about? How could
it be him?"

"Never mind. He'll be here soon. Forget it." His hand shook so he
held the cigarette with his teeth and talked through it. "You'll see.
It's okay. I wanted to talk to him." Turning around several times to
see if he'd entered the cove yet, his shaking subsided.

"What should I do? What do you want me to do?" Now she felt
a bit panicky.

"What can you do?" He had calmed. "You're here." He sat beside
her to wait.

Wallensky maintained his slow, but steady course toward them.
He saw them, made no gesture of greeting, but stared at the sand until he stood a few feet from Chris. "I've returned," he panted out of
breath. "Perhaps, you're in a better mood, Dr. Alterberg?"

Rage obstructed his vision with flashes of light, and he felt incapable of words. He hadn't expected this sort of blinding anger. He
stammered, spitting out his words, "So you know my name now.
And I know yours. I know too much about you, you bastard." It
slipped from his tongue, unwanted, not conducive to his goal.

"I suppose you've read it?" Wallensky was unaffected by his venom.

"You suppose right."

"Well, there may be much you know, but there's much you don't know." His shoulders rose and fell in resignation. He turned to Pat. "How do you do. I'm Ivan Wallensky, friend of the late Dr. Keller."

"I'm Pat, friend of him." For reasons that entirely escaped her she found this man charming. His accent, she thought. She was always a sucker for Latin accents and unconventional twists of language. It was romantic.

"Ah, well, you may be of help to me in communicating to your friend. He's very upset, no?"

"Yes." Pat began to sweat, a response to her growing apprehension of Chris's unpredictability. A fight would never do; she had no tolerance for such things. "Why don't you sit down?" This seemed the only solution to the maintenance of civility.

"Si, yes, thank you, kind lady. It is quite a hike from the car lot." He sat on the ledge, extracting a full pack of Dunhills from his jacket, offering one to Pat, then one to Chris.

"No thank you, I don't smoke."

Chris greedily accepted the offer. "Okay, Wallensky, I want to know why you encouraged her with the drugs. You knew she wasn't up to it, psychologically. She came to you for help. You shoved her face in it. You took advantage."

"Don't be too righteous, my friend. She was not — how do you say — a babe in the woods. Much beside the point now, don't you agree?"

"What drugs?" Her curiosity piqued.

"Stay out of this."

"I am not here to annoy you further, Dr. Alterberg. I have some information you might like to know. I have some questions of my own. We both want to know why she went, well, to such an extreme? For me it's not much surprise, but there are concerns."

"What concerns? What information?"

Wallensky hung his head. Pat was certain he was going to cry. But he didn't. He struggled for something, words, she guessed. "She is dead. You must know — in your way — but I can tell you for sure. Before when I came here I wasn't certain. I thought she had pulled one over, as you say, ran away. For reasons. . . . But, I had to find out. I went to the police. Some fisherman found a silk blouse and a shoe floating. They fit the description given by the woman in her laboratory of what she was wearing that day. She identified them. Case is closed." He never looked up, drew heavily on his cigarette, lighting a new one before tossing the first into the sand.

Pat couldn't look at Chris either. Tears, from a subterranean origin, unhinged her. How would he take this?

It was a fact he already knew, but the thunderbolt impact of hearing the words, "silk blouse," "a shoe," ordinary words, hit with the force of a Pacific tidal wave. The absolute end of hope. Death. He was still prepared to resist. "How can they be sure?"

Wallensky shook his head from side to side. "She is dead. We must accept it. There are other considerations."

Without a moment's thought, Chris bolted toward him, grabbed his necktie and jerked his head up, forcing him to stare into wild, refusing eyes. Pat jumped up and tried to pull him backwards, but only succeeded in choking Wallensky further. "Let go! Chris, let go of him!" Her fists pounded on his back, all her own fury unleashed, out of control.

He did let go, and Pat fell back into the sand, sobbing. Wallensky seemed undisturbed and took off his necktie with his characteristic appreciation of the inevitable. Chris paced in front of him, wishing he could ignore Pat's sobbing, not giving a damn about it, an interference in the overload of thoughts, memories, questions that were twisting his head in the noose around his own neck. There was something cancerous and hard growing inside him, a tumor that would block all sentiment. He welcomed it. "Okay, all right, Wallensky. She's dead. Is that why you came here? To tell me she is dead?"

"To an extent. It is over for her, but she was working on something, the case of my friend. He was very sick. I want to know what she discovered about him. It's important to me. I thought, the journal perhaps?"

"It's in there. Your friend," a foul, acid taste distorted his mouth, "the drug addict, the bisexual, is that the friend you mean?"

Wallensky laughed, a sardonic guffaw. "Yes, that one. He died two days ago. No great loss, Si?"

"He died?" Pat sat up, listening with exaggerated emotion, aware and frightened that some unwanted, strange revelation was upon them.

"Good riddance." Chris cleared his throat and spat in the sand.

"Chris!"

"Suzanne was trying to find out what was the reason for his illness. She had promised to find out for me. A last favor, so to speak. The hospital rules — he was at General — they wanted to contact his next of kin. They wouldn't tell me. I asked them if it was AIDS. They said they couldn't tell me. She said she would try to get some tests done, a broncoscophy, I think. These results would tell me." He stopped. "His step-mother — they finally found her — refused to allow an autopsy. Yesterday she took him back to Kansas to be cremated. She didn't want to know."

"AIDS?" She felt a huge lump rising in her throat.

Chris looked at her tentatively. "It's nothing," he addressed her too adamantly.

"Nothing!"

Chris sank into the sand beside her. Sympathy. A feeling he was determined to block out. Yet the pieces were too easy to fit together. The puzzle of a child. "So you wanted her journal to find out if she knew your friend had AIDS? Well, it isn't in there, Wallensky. She wasn't in the habit of writing medical notes in her diary." This protectiveness toward Pat wouldn't subside. All his intellectual faculties were mustered to repress what he feared. Wallensky was worried that he had been exposed. No, it was worse than that. He knew he had been exposed. That was in the journal, the allusions to Wallensky's bisexuality, the orgies. The two of them knew more than they wanted.

"You work in the same hospital with the same, ahh, problem. You can find the results in her medical notes. Isn't that possible?"

"Why should I do anything to help you?"

"You might wish to help yourself?" He glanced toward Pat.

"What are you implying?"

"I'm no doctor of medicine. I don't even care much about dying. Perhaps, you're right, there is no reason you should help me. It doesn't matter now. I have nothing to hide. Or to protect." Wallensky rose to leave. What did it matter? The stress, the pressure, it had pushed him too far into the realm of concern. Death. It was no stranger to him. He scoffed at it. He found the idea amusing, another twist of his own checkered history, his fate, that pathetic and absurd notion. I am sorry she is dead, but I can understand her choice. This man, he loved her too much. His knowledge of her was therefore limited. In this way he felt sympathy for Chris. It was a time to be philosophical. Why couldn't they be comrades? Shouldn't such grief — like such women — be shared? Resigned, he thought, shouldn't there be comfort for the living? "I shall go now." He bowed to Pat.

"No! Don't go yet." She wanted him to stay. Chris was hiding something; of that she was sure. There were questions. She had questions. Why had Suzanne killed herself? Just when she was about to marry Chris whom she supposedly loved? It didn't make sense. She put out her hand to push Chris away from her. "I want to know, Ivan, why do you think she killed herself?"

"Despair, of course, my dear lady. She lived on the edge of passion and despair. Despair usually wins." He had no reason to alarm this unfortunate young woman.

"No. You're wrong. That's your own dismal, pseudo-philosophy, some Nietzschean, nihilistic bullshit you dispense for lack of . . ." He knew Wallensky was right in a way, but couldn't bear that he should say it out loud.

Pat interrupted him, "Well, why do you think she did it, Chris? Is there some reason? Is there any sense to it?" Her first confrontation with him. It felt good, liberating. "If she wasn't depressed or out of her mind why would she kill herself?"

"Stay out of this, Pat."

"Why should I?"

Before any of them noticed Julia and Dan were standing next to them. A very uncomfortable, awkward silence ensued. Pat couldn't stand it. She went over to Julia and put out her hand. "You must be Julia. I'm Pat, I talked to you yesterday. This is Chris." She pointed to him. "And this is Ivan Wallensky, another friend of Suzanne's." Wallensky bowed and held out his hand, the gentleman that he was.

Julia took his hand, then turned to her side. "This is Dan."

Wallensky extended his hand to Dan, but got no response. "Dan, yes, I knew of you, Suzanne spoke about you very much." He had never seen anyone looking quite so recently out of the grave, dismal, spectral, reminiscent of poor Peter.

Daniel limped toward Chris until he stood inches from his face. "You killed her."

Chris bowed his head, overcome with shame, remorse, guilt, and pity. He fought to regain his rocklike barrier to emotion, but the sight of Dan caused him to crumble, like a grenade against an old stone wall.

"Don't be silly." Pat tried to squeeze herself between them. "She killed herself. It wasn't his fault. It was nobody's fault." Her endurance gave way. "Goddammit, God damn this woman to hell!" She walked away and threw up her hands. "Look what she's done to you! All of you!" A flood of anger gushed out in tears.

Julia burst into tears, covering her face and collapsing into the sand. "Please, no. Don't say that. Don't say that."

Dan stepped back from Chris and stared at Pat, his glazed eyes popping from his skull, showing total incomprehension. Chris wanted to put his arms around Dan; he was the closest. He had loved her. They had both loved her. She had loved them both; they were the same. He put his hands on Dan's shoulders and turned him back to look in his eyes. "I loved her. I want you to know that. I want you to understand that."

Dan began to cry, much to his own horror. "I don't understand that. I don't understand." The coughing began, gagging him until he was forced to sit down. "I can't believe she would do this to me. I can't believe it."

"That's an understatement!" Wallensky scoffed.

Julia pulled herself together and went to him. "Dan, please, try to calm down." She tried to find her way to acting the arbiter, the mediator, the one who would make it all right. Do the impossible. But she too was exhausted and miserable, blaming herself, wanting relief. She understood Pat's anger. She understood Dan's desire to blame Chris. She understood Chris's remorse and shame for failing to prevent this. It was too much to understand everyone and to want to understand, more than anyone, the one who wasn't there. On top of her own lover's mental breakdown, this was unendurable. Losing her best friend for whom she hadn't been there. She had not been there.

Wallensky studied Dan. Then spoke to Chris. "He's sick."

Chris resisted the impulse to punch him in the face. God, how he wanted to smash that face. The face of objectivity, of observation, of honest appraisal — humanity be damned. "Shut the fuck up, Wallensky."

Dan, still hacking, gazed at Chris confused, furious, befuddled, full of sorrow. He didn't feel any comradery with this . . . this . . . this man whom he saw like all the others of the past three years, another one of her "experiments." Julia had tried to tell him in the past few days that Suzanne had been serious about Chris, that she had mentioned the possibility of marrying him, but he didn't believe it. Suzanne had said nothing about any serious involvement when he saw her in New York a mere three weeks ago. Yes, she indicated she was seeing someone, a doctor, but she was always seeing someone — a doctor, a lawyer, a stock broker, a shrink. Why was this guy any different from the rest? Only one reason. He was the last. "I am sick." Not that he cared one whit about Wallensky, obviously another of Suzanne's weirdos, but he refused to accept any alliance with her murderer. "Answer my question, Alterberg. Did you kill her?"

"No."

"Dan." Julia put her arm around him.

"What's wrong with you?" Wallensky persisted.

"He's got mono!" Julia glared at him.

"How long have you been sick?"

"Why are you asking these questions? We came here to find out about Suzanne. Who are you anyway?"

"Ivan Wallensky. Psychologist of sorts. I think I know why she killed herself." He started to continue, but Dan interrupted him.

"You too?" For some odd reason he found himself smiling at Wallensky.

"Yes. I suppose so. Me too." Wallensky smiled back.

Julia addressed Pat who was balled up inside the cave in a catatonic posture. "You said her journal was here. I'd like to read it. I'd like to know if there's any doubt."

"There's no doubt," Wallensky answered. "Haven't you been to the police?"

"No. What do you mean? They've found her body?" Hysteria rose in her chest. "I knew her. I knew her very, very well. She could have left, she could have run away. She could still be alive. There's a chance."

"Some fisherman found her blouse and a shoe a mile off shore down toward the Bay from here. There's no doubt."

Julia flung herself on Dan and buried her head in his shoulder. A long silence ensued. The peaceful wash of the waves sang around them. The sun was hot for this time of year, the breeze gentle. A group of children — their parents looking on — romped around on a nearby dune, a few other hikers strolled by, an old couple with binoculars, two gay men hunting for privacy. The tide was out and the normally deserted cove where gale force winds and very little beach kept people away was becoming the public domain, a place they didn't possess, a place in which the norms of society raised scrutiny. They looked unawares, a sorry lot.

Chris paced up and down in front of the others, himself aware only of the nuisance of these intrusions. Invasions he had experienced before. He thought about the journal. About Dan. About Wallensky's friend. Dead. She was getting some blood samples back that morning. He knew about them, a series of controls included. He thought about the look on her face the morning after he read her *The Wasteland* in the cabin, the blood she'd drawn from herself and later from him. He thought about her trip to Boston, the four hours of silence on the way home from that weekend. He thought about her hasty trip to New York a few weeks ago. He thought about her tears in the restaurant parking lot at Princeton. Had she consciously been hiding it from him? His medical mind went into action. There was no real evidence of heterosexual transmission of AIDS without some other risk factor: hemophilia, blood transfusions, drug addicts who shared needles. She had told him Dan had a bad case of mono, Epstein Barr virus, she said. So? What if she had had sex with Wallensky's friend? What if he did die of pneumocystis? She wrote in her journal that she had boiled the needles the night she shot heroin with them or was it coke? He remembered she specifically said she boiled the needles. But he'd seen a lot of ARC in the clinics, a lot of AIDS. In many of the patients, EBV and CMV was cultured from their blood. He glanced at Dan, not wanting to, but not able to stop himself. There was that pallor, that gauntness, a receding hairline, protruding bones, that strange gait.

They didn't know it *wasn't* heterosexually transmitted. There were several cases of female patients who could have only gotten it from their husbands. At least, no other risk factors were found. Suzanne told him this was reported in the CDC Bulletin. He chewed on his tongue, wishing he could swallow it. He'd been too busy taking care of patients to read the latest scientific articles, the unpublished reports she carried around in her briefcase. What he knew of the research in progress, he knew from her. The case of Mrs. Canner. Yes, he remembered Suzanne carrying on at length about that case. She was convinced the woman had AIDS, sexually contracted from her husband who had multiple transfusions. But they never really knew. He was skeptical. His normal medical instincts, skepticism, conservatism, no assumptions without evidence, hard evidence, scientific evidence. What if? What if Dan had the pre-AIDS syndrome? Did she know? Would that have done it? There was more than enough misery in her journal, or was there? Did there have to be a reason? No. Yes. The misery had preceded him, he couldn't accept that he hadn't changed all that, erased the loneliness, reached her completely. She had let go of Dan. She chose not to marry him before they ever met. Even if he had ARC, she couldn't know he would die. Nobody knew that. She was too smart. There seemed to be many ARC patients who got better, even AIDS patients improved. And what did it have to do with her? Sure, she'd be upset, sad, but not kill herself. Unless? Maybe. . . .

The more he thought, the more confused he became, the less it made sense. Who she had been grew obscure, vague, remote. The conviction that he had to understand her was losing ground to the potential curative of not knowing. It was better that *they* didn't know. He had to destroy the journal. Every moment brought him closer to understanding why she had written that she didn't understand herself, that she didn't want to understand. But the irony of it.

"Chris, did you hear me?" Julia followed him back and forth. "I'd like to read her journal. I have a right to know."

"It's gone." He peeked toward Pat who didn't move a muscle.

"What do you mean it's gone?"

"I threw it into the ocean, off that rock," his finger pointed the way.

"What! How could you? What right do you have?" Julia snatched his arm with all the force she could muster. "Look who do you think you are? I knew her for fifteen years. I watched her go through the pain of two marriages and more relationships than I can count. You men!" She snarled at all of them. The tears were coming. "Can't you see how hurt she was, how you hurt her? The only way she could have herself was this. It was the only real power she had," she heaved with sobs, "to die."

Dan went to her and tried to comfort her. He had not actually understood her words. She couldn't be expected to make sense anyway. It was time she cracked after three days of comforting him, but it hurt to see her crumble to pieces. She waved him away and straggled down the beach.

Pat had not moved — her head still between her knees — but she heard Julia perfectly well. I'll go along with that, she thought. Wallensky remained fascinated, but felt he would soon grow bored with a continuance of such diatribes and antics. Chris stood like stone, determined that he was doing the right thing, that Suzanne's journal could only increase the agony for each of them.

"Look, you didn't have the right to destroy her journal. You had no right. But since you did Julia might feel better if you told us anything that would. . . ." Would what? Words seemed to be on the tip of his tongue, then gone again. He stuttered, "Would, would help us understand. I mean, in the last few weeks, did anything happen? Do you know what she was thinking? Why?"

"I can tell you," he raised his voice hoping Julia would hear, "that she loved you both very much." His voice cracked, "I don't really know why. But I know she missed you. She worried about you. She had very mixed up feelings about your moving to Boston. She loved you both."

"I can't take this. It is too much, as you say." Wallensky smirked. "This man is trying to be a 'do-gooder,' but it's too late, Dr. Alterberg. Too late to play God."

"What do you mean?" Dan grew suspicious.

"He doesn't want you to know, but you'll know sooner or later. A friend of mine — someone close to me, someone with whom Suzanne had some passing contact — died of AIDS two days ago. She killed herself because she had no other choice. It only makes sense. She didn't really want to die. I think not. But, well, you, you are a sick man. He can see this. He wants to cover it up. Because he knows there's nothing to be done, no treatment, no cures. Do you imagine that she didn't know this? Why are we here anyway? This five of us, what connection do we have? The lady made a point. We all knew Suzanne. In the biblical sense, if you'll pardon the expression."

"Don't listen to him. He's some quack psychologist. He doesn't know shit about AIDS."

Pat got up and slid across the sand near to where Wallensky stood.

She looked at Dan carefully. She looked at Chris. "Why did you lie then? Why did you lie, Chris, if he's got no point?" They all ignored her, too deep in their own unspoken thoughts.

"Don't think I don't know." Dan sat down next to Pat and noticed the bottle of tequila. He opened it and took a big swallow, then passed it to Wallensky. "I've suspected this *mono* wasn't just *mono* for a long time."

Wallensky relished the tequila. "What about it, Herr Docktor? How long do we have? Are we all going to die?"

Chris bent his head. The reality was he didn't know. "Of course. There's no doubt about it, Wallensky." A faint smile passed across his face.

Julia wandered back. She'd heard it all. "I suppose I should tell you now that Suzanne confided in me several months ago that she was worried she might have it." A furtive glance went to Dan. The tequila bottle was accepted, and she, too, relished the smooth burn in her throat. "Did you ever discuss it with her, Dan?"

"No. When she was in Boston in September I tried to tell her I thought this mono thing was a crock of shit, but she wouldn't listen. When we had lunch in New York she asked me if I would request my medical records from the doctor in Boston. I said fine, but I wanted to know the truth. She said from all that was known I had no risk factors and that there were many diseases that could cause these symptoms. That this Epstein-Barr virus looked a lot like AIDS-related-complex, but that healthy people recovered. It took a long time. Sound familiar, Alterberg? She didn't want to talk about it after that." He lay back in the sand, resting, his arm over his eyes. "But I know."

Pat slugged down the last of the tequila. "So if, just IF, you've got ARC, and you might get AIDS, and your friend died of AIDS, then Suzanne might have had it too. She might have given it to you." She stared at Chris. "She might have given it to you. And you might have given it to me!"

"Don't be ridiculous. This is utter nonsense." He wanted to be the voice of reason, but his heart, which he did have, wasn't in it.

"Sooo . . ." Pat was drunk. She had always been a cheap drunk, one glass of wine put her under the table. "We could all have AIDS!"

Julia stood, quite paralyzed, left out. "It's a bit unlikely, don't you think?" An absurd resentment that her connection with Suzanne was over, that they all might still share something of her, something deadly, but real. It was insane.

"Well, you're safe. Unless there's something I never knew about you and Suzanne?"

"Dan! That's cruel. How can you be so blase about this?"

"How can he afford not to be?" Wallensky liked this new atmosphere. They were in it together up to their necks. Julia sat down and bawled, her hands over her face. Pat, beside her, doled out handkerchiefs and kleenex, sliding an arm around her shoulders. Dan and Wallensky lay back and began a conversation in Russian, a jest of poetic quotations.

Chris, aware that this could be his only chance, casually picked up the pack and walked toward the rocks. He climbed to his roost where he'd spent many hours of contemplation, frustration, anger, agony, and he luxuriated in a moment of freedom. The wind in his face, the ocean spray, was welcome. His stomach knotted into a ball when he took out the journal. He wanted to keep it. But he had to say goodbye. The worst was over, or was it? He was desperate to laugh, a howling roar. He hurled the book far off the rock and watched it fall, bouncing off smaller rocks, sinking finally into the black hole, covered instantly by the waves. He had made an honest man of himself at the very least. And it made no difference at all nor did he care. She was free, and they were left to face it. "I'm not like you," he whispered to her. "You were one of a kind, my love. You were right."

* * *

241

part four

death

THE CLOCK SAID SIX when she opened her eyes. Chris was snoring, sound asleep. The blood samples were to be ready by seven, and she wanted to look at the results of Peter's bronchial washings before she began looking at the other cells. The dream disturbed her. Why is someone always after me? She sluffed it off, a distorted memory of the tourists in Death Valley. *Go back to the edge of the earth.* A familiar, frightening compulsion she had had routinely while driving to work, but that was behind her now, relegated to the world of dreams. She turned over and kissed his snoring head, ran her fingers through his soft, brown curls, and whispered, "You're too cute, good enough to eat." He groaned but never woke up.

The shower was brief and scalding hot, the way she liked it. In it she decided to wear her maroon silk blouse and white pants. She felt guilty about that blouse. She had paid $200 for it on impulse at Saks and had never worn it. It's too expensive to wear, she told herself whenever it passed by on the hanger as she surveyed the selection of possibilities. Next time. Today is the day, she insisted to her conscience. Time to exorcize that needless guilt, perpetual worry that if she wore her best clothes they might get worn out or stained, dirty or torn. The point was that she wanted to look smashing when Chris picked her up for lunch. She relished that old wish to look pretty for a man, for him. Checking herself in the full-length mirror, she was satisfied with her choice. The burgundy leather shoes were a perfect color match, simple and sleek. He'd like it.

She made the coffee, left him a note and took her mug with her to the car. A manilla envelope was lying by the door under the mailbox. Mail she must have overlooked in her exhaustion the night before. The return address gave her an unpleasant pause and interfered with her premonition that the day would be a good one. It was from Daniel. She immediately decided to wait until she got to the lab to open it. All news was better when gotten in the security of her well-organized, clean, white laboratory. Into the African bag it went along with the usual overload of stuff she toted around. Just in case. She smiled, remembering how Chris teased her about it. Who needed two Swiss army knives, three colors of eyeliner, several lipsticks, barrettes, eye-shadows, assortments of sugarfree gum, dope boxes, coke mirrors, razor blades, rolling papers, scissors, tweezers, clamps, two wallets, credit card holders, et cetera, et cetera? Her armor, she always retorted. It probably was nuts.

The traffic was light this time of morning ahead of the worst rush hours. The sky turned before her from dusty grey to tangerine. Another gorgeous, cloudless October day, a beach day, she wished. The rainy season, if they were lucky, was two months off. The vines would be brilliant shades of orange, red and yellow in Napa this weekend. The wine country. They could take their bicycles, their new ten speeds, and bike along the Siverado trail. They would end up in Calistoga where she for one would take a mud bath and have a massage. He could bask in the mineral water or swim in the pool if he preferred. They could eat at the Calistoga Inn where the duck liver mousse made her mouth water. She made a mental note to call them for Saturday night reservations. They should try and stay overnight in one of the many quaint, luxurious inns, but this time of year, on such short notice, they might be full up. Don't forget to call, she instructed herself, and don't forget to remember.

The blood cells were spun down and waiting for her. Several messages, most about consults, sat on her desk. Carol, who somehow managed to arrive earlier than she, said Dr. Thomas had already been around about some AIDS patient admitted during the night. She struggled into her lab coat, searched for her stethoscope and started toward the wards. "Separate the cells and get the FACS set up, will you please, Carol? And arrange the specimens, controls first. By the way, did anything come by courier from General?"

"Yeah. This." Carol handed her an envelope, thick with records.

While she walked, she looked at Peter's test results. Pneumocystis carinii pneumonia was confirmed, along with candidiasis, disseminated herpes virus in the gastrointestinal tract. *The patient presents with the CDC definition of acquired immuno-deficiency syndrome*, the resident wrote. She glanced at the clinical notes. He was already on a respirator. He was going to die soon. Not good news. Not good news at all. She put the records back into the envelope and tried to forget it for the moment. The nurses' station was bustling with activity. They hardly had time for "good morning's" before launching into recitations of the patients' conditions. There was a new one, but they moved him to the ICU about an hour ago. Seizures. Dr. Thomas had been here, then rushed off to some meeting. She decided not to make rounds and told the nurse to have the resident call her in the lab if she was needed for a consult.

Forget it. Forget it. She repeated this over and over. A wave of sympathy for Ivan washed over her. This guy, whether she understood it or not, was like a son to him. The kid always reeked of an orphan quality, and Ivan played the older, wiser man, the fully available Dad. Perverted? Yes. But he did like Peter, and that Peter worshiped him was plain to see. The all-approving, pleasure-affirming, permissive Father; the one Peter had never known or seen or heard of, the one who donated nothing but a lone sperm in a dark night to his life, never to be identified or identifiable. He was an intelligent young man, twenty-three and finished with his Master's Degree in psychology, a former Ph.D. candidate until he left to pursue learning under Ivan's tutelage. She had never actually held a conversation with him — more like a disjointed dialogue from a play, an Artaud play, she thought, *The Theater of Cruelty.* Ivan was their mutual kingpin. They talked through him, even fucked through him. Her heart began to race. She quickly tossed two Lorazepam into her mouth and headed to the water fountain. What will I tell him? The truth, what else? Peter is dying of AIDS, Ivan. No, I don't know if you have it. Yes, you could be exposed. But didn't you know the risks, even then? I did. I think I did.

The walls seemed to be drawing too close around her, the corridor suddenly felt too narrow. She caught herself running down the hall toward the elevator, but not before tripping over a small bit of rubber loosened from a carpet edgings. She found herself down on her knees, her hands in front of her pushing her up. The walls were going to crush her. The lobby into which she spilled was spinning around her. An elderly lady leaned on her cane and bent over to help pick her up. "Oh my, my, oh my, what a spill." She held onto the cane and managed to stand. The elevator opened and she bolted in, many "thank you's" and "it's nothing's" murmured to the lady. The entire lobby had stopped. Everyone in it stood frozen like in the game she played as a child in which everyone was spun around and let go until someone yelled "Freeze!" Whoever moved first was IT. They all stared at her, dead stares, at her, through her. It's in my imagination, she prayed, as the doors shut on this immediate nightmare. Get hold of yourself, Suzanne.

Carol had everything ready, but Suzanne had trouble settling down. She paced about the lab, cleaning up the lab benches, organizing shelves, arranging and rearranging the serums, the tools, the chairs, the tubes, until Carol asked if something was wrong, much to her regret. "Of course not. I simply can't function in this mess. Everything's out of place. Look at this, these aren't labeled!" It was a plot; she was the victim in a conspiracy against her. Carol, never having seen this sort of outburst from her, not having had a clue that it was on its way, was stunned. Since everything wasn't a mess and

Suzanne had herself painstakingly organized the entire lab, no reply seemed the most appropriate. Something was the matter, but she'd let her cool off first.

After much shifting about, Suzanne sat down at the microscope, her notebooks and the slides within reach, and Carol went back to the computer closet where she was feeding in volumes of data. She heard her get up and leave the microscope several times. She gritted her teeth in anticipation of another outburst, but none came. At one point, there was an enormous sigh as if she had sucked in all the air in the room and released it again. Carol looked around the corner to see if she was all right. Then the phone that sat within Suzanne's reach rang, several times, ignored. Just when Carol was about to answer it, Suzanne grumbled and picked it up. There was a muffled conversation. She knew it had to be Chris from the way Suzanne whispered. With other calls she invariably turned to face the middle of the lab and spoke in a studied, professional voice.

The joys of love, Carol brooded, her concern for Pat roused, even her concern for Suzanne. Although she didn't know her well, she respected her, and in spite of her disapproval where Chris was concerned, she liked her. Their too infrequent lunches left her intrigued and looking forward to a new friendship, maybe a close one. They might someday get down to earth with each other in those inextricable ways women did. Suzanne's reaction to her gun had pleased her, eased her own guilt about being too paranoid. They had gotten drunk together that night on sake in a Japanese restaurant. She saw a side of Suzanne she really liked, carefree, sardonically funny, gutsy, and not afraid of it. The distance Suzanne invoked the next few days was quite predictable. They were colleagues, co-workers. Anyway, she wasn't sure if Suzanne knew she was a lesbian. Maybe it put her off, frightened her the way it did many of her non-lesbian women friends. At first. Lost in thought, she heard the receiver slam down with a reverberating ring. Jesus Christ! What is going on?

For fifteen minutes Suzanne studied the slide under the microscope. The cells of one of the controls, a healthy heterosexual. It could be her cells. It could be Chris's. It could be one of forty-eight others. What she needed only minutes to discover was taking forever: the T4 to T8 ratio was 2:1, perfectly normal. She took out the slide and put in another, normal; another, normal; another, normal. She ought to finish this by lunchtime. The next: something was off; this one wasn't normal. She took it out and looked at it. Each one was number coded. Back under the scope. Perhaps it had gotten mixed up, but the code was definitely one of the controls. The count was slightly less than 1 for T4's and 1 for T8's, .9:1. Something was wrong here. Either this wasn't one of the controls or this person was immuno-compromised. This happened occasionally. She found ratios indicative of a borderline ARC pattern among the controls. Usually there was a plausible explanation, and the reasons would come to light on further examination of the person. There were many assymptomatic persons who, unbeknownst to them, were immuno-compromised. It was rare that she bothered with concerns about individuals in the midst of her research, but she didn't trust her eyes today. The need to know who this number was obsessed her with no mercy. Don't stop, she ordered herself. Don't look it up now. But it could be. She took the coded list out of the drawer.

Carol heard another round of thrashing about, books slamming on the lab bench, glass breaking. "Suzanne, need some help?" No answer. She got up and went into the lab proper. A beaker had fallen on the floor, nothing major. Suzanne sat at the microscope in a trance. "Listen, how about a coffee break?" She didn't seem to hear her. "Suzanne, what's . . ."

"It's nothing. Nothing." Her eyes were red from strain. She pushed herself away from the microscope, rolling on the lab stool into the middle of the room and almost bumping into the refrigerator. "I think that's a good idea."

"What?" Her face was still hypnotized, trancelike. Carol stared at her perplexed.

"Some coffee. Isn't that what you said? Coffee break?"

"Sure. Yeah. Let's go together. Or do you want me to make some here?"

"No!" She modulated her voice, "No, I think I need some fresh air. To think a bit. I'll go down the street away from this for a while." She gestured toward the lab bench where the slides were spread about. In a start, she hopped off the stool and grabbed her African bag. "I'll bring you some." She ran out, very unlike herself, leaving everything where it sat.

"Okay." Carol shrugged her shoulders. Bad day, she's having. She was only a little hurt that Suzanne didn't want to share it with her. Back to the computer room she went. Out of curiosity she stole a look at the papers, the list of controls in the lymphocyte study. She saw her own name down there. It made her nervous. She saw most of the other lab techs, several doctors on the staff, including Chris and Suzanne, even some of the secretaries. What would she do if one of us . . . ? No wonder she's bent out of shape. This is too much responsibility, pressure, emotional baggage. She dismissed all con- sideration of this stuff. There was no way to work around it and take it personally. The demands of Lotus drew her back to something comprehensible. When Chris stormed in, she wasn't aware of how much time had passed.

Once out of the building Suzanne walked automatically to her car. The dark concrete parking structure was soothing. Her car, her haven from the world, her own steel box on wheels, once inside it she began to stop suffocating. She relaxed; her head fell onto the headrest and her hands gripped the wheel. She could go now. She was free to go. For the first time that day she felt in no hurry. She felt she had all the time in the world. After some moments rest, she knew exactly where she was going. She knew she wasn't coming back. The dream, now it made sense; it was prophecy. *To the edge of the earth.*

She opened her bag to find some Valium and confronted the unopened envelope from Daniel. Why not? She tore it open. As she suspected, there were his medical records he had photocopied for her with all the pink lab slips arranged on one sheet of paper. A cassette tape fell out on her lap. Why not? She examined the blood count, not that it took much time or genius to figure out what she already knew. The CBC and differentials might puzzle the doctor in Boston, but they were clear to her. Of course, he did have EBV. She supposed that future research would find EBV in the blood of most ARC and AIDS victims. Future research. Well, it won't be me handing out the bad news. There it was — his white count was much less than 2,000, lymphopenia. Sure. Sure, it could be caused by other things, but it wasn't. Ignorance *is* bliss. Too late. Too late now. She ripped the xerox sheets into tiny shreds and scattered them over the parking lot. That part was over.

She picked up the cassette: *The Pros and Cons of Hitchhiking*, Roger Waters. What? He had enclosed a letter which she debated tearing up, but didn't. Couldn't.

Dear Suzie,
    Enclosed are the records you wanted. Dr. Katz said anything you could make of it would be greatly appreciated. He's a nice guy, for a doctor. I'm about the same, better some days, worse others. My teaching load is pretty light here, and the students no worse than Berkeley. Thought you'd like this tape. One of my brighter students turned me on to this album. A reminder of all those hours we spent in the car. Listen to it. We could have written the lyrics. Do you remember the graffiti in the underpass to the beach in Santa Monica? I know you have a memory like a steel trap. "Roger Waters is God." Well, why not? I miss you terribly. The only benefit to being sick is that

my normal desire to ravish you daily is suppressed by exhaustion. I haven't given up on you coming here. Not at all. And you can tell this new guy to get lost. What more can I say? I love you. Dan

Okay. She mouthed the words, get lost. Get lost.

She started the car and pulled out into the bright sunlight. The light hurt her eyes. There was Dr. Thomas, his head bent forward his hand flying through the air with explanatory meaning for the residents and interns who followed him into the building. Some had to jog to keep up with him. Good to leave that behind. No more of that. The graffiti in the underpass in Santa Monica — she did remember it. She put the tape into the recorder and turned the volume up high.

Maybe Roger Waters was God. If not, he could still play guitar. The Golden Gate bridge moved unfettered in mid-day. It took minutes to get to it and minutes to cross it, but for her it seemed forever.

A timeless sojourn into memory. Not unusual. She gave herself over to it. Nothing to lose. But it was different from her usual ruminations on the men she'd loved. Men. What could be said about them really? They were impossible. She loved them. She loved him and him and him and, well, what more need be said?

"Is anyone hungry?" She turned up the tape, reversed it and ran that by again. It did say "Is anyone hungry?" Her mother, with her disarming repertoire of facial expressions appeared before her, clear as day. I'm really sorry, Mom. Sorry we never got to talk. Sorry we didn't know each other. Sorry I was a difficult and rebellious child. Sorry I wasn't like the other girls. Sorry you weren't happy most of the time. Sorry. Very sorry. But I couldn't change it, and it's too late now. And I'm not sorry you were a lousy cook. Dad, you'll never accept it, but somehow you'll understand. I don't want to know anymore if you really understood me like I thought you did. How could you anyway? Thinking you were on my side was enough. Enough to get me into plenty of trouble. Go ahead, Dad. Blame me. What else can you do? Blame yourself? No. It is my fault. I'll take it, just like the little toy soldier. Remember that story? His leg chopped off, he floated down the river to his doom, all for the love of the ballerina. You read it to me. It always made me cry. Did you ever cry, Dad?

Tears flooded her face. The wet silk stuck to her breasts. It had to stop. It had to end. Everything has to end sometime. The guitar was wailing, a fantastic range of screaming electronic soul. "Hey girl.

Take out the dagger . . . and do something sexual." She struggled to hear the words, reversing the tape again and again. It was apparent why Dan sent it to her. Reminiscent of more than their hours in the car, it was the sound of their youth, rock, hard rock, sixties rock. Good ole Jimmy, Janis, and, the one and only, Jim Morrison. "Death, death and my cock is the world." That tape might be in the glove compartment. She opened it and began pulling tapes out. There were so many she wanted to hear, *An American Prayer*, she had to hear that, *Big Brother and the Holding Company* with Janis, that one absolutely, and Hendrix's rendition of *The Star Spangled Banner*, the one he did at Woodstock; one irreplacable moment in which time had stood still, in which she experienced, peaking on LSD, her first and only twinge of patriotism, of good old-fashioned American pride. The guy on the stage was an American and so, damned as we are, was she. Luck was with her. They were all in there among twenty others she wanted to hear. A plan. A plan had to be formulated. Drive straight up the coast to Canada. Plenty of time. Plenty of time to hear them all once. What then? Where could she possibly hide? Was there any escape?

"ONLY THE DEAD GO FREE."

Did he say that? Is that what she heard? She played it back again. "ONLY THE DEAD GO FREE."

Okay. It wasn't something she didn't already know. It's just that she wanted to hear more music. More music. You can't do it all over again, Suzanne. The past is past. It's all in your head, and what's there can't go around again. You're not an auto-reverse cassette recorder; you're a slave of it. Enslaved to memories which are life itself in the end.

The new Prelude seemed to hover a few feet off the ground and glide along Lucas Valley Road. That glorious, unbeatable scenery, the rolling dales in shades of green and brown, gold and mauve. She really was a space invader, an alien seeing this familar landscape, the material of her loveliest fantasies, from a new vantage point. The moment of death couldn't be other than a release to hover here and keep watch over these hills for eternity. The turns to the left and the right, the curves of the road rocked her almost to sleep. If she hadn't heard the horn blaring she would have crashed head on into a two-ton truck. Adrenalin rushed through her, and she broke into a clammy sweat. The driver's fist was shaking in rage and dismay. Christ! For God's sake, don't take anyone with you.

Her hand trembled as she lit a cigarette. A Jakarta cigarette. They'd never find her there. Indonesia. High on her list of exotic vacations, the ones she never took. Nepal. Sri Lanka. Africa. There was a beach somewhere, in Sri Lanka, she thought, where everyone chewed mushrooms all day. They ate mushrooms and travelled to distant galaxies until they passed out, died, reached Nirvana. That sounded fun. Until she grew tired of it. Until her body gave out. Until someone murdered her to steal all her money. It was a way to go. Without taking anyone with you.

My affairs. Are my affairs in order? There are certainly things I haven't attended to. I have no will. Who is listed as beneficiary on the life insurance? My brother? I think so. He will be sad about this. He will miss me. Of everyone in the family he will be the most upset and the most unforgiving. He always took everything too personally, poor sensitive darling.

Regrets. Do I have any regrets? Is there anything I don't regret?

It *is* better this way. I wish I could say goodbye to all of you. I want to, but that, you know, would ruin my plan. To see you once more, to say I love you, to ask forgiveness, I'd have to stay.

It hurt too much to think of Chris, of the future they might have had. Speaking of regrets. That disgusting secret she never managed to tell him. The botched abortion that left her sterile. She never even told Dan in their three long years together. Simone de Beauvoir had written she had only one regret about her life and that was never having had a child. Well, she'd always agreed with Simone. A pain seared up from her abdomen into her throat, her head. An unbelievable fatigue came over her. She couldn't wait to be there, renewed by the ocean, freshened by the wind, enlivened by the waves on the rocks.

There was a tiny green road sign, Highway 1, with an arrow pointing to the right. The time for decision. Should she try to escape? The car said, no. We go left. We go to the ocean. We've been round this bend before. It leads nowhere new. It leads only backwards. We are going to the edge of the earth. Fine. Let the car decide. I'm tired of making decisions. I can't do it anymore. I'm tired of being responsible, not that I was, very. Anyway I'm tired. Is that so hard to understand?

Time collapsed. All thought, all memories banished. Just like Koestler said. If nothing happens, time collapses. The car pulled into the parking lot, gravel flying everywhere. As she rounded the corner, she frightened a herd of elk, most of which dashed elegantly across the field; a lone bull stood confronting this larger metal animal. She stared at him and saw him snort, scoff at her. This was his territory. The wind was quite violent and the stand of craggy eucalyptus were creaking like loose boards in an abandoned house. She sat in her car for some time, watching the world go by. She put the tapes back into the glove compartment and rummaged through her purse one last time. She decided to roll a joint, then decided against it. The Valium and Lorazepam together would be better, not that she had enough to do permanent damage by themselves. And whatever happened she was not going to wake up in some hospital bed with friends and shrinks gathered around. Her pride. No gestures. No pleas for help. No cries for rescue. That was too abhorrent.

The wind howled, but the sun was warm, and the trail to the beach afforded her that renewal she hoped for. Some sturdy wild flowers clung to the hill slopes. A dry summer. The red dust of the trail flew into her face, and her white pants were soon covered with dirt. She folded her arms under her breasts and felt the silk next to her skin, glad she had chosen it for today. An extraordinary calm embraced her. The drugs, she supposed. At the same time, she was exhilarated and light at heart, that sensation of freedom, of complete liberation stayed with her. This must be how it feels to win a revolution after much hardship and many deaths — an exuberant charge from victory with total relaxation close at hand. The ocean pulsed, as forever, in front of her, waving its arms, beckoning a welcome. A mighty force. She walked toward the cove after searching the beach to see if she was indeed alone. There were no other cars in the parking lot, but sometimes people made their way here to camp from the hiking trails. No matter. She didn't see anyone.

The one thing she dreaded more than anything else was being cold. Her spiritual love for the Pacific had never been translated into a love of touch. On the hottest days imaginable, she might put a toe in, then run out in cowardly distress. Her idea of pleasant swimming temperature was closer to that of a hottub. She loved the water in Ixtapa in August when she had to run across the burning sand and plunge into hot, salty waves. But this would make it easier after all and faster. She sat down on the sand in the cove where she'd sat with Ivan and Dan and Chris. She debated taking her clothes off, but decided against it. She held onto these moments passing by her with the wind, seconds on a clock that controls a time bomb. It has to be without thinking because thinking will stop it. She brushed the sand off and walked toward the waves. A seal was out there cavorting about, free and easy, a friend. The water wasn't as cold as she expected. Her clothes afforded enough illusive protection. She began to swim when the water was up to her waist.

A wave crashed down on her back, sending her sprawling in circles toward the rocky bottom. Her arms instinctly reached upward toward the surface, but the mountain of water hit her a second time before she reached the air. Her body was pulled in every direction at once, and her legs thrashed about with her arms for a measure of control that she hadn't known she wanted. The undertow jerked her out, her body light as dust sucked into a vacuum. A hairy creature floated by her head. A fright of seaweed to tangle with, she clutched at it, her own hair.

Surrender. Surrender, she begged herself, not able to close her eyes against the burning salt water, not able to give up an involuntary struggle to see the sun in the sky once more.

Her body had no weight, no matter, and the more she wrestled with the waves, the more rapidly her muscles grew weary. A hard black surface rushed at her with incredible speed. She put out her arms to shield her face, the absurdity of it irrelevant. Her side crashed against the rock, and for a moment she surfaced. She saw the blue of the sky. A warm red color flowed around her, she couldn't feel her right leg at all. She couldn't feel anything in her body.

This is a mistake. I can't go. I can't do it.

Water crushed her again, pulling her a long way from the rock out to sea. She let go within this smothering ton of water. Her will, stronger, more stubborn than she perceived, retreated in defeat. It backed down a long, dark hall; she could see it and wanted to go with it or wave goodbye. Her hand waved, a white petal in a blue black night.

I can. I can go.

Her arms went limp and floated straight up while her body sank deep under the waves, heavy now, a stone. She breathed in water, gasping for air, and strangled, her lungs choked with unnatural fullness. The pressure, in seconds, would implode her lungs. Inside out, she was turning upside down and inside out. She faltered again in her determination to finish this, to give herself over, to surrender to the sea. She fought to swim up to the surface and saw rays of light shining down toward her through the water. The light faded as she thought she reached it. There was only a dark corridor down which she had to go until the faintest glimmer of light at the end was gone.

*　*　*